Walking the Lights

Walking the Lights

Deborah Andrews

**FREIGHT
BOOKS**

First published 2016

Freight Books
49-53 Virginia Street
Glasgow, G1 1TS
www.freightbooks.co.uk

ISBN 978-1-910449-88-2
eISBN 978-1-910449-89-9

Typeset by Freight
Printed and bound by Bell and Bain, Glasgow

the publisher acknowledges investment from
Creative Scotland toward the publication of this book

Deborah Andrews is an award-winning theatre practitioner turned novelist. Her theatrical adaptation of *Dream State: The New Scottish Poets* won a Scotsman Fringe First Award; she established the first year-round Deaf Youth Theatre in the UK; and she co-founded Solar Bear theatre company (of which she was Artistic Director 2002-09). Born in Windsor, Deborah moved to Glasgow to study at the Royal Scottish Academy of Music and Drama (Norah Cooper Award for the Speaking of Verse). She went on to work as a performer, director, workshop facilitator and writer, and gained an MLitt (Distinction) and a PhD (AHRC funded) in creative writing from the University of Glasgow. Her short stories have been published in several anthologies. She now lives in Lancaster, where she teaches creative writing.

For Heather, David and a host of brilliant friends.

1
AUTUMN
1996

One

Somewhere, the river monster. The rubber ring creaked against her pink swimming costume as she turned, using her cupped hands like paddles, searching for signs. Too deep to see down there, and the sun too bright in her eyes, the surface all diamonds and dazzle. She rested her arms on the inflated blue and white plastic. The bank looked odd this far away, blanket no longer visible, butterfly bushes getting smaller. Her legs dangled down, her feet caught in a rush of colder water. He liked toes, the river monster. She pulled her legs up, giggled. Where was he?

The water around her, faster, her toes aching with the cold.

'Dad…?'

A bubble popped.

'Dad!'

'Wraaar!' He rose up, massive, drops flying off him. She blinked them out of her eyes, shrieked, beat the water with flat hands, blinded by a wall of leaping white.

Lifted up, clean out of the rubber ring, she laughed, coughed.

On his shoulders, she stretched out her arms, water dripping from twinkling starfish fingers, sunlight sparkling in tiny domes along her summer-brown arms with their five new freckles.

'Merrily, merrily, life is but a dream.'

'Sing the one about the fishy.' She pressed her cheek against his wet hair and wrapped her arms around his head, stroking his sandpaper chin.

He bobbed and she held tight. *'Dance tae yer daddy, ma bonnie lassie…'*

On the warm tartan blanket, a ladybird struggled over brown

and green fibres. She set a finger in its path and it climbed up, bigger than her fingernail, shiny red cape with a spot on each wing. She touched her dad's big toe and it crawled on.

Stretched out on his back, large feet crossed, open newspaper a tent over his face, he took up most of the blanket. Her shoulders nipped, nothing there, just skin dried tight, hot under her palm. The rubber ring was almost too hot to touch. She squeezed the soft valve and air hissed out. One day she'd be able to swim, strong like him. She'd stay under for hours, grab his leg when he least expected.

Opening its red cape, the ladybird took flight. She followed it to the water's edge and onto the skinny crescent of sandy mud. Something streaked out towards the weir, electric blue – a dragonfly? They'd walked down there once, seen the frothy water tumbling out the other side.

Cool water rippled around her ankles, leaf skeletons floated, a shred of waterweed plastered against her shin. She stepped forward and a brown cloud billowed, hiding her feet. She felt them sink, stepped again and there was nothing but a mass of bubbles and a cold muffled voice calling her name.

'Maddie…'

Then spinning, free-fall, something soft beneath, her body pressed against it. All that weight, of water, of air. She tried to struggle up out of the dark towards distant noises. A chair scraping against the kitchen floor, the thud of a bag on the tabletop. She knew what this meant, he was leaving again. He'd shoved some stuff into the black holdall and was about to slip the wedding ring from his finger, place it on top of the jam jar. She wanted to run down, to tell him she was sorry, that she shouldn't have gone back in, but she couldn't move, her legs were leaden.

The phone rang but he didn't stop to answer it. In a moment he'd open the front door, start the car, then he'd be gone.

Ringing, ringing, ringing…

She opened her eyes, took a moment to place where she was. White wood-chipped walls, brown ceiling, single bulb hanging from a crumbling centre rose. She wasn't at home in Stirling, but in the room she shared with Mike in her student flat in Glasgow. Though neither of them was a student anymore.

Out in the hall the answering machine clicked, reset. She swallowed, throat dry. Images at the edges of her mind dissolved when she tried to bring them to centre. She curled up behind Mike, pressed her face against his shoulder blade, but his skin was slightly tacky and her legs were restless.

Slipping out of bed, she picked her way over clothes and dirty dishes to the sofa. In the pocket of his leather jacket she found his hash tin – empty. She poked through the ashtray. All the joints had been smoked right down to the roach.

Pulling on socks and a jumper over her pyjamas, she padded down the hall, passing Callum's room and the empty room that Bea stayed in before she went to London. On the hall table the answering machine was flashing. Turning the volume down, she pressed play. The tape rewound.

'Maddie… it's Mum again. Are you there? It's Sunday morning. Can you please give me a wee ring back, even just to let me know you're okay?'

She should ring back, but not now. Maybe after she'd had a smoke. Later on today. Or tomorrow. Tomorrow evening, maybe. Delete.

The brittle light in the narrow communal kitchen made the back of her eyeballs ache. Trying to ignore the stench of onions, she raked through the bin and found four joint butts. They were damp, so she cut them open, spreading the tobacco on a baking tray to dry off under the grill. In the stack of dishes in the sink she found a mug, rinsed it. Her fingertips stung with the cold.

Waiting for the kettle to boil, she stood at the tall sash window and looked out onto the back alley. The city took a long time to wake up on Sundays. Some folk had only just gone to bed.

Jo, her best friend from college, would say, 'Come out. It'll do you good. We'll have a laugh. You, me and Roger, like old times.' If she wasn't permanently skint... Her dole hardly lasted out the first week of the fortnight.

'Mike always seems to manage,' Jo said.

Which was true. Last night it was 2am when he finally got home. She'd paced the room – had he gone off with someone else, was he lying in a pool of blood with a knife in his gut? Which was partly why she didn't want to go out anyway. Saturday nights were lurid and loud, folk staggering and leching and vomiting. That's what drink did. Rab, her mum's second husband, taught her that. Dope, on the other hand, was a peaceful drug.

She rolled a single skinner then poured boiling water into the mug. The fridge was nearly empty – a few sauce bottles and a packet of bacon, Callum's. No milk. But Mike said he'd borrowed some money off Gnasher. Later they'd have a full cooked breakfast. There might even be enough to buy shampoo. She'd used washing-up liquid last time, now even that had run out.

Back in her room she switched on the TV, turning the sound to mute. Dunblane Primary School, cordoned off with police tape, flowers heaped outside. On the news again lately, since some report had been published. In Glasgow, people talked about the massacre, but in Stirling shock was followed by silence then small muttered comments. Inconceivable – just up the road. In big American high schools, aye, but not in a wee Scottish town. In a primary.

On the screen, a picture of handguns, then Tony Blair grasping a podium and punctuating with emphatic nods of his head.

She sparked up. The smoke was hot and harsh and caught in the back of her throat. Mike whimpered. The duvet slipped from his shoulder. He'd sleep all day if she didn't wake him.

'Hey…' She edged onto the mattress.

He groaned and pulled the duvet up round his neck.

'Want something to drink?'

He rolled over. Grunted no.

'Smoke?'

Struggling onto one elbow, he rubbed his eyes with the heels of his hands. Ricky Ross from Deacon Blue, that's who he looked like when they first met. Even had the gap between his teeth. Now he just looked gaunt, with a beard and moustache she wished he'd shave off.

He reached for the joint and took a long drag, squinting up at her. 'What time is it?'

'Gone midday.' She held out her mug towards him. 'Tea?'

He took it, sipped. 'Fuck, too hot.' He handed it back. 'What is there to eat?'

'Nothing, yet.'

'Must be something.'

'Half a bag of pearl barley and some Salad Cream.'

He passed her the joint. 'Whose turn is it to go to the shops?'

Like he ever took a turn. 'I'll go if you give me that cash.'

'What cash?'

'That you said you'd borrowed?'

He reached for his jeans, checked the pockets then dropped them back on the floor.

'Mike!'

'It was only a tenner. And I had to buy a round.'

She smoked the joint till it tasted of charred cardboard, then stubbed it out. Had there been anything in it? She felt queasy.

He sat up and rubbed his face. 'Can't you borrow some money off your mum?'

'Can't you borrow some off yours?'

'She gave us thirty quid last time I saw her.'

'Yeah, which you spent on booze.'

It was like striking flint with steel. 'I didn't spend it *all* on booze. I bought some grass. Most of which you smoked.'

'You didn't buy it, you got it on tick. Which I then had to pay off when I got my dole.'

'Ah man, I can't be dealing with this.' He swung his legs from the bed and started pulling on his jeans. She stood. Leaning against the chest of drawers, she sipped her tea.

One of the first mornings after they'd got together, just over three years ago, they walked through the park to get breakfast at The Big Blue. Halfway down the alley of flowers, the heavens opened. He sheltered them both, holding his greatcoat over their heads. When they reached the fountain, he dashed out to perform his Queen Mab speech for her. He'd played Mercutio in his end-of-second-year production. Everyone talked about how impressive he'd been. There in the park, he didn't care about the rain streaking down his face, or the dog walkers who looked at him as if he was mad.

And in this state she gallops night by night,

Through lovers' brains, and then they dream of love;

That blush and the tingle in her stomach. What'd happened to all that?

She watched him push his feet into his shoes. He stood, unsteady, and clipped a plate with the edge of his foot. Some cutlery clattered.

'Where are you going?'

He snatched up his jacket. 'Fuck knows. Someone somewhere must owe me a drink.'

'Wait…'

He opened the bedroom door. 'You should call your mother. She's worried about you.' He knew how to strike back.

'Like you give a shit. You're just thinking about who you can tap.'

'I'm not getting into this.' He was out in the hall, opening the front door. 'It's Sunday for fuck's sake.'

The door slammed. She dashed over, pulled it open, stepped into the stairwell. Bending over the bannister, she saw him halfway down the stairs. 'Don't forget to think about yourself!'

He didn't look up.

'Fuck off then. Fuck off and don't come back.'

At the bottom of the stairs he headed for the close door, disappearing.

'Mike…?'

The close door clicked shut.

Back in the bedroom she pulled open the curtains, lifted the sash window and leaned out. Mike was walking towards the traffic lights with his head low, his hands jammed into his pockets.

'Mike!'

Three people standing beside a car looked up. She lowered the window then struck a candleholder. It flew across the room, hit the edge of the wardrobe and shattered.

A knock on the bedroom door. She jumped.

'Maddie?' Callum's voice. 'You alright?'

'Yeah. Sorry.'

'Okay.' The bathroom fan began to whirr.

Kneeling, she picked the china splinters from the carpet. The candleholder was the nicest thing anybody ever gave her, even if Mike had stolen it from the props department at college. Her eyes filled. Selfish, spoilt girl. But she caught sight of herself in the mirror.

'Don't cry,' Rab used to say to her. 'You're even uglier when you cry.'

Outside, a fine rain fell. She walked along Sauchiehall Street towards the station with her hood up. Her fists, stuffed deep inside the pockets of her duffle coat, strained the stitching of the cold lining. She'd managed to borrow another fiver off Callum.

Enough for a single ticket to her mum's.

As she passed the Variety Bar, she tried to see in through the narrow black slats of the venetian blinds. No sign of Mike. Not in Nico's either, though Nico's was more somewhere she used to hang out with Jo and Roger.

Arriving at the station with her bus about to leave, she sprinted across the stance area, mounted its steps as it shuddered to life. At the back, she dumped down her bag and peeled off her damp coat. The bus reversed, then set off. Wiping a patch in the condensation, she rested her head against the window and shut her eyes. Two free seats and the void of the journey ahead. With any luck, by the time she arrived, Rab would be off down the local. Felt as if she'd been wishing forever that her mum would leave Rab, like his sensible first wife had done.

Years ago, when she was about eight years old, there'd been a massive row. Her mum threw some things in a case, Auntie Irene picked them up, and they stayed at Gran's. No supper that night, just digestive biscuits, soft from the old Quality Street tin and tasting of coffee creams. She lay awake till her mum came upstairs. Her mum and Auntie Irene used to share the room, when they were growing up, and the two single beds, side by side, had matching peach candlewick bedspreads. As her mum climbed into the other bed, she felt that, at last, someone had answered her prayers. But the next day, at the end of school, Rab was standing at the gates.

'Your mother asked me to pick you up.' His hand landed heavily on her shoulder. Under each of his fingernails was a black line, from working on the engines. He hauled her back from the edge of the kerb, then pushed her forward suddenly so she stumbled. When they arrived home, her mum came out of the kitchen with a lightness about her, like a sheet blowing in a spring breeze. Behind, on the table, a vase of flowers. Shortly after that he'd suggested she call him Dad. As if she had a choice.

The bus picked up speed. They were on the motorway now,

heading north. Some of the last leaves on the trees glowed fluorescent yellow against the low grey cloud, clinging on.

Nearly an hour later, the bus pulled in at the Thistles Centre. Two women got up from their seats a couple of rows in front and reached overhead for their rucksacks. They looked like tourists, but who in their right minds would come to Stirling in October? She followed as they inched their way to the front.

The fine rain had turned sleety. She swung her bag over her shoulder and put her hood up. The whizz and pop of a firecracker – it was a couple of weeks until bonfire night, but kids had started to let off random fireworks in the streets already. She shivered. In an hour or two the damp pavements would be icy. To her right, the Wallace Monument loomed ghostly, the Ochils invisible behind, swallowed in the twilight. Did Auntie Irene still live over that way, towards Cambuskenneth? She hadn't seen her since the night after that big row.

She'd been upstairs getting ready for bed when Auntie Irene came over. Ear pressed to the floorboards, she listened to the murmur of voices, catching the occasional phrase: 'control your temper', 'keep your nose out', 'she's my sister'; and her mum's voice, 'leave it, Irene'. The voices rising, till Rab was shouting about his father: 'if you want to see what a fucking temper looks like…' – a riff on one of his favourite themes. Then they were out in the hall. She'd watched from the landing as Rab shoved Irene's coat into her arms and pushed her out the front door.

As she entered the estate she put her head down, hoping not to see anyone she knew. All the houses were pretty much the same: grey, pebble-dashed, semi-detached. They might have been designed to appear grand, with their turreted roofs, but they looked rundown. Some folk had tried to make an effort, with lacy net curtains and hanging baskets, but for every house like that there was another with sheets pinned up at the windows and a front lawn serving as a skip.

She crossed to number thirty-six. Lights were on in the living room and hall, and the deep bark came on cue as she approached. Marshall. Poor thing, he was neurotic, barked at everyone. Her breath billowed and rose in the night air – oh, for a smoke. She knocked, peered through the letterbox. Marshall's barking upped a gear. Straightening, she searched through her bag for her old set of keys.

'Hello?' She squeezed herself through the door so Marshall didn't have enough room to dash out into the street. He turned and ran into the living room as her mum appeared in the kitchen doorway, pulling off her washing-up gloves. She was wearing the hideous bikini-body apron Rab had given her.

'Oh my God, Maddie, where've you been?' She walked over as if she might gather her up in a hug, or at least put a hand on her arm. 'I've been calling you. Didn't you get my messages?'

Maddie hung her bag over the stair post. 'Yeah, sorry. I've been busy.'

Realising now there was no cause for alarm, Marshall pushed past, his back legs stiff.

She bent down to fuss him. 'Hey, old friend…'

He kept his head low but his undocked tail swung a wide arc.

'Couldn't you have found five minutes to give me a wee ring?'

'The line's been changed to incoming calls only.' It probably would be, soon. She scratched behind Marshall's ears. His mouth stretched back, showing ragged lips, pink and black, with yellowed molars set in too-red gums. 'I don't mind if your breath smells…' She kissed his nose. He'd always been ready to curl up beside her whenever she was upset.

'Don't they have phone boxes in Glasgow?'

'Sorry.' As she swept her hands along Marshall's sides, some of his oily brown fur came loose and gathered in two mounds on his hipbones.

She felt her mum soften.

'He needs a brush,' her mum said.

'He needs a bath.'

'Same could be said.' Her eyes darted over Maddie.

In the kitchen, her mum swung open a cupboard door. 'We ate, but I could rustle you up a wee bite.'

Leaning against the sideboard as her mum heated up a tin of beans, Maddie half-listened to stories about people at work, the woman next door, so-and-so's son who'd been involved in a ruckus in town.

'There've been a few random attacks by teenagers lately.' Her mum took a tub of Stork from the fridge. 'A *solicitor* got beaten up near the Sheriff Court a month or so back. They've no respect, the young folk, they just hang about with nothing better to do than get pissed and cause mischief.' The toast popped up charred. She scraped it over the sink. 'People have been petitioning for spy cameras to be made more obvious.'

Carrying some cutlery and a square of kitchen roll through, she set a place for Maddie at Gran's old round dining table that was squashed at the far end of the living room. 'Spy cameras. What they need is jobs, and more than a good bit of discipline.'

The first bite of toast stuck in a ball in Maddie's throat. She forced it down with a swig of orange squash. Even without Rab home, the place felt like his. His armchair occupied the prime spot, square in front of the TV. His leather slippers waited beside the nest of tables. In the living room and hall he'd hung a heavy brown paper with a knotted pattern. It took loads of paste, but still slid down the walls. He swore himself blue, eventually getting one of the guys from work to come over and give him a hand. Before the guy left, she saw Rab give him some money. He hadn't been a friend. Above the cabinet, a corner of the paper curled away from the wall, revealing the bright chintz beneath.

Her mum set her mug on the table, the apron gone and her long cardigan on instead. Small undissolved lumps of creamer floated on the surface of her coffee. Maddie fed the remains of her toast to Marshall then pushed her plate to one side.

Her mum tutted. 'You spoil that dog.'

She stroked his head. 'He deserves it.'

From her cardigan pocket, her mum pulled a packet of Superkings, offering Maddie one. The two of them lit up. 'Enough about things here. What about you?'

'Things are okay. So-so.'

'Work?'

'Still looking. Hoping something might come up for the panto season.'

Her mum blew smoke high into the air and ran her fingers through her hair a few times. Maddie didn't like it cut quite so short. It jumped up at the crown, and the grey showed through more.

'And Mike?'

'Same.'

'How long can you go on like this, living on the dole?'

'It can be tricky getting your foot in the door. I only graduated a year ago.'

'Not Mike though. He's been out two years.'

She made it sound as if he'd been in the nick. Maddie turned the end of her cigarette against the ashtray. The ash flaked off leaving a glowing red cone. 'He had an audition last week.' A lie, but it might be enough to divert the lecture.

Her mum raised her eyebrows and made a puffing sound. 'Audition. Auditions aren't going to put food on the table. He's too proud. He needs to get a job. Any job. We all need to work.'

Her knuckles were swollen from years of polishing the floors of school halls. What did working matter, what did eating matter, if it meant living in a dive like this, selling your soul for a crust?

'And *you* could get something. Something half-decent. In an office. That degree of yours must count for something.'

Something, something, something. 'A Mickey Mouse degree.' That's what Rab called it. 'A waste of time. A waste of taxpayers' money.'

'I need to get new photographs done.'

Her mum blew on her coffee. 'I hope you're not expecting me to dip into my pocket.'

Unbelievable. Maybe she occasionally helped out with the odd twenty, thirty quid, but Maddie never asked for anything. Well, there'd been that one time back in spring, but the electricity was about to be cut off. An emergency.

Setting her coffee down, her mum thumbed the edge of the coaster. 'I'm just worried for you. D'you not think, *I've had my fun, I gave it a go, time to get back to the real world now*? You ran up a lot of debt at that college. How are you going to pay it off?'

Maddie stubbed her cigarette out.

Upstairs in the bathroom, more of the sealant had peeled away from round the rim of the plastic coffee-coloured bath, and the edge of the mirror had rusted. Her hair *did* need a wash.

At the end of the landing, her mum's bedroom door was standing open, the streetlight casting a glow over the bed she shared with Rab.

For years, she'd wished, prayed, her dad would come back, preferably with a big axe to scare Rab off, or chop him to pieces. For a while there were photos of him in a box under the bed. But one day, when she went to look at them again, she found they'd all gone. When she tried to picture him now all she could remember was his shoulder-length brown hair. A pang – what if Mike did what she said, and didn't come back? 'I'm sorry,' she whispered.

The bottle of Charlie perfume on her mum's dressing table had been replaced by Poison in the Eighties. Now there was just a roll-on deodorant, next to a photo frame and her old jewellery box. She picked up the frame, surprised to see it held a picture from her graduation day. She was smiling, but remembered feeling miserable. Mike spent the day nursing a hangover; her mum turned up late and missed the ceremony; and Rab had hung around, wearing jeans and trainers, sneering at other families.

She set the frame back down and lifted the lid of the blue leatherette jewellery box. Inside, a silver cross on a chain, the one her mum wore when she'd had long hair like Maddie's. In the shallow drawer beneath were several metal bangles, a red plastic bracelet, and, at the very back, her dad's wedding ring. She pulled it out. Slipped it on. It was still far too big for her. Outside, the bang and crackle of a rocket. A couple of boys shouted something as they ran away and Marshall barked.

'Be quiet,' her mum called from the kitchen, but he kept barking.

Her dad's ring was still on her finger when she heard the front door swing open.

'Shut up, for fuck's sake, it's just me.' Rab's voice.

She slid the drawer of the jewellery box shut and pushed the ring into her trouser pocket.

'Fucking idiot.' He went into the kitchen.

She tiptoed downstairs. Although it'd been hung in front of the gas fire, her coat was still damp.

'Maddie came to visit,' she heard her mum say.

'Who? I thought she was dead.'

'That's me away then,' she called, heading for the hall.

Stepping into the living room doorway, Rab blocked her path. 'What, not gonna say hello to your old man?'

He'd lost a bit of weight, and his hair was thinner, but he still looked troll-like, with his bulbous nose, heavy jowls and hard green eyes. 'Hi.'

He shook his head, collapsed in his chair and called out, 'Jean, put the kettle on.'

Marshall followed her down the hall. She wrapped her arms around him, pressing her face against his warm neck. As she reached for the front door her mum hurried from the kitchen.

'Off already? Why don't you stay? It's no bother to make your bed up.'

'I need to get back.'

She pressed a note into Maddie's hand.

'No, it's okay, I don't need it.'

'Take it. Get yourself something nice. Or pay a bill.'

Maddie turned and waved from the bottom of the path, then set off towards town. Black sky stretched over the houses and a thin blanket of frost covered car windscreens and sparkled along the edge of the kerb. She'd have to wait nearly an hour for a bus. At the end of the road she unfolded the note. Twenty quid. Enough to get back to Glasgow, pop across to Liam's for some dope, and buy a loaf. With each stride, her dad's ring – a small circle of gold – pressed against her right thigh.

The winter before he'd left, he'd taken her to the town's fireworks display. Rockets soared above them, booming into fountains of glittering sparks – yellow, red, and ice-blue. The bonfire raging, they wandered round the stalls and ate hotdogs with sticky, sweet onions. She rode in a giant swirling teacup, waving at her dad each time he spun into view. And he was there at the end, as she half-tripped, dizzy, down the wooden ramp. He hoisted her onto his shoulders. The smoky air had smelled of warm, gloss-red toffee apples.

Please God let Mike be home when she got back. She stopped at a shop to break the twenty so she could use the phone box, which reeked of pee. Brushing some small cubes of shattered glass to one side with the toe of her shoe, she dialled the flat. The answer machine kicked in, her own voice, sounding cheery. She had been cheery. A new flat, a new life, it was all ahead of her.

'Hi, Mike. It's me. I'm in Stirling.' She paused, hoping he'd pick up. 'I should be back in a couple of hours. I'll ring again when I get to Glasgow.'

But when she rang from Buchanan Street station, there was still no one home.

Liam lived just up from Great Western Road, over the river. Although his flat was on the third floor, the sound of heavy bass and voices could be heard from street level. He answered the door wearing his ubiquitous yellow towelling dressing gown, his waist-length blonde hair coming loose from a red scrunchie.

'Hey, wee Madster.' He held a joint between his fingers and gestured for her to come in with a wide sweep of his arm.

The flat honked of garlic. At the far end of the wonky hall, in the kitchen, Liam's girlfriend, Hanna, was cooking chilli.

'Hey!' She waved, wooden spoon in hand.

Five of their friends were sitting round the kitchen table shouting over one another to be heard. Liam whizzed through their names. A thin-faced guy nodded hello. Fairy lights around the window, and tall green candles stuck in wine bottles, gave the room a soft sheen. If it wasn't for the way the lino sucked at the soles of her shoes...

'Beer.' Liam placed a bottle in front of her, flipping off the cap.

'There's plenty to eat if you'd like to stay for tea?' Hanna said, draining a can of kidney beans and emptying them into the massive cast iron pot.

'Thanks, but I said I'd see Mike back at the flat.'

'Too bad.' Hanna opened a tin of tomatoes. 'My brother, Alex, is coming up. I reckon you guys would really get on.'

'Is he the one that does the circus stuff?'

Liam stood at the end of the counter, setting up his scales. 'Yep, he's the clown.'

'He's not a clown!' Hanna used the scorched tea towel that was draped over her arm to whip his legs. 'He's an *artiste*.'

The thin-faced guy looked up. 'D'you work in a circus?'

'Oh no. I trained in drama. We did a bit of juggling. I was

rubbish.'

'And mime.' Liam had been on the stage management course, but dropped out halfway through second year.

'Yeah. I'm well qualified to punt an imaginary barge.'

The guy smiled. His hair was lank around his thin face, but he had big eyes like a deer's. 'Bet there's a lot of call for that.'

She laughed, the gurgling sensation odd in her throat. Since when had life become so serious? 'You wouldn't believe how in demand I am!'

The guy rejoined the conversation at the table. Did her words sound wrong – if not flirtatious, then egotistical?

Hanna yelped as the bubbling chilli spat from the pot.

'What're you for?' Liam asked.

'Just a 'teenth.'

She stayed to roll a joint, for etiquette's sake. Taking a seat, she chatted to a girl who'd been at uni with Hanna. The thin-faced guy started telling an anecdote about travelling in the boot of someone's car after a gig, then everyone was shouting, pitching in with other bits of the story, insults and quips. A girl opposite laughed so hard she had to wipe her eyes. When Hanna plonked a load of cutlery down in the middle of the table, she almost regretted saying she had to go. But if Mike was home…

Out in the night, the streetlights were orbed by orange haze. She skirted round frozen puddles, scanning the pavement for the telltale gloss of black ice. At the top of Kelvin Way, a young guy wearing tight jeans hugged a bomber jacket to him and eyed her suspiciously. She stumbled. Tree roots were rising up, trying to break free from the concrete. At any moment, one of them might whip its tapered root round her neck, claim her as compensation for all the years they'd been trapped there, suffocating in exhaust fumes.

Stepping into the gutter, she hurried past dark voids where entrances led to the park and gardens. At the bridge with the figurative bronze sculptures, the old man representing Philosophy gazed down at a skull in which someone had placed ping-pong balls for eyes. They'd coloured in black spots for irises and set them at an angle that gave the whole tableau a cartoonish look. The brighter lights of Sauchiehall Street were within reach.

The flat was dark, and only the message she'd left for Mike was on the answering machine. Should she call Mike's mum? She'd probably be in bed. At least with Callum out she didn't need to invent an excuse for not being able to pay him back. She sat on the loo. Her thighs were mottled red with the cold. The stench of mould and damp carpet was overpowering. Something caught her eye. A hairy beetle larva inched its way along by the bath. She reached for a square of loo roll to pick it up, but there was only a wisp left on the tube. Outside in the hall something creaked. Easing the lock back she peeked out.

In the bedroom, she switched on the electric fire, pulling it closer as the ashen bars turned orange. Her ears rang with the silence, but in her head she still heard the chatter of folk over at Liam's.

02:12, the scuff of feet in the stairwell signalled Mike's return. It took him a while to get his key in the lock. She picked up a magazine to try and make the scene look casual, as if she hadn't been sitting up for hours, worrying.

He opened the bedroom door, bounced off the wall, came to rest leaning against the wardrobe. 'I'm sorry.' His mouth was rubbery, like he'd been to the dentist's. 'I don't want to fight.'

The fist in her chest relaxed its grip. 'Me neither.'

'I wanted to call, but I didn't have any cash.'

The room shimmered as her eyes filled. 'I rolled you a joint.'

Like a boy on a Cake Walk he staggered to the sofa then collapsed down beside her. Her eyes spilled. Quickly she brushed her cheeks.

'Hey, come here.' He pulled her into a hug.

18

Two

Tuesday morning. She switched the lava lamp off at the wall then switched it back on again. It glowed green, but the red wax at the bottom remained a solid lump. The phone rang.

'Hi, Maddie.' Jo's voice. 'Are you screening?'

She ought to answer.

'I'm at Wren's. He's gone out to a meeting and I was gonna pass by.'

Jo's boyfriend lived a couple of streets away.

She threw some clothes into the wardrobe and shook the duvet so it covered the bed. Not that there was anything to hide, when had they last had sex? In the bathroom, she ran a basin of water and put her face in.

Who could hold their breath the longest, that was one of the games she and her dad used to play when they drove through the Clyde tunnel. How many journeys did it take her to figure out that, although he went beetroot and looked fit to burst, he was actually breathing through his nose?

She buried her face in Callum's towel and swallowed hard. When her breath settled, she smeared a line of concealer beneath her eyes.

The 'teenth had been smoked, but she made a single skinner with the dust and woody bits of tobacco left in the corner of the tin. It burned unevenly and caught in the back of her throat. The whole world was grey and tinny and hummed like a refrigerator.

The rap on the letterbox made her jump. The spy hole showed the back of Jo's henna-red bob. As she opened the door Jo turned.

She was wearing an enormous pair of spectacles, one leg held on with sellotape. 'No need to say anything.'

In the kitchen, Maddie filled the kettle.

'Mike still in bed?'

'He went out for Harry's birthday last night. He's not come home yet.'

'I heard Gnasher had some liquid acid on him.'

'Lucky bastard.' She rinsed some mugs.

'Maybe. Roger had a few drops of that stuff once. Thought he was growing ears like a donkey's. Went home in search of a bread knife, but luckily conked out before he did anything with it.'

'How is Roger?'

'Okay. Still working in Gandolfi and waiting to hear back about that *Taggart* audition.' Jo unpacked her tin. She was more of an occasional smoker, had given up trying to master the art of rolling by hand. Instead she had a machine, king-size skins, a collection of tickets, and a pair of nail scissors – to cut the tickets into neat little roaches. 'We should get a night out soon. Tessa's birthday on Saturday, pub then club?'

'I'll ask Mike.'

'Fuck Mike. You should come. It'd do you good to get out of this dump for a while.'

Her words stung. She yanked open the cutlery drawer. 'Tea?'

'Coffee?'

'Sorry. All out. I don't get my dole till next week.'

'Forget it. Let's just smoke this and go.'

Along the walkway that led to the fountain, yellowed leaves and brown stalks tangled on the flowerbeds. In summer, the flowers grew up past head height. Massive purple pompoms; giant poppies with crepe-like skirts; foxgloves with speckled bee-width bells.

After one of their first nights out, on the way back from the pub, she, Jo and Roger had skipped along here, arm-in-arm, singing 'Follow the Yellow Brick Road'. Nails down a blackboard to anyone in earshot. Roger was six years older, but just as daft. He climbed the fountain and she followed. Water flooded her trainers, tugged the bottom of her jeans, thundered on her head. Jo stood below shouting, 'You're mad. You're both bonkers!' They dripped their way back to Maddie's flat, where they gathered round the toaster, staring at it for some time before Jo saw it wasn't switched on at the wall.

Walking now at Jo's side, she tried to think of something to say. Maybe the smoke had emptied her brain, even if it was weak, in classic Jo style.

Jo tucked her hair behind her ears. 'I got a phone call from that guy, Graham.'

'What guy?'

'The one that set up the agency.'

'Oh yeah.'

A poster had gone up near the pigeonholes at college three weeks before graduation, inviting students to submit their photos and CVs for consideration.

'I've been offered a panto.'

'No way! Why didn't you say?'

'I am saying. Besides, it's not a big deal.'

At the end of the flowerbeds they rounded the fountain. The leaves on the smaller trees had turned brilliant reds, some the colour of Jo's hair, others darker.

'What are you playing?'

'Lots of bit parts. It's a reworking of *Little Red Riding Hood*. I play like the mum and the wolf and the granny or something.'

'You have to eat yourself?'

'Hmm... maybe not the granny then.'

They climbed the steep bank of lawn where students sat in summer.

'Where's it on?'

'It's just a T.I.E. tour.'

'What's T.I.E.?'

'Theatre in Education. Shit, didn't you come to any lectures?'

'I came to some.'

'Yeah, before Mike.'

She crossed her arms, a tight knot. 'When do you start?'

'Middle of next month.'

She tried not to pant. The hill was easier for Jo, lean and long-legged. 'How are you going to manage the buroo?'

'I don't need to. It's paid. I'm gonna sign off for a while.'

'Cool.' She meant it, but her voice sounded thin.

They leant on the railings round the statue of Lord Roberts in his army regalia, mounted on a horse. One of her favourite spots, beside the fir trees, looking out onto the spires of the uni and the turrets of the art gallery – a fairy-tale picture. Beyond were flats, houses, cranes, and high-rise blocks that stretched out to the hills. It usually gave her a tingling feeling, as if anything was possible.

'Anyway, what *is* the story with the glasses?'

'I fell asleep with my contact lenses in. Couldn't open one eye this morning. Had to prise up my eyelid, peel the lens off my eyeball.'

'Too much information! Nice specs though.'

'Very funny. They're an old pair of my sister's. She gave them to me after she got her new ones.'

'Generous.'

Jo turned. 'You know, Maddie, I've been thinking, I'd still like to do something with *The Tempest*.'

'Really?'

'That speech you did at the Grad show was brilliant. You'd make a great Miranda, and Roger would be a fab Prospero – don't you think?'

'Roger playing my father? I don't think he'd thank you for that!'

'We could grey him up a bit.'

'But how…? Like a profit share?'

'Maybe.'

Too much to dare dream. Yet she could almost feel the sand, hot beneath her feet. Looking out – nothing but sea. Stranded there on that island with her father, for almost as long as she'd been without her dad…

Jo swivelled her watch on her wrist. 'Shit. I said I'd meet Wren for lunch. Why don't you come?'

Had she forgotten she'd said she was skint? 'I thought I'd get the flat sorted a bit this afternoon.'

'Okay. I get my dole on Thursday, will probably pop up to Liam's if you fancy?'

They hugged. Beneath her denim jacket Jo wore a blue lambswool jumper. It smelled of vanilla. Her long silver necklace with the amber pendant pulled at the fibres of Maddie's coat as they separated. She always coordinated her outfits well.

After Jo had gone, she sat on a bench soaking up the dark peatyness and the tang of pine needles. *The Tempest…* Surely it wouldn't be long till Jo's career took off, then she wouldn't have time for some stupid profit share. A light rain fell. She followed the curve of the path down the hill.

By the duck pond an old man was feeding squirrels, throwing monkey nuts from a white carrier bag. 'So tame now. Had one on my shoulder earlier.'

'They're cute.'

He looked up. The left side of his mouth was twisted – scar or deep wrinkle? 'They're vermin. Rats with tails. What you really want are the birds. Here…' He peeled open a nut and worked its papery red skin off between forefinger and thumb. Beckoning, he took her by the wrist, led her to a holly bush, and placed the nut on her outstretched hand. 'Now keep very still.'

Another day, another loon. Always seemed to be someone who

wanted help, or to offload.

'You're too gullible,' Jo would say, after she'd got drawn in then asked for 10p for a cup of tea.

One time there'd been a guy down near Trongate. 'I know this is gonna sound weird, hen, but my bus fare's in my front pocket and my jeans are too tight for me to get it out. Could you...?'

She'd frowned.

Jo had pulled her on. 'Aye right, mate. Anything else you'd like a hand with down there?'

Just then something rustled the leaves. A little bird, blue with a yellow chest, hopped along a branch. With tiny brisk movements of its head it flitted onto her hand, secured the nut in its beak, and was gone.

'Aha! You've got the knack.' The old man held out the bag. 'Here, you can have my job.'

'Thank you.'

'The wife used to love coming down here. She'd feed ducks, pigeons, all sorts.'

As he headed for the bridge, one of his pockets flapped loose. Hardly looked like he could feed himself.

She turned back to the bushes and held out another nut.

Nine years old, lying on her bed reading, she'd heard something odd going on downstairs. Her mum said a bird with a broken wing had landed in the garden – using the word 'garden' loosely: there'd been grass out there once, before Rab said it was unsuitable for dogs, laid down some concrete slabs and erected a six-foot fence. She didn't see the bird, just Rab at the kitchen sink. The muscles in his arms flexed as he held something under water. Something that was struggling.

No more birds came, so she threw a handful of nuts to the squirrels. How brilliant would it be to have work over Christmas? She'd make a good Little Red Riding Hood. Or Snow White.

In third year, everyone had to supply a headshot for the

graduation programme. A friend of Wren's offered to take photos for her for the cost of materials. She thought they were good, but next to everyone else's they looked shoddy – no proper lighting, not framed the same. No way she was sending one of those to that agent. If she hadn't spent all her student loan helping Mike out...

One of the squirrels buried a nut and came back for more. Another squirrel scampered across and the two squirrels went for the same nut, rolling over each other.

'There's plenty of nuts.' She emptied the bag onto the grass. 'You don't have to fight over the same one.'

The flat was still deserted. Callum was hardly ever about these days. They used to play cards while Bea cooked, and one time, when Maddie was upset about a guy from the music school she'd had a fling with, Callum sat up with her for hours.

On his door, she straightened the child's nameplate she'd bought him for a laugh. Taking her dad's ring from her pocket she pressed it against her cheek.

She was about six when she found it on the jam jar. That afternoon she sat sentry at her mum's bedroom door, listening to her howl and sob.

Risky keeping it in her jeans, it needed a safe place. She settled on a box of bath cubes at the back of her underwear drawer. Funny how she'd stopped looking at the poster pinned above the dresser – John Waterhouse's *Miranda*, yellowed and buckled. Mrs Hughes had been her favourite teacher at secondary school. When they starting studying *The Tempest* in English, she'd asked Maddie to read the part of Miranda; it'd been the first time she'd done well at something.

The phone rang.

'Hi, Maddie. It's me...'

Mike. Rushing into the hall she grabbed the receiver. 'Hi.'

'Hey, babe. Guess what? My bro's in town. He's lent us forty quid. We're in Brel. Coming?'

By the time she reached Ashton Lane the rain was battering down, bouncing off the cobblestones. A rush of heat hit her at the pub door. Making her way to the back, she smelled French onion soup. Her stomach rumbled.

At a table at the far end of the narrow conservatory, Raymond raised his hand. Older than Mike, taller, hair reddish, a ginger goatee. Mike downed his beer as she approached.

Raymond kissed her on both cheeks, his goatee bristly. 'Maddie. You're drenched.'

She'd only met him once before, at a family do, when he'd told stories that entertained the aunts, took photos, impressed the uncles with some fancy cigars and got everybody clapping and stamping their feet along to The Proclaimers. On the opposite side of the hall, Mike had stood alone at the bar.

Rising now from his seat, his clothes crumpled and eyes lilac-hooded, Mike mustered a crooked smile. 'Hey, babe.' The cheerful tone in his voice sounded forced. 'Let me get you a drink.' Edging past, he put a hand on her shoulder.

'Bet you miss this good old west coast weather.' She peeled off her coat.

Raymond helped her hang it over the back of a chair. 'You need a towel.'

'At least it's warm in here.' She swept strands of hair from her forehead.

'So, how are you?' he asked.

She sat across from him. 'Good. You?'

'Very well. Was up for a meeting with a new client. Chances of bumping into Mike on the street.'

Raymond rang the flat occasionally. Sometimes Mike sneered, other times just frowned, but he never picked up or returned Raymond's calls.

'How's London?'

'Good. Great. But the best news is Sara and I are engaged, we're getting married in April.'

'Congratulations!'

Mike arrived back carrying three drinks: a vodka-and-Coke, a beer, and a glass of white wine. Some of the beer spilled as he set the drinks on the table.

'Mike, I don't need another.' Raymond referenced his still half-full glass. 'And I've gotta go in ten.'

'What?' Mike sucked the beer from his knuckles. 'It's not everyday you hear your brother's getting married. I'd like to propose a toast, to Raymond and Sara, may you live long and prosper.'

'To Raymond and Sara.' She raised her glass.

Raymond raised his too, but didn't drink. 'Mike was saying he's got some work lined up.'

She glanced at Mike. He avoided her gaze.

'As good as.'

'Oh,' Raymond said, 'it's not definite?'

'It's just a matter of time. You've got to go in big. Once a spear carrier always a spear carrier.'

'Is that how it works? Don't you have to be a bit more entrepreneurial about it?'

'Talent will out.'

She sipped her vodka-and-Coke, lovely sweet burst of bubbles.

Raymond turned to her. 'What do you think, Maddie?'

A bit of her drink slipped down her windpipe. She coughed. 'I don't know.'

Raymond scratched his goatee. 'With most forms of employment you have to serve an apprenticeship. There's nothing more you could be doing?'

'They saw me at the Dip show. Let them come to me.'

'I just don't want to see you miss the boat.'

Mike fixed him with a stare. His pupils narrowed. 'And I don't want to jump on a dinghy when there's a cruise liner coming up behind.'

The sound of a big brass band blared over the speakers, the opening of Dean Martin's 'Ain't that a Kick in the Head'. Someone tempered the volume.

Raymond stretched. His knuckles cracked. 'You're right. What do I know? It's not my field. I better go though, guys, might take a while to get to the airport with the after-school traffic. Sorry to dash off, Maddie.' He pulled on his wool overcoat.

Mike sniffed. 'I'll get that forty quid to you by the end of next week.'

'Don't worry about it. I'll give you a bell about Christmas. I'm not sure if we'll make it up. Good to see you.' He squeezed Maddie's shoulder then slapped Mike on the back. 'We'll send you an invite for April.' At the step he turned and gave a wave. It looked more like a salute.

Mike folded his arms and sunk his head onto them.

'Nice to see him?'

He groaned.

'Nice of him to give us a lend.'

'Hardly the handout of the century.'

She ran a finger through the condensation on her glass. 'How was Harry's birthday?'

'Okay.' Mike rubbed his eyes. 'Feeling it now.' He slid Raymond's untouched drink towards her. 'Want his wine?'

'Not really. Look, why don't we go home. Stop in at Blockbuster and rent a video. Maybe treat ourselves to a Chinese?'

He put a hand on her arm and let out a long sigh. 'Sounds good.'

Someone peered round at them from the front bar. 'No way! Mike?'

It was Ade, a guy from Mike's year.

'Hey hey hey.' Mike stood up. They clapped each other on the back.

'Long time no see. You're never gonna guess who's at the bar?'

'Surprise me.'

'Nick.'

'What? That old badger?'

Ade threw his head back and let out a throaty laugh. 'What are you guys drinking?'

By ten o'clock, the crowds that had gathered in the bar started to thin out. Through the front, people on the mezzanine had dined and were finishing their drinks. She climbed the spiral staircase, paused at the top to let a head rush pass. The shape of the bar made it look like the deck of a ship, with her in the crow's nest.

As she sat on the loo, the tiled floor tilted up to meet her. 'Fuck it,' she whispered, unsure what she was responding to. In the mirror above the sink her face looked like that of a sad ten-year-old's. Beside her, a blonde woman scrunched her hair and adjusted her bra. Time to go home.

Downstairs, Ade was at the bar. Mike was sitting alone through the back.

She rubbed his shoulder. 'I think I'm gonna head.'

'But Ade's getting you a drink.' He helped himself to one of Ade's Marlboro Lights.

As she sat next to him, their knees touched. 'Why don't you come with me? You've been out a few nights on the trot. We had a good plan.'

But she'd already heard Ade mention the casino and offer to lend Mike fifty quid.

Mike looked round, then leant in. 'Nick's nipped up to his dealer's. Said he's got some good quality charlie in. Stay. It'll be fun.'

Almost tempting, but she'd had enough of hearing him slag

Nick and Ade, telling them they'd sold out by taking work on *Rab C*. Even if he *was* funny, a good mimic, acting out all the parts.

She lifted her coat, still heavy with rain.

Mike stroked the back of her leg. 'We'll get another night to ourselves. Tomorrow. Nick's got some great connections up at the Beeb, it's kinda important I stay.'

Her fingers snapped the toggles through their loops.

'Don't be angry with me. Here…' He dug into his pocket and pulled out a fiver and a handful of smash. 'I won't be late.'

The rain had eased and the cobblestones shone beneath strings of fairy lights. Quicker to head left, but it was dark that way, along the back of a university building with its industrial-sized bins. Better to go the long route.

Round the corner by the Ubiquitous Chip, a man played the fiddle. His border collie, a red scarf tied round its neck, guarded the collection hat. The cold air smelled of wood smoke. Eyes on the pavement, she snaked a path down Byres Road. At the traffic lights the words of Valerie Dawes, the voice tutor from college, rang in her head. 'And pull yourself up by an invisible thread… like a puppet on a string.' She'd become such a sloucher.

Halfway up University Avenue, a holler made her start. Three folk in white sheets and *Scream* masks tore down the centre of the road. They circled her, flapped their arms and whooped, then fled on. Behind them, a short girl in a pumpkin suit struggled to keep up. She shoved a leaflet in Maddie's direction then cried, 'Guys, wait up.'

Prickles of fright at her temples. She watched the girl waddle on, through patches of streetlight, becoming an odd rotund silhouette. There were a few other folk on the street in pairs and groups. In her hand, the flyer advertised cheap vodka mixers, a Halloween special at Clatty Pat's on Saturday. Had Jo said where Tessa was going for her birthday? It was ages since she'd seen any of her friends, other than Jo.

The flat was dark. Opening her bedroom door she flicked on the light. On the floor was a folded sheet of A4 – a note from Callum, he needed his thirty quid back ASAP.

A buzz built like a trapped bee, then Pop! and a chink of glass. Blackout. The bulb had gone. Heart thumping, she groped her way to the far wall. As her eyes adjusted, crouching shapes of furniture emerged. Fumbling for the socket, she switched on the lava lamp and fire. In the green glow she changed into her pyjamas. The wax at the bottom of the lamp refused to budge.

Three

Thursday brought a clear sky after days of rain, a bright blustery autumn day. She would've preferred an excuse to hide beneath her hood. The bottom end of Great Western Road was usually quiet though, please God she wouldn't see anyone she knew. Outside the chemist's, a group of skinny guys were smoking and shifting from foot to foot – waiting to get their meth? She crossed over, passing an Indian woman pushing a pram. The woman's embroidered lilac salwar kameez billowed in the wind. Above a doorway, the number read 290. She was looking for 170.

The morning before, she'd woken to the sound of knocking on her bedroom door.

'Maddie?' Callum's voice.

'Just a minute.' She pulled a jumper over her pyjamas.

He looked tense. 'Did you get my note? Have you got my thirty quid?'

'Oh. I will have, tomorrow.'

He flung his hands up. 'I need it today! I don't get paid till Friday. I've got to get down to Paisley. Haven't you got any of it?'

She retrieved the fiver Mike had given her, then nudged him awake. He gestured to his jeans, but she only found a couple of quid in his pockets.

'Seven pound fifty.' She offered it to Callum who snatched it up.

'Jeezo, Maddie. You promised to pay me back on Sunday. I'll need the rest tomorrow.' He swung the front door open. 'I shouldn't have to hound you like this. I feel like a fucking loan shark.' Slam.

Standing inside her room, her back against the door, she stared at the lump under the duvet. 'I thought Ade was going to lend you fifty quid?'

He pulled the duvet over his head. She wrestled it off him. 'Callum needs his money back.'

'He doesn't. He's just making a point.'

'It's his money and...' Her eyes started to stream. She moved to the sofa and wiped her tears with the end of her sleeve, scratchy against her face. The vinegary smell from the fish supper Mike had reeled home with spiked the back of her nose. She bundled it up and hurled it across the room. In the afternoon she walked round the park. Sometimes she'd found coins in the gutter, but not today. Listing all the people she knew, she realised she already owed them money, or she'd be too mortified to ask.

Passing St. Mary's Cathedral now she saw the symbol for the shop. A curly wrought iron bracket strung with a triangle of golden globes.

James Hempseed & Son. Steps led to a basement where two windows displayed jewellery on faded green velvet trays. Beneath the windows, two trough-shaped terracotta plant pots. Whatever had been growing in them was now dead.

A board at one side of the windows was painted with green italics. *Confidential Service.* She adjusted the strap of her bag. Her palms were damp. Though the paint on a corresponding board was peeling, the words were still legible. *Cash advances on items of gold, jewellery, diamonds and gems, musical instruments and a variety of other goods...* The door swung open and a white-haired woman edged out, negotiating her way with a stick. Maddie rooted in her bag, pretending to be looking for something. Her hand touched and turned the little black box she'd put her dad's ring in. Did her mum ever look in the bottom of her jewellery box? Would she notice it gone?

The shop was empty, but a radio played somewhere in the

back. Behind a glass counter, a range of electric guitars hung beside a shelf stacked with jars of jewellery cleaner. A musty smell, like in charity shops. She stifled a sneeze.

A thin blonde-haired woman carried a hoover through and propped it up in a corner. 'Can I help you, hen, or are you just looking?' Her orangey foundation had settled into creases round her mouth.

'Just looking, thanks.'

Beneath the counter, necklaces on velvet trays, with prices on little white tags.

The door, sunk on its hinges, brushed against the worn beige carpet as a big man wearing a navy bomber jacket came in.

He placed a long black bag on the counter. 'Want to pawn the golf clubs.'

'I don't think we take them. Sandra? Do we take golf clubs?'

'No,' a voice came back, then Sandra appeared on the shop floor. 'Not anymore.'

The man sighed, picked up the bag and headed back out.

'Are you okay there?' Sandra was plump with an upturned nose and dark hair cut in a long bob.

Maddie's coat felt tight across her chest, she undid the top toggle. 'I've never been in a pawnshop before.'

'Is there anything you'd like to know?'

She swallowed, her throat dry. 'How does it work?'

Sandra rested a hand on the counter, her manicured nails painted baby pink. 'If you're looking to pawn something, we give you a ticket for six months. It's six percent interest. You can pay the interest monthly, if you like, it can go towards your loan. And we're obliged not to do anything with the item for the six months.'

'What if someone needs longer than six months?'

'You can increase the time on the ticket. We send you out a letter the month before your time's up, just in case you've forgotten.'

Did she look like the type who'd forget? 'How much would the loan be?'

'The loan's based on the second-hand price of the item. What is it you're looking to pawn?'

She hesitated. 'A ring. A gold ring.'

'The price is determined by weight. Or by carat. If there's no hallmark, we do an acid test.' Sandra sounded matter-of-fact, but her eyes were soft.

From her bag, Maddie took the little black box. Inside, she'd wrapped the ring in an old piece of tissue paper. Sandra picked it up.

In a glass cabinet, earrings on slowly rotating shelves. And trays of rings studded with diamonds that spelled MUM, others that said SISTER.

The first time she went out with Jo and Roger and some of the others from college, Jo asked her about her dad and she said, 'I haven't got one.' Everyone laughed. What was funny?

'Everyone's *got* a dad,' Jo said.

Later on, when just the two of them were sitting on a windowsill, smoking, Jo asked, 'Is he dead, your dad?'

'No.'

'Where is he then?'

'I don't know.'

Jo peered at her. 'Don't you want to know?'

She shrugged. He'd walked away.

Beneath the rings, on the rotating shelves, bracelets and necklaces with signs above them that read *Child Sizes*.

'Are you okay?' Sandra placed the ring on the counter.

'Yes,' she said, but her voice wavered.

Outside, the sky had clouded over. At the corner, two boys were sitting on steps leading up to a close.

'Trick or treat, Miss?'

'Miss,' the second boy joined in. 'Oi, Missus!'

'I haven't got anything.'

The first boy stood up. 'Penny for the Guy, then?'

She stopped. 'What "Guy"?'

'Pie-in-the-sky Guy, Miss.'

She shook her head and walked on. 'I've not got any change.'

'We'll accept a note.'

The green man on the pedestrian crossing faded. She broke into a jog.

'You're getting tricked, Miss. You're so getting tricked.'

A woman crossed the street, striding towards her. 'Maddie!'

Disconcerted, she did a double take. It *was* Jo.

'You probably didn't recognise me without the stylish specs. I've just passed by yours. I'm on my way to Liam's. Wanna come?'

'Yeah, actually. I could murder a smoke.'

Hanna answered the door wearing dungarees, her strawberry-blonde curls tied up in a scarf.

'Hey, gals. Come in.'

The living room curtains were still shut. Heavy smog hung just above head height. Blue ribbons of smoke, rising from an incense stick, unfurled an illegible script.

Liam was sitting in his Ernst Blofeld chair. His dressing gown gaped at the thigh, threatening Maddie with more than she'd like to see. His flatmates Iggy and Keith were lying on the floor playing Virtua Racing on the Mega Drive. Up at the decks, a tall guy with wild shoulder-length black hair.

Hanna gestured towards him. 'Jo, Maddie, this is Brendan.' She flopped down on the sofa.

'Hi, Brendan.' Jo moved a packet of Jammie Dodgers onto the coffee table and sat beside Hanna.

Brendan looked up at Liam. 'Haven't you got any techno?'

'Techno's a load of shite.'

'Not gabber, man. Gabber's class.'

Maddie sat on a green velvet beanbag next to Jo.

As Brendan pushed his fingers through his hair, his eyes elongated like a cat's. 'Just the Chili Peppers are doing my box in, man.'

Liam swivelled round. From the ghetto blaster at his feet, he ejected a tape, turned it over and pressed play. Toots and the Maytals came on. He spun back round. 'Hi guys. Got some quality skunk in, if you're interested?'

It looked quite full of seeds, but smelled pungent, a sweet field of wet hay.

'Cool.' Maddie took her purse from her bag. 'Can I get an eighth?'

The fifty pounds came out as a thin wad. The notes were soft, like chamois leather, and smelled of the shop. Her hands shook as she peeled off a twenty and handed it to Liam.

Jo cleared a bit of space on the table and began laying out her skinning-up paraphernalia.

'Man, you should've been out last night.' Brendan moved to the front of the decks to take a pipe from Liam. 'We were sitting down by the river when these guys appeared with drums and started playing. Then these chicks turned up with a load of booze. Before you knew it there was like twenty, thirty of us. Then some geezer came by with a shit load of microdots and just started handing them out.'

He puffed on the pipe. 'Then the geezer built a fire, and another fella got some poles out and twirled the fire over his head and behind his back and swallowed the flames down, like, breathing them out again in roaring jets, filling the sky with a thousand multi-coloured rainbows, all sparking and flying in time with the drums.'

As he used his hands to draw the images in the air, his jeans – baggy at the knee and scuffed with mud and grass – slipped a little showing a thin line of hair running from his navel.

Iggy whistled the *Rainbow* theme tune.

'Shut it, Zippy.' On screen, Keith's car nudged Iggy's onto a verge. 'And take that.'

'Fuck you, Bungle.'

Brendan seemed unfazed. 'Then the flames took on a fucking life of their own, man. They swooped about the sky, spelled out our names, made pictures. One of them became this great big devil dragon, like a Chinese dragon, that danced round the moon.'

Liam raised a leg, Karate-Kid style, and said in a dodgy Chinese accent, '*Enter the Dragon.*'

Iggy coughed and looked up from the screen. 'What the fuck's that supposed to be?'

'Bruce Lee.'

Keith laughed. 'Was he Welsh?'

Liam tutted. 'Bunch of fucking cultural idiots.'

Brendan took a lighter from the coffee table and sucked a flame into the bowl of the pipe. 'Then the dragon's face came right up close to mine and it opened its mouth and it'd got these great big fuck-off horrible teeth, man. And there was like blood in its eyes, and I was scared.'

He passed Maddie the pipe. A tattoo of thorns around his hand. She inhaled and almost choked on the thick smoke. A rush sped up her legs to the tips of her ears, then tingled down her arms. With rubber fingers, she passed the pipe to Jo.

'I was scared shitless. But the geezer who'd given us the microdots, he put his hand on my shoulder and said, "It's okay. Just dance with the beast, man. You'll feel the heat of his breath on your belly right enough, but you ain't gonna come to no harm." So I got up on my feet, and sure enough the dragon closed his mouth. I started dancing and the dragon turned round and – can you believe this? – the dragon shook his fucking ass.'

Shafts of silvery-white burst through the gap in the curtains, backlighting Brendan as though he was some kind of saint.

'He looked over his shoulder, winked at me and shook his ass. I laughed but I knew what he wanted. He wanted me to take hold of his tail. So I did, and I was doing the conga. I was doing the fucking conga with the dragon!'

He shoved his hands in his back pockets. 'But some bitch grabbed my ankle and said, "Hey, watch out for the fire." When I looked back up the dragon had gone. I thought I was gonna go into a real downer then 'cos that dragon was like the best fucking friend I ever had.'

Liam played an imaginary violin.

'But then I met up with a whole load of guys and went back with them to a flat and sat around in front of an oven. Every now and then one of us started laughing. It was so funny, man. It was so fucking funny I had to crawl to the freezer and put my head in it 'cos my eyes were melting. I fucking love this city, man. There's always something going on, you know?'

Maddie sealed the joint she'd been building and offered it to him. He should have the honour of sparking it up.

As he leant forward to take it, sunlight glinted off the anodised blue barbell bolted through his eyebrow. 'Then someone passes me a joint. Could life be any fucking better I ask you?'

What would it be like to dance with a dragon – to hold its tail and sail around the stars? *Swinging on a Star*…wasn't that some old song her dad used to sing?

Jo handed her a machine-rolled joint. It was mostly tobacco. She was slightly embarrassed to pass it on. Liam took a drag, frowned, then left it in an ashtray. 'I've got fucking hundreds of those microdots if anyone wants one?'

She looked at Jo, who'd wandered over to the terrapin tank.

'Nah,' Jo said. 'You're alright.'

'Get it up ye!' Keith punched the air.

Iggy threw his controller towards the telly, got up and plonked himself down on the sofa next to Hanna. 'Fucking stupid game.'

'I'll take a handful off you later,' Brendan said, sitting next to Keith and picking up Iggy's controller.

'Alex…?' Hanna called.

'Yeah?' a voice came back from the hall.

'You off somewhere?'

'Thought I'd take the unicycle out for a bit.'

'Want my keys?'

'Okay.'

Alex appeared in the doorway, juggling four balls with one hand. With his turquoise trousers, checked shirt under holey v-neck and cherry-red Doc Martens, he reminded Maddie of someone, maybe a character she'd seen in a film at the GFT.

Hanna chucked her keys at him, but they hit one of his juggling balls. He caught three of them, but the fourth, and the keys, fell to the ground.

Hanna turned to her. 'This is my brother, Alex, I was telling you about.'

'Hi.'

Alex picked up the juggling ball and keys, looking sheepish. His blonde hair fell forward over his brow. 'Hey.'

Hanna proffered Liam's pipe. 'Wanna toke?'

'Nah. Gonna do a couple of hours' busking.'

'Catch ya later then.'

'See ya.'

His eyes caught Maddie's as he turned to leave and blood rushed into her cheeks.

'Some busking.' Liam sniggered.

'Ach, leave him.'

'Told you the boy's a clown.' Liam laughed more openly.

'I've seen him on that unicycle,' Iggy chipped in. 'He can ride that thing.'

Hanna glared at Liam. 'He's not a boy. He's only a year younger than you. And he's not a clown.'

Maddie rescued herself from the mouth of the beanbag, straightening her legs. She kept her chin low as her cheeks still felt tingly. 'How long's he here for?'

'Dunno. He dropped out of art school.'

Liam spun circles in his chair. 'He's not from this planet.'

'He's just been travelling around for a bit.'

Keith glanced up from the screen. 'On his unicycle?'

'Hey! He can make good money on that thing.'

Liam, Iggy and Keith laughed.

'Fuck you all.' The cups clanked as Hanna gathered them together. 'Maddie and Jo are getting coffee, the rest of you can get to…'

Brendan looked round from the TV, suddenly more hobbit than shaman. 'Am I not getting coffee?' His car fell from a bridge and burst into flames.

Liam shook his head. 'No luck, brother.'

'Hey, Liam'—Jo's voice sounded edgy—'what happened to Madge?'

Maddie grabbed the corner of the coffee table and pulled herself up. The purple swirls of the carpet made her giddy as she stepped over newspapers, beer cans and polystyrene carryout boxes. In the tank, Harold the terrapin was sitting up on a rock staring back at Jo, but Madge was floating upside down in the water.

'Oh, I don't know.' Liam stretched some tobacco over fresh skins. 'She's been like that for days now.'

Maddie and Jo walked back through the park. There'd been a shower and the yellow leaves underfoot were like slippery bat wings.

'You know,' Jo said, 'the more I think about it, the more I'm convinced we should do something with *The Tempest*. It seems so now.'

'What d'you mean?'

'Oh, lots of stuff... Prospero being robbed of his state, reclaiming it – stuff that'd resonate with the push for devolution. Post-colonial stuff. Especially if we did something a bit more experimental with it – basing it on the play, rather than just a straight production. That way we could balance out the fact that women get a bit of a raw deal in it too.'

'Cool!'

'Why should we wait around for the kind of work we want when we could make it happen ourselves?'

Behind them, a bicycle trilled. She jumped. The beam of its headlight showed gloom had gathered between the trees – Mr Tumnus' hour.

'It'd be amazing, but how...?'

'I've got some thoughts.' Jo produced striped fingerless gloves from her bag and pulled them on. 'The Tramway's got this Dark Lights commission thing. I'm gonna look into it once I've got this stupid panto out the way. Which reminds me, you know that woman I do some work for sometimes in Edinburgh?'

'Who?'

'Margaret. She runs ACTive Training, the role-play company.'

'Oh yeah.'

'She's asked me to do a job in a few weeks' time, but I'll have started rehearsals by then. Shall I give her your number?'

'What kind of job is it?'

'Training for police and social workers. Mostly improv. Last time I played a young girl with depression. You'd waltz through it. And the pay's really good.'

'That'd be great.' Maddie stopped, they'd reached the point where their paths split.

'I'm not going to see you on Saturday am I?'

'I'll try.'

'Well, let's get a night out together soon, the three of us – you, me and Roger.'

'Definitely.'

A collar of flashing red lights bounded towards them, circled them as they hugged, then bolted off in the direction of the slope, pursued by a woman shouting, 'Bonzo! Bonzo, come here you wee swine…'

Jo laughed and waved a stripy hand as she headed for the tall iron gates.

Maddie stopped at Londis, then made her way back to the flat. The hall light was on.

'Hello…?'

'Hi.' It was Callum.

She carried the groceries through to the kitchen. Callum was spooning a tin of tuna onto some boiled potatoes.

'You've just missed Mike. He phoned from his mum's. He said he'll be back in an hour.'

'Cool.' She set her bags down. 'I've got the rest of that money I owe you. Sorry about the delay.'

'No worries.' He took a couple of beers from the fridge and offered her one. 'I just found out I got that assistant stage manager job at the Tron. I start next week.'

'Nice one!' She cracked open the beer.

Sitting together, it was almost like old times. She told him about Jo's ideas for a production, and the potential role-play job. He had a story about the kids show he was working on, how the actor playing the spider got angry with the director – how ridiculous he'd looked in his costume, shouting, four false legs quivering with rage.

'Still'—he pushed his chair back—'I better make tracks. I'm meeting the guys for a few drinks to celebrate.' He carried his plate to the sink.

'Just leave that. I've been meaning to make inroads on that stack.'

'Cheers, Maddie.' He headed down the hall. The bathroom fan

whirred.

She was up to her elbows in suds when he popped his head back round. 'Did you say you had the rest of that dough?'

So much for a stay of execution. 'Sure.' She nodded towards her bag. 'Just take it from my purse.'

She did half the washing up, then made a sauce, so she'd just have to boil some pasta when Mike came in. She tidied her room, putting things in piles, rolled a joint and angled it ready to be lit. Taking the black box from her bag, she clasped her hands round it. 'I'm sorry. I'm going to get you back soon. I promise.'

She put on the blue dress Mike liked, applied some make-up and clipped up her hair. Maybe he wasn't the only one who'd stopped making an effort.

By half ten, a rock had formed in her chest. She changed into her pyjamas, smoked half the joint and lay on the sofa in the green glow from the lava lamp – she'd forgotten to buy bulbs.

An hour later, she stared at the phone as the rock sank to the pit of her stomach. Back in the kitchen, she stirred the cold pasta sauce. Should she eat something?

She sat at the table and flicked through an old copy of the *Evening Times*.

People were losing their jobs; abuse was rife in children's homes; refugees were fleeing Zaire; Scottish young offenders were to be electronically tagged; council tax was set to rise by 25%; the Taleban refused to leave Kabul; Lady Di had been voted the best role model for 90's women; air pollution was costing Scotland millions each year.

Most of it depressing, but if Labour could come good in the election next year…

A key in the lock. She closed the paper. 'Hello?'

No reply. In the bedroom, Mike was collapsed on the bed.

'Are you okay?'

'Fucked,' he murmured.

'What happened?'

'Bumped into Gnasher.'

'Couldn't you have phoned? I've been waiting.'

'Did phone. You weren't in.'

'That was ages ago! I got home just after. Callum said you'd be back in an hour.'

His upper body was still, just his legs jerked as he kicked off his shoes.

She didn't want to be angry. Not tonight. Not when she had good news. 'D'you want something to eat?'

He groaned.

'Smoke then?'

He shuffled under the duvet and pulled it up over his head.

Sitting on the edge of the bed, she slid her feet into his shoes. They were five sizes too big for her, and the sole was coming away from one of them. The insoles were damp.

Mike mumbled something from beneath the covers.

She turned. 'What's that?'

He cleared his throat. 'I said, can you turn off the lamp?'

Four

Three weeks later she was looking out of a bus window at a blur of shops, trying to make sense of the directions Margaret had given her on the phone. Was that the Merlin pub? She jumped up, grabbed her rucksack and pressed the bell. The bus shelter flashed by. The driver pulled over at the next stop.

'Pressed that too late, hen,' he said, before opening the doors.

Driving too fucking fast, she wanted to say.

Beneath a streetlamp she checked her map before doubling back. Cold mist crept under her scarf, making the wool feel damp against her neck.

Margaret's road was wide and tree-lined. The big granite houses looked like miniature castles. They had the kind of front rooms that could accommodate proper Christmas trees. Families would gather round them to open their presents on Christmas morning, before the children went outside to play in the snow and relatives came over for dinner. And in the evening, when the relatives had gone, and the children had fallen into deep contented sleep, the parents would sit in the quiet glow of fairy lights, sipping nightcaps and watching the embers pulse red then crumble through the grates onto piles of grey-white ash.

God rest ye merry gentlemen…

Her mum had been leaving messages again, but she dreaded phoning back, knowing she'd want to arrange Christmas. The plastic tree would be dragged from the attic; the dinner would be overdone because Rab would dally at his sister's; he'd finally get back, pissed, then nip nip nip at her mum till she jumped up from the table and slammed the dishes onto the draining board.

Maddie would count off the hours in front of the telly, praying a full-scale row wouldn't erupt, till she could justifiably go to bed. Then she'd pack the nail varnish and eye-shadow kits her mum had saved up for, feeling guilty, knowing she'd never use them.

A gravel drive led up to Margaret's house where the porch was lit by a stained glass lamp. She felt lightheaded – ridiculous to be shy. She'd been given a chance to act again, and she needed the money. Besides, it might lead to more work. Taking a deep breath she pressed the brass bell.

Margaret was smaller than she'd imagined, given her deep, resonant voice on the phone. Low-lighted curls framed her face, which had probably been leading lady material in her youth and was still striking now. She welcomed Maddie with a kiss on both cheeks and asked how her journey had been. Taking note of a row of shoes, Maddie slipped off her trainers, then followed Margaret down the hall into the kitchen.

'Camomile, green, mint, cranberry and raspberry, earl grey or builders'?' Margaret asked, swinging open a cupboard door.

Maddie sat at the end of the large oak table. 'Anything, really, will be fine.'

'No preference?' Margaret frowned and flicked on the kettle. 'Just a minute.' She headed back out into the hall.

As Maddie wandered to the window, warmth seeped through her socks. She pressed her toes against the flagstones – underfloor heating? It was too dark to see into the garden, but to the left there was a conservatory where a man, spectacles perched on the end of his nose, sat in a wicker armchair reading a magazine. Along the sill, herbs grew in ceramic pots. She rubbed one of the leaves – it smelled lemony.

Margaret reappeared holding out a blue and cream striped jumper. 'Here. It's my daughter Emily's. You look frozen.'

She pulled it on. The soft mohair smelled of fabric conditioner. Over a pot of earl grey, Margaret talked about her days as an actress, how she got fed up traipsing the country, staying in dodgy digs, so decided to retire and set up ACTive Training.

'We'll discuss the job in hand when Ian gets here.' She offered Maddie another flapjack. 'He's one of the main trainers who organises things on the social work and police side. He'll be arriving with the two Edinburgh actresses about eight.'

'Thank you.' The flapjacks tasted homemade, treacly, studded with toasted walnuts and juicy raisins.

'So I thought it made sense for you to stay the night. Otherwise you'd be really late back to Glasgow, with a painfully early start tomorrow.'

'Thank you.' Thank you again? Were there no other words in her vocabulary? 'Jo said she always stays.'

'I remember what it's like, when you're starting out. And now we've got an empty nest…'

On the other side of the kitchen, a radiator ran the length of the wall. Some kind of fleecy basket was hooked over one end of it.

Margaret smiled. 'That belongs to Mr Mistoffelees.'

Inside, stretched out on his back fast asleep, was a large black cat. His mouth, pulled down by gravity, showed the tips of his incisor teeth.

A light knock on the kitchen door. She turned and saw the man from the conservatory.

'Am I interrupting?'

'No, not at all,' Margaret said. 'Maddie, this is my husband, Geoff.'

'Hi.' She extended her hand.

Geoff took it in both of his. 'Very nice to meet you.'

'I was just about to show Maddie her room.' Margaret turned to her. 'Give you a chance to unpack before the others arrive.'

The wooden stairs had a pinstripe runner held down by brass rods. They curved up to a first floor landing where framed photographs hung on the wall.

Margaret stopped. 'Juliet. 1962.'

A young woman with a mass of red curls sat at the feet of a stone angel.

'You look stunning.'

'Publicity shot.' Margaret adjusted the frame. 'One minute Juliet, the next Lady Capulet.' She put her hand on the bannister and continued up. '*Gather ye rosebuds while ye may…*'

On the second floor, she pushed open a white panelled door. 'I've put you in here. Emily's room. She was the last to leave, went off to university in September.'

'Do you miss her?'

As Margaret drew close the floor-length curtains, the rings clinked along a wrought iron pole. Was the question too personal?

'I miss them all. But Emily's just in St Andrews. And they'll all be home for Christmas.' She put a hand on Maddie's arm. 'Are you sure you don't want something more substantial to eat?'

'No, I'm fine. I had something before I came.'

'Well, take your time to settle. Come down when you're ready.'

She sat on the edge of Emily's bed. It was a double, with a big feather duvet in a cream cover embroidered with little pink roses. Opposite, a dressing table. A few hair slides and necklaces lay on its glass surface beside a big oval brush that had blonde hair woven through its soft bristles. In the mirror she looked tired and out of place – a mangy forest bear crashing about in Goldilocks's room. Couldn't she have worn something smarter than her jeans?

Parting the curtains, she looked out onto the conservatory. Margaret's garden backed onto another. In a lighted window in a house at the far end, a young girl was playing the violin.

Mike hadn't been as impressed about the job as she hoped – it wasn't 'a proper acting job' – though he seemed interested enough in how much she'd be paid, and when. *Starting out*, Margaret said. All those old promises she'd made to herself: she was going to London, to the Royal Shakespeare Company, but also to the

Almeida and the Royal Court and the Donmar Warehouse where she was going to do new work, work that was going to make a difference. Her breath steamed a small patch against the glass. She wrote her initials, then quickly rubbed them out.

From her rucksack she pulled a skirt and jumper and hung them over the back of a chair, hoping the creases would drop. The nylon wash bag her mum had given her the Christmas before looked cheap and tatty. She was too ashamed to take it out and put it on the dressing table.

The doorbell rang an hour later and the hall filled with voices. Her hair had dried to a frizz. She tried to smooth it. If only she had a smoke to steady her nerves. By the time she descended, the voices had moved to the front room.

Margaret turned. 'Here's our Glasgow gal, Maddie.'

Ian extended his hand and introduced himself.

'And Alisa…' Margaret gestured to a blonde girl with a soft, childlike face.

'Hi!' Alisa grinned, raising her hand.

'And, last but not least, Rachel.'

Rachel was tall, thin and dark-haired. Maddie smiled and nodded hello.

Margaret brought through a tea tray, and, after some general preamble, Ian opened his briefcase, handed out some character studies and began to talk through the plan for the following day. They'd each be playing Kelly – he wagged his set of papers at them – but in different rooms with different groups.

The pool of light from the modern lamp that hung over the Chesterfield armchair on a steel arc made him look like a detective in *Taggart*. Behind him were a grand piano and a cheese plant with huge rubbery leaves that stretched towards the high, corniced ceiling. Bookshelves covered two walls and along a third ran a radiator, over the end of which hung another fleecy basket.

'Any questions?' Ian asked.

Sipping her tea, she flicked through the character study.

Margaret offered round more flapjacks. 'Rachel's done this gig before, so if anything comes up tomorrow, she'll keep you right.'

Rachel gathered her hair in a high ponytail. 'After the first one you'll get the hang of it.'

'There's also a break of about fifteen minutes between each session when I'll be around to answer any questions.' Ian put his papers back in his briefcase and snapped it shut. 'It's not the cheeriest of jobs, but we've found it really makes a difference to our training.'

As Margaret saw everyone out, Maddie sank into the red sofa, listening to the voices at the door. Night air drifted in, smelling of cold tin. The seat where Ian had been sitting creaked as it recovered from the indentation he'd made.

After the goodbyes, Margaret closed the front door. 'Brrrrr…'

The gravel crunched down the drive.

Margaret popped her head in. 'Do you feel okay about everything?'

'Yes. It sounds fine.'

'I wondered if you'd like a nice hot bath. Then I'll make you some cocoa before bed.'

'No, that's okay.'

'Go on, you look like you could do with a nice relax. There's plenty of hot water, and I've put a towel on the radiator for you. Use whatever smellies you fancy.'

The square bathroom had a large clawfoot bath. As she turned on the hot tap, water spluttered then thundered into the tub. Clouds of steam swelled in the air. She selected one of the frosted bottles of bubble bath from a glass shelf and sniffed. Orange and clove. She poured a little beneath the running water then undressed, laying her clothes across a wicker chair. The white towel Margaret had put on the radiator for her was thick and fluffy.

Sitting in the porcelain bath with her knees pulled up, she

watched the glistening suds swirl and regroup. Rainbows slid over the surface of the bigger bubbles as they thinned, then popped. The water was deep, almost too hot. She put her head on her knees and closed her eyes.

Growing up, the towels had been rough and frayed, the soap a hard cracked sliver. Downstairs, the TV was always on too loud over which Rab and her mum yelled at each other.

'Shut up,' she'd whisper, 'shut up, shut up.'

Putting the heels of her hands over her eyes she pressed hard till green shapes pulsed in circular patterns behind her eyelids. Then the centre turned red, and lastly a fuzzy black.

Five

The next day, a taxi took her a short distance out of town to a modern building that was part of the Heriot-Watt University complex. The sky was a high winter blue – oh, to be out walking in the woods somewhere. Or better still, back at her flat, curled up in bed. It was too long since she'd done any acting. She was bound to be shit.

Last night she'd read over and over the notes Ian had given her, then lain awake for hours. When she finally drifted off, she dreamt she was in a derelict house, running from room to room, searching for someone as floorboards splintered beneath her feet – dark ocean waves below.

The driver handed her a receipt. Her eyes felt gritty. She'd probably have a headache by lunchtime.

At the reception desk she gave her name, but Ian appeared and beckoned her from across the foyer. He opened a door to what looked like a small common room. 'This is where you guys will be based for the day, between interviews.'

Rachel and Alisa were already there, reading the character study.

'Hi.'

Rachel raised her hand. 'Hey, Maddie.'

'We're just setting up, so grab yourself a coffee if you'd like one.' Ian closed the door behind him.

'How are you getting on with the notes?' Alisa asked, pulling her hair over her shoulder and starting to plait it.

Maddie pulled up a chair. 'I could do with having another look through them.'

Alisa nodded. 'I'm a bit worried about remembering all the dates.'

'They're just for our info really,' Rachel said, turning a page of her *Heat* magazine. 'It's unlikely you'll need them.'

Maddie took her notes from her bag and looked at the main body of the story.

Kelly is a twelve-year-old girl who lives at home with her mum, her younger sister, and her mum's boyfriend, Pete. Kelly hasn't seen her birth father since she was eight years old. She remembers huge fights between her mum and dad that were often violent. The family moved around a lot and, last year, Kelly, her mum and her sister moved from Manchester to Edinburgh, where Kelly's mum met Pete. Pete quickly moved into the family home. He also has a temper, and Kelly is frightened of him. It was Kelly's birthday last weekend and Kelly had a small party – family, and a couple of the neighbours' children. Later that night, after the party, Pete came into Kelly's bedroom and woke her up. He said she was becoming a woman and it was important for her to understand 'how things worked'. He showed her some pornographic pictures in a magazine and made her touch him. He touched her in ways that made her feel uncomfortable. Kelly asked him to stop and he squeezed her neck and said he'd kill her if she told him what to do. As he left her room, he told her this was just between them, making a gesture as if he'd strangle her if she said anything. Kelly has always been a nervy and anxious child and over the past week this has increased. She has been plagued by nightmares. She doesn't really have any friends at school, but she asked Marianne, a girl she sits next to in class, about how you become pregnant. She began to talk about Pete, but quickly backtracked.

Maddie cringed.

The door opened and Ian peered round. 'About ready?'

Rachel yawned.

'Maddie, if you come with me just now. One of the other trainers will be through for the two of you in a couple of minutes.'

Alisa looked up. 'Good luck.'

'Ach'—Rachel rolled her shoulders—'you'll both be fine.'

Tables draped with white tablecloths were end-to-end along the back wall of the foyer. On them, glasses, cups and saucers arranged in rows beside bottles of sparkling water, jugs of orange juice, and metal pots of tea, coffee, and hot water. A woman with a clipboard was giving directions to a man in a grey suit. They glanced at Maddie as she followed Ian into an office.

'It's a wee bit small in here, but it'll suit our purposes.' He closed the venetian blinds, checked through the viewfinder, and pulled the tripod a little further from the three chairs. 'I'll give you five minutes then I'll come back and switch on the camera. I'll send the first pair in after that.'

She sat in the corner chair.

'Don't make it too easy for them.'

She pinched her thigh to focus herself – whether she was shit or not, she had to do her best. Running through the facts again, she rehearsed how Kelly might tell the story of her birthday in her own words. Then she tried to immerse herself in the world of the scene. She was at school, the bell had rung, Kelly had been asked to stay behind, in the classroom. Outside, footfalls and hollers echoed down the corridor as pupils hurtled to their lockers, jostled on the steps and burst into the playground.

Kelly was anxious – Maddie was nervous too, she could use that. Her school shirt was damp under the arms. Maddie remembered how the boys round the swimming pool used to cup their hands under their armpits and flap their elbows to make farting noises. One of them might've thrown a stink bomb at Kelly. Then they'd all point at her as the girls mimed squirting aerosols, their singsong voices calling, 'Smelly Kelly! Smelly Kelly!'

Ian came back in, but she didn't look at him. Then two people appeared in the doorway. She glanced up. A stocky man in brown cords and a cream shirt, and a short red-haired woman wearing an olive-green trouser suit.

'Kelly?' the woman asked. 'My name's Hazel, and this is Bill.'

Looking between them, Maddie shifted in her seat, sat on her hands.

'I work for the police, and Bill is from social services. Do you know why we've come here to talk to you today?'

She'd widened her eyes at the mention of police. She shook her head.

Hazel and Bill looked a bit stuck.

'Am I in trouble?'

Hazel slipped her bag from her shoulder. 'First of all we want you to know that you're absolutely not in any trouble whatsoever. Okay?'

She nodded.

'D'you mind if we sit down? There's a few things we'd like to chat with you about.'

She nodded again, but Kelly wanted to run, grab her school bag and run.

Bill sat first. 'It's a nice school.'

She shrugged.

'What lessons have you had this afternoon?'

'Double Maths and English.'

'Oooh…Maths.' He grimaced. 'What's your *favourite* subject?'

'Art.' But she wasn't sure there was really anything Kelly liked about school.

'Yeah,' Bill said, 'I liked Art too.'

Something tapped against the window and pulled their attention. Probably one of those boys throwing stones.

Hazel leant forward. Beneath her face powder, freckles were

visible across her nose and cheeks. 'We've come here today because your form teacher, Mrs McGregor, is a bit concerned about you.'

Maddie scratched her leg. A patch of eczema had flared up recently around Kelly's knees.

'Do you have a friend named Marianne?'

'She's not my friend, I just sit next to her in class.'

'Well Marianne spoke to Mrs McGregor about things that might be happening for you at home. We've come here today so you can tell us about that.'

Looking down, she saw the school skirt Kelly's mum had bought second hand. It was way too big and hung in wide pleats. Kelly's skirt, but also her own skirt, from when she'd been about twelve years old.

Bill took a turn, his voice light. 'Do you live near the school?'

She nodded.

'Have you always lived round here?'

She shook her head, then felt as if she should give them something. 'We just moved here about a year ago.'

'Where were you before that?'

'Near Manchester.'

'Big change?'

She looked at Bill, then back down at her knees.

'What do you think of it up here?' he asked.

She shrugged. 'S'alright.'

During the silence, Hazel re-crossed her legs. 'So you live with your mum…?'

Maddie chewed her lip.

'Have you got any brothers or sisters?'

'I've got a sister called Stacy.'

'Is she at school too?'

'No. She's at the primary.'

'Is there anyone else at home?'

She tucked her hands inside the sleeves of her jumper. Outside, the strange rattling call of a magpie. Kelly whispered, 'My mum's boyfriend, Pete.'

'What's he like?'

I hate him, I hate him, I wish he was dead! Kelly wanted to shout. Instead, she drew her legs under the chair. 'He's big.'

Hazel looked stuck again.

Bill twisted his wedding ring. 'Looking forward to the weekend?'

She wrinkled her nose.

'I'm looking forward to it.' He interlaced his fingers. 'It was my birthday yesterday, but I'm celebrating on Saturday.'

Something soft about his face, friendly really.

'When's your birthday?' he asked.

'It was last week.'

'Ha – a fellow Scorpio. Snap!'

He sounded silly, and the corner of her mouth almost curled into a smile.

'What did you do for your birthday?'

'Nothing much…' But Kelly had warmed to him. 'I had a cake.'

'Oooh… what type?'

'It was white and it had pink icing on it.'

'I love cake.'

And slowly the whole sorry story came out. Hazel sat back and let Bill take the lead, but he only asked gentle questions when Kelly came to a stop. Some of it was so hard to put into words it hurt. Hazel reached into her bag and offered a tissue when Kelly couldn't swallow back the tears any longer.

Then Hazel glanced at her watch. 'Kelly, Bill and I need to go now, but we'll come back and see you tomorrow.'

A shiver ran through her. 'You won't tell anyone what I said, will you?'

'We'll need to speak to your mum. And Pete.'

Her heart started to race.

'What Pete's done is very serious.'

'But he said he'd kill me if I said anything.' She looked to Bill, her eyes watering again.

'You've done absolutely the right thing speaking to us,' Bill said.

'He'll say I'm lying, and then...'

'I believe everything you've told us, Kelly. You're not to worry about anything.'

'We'll come back and see you tomorrow,' Hazel repeated as she stood.

Was it time to wrap up? Like a weather house reacting to a change in humidity, she swung Kelly to the back and brought herself to the fore. She nodded and looked down.

After they'd gone, she spread the damp tissue across her knees. What would happen to Kelly? Was she supposed to go home now, to her mum and Pete? Would he do something to punish her? In the very least, he'd deny everything. It was doubtful her mum would leave him. Perhaps she'd end up being fostered or living in a children's home. Please God, with some nice people.

She curled the edge of the tissue.

The first time her mum and Rab had rowed she'd been in her pyjamas, in bed, reading by the light from the streetlamp outside. She crept downstairs and huddled against the bannister. Her mum came to the front door, wiping her face and pulling on her jacket. Rab was shouting, and her mum yelled back with a strained and breaking voice, 'Fuck you, fuck you!' She slammed out. Maddie was scared, but stood up and shouted at Rab, 'Now look what you've done!'

When he turned towards her, his face was tight with rage. She ran back upstairs. He chased her into her room. She jumped on her bed and pulled her knees up into the corner. His face came close. Wild green eyes. 'It's none of your fucking business,' he hissed. His breath was sour. He slammed her bedroom door on the way out. She sat for a long time, breathing shallowly, then shuffled under her duvet, crying 'Mum…' into her pillow.

She'd woken to the sound of laughter coming from her mum's room. It was morning. She went out onto the landing and Rab called, 'Make yourself useful and put the kettle on.' She was halfway downstairs when he added, 'Lurking out there like your mother's fucking shadow.' Her mum had giggled and said 'Rab…' in a playful, admonishing tone.

She folded the tissue and put it in her pocket. She was lucky.

Ian came in and switched off the camera. 'How did it go?'

'Good. They did really well. I hope I did okay.'

'They certainly looked pretty pale coming out. If you can write everything down for the feedback session… But get yourself a coffee first.'

A dozen or so people in the foyer, Hazel and Bill over at the front doors. She joined Rachel at the refreshment tables.

'Hey, how'd you get on?' Rachel asked.

She raised her eyebrows and blew out some air.

'Don't worry, it gets easier. Coffee?'

The cup rattled on the saucer as she took it.

'Ciggie?' Rachel flashed a packet of Berkeley Menthols.

'Have you got enough?'

'Aye.'

She followed Rachel back to their room.

The pair after the break brought a completely different atmosphere with them. The female social worker tried her best, but the policeman was bullish. He shunted his chair forward and pressed Kelly for information as if she were a hardened criminal. Maddie was shaking by the end. The interview felt a kind of trauma in itself.

'How was that?' Ian asked.

'The policeman…'

She struggled to find the words, but Ian cut in, 'Yes. Write it down. It'd be good for him to hear it.'

The third pair seemed anxious. She talked more than she believed Kelly would, just to keep the interview going.

Then it was lunch. The foyer was packed. Ian accompanied her to the queue for the buffet, but was called away.

In front, the woman she'd seen earlier with the clipboard was chatting to an older lady wearing silver spectacles. 'He's been with his carer for four years, but she says she can't cope with him anymore. She's bringing him back to us tomorrow, but we've nowhere to put him. Twelve years old and all alone in the world.'

The older lady shook her head. 'Tragic. But then you know the parents have had it shit too. Just passes on down, doesn't it, like some terrible legacy.'

'That's the bleeding-heart explanation. But I'm not sure where that leaves us, removing personal agency and responsibility from individuals.'

At the table, Maddie put a couple of sandwiches on a paper plate with a handful of crisps then headed back to the room, keeping her head low, hoping no one from the morning's sessions would stop her. She wouldn't know how to behave, and didn't have the energy to muster up an actor's persona.

Rachel and Alisa were sitting at a small square table.

'The script was good, but the director was a complete prick,' Rachel said, sawing an apple with a plastic knife.

'I've heard he always casts his boyfriend.'

'Yep. And the guy can't act for toffee. He's a complete ham. And a bit of a lech.'

'Hey.' Maddie joined them.

Rachel crunched into a quarter of her apple. 'What's the goss on the Glasgow theatre scene?'

'Oh, the usual.' She lifted a triangle of sandwich. The cheese looked like shreds of orange plastic. 'To be honest, I've been caught up with family stuff since I graduated, so I'm only just getting into it now.' Rachel and Alisa were still looking at her. 'I'm playing Miranda at the Tramway soon.' More than a bit presumptuous, but hopefully enough to get her off the hook.

'The Tramway's fantastic,' Alisa said, peeling a fluted paper case away from the sides of a cupcake.

Rachel nodded. 'They host some amazing European productions.'

It was enough. They were off talking about shows they'd seen and folk they both knew from QMUC.

She bit into the sandwich. The cut edges had hardened slightly. The clock on the wall said over four and a half hours till the end of the day, ticking them off with a slender red hand, one second at a time.

Three more pairs in the afternoon, then a break before the feedback session. She was smoking another of Rachel's menthols when Ian came in.

'So, how was it, overall?'

She looked at Rachel and Alisa.

'Some better than others,' Rachel said.

'That's what makes this bit so important. We'll review the video footage with them all tomorrow, but they don't normally get feedback from the child – obviously. *Your* feedback is the nearest we can get to it.'

She scanned the notes she'd made. Her comments on the pair immediately after lunch seemed a bit thin on the ground and she couldn't remember the interview properly.

'So, Maddie, when you're ready…'

In the meeting room, lots of square tables had been pushed together to form one big rectangle. All the police and social workers were sitting round it, some still in their pairs, others separated. Their conversations tailed off as she and Ian entered.

'Right folks'—Ian gestured for her to sit—'it's the end of a long day, but as far as I'm concerned the most important part of it. So if I can ask you to dredge up the last of your energy…'

People sat up in their chairs, put their coffee cups down, took out notepads. Bill, the first social worker to interview Kelly, caught Maddie's eye and smiled. A nice policewoman from an afternoon session waved.

'Firstly I'd like to introduce you to Maddie, our actress.'

She looked round. 'Hi.'

Folk nodded, smiled, murmured in return.

'From what I've heard, she's done an excellent job in a very difficult role.'

Bill started a round of applause and a few others joined in, but it didn't really take off. A bit mortifying.

'I'm going to ask Maddie to give her feedback to each pair, and I'd like you to listen and take what she has to say on board. We can discuss any arising issues tomorrow.'

Ian's gaze was encouraging and, after a few minutes, her voice stopped wavering. Most folk seemed to take the feedback well. At the end she folded her notes.

'God,' Bill said, 'if I can just say, I thought it was going to feel really awkward, but within a couple of minutes I didn't see *you* anymore. It was like a real interview.'

'It was so real,' Hazel from the police said. '*Too* real.'

'I just wanted to give you a hug,' said the nice policewoman from the afternoon session.

'I don't know…' It was the bullish policeman. He'd sat in heavy silence when she told him she'd felt cornered, pressured to tell him what'd happened. 'Maybe if you've never interviewed kids before. It's old hat to me. I couldn't take it seriously.'

'But this is about good practice, Roy. Looking at ways we can achieve best evidence.' Ian clicked his ballpoint pen. 'And it's about retraining for *joint* interviewing.'

Roy pushed his chair back and lifted a leg, crossing it ankle on knee. 'Too softly softly. Too much pissing about. There's people out there being murdered while we're supposed to spend how long with kids, pussyfooting around?'

The social worker that was paired with him piped up. 'This is about trying to respect and protect the child...'

'Protect the child! The best way to protect the child is to find out what the bastard's done, and get him banged up.'

'I don't think it's right...' Her voice was small; she cleared her throat. 'I don't think it's right to treat a child that way.'

He stared at her. Her cheeks burned, but she held his gaze.

'Well, a lot for us to think about and discuss tomorrow,' Ian said. 'But just now I think we should let Maddie go. It's been a long day and she's got a train to catch back to Glasgow.'

Roy snatched up his papers and shoved them in a file.

On the way out the door, the nice policewoman caught her eye again and gave another little wave. She smiled and waved back. Somehow the offer of that hug seemed appealing. She turned, looked up and blinked rapidly. Salty wet at the back of her nose.

It was dark when they stepped outside. A taxi took them into town and dropped them off at Waverley station. The street was busy.

'What time's your train?' Rachel asked, pulling on a fur-trimmed hat that made her look like a Russian empress.

'I'm not sure, but they're pretty regular.'

'I'd suggest a pint, but some friends are coming over.'

'No worries, I'm quite keen to get back anyway.'

Alisa and Rachel crossed towards Leith Street. She waited till they were out of sight before heading to the bus station. From a phone box on the way she called the flat – no one home.

The bus filled quickly and a big guy sat down next to her. She pressed against the window but his legs splayed, devouring the extra space. The heating went into overdrive and the windows steamed up. She closed her eyes. The stench of damp coats and the out-of-order toilet seemed stronger.

The M8 was jammed and the journey slow, but finally she caught a glimpse of George Square. It was strung with Christmas lights. Massive golden bells that illuminated back and forth through three stages giving the illusion they were swinging; giant leaves of holly, each with three red berries; and her favourite, 3D neon blue angels complete with yellow haloes.

Eighty quid for the day's work. As soon as the cheque arrived, she'd go straight down Great Western Road and get her dad's ring back. And there'd still be enough left over for some food and a piece of blow.

Glasgow felt colder than Edinburgh, but the fresh air was a relief. No point rushing back to an empty flat. Doing up her coat, she decided to walk.

Sauchiehall Street was packed with Christmas shoppers. A duo playing a medley of Oasis songs competed with the Salvation Army's 'Hark the Herald Angels Sing'. Along past M&S a small crowd had gathered. It broke into enthusiastic applause. Rising on tiptoes to see why, a thrill ran through her. Alex. Her instinct was to put her head down and hurry away, but she didn't.

Iggy was right, Alex rode well. His feet cycled back and forth through 180° enabling him to balance as, with utter concentration, he juggled what looked like five snowballs. Turning a full circle, he tossed three of them to a group of kids. The fourth he splattered against one of the father's chests, feigning an exaggerated apology. Then he spotted Maddie, smiled and broke the fifth in two. In its centre was the head of a rose. He leant back and landed on his feet, catching his bike by its post. Bowing, he presented her with the flower, but, as she reached to take it, the petals transformed into a butterfly that fluttered rapid spirals up into the night sky.

She laughed and the crowd cheered. Alex grabbed her hand and pulled her into the circle, raising her arm and having her bow too, as if they'd been a double act.

One of the mums ushered her daughter forward to put some money in his pirate hat, and another couple of kids came to stare at the unicycle.

'How long have you had the unicycle?' the snowballed man asked.

'My dad took us to the circus when I was eight. I pestered for one after that, got one for my birthday. This fella I saved up for and bought about three years ago.'

'Impressive act.'

'Thanks.' Alex gestured to the man's jacket. 'Sorry about the attack.'

'He got you, Daddy!' A little boy wrestled the man's legs and was hoisted onto his shoulders.

'Certainly did.' The man counted out some change and dropped it into the hat. 'Get yourself and the lady a drink.'

She blushed – did they look like a couple?

As the crowd dispersed, Alex turned to her. 'Can I buy my fair assistant a beverage?'

'I didn't do anything.'

'Au contraire.' He collapsed the unicycle, tipped the coins into a small cloth bag, then landed the pirate hat on her head.

No make-up, a day of crying, now sporting a pirate hat – surely not a good look.

'Besides,' he said, pulling on his jacket, 'it was a condition of the donation.'

She glanced at the phone boxes, would Mike be home yet?

Alex wrapped a houndstooth scarf round his neck.

'It wasn't a real butterfly, was it? How would it survive?'

The corner of his mouth quivered. 'Come for a drink and I

might tell you.' He ran his fingers through his hair but his fringe fell back over his brow.

Stupid to be nervous, how would she ever manage a conversation? She slid the hat from her head, but he linked his arm through hers.

'I'll take that as a yes then.'

They came out of Nico's about half nine. A group of women sashayed past singing, *'Olé, olé olé olé!'*

'See'—he pointed to the ground—'there's some of those flowers I was telling you about.'

Beneath a grid of glass cobbles, the heads of what looked like chrysanthemums were set against coloured backgrounds and lit from beneath.

She leant forward. 'I'd not noticed them before.'

'They're fairly recent. Part of an environmental art project.'

'But the glass paving's always been there?'

'Yeah. At least, since Victorian times. They used to let daylight into cellars and shop basements.'

'The things you don't know… Which reminds me! What about that butterfly?'

'Ah…' He seemed to consider it. 'Let's just say it's one of life's mysteries.'

'Oh, come on. What about the snowballs then, what were they made of?'

'Hmm. The nature of mysteries… I mean like now – life expects us to walk to Charing Cross and say goodbye and that's that, right? But what if we turned round and walked this street again – would we upend life's plan, or would that be *part* of its plan?'

'You're assuming life has a plan.'

'A libertarian?'

'Maybe. Just seems an awful lot of us to each have an individual fate.'

'But we don't know for sure, right? It's a mystery. Don't you look up at the stars sometimes and feel almost decimated with awe?'

'Like a coconut?'

He peered down at her with a playful stern stare.

'Sorry. You were saying…?'

'D'you ever get an overwhelming fizzy feeling that you have to, like, just run off?'

'I can't say that's something I can really relate to.'

He laughed.

At the street corner a man was selling copies of the *Big Issue*. Alex took a couple of quid from his cloth bag.

'Help the homeless, mate?'

'Cheers. Keep the change.' Folding the magazine, he tucked it in his jacket pocket. 'Actually, are you going to be here for the next ten minutes or so?'

The man sipped from a polystyrene cup. 'Aye. Why'd you ask?'

'Could you keep an eye on the unicycle for me?' He propped it up beside the cash point.

The man shrugged. 'No problem.'

Securing his hat on his head, Alex cocked an eyebrow. 'Last one back to the Christmas tree's a numpty!'

She watched him run. In her head she heard Roger declare that the position of numpty seemed to have already been filled. She laughed and set off after him, weaving between people coming out of pubs and couples perusing restaurant menus. The cold night air rushed against her face and the world shone.

Just past Bradford's she called, 'Alex. Hey, Alex!'

He turned.

Pointing down, she asked, 'Is this part of that environmental art project?'

He made his way back towards her, peering at the pavement.

When he was close enough to touch, she took off, sprinting past him.

'Hey!'

She was within reach of the Christmas tree when he grabbed her round the waist, picked her up and spun her round. 'A cheat. A total cheat!'

'A numpty. A total numpty!' She laughed, panting clouds of breath.

Setting her down, he turned her round and led her in stumbling circles that became a polka, singing, '*Oh Christmas tree, oh Christmas tree, of all the trees most lovely…*'

Behind him, the world was a blur of people in hats and scarves and the arms of the fir tree laced with coloured bulbs.

When they stopped, the world seemed to keep on spinning.

'Look, angels are having a pillow fight…'

Following his gaze, she saw soft feathers of snow drifting down to them out of a sodium sky. He still had hold of her hand. In a rush of awkwardness she crouched down, pretending her laces needed retied.

All the way back down Sauchiehall Street she could feel how his hand had held hers – its heat, width, slightly rougher skin. Artist's hands. He'd said he liked sculpture best at art school, and hoped to get back to it soon. 'But it's hard. Sometimes I feel like there's sixty lives I want to lead. How am I supposed to pick just one?'

At the corner, a small group of blokes had gathered. One of them was propped between two friends, holding onto their shoulders as he tried to balance on the unicycle. The wheel slipped beneath him and he was catapulted forwards, only just finding his feet. The unicycle bounced on the ground.

'Sorry'—the *Big Issue* seller pointed with his thumb—'couldn't keep them off it.'

'Oi, Calico Jack,' one of the guys called. 'Is this yours?'

'Yep.'

'Bloody impossible!'

'Takes practice.'

'Let's see then.'

'Nah, I'm done for tonight.'

'Come on, man. Just a wee turn.'

Alex stepped on a pedal and, like an obedient witch's broom, the unicycle sprang up under him.

'No way, man!'

He balanced along the kerb, hopped off, cycled back and forth then spun three times like an ice skater.

The guys clapped. 'Hats off to Calico Jack!'

'Hey,' one of them called, 'why are pirates pirates?'

'Cos they arrrr!' the others replied, grabbing their friend round the neck and ruffling his hair.

'Do you get that a lot?' she asked as they walked on.

'I don't mind when it's friendly.' He stopped outside the Canton Express. 'Noodles?'

If she had any money left... 'I better be getting back. It's been a long day.'

'Can I walk you?'

'It's okay. I'm used to getting about by myself.' A twinge of guilt, she'd not mentioned Mike. Please God they wouldn't bump into him, rolling out of somewhere, steaming.

'D'you know it's a gibbous moon tonight. If we could see it. Well, it is a gibbous moon. Whether we can see it or not is incidental.'

'A gibbon moon?'

'Gibbous! *Gibbous.*'

'Stop monkeying around.'

'Oh, ah ha ha. Look it up.'

'No such word.'

'A pound says I'm right.'

'Deal!'

They shook on it. For a moment, her hand back in his.

The corners of his mouth curled. He doffed his hat and bowed. 'I look forward to collecting my pound.'

As she headed west, away from the city centre, the sky lost its orange glow, becoming blacker. Stars appeared. 'Gibbous moon...' She laughed. Beneath the street lamps the snow sparkled like glitter.

Looking up at the unlit windows of her flat, she almost didn't want to go in. Alex would be arriving back at Liam and Hanna's about now. There'd probably be a group there, sitting around, telling jokes and stories.

In the hall, the answering machine was flashing – five messages. She pressed play. The first was for Callum; the second, the one she'd left for Mike from Edinburgh; the third, her mum, again; next, Mike slurring something about being home soon; and, lastly, a voice that was initially unfamiliar.

'Hello. This is a message for Maddie. I just wanted to let you know I've had some excellent feedback from Ian about your work today. It was a pleasure meeting you, and I hope you'll come and work with us again. I'll certainly be in touch when something suitable next comes up. In the meantime, wishing you the very best with all your endeavours.'

She listened to the message again, then stood in her bedroom in the dark, looking out. Flinging up the window she was met with a fresh chill and the sound of distant traffic. The snow was falling thickly now and the roofs leading back to the city centre were already laced white. *Excellent feedback... more work in the future...* Something bubbled up in her, that fizzy feeling Alex described, and she *did* want to run, out over the rooftops, run and run and run till her feet hardly touched the tiles and she started floating up – up and up and up, twisting and turning as snowflakes melted on her hands and face.

Then she remembered to look in the dictionary.

Six

Over the next couple of weeks she wandered into town a few times and saw various acts: a man painted bronze posing on a plinth; a blind couple singing love songs; a group of Native Americans playing panpipes. But no Alex. Eventually, at Liam's one night, she plucked up the courage to ask after him. Hanna said he'd gone back to Keswick to help their folks out in the restaurant. Ridiculous, all the time she'd spent pacing the streets and he wasn't even in the same country. What had she been thinking anyway? Some lame excuse about wanting to give him that pound.

Meanwhile, Nick had got Mike an audition up at the BBC Comedy Unit, and he'd been dining, or rather drinking, out on it since. Whether it'd actually lead to a job was debatable, certainly no sign of anything yet. Then Jo passed her another bit of work, this time playing a dead body for a murder mystery weekend at a hotel near Loch Lomond. She'd been nervous, but she knew a couple of the other actors from college, and Alison – the woman who ran the company – was easy to get along with. All her anxiety turned out for nothing anyway, she'd only had to sit through dinner looking like one of the guests, then choke on her pudding.

When she got back to her flat on Sunday afternoon, there'd been a message from Jo.

'Wednesday night,' Jo said, 'keep it free. You, me and Roger – pre-Christmas drink.'

She couldn't keep putting it off. And she wanted to see Roger. She rifled through her wardrobe and found a lacy top that she wore with leggings when they used to go out clubbing. It smelled musty so she hung it by the window.

Wednesday evening, Jo called round at seven. After a quick smoke they headed down Sauchiehall Street. For most of the week, days had only managed to drag themselves briefly into heavy grey light, but today brought a clear sky, alpine blue. Now crisp black. The blood in her cheeks felt as if it was already starting to crystallise.

Jo linked her arm through. 'Slippy.'

An awkward partnering given the height difference.

'You've not said how the panto's going?'

'Okay. Some of the kids are really sweet.'

'I'd like to see it.'

'No way. Besides, we finish up tomorrow. How did you get on with the murder mystery gig?'

'It was fine. Easy life. Alison seems nice.'

'She phoned earlier about another gig this weekend and was wondering if you were free. I said I was seeing you tonight and would ask.'

'Really? To play the deadie again?'

'Actually I was wondering if you'd take my part and I'd play the deadie.'

'But that'd be less money for you.'

'I know, but I've had a busy week. I'd be happy to collapse in the first half hour then hang out in a bedroom. Roger's coming – it'd be fun, the three of us.'

Was there any point checking with Mike? A bit of extra cash might enable her to buy a few Christmas presents. And she owed Callum some money again. 'That'd be great actually. Can you tell her yes from me?'

'Cool. Will do.'

They crossed the motorway. To the right, the bronze statue of Minerva, illuminated on top of the dome of the Mitchell library, was striking against the sky. Like Alex said, there was stunning architecture in so many parts of the city, sometimes you just had to look up.

A group of people on a work night out funnelled through the doors of the Loon Fung, a couple of them sporting paper hats. Her mum had finally caught up with her and she'd arranged to go north on Christmas Eve, come back Boxing Day, transport allowing.

'When d'you think I might get a cheque from Margaret, by the way?'

'Usually takes just over a month. Why, d'you need a lend?'

'Nah. Was just wondering.'

She'd been paid cash-in-hand for the murder mystery, but it wasn't enough to buy back her dad's ring, it was just enough to tide her over. What did the woman in the pawnshop say? They were obliged not to do anything with the ring for the first six months. Still, she'd feel better having it back in her possession. If she could get it by next week, she could return it to her mum's jewellery box over Christmas.

'Won't be a mo, just need to get some money out.' Jo sprinted across to the cash point.

It was the corner where Alex had parked his unicycle that night; where he'd challenged her to a race; where he'd done some tricks, impressing the group of guys.

The Variety was busy, but a couple got up from one of the large curved sofas that looked like waltzers without the safety bars. She made a beeline for it. Suddenly too hot, she peeled off her coat. 'Teenage Kicks' was blaring, and folk were shouting at each other to be heard. Her heart thumped. Perhaps she should've had more for dinner than that Findus Crispy Pancake stolen from Callum's supplies.

The door swung open. Roger spotted her immediately but pretended not to. Leaning against a pillar and sliding his scarf from his neck, he threw her smouldering looks. She played coy, fanning herself with her hand. He looked as she remembered, only his ginger curls were a little wilder. Mick Hucknall hair. Must tell him that, he'd be outraged.

Finally he dashed over and lifted her up in a rib-cracking squeeze. 'Hey, stranger. Where have you been?'

'Oh, Hollywood, Cannes, Berlin. You know how it is.'

'Ah, yes. And how was the premiere, the festivals, the award ceremonies?'

'I'm sorry to report that, frankly, I think the film industry's corrupt. From now on, I'm staying here in the dear green place. Maybe I'll grace a profit-share piece of theatre at most.'

'Wise. Very wise. I felt the same about the West End and Broadway.' He cupped his hands round her face and planted a kiss on her cheek. 'Been too long, baby.'

Jo appeared with three vodka-and-Cokes. Manoeuvring her grip on the wet glasses she released their drinks to them, then hooked Roger round the neck. 'Hey, handsome. What's the news?'

'Seeing you two lovely ladies, all's well. Day up till now, total nightmare.'

They sidled onto the sofa.

Jo wriggled out of her jacket. 'Tell us all about it.'

'Where to begin…' Roger rummaged in his coat pocket and pulled out a packet of B&H. 'I saw an advert in the *Evening Times* last Tuesday. I've been looking for something, anything, I'm sick of being skint.'

'No luck with the *Taggart* audition then?' Maddie asked.

Jo winced.

Roger's stern look melted into a sigh. 'And from the shifts at the Gandolfi I only earn enough to reduce my dole.' He peeled the cellophane off the cigarettes, flicked open the top, pulled out the lip of gold foil and gave it to Maddie. The music student she'd had a fling with had shown her how to fold butterflies and, for a while, she'd been obsessed with making them.

'So the advert…?' Jo prompted.

'Yes. It said, Actors required for promotional work. Well I thought, it's probably phone sales, but I'll give them a ring.' He raised his glass. 'Up yer bum!'

They clinked over a nightlight in the middle of the black half-moon table.

'Sleeves! Sleeves!' Roger shooed them away, gesturing to Jo's 70s-style top. 'Especially angel sleeves.' He offered round his cigarettes.

Maddie took one, but Jo shook her head and said, 'I'm trying to give up. Even cutting down on doobies.'

Roger grabbed their hands. 'Oh my God, yes, what about you? It's not all about me.' He squeezed Maddie's hand. 'I've not seen *you* for ages.'

She shrugged. 'Been getting by. Jo passed me a couple of bits of work. I'm going to join you for the murder mystery this weekend…'

He threw his hands up. 'Okay, enough about you!'

They laughed.

Jo nudged him. 'Come on then, what happened with the advert?'

'If you insist.' He bent over the flame and lit up. 'I phoned. A man answered and asked if I was free to work today. I said I was, but asked what the job entailed. "Well," the man said, "it's quite basic promotional work at Thomas Cook. You'll be based within St Enoch's Centre." I reckoned I was right. Sales.'

He slid the nightlight towards Maddie. 'He told me how much the hourly rate was – which was pants, but cash-in-hand – and we agreed to meet.'

The long wick glowed red at the end, its tip about to fall off into the wax. She lit up, her lungs filled with smoke.

'Thomas Cook was still locked up when I got there this

morning. I waited ten minutes and was just thinking I should've taken a note of the contact number when this scraggy-looking guy came up and said, "Roger? I'm Richard. We're actually going to be working a little further down here today."

'I followed him to the far end of the precinct, near the toilets, where there was a food wagon beside the Christmas market. It had a sign over the hatch that said Dick's Dogs.'

Jo leant in. 'What?'

He took another gulp of his vodka-and-Coke and sucked his lips together. 'Turned out Richard owned a hotdog van and wanted some leaflets distributed around the precinct. Half-price hotdog for anyone who handed him back a leaflet.'

Maddie glanced at Jo. 'Not very glam, but not too bad.'

'That's what I thought, until I saw the costume.'

Jo kept her gaze steady. 'Costume?'

He pounded the table. 'It's not funny!'

A guffaw escaped Jo's mouth. She coughed and looked down. 'Sorry.'

He sighed. 'Yes. With holes for my face and arms.'

Jo flicked her eyes up at Maddie.

'I asked Richard if it was a joke, but he looked pretty hurt. I didn't have the heart to say no. So there I was in the gents climbing into this giant foam hotdog suit. Richard stood behind me zipping me in saying, "You look great!" I thought, *Oh my God, if Grandpa could see me now...* Then he stuffed a bundle of leaflets in my hand and I spent the whole morning trying to give the damn things out.'

He took a long draw on his cigarette and blew three smoke rings.

'Nightmare.' Maddie tapped a long catkin of ash from the end of her cigarette. 'I'd be terrified I'd see someone I knew.'

'Funny you should say that... Just after lunch, I wandered down by the escalator, got a bit distracted looking in shop windows, when who should I see walking towards me? Valerie Dawes.' He adopted his Queen's English voice. Valerie was always on his case about Received Pronunciation in class.

Jo's eyes widened. 'Oh my…'

'Yes. I saw her beehive first. No mistaking it was her.'

'What did you do?' Maddie curled the edge of the gold foil tab.

'Panicked. Looked around for somewhere to hide. Everywhere seems rather exposed when you're a giant hotdog. So I just thought, *Right, head back to the wagon.* But my legs could only go so fast because of the stupid suit. Eventually I got there. Amazingly, Richard had a queue. He gave me the thumbs-up. I dashed into the gents, squeezed myself sideways into a cubicle and locked the door.'

Jo raised her eyebrows. 'Relief.'

'Yes, but then I realised I couldn't sit down. I tried to reach round for the zip – no luck. Then I actually did need a pee.'

He stubbed his cigarette out and took another drink. 'I thought, *I'll have to go and ask Richard to unzip me.* There was still a queue at the wagon. I stood to the side, waiting. Which was when this group of neds came up…'

He pressed the sides of the nightlight so the wax rose, chasing the flame to a small yellow orb at the end of the wick. 'There were only three of them, and they must've only been about twelve years old, but I sensed trouble. One of them was wearing a white baseball cap. He called out, "Hey, dickhead!" I ignored him. "Look at the size of that guy's banger!" another one shouted. Which they all thought was really hilarious. I looked at the ground. "Yeah," shouted white baseball cap, "but check out his baps!"

'He prodded me. Now, okay, I didn't feel it because of the foam suit, but even so… "That's enough," I said. Big mistake. He pushed me. I wobbled for a moment… then toppled. I actually bounced. They legged it. Just when I thought I'd be left thrashing about on the floor forever, Richard and some other guy appeared. Lifted me back onto my feet.'

'Thank God.' Jo ran her amber pendant from side to side along its chain.

'Which is when I had the joy of realising a crowd had gathered.' He dipped his fingertips in the wax and let it harden to white caps. 'And at the back of the crowd who should I see?'

'Oh!' Jo pressed the pendant to her chin. 'She might not have known it was you?'

'Bless you, angel-eyes.' He peeled the wax from his fingertips. 'She knew. We had a moment. Then she turned, put her head down, walked away. Meanwhile Richard was shouting, "Right folks, the show's over!" waving his arms about. He asked if I was okay. I couldn't speak. On the way back to the wagon we saw that, during all the commotion, some clown had climbed up and swapped his sign about over the top of the hatch. So that it read Dogs Dicks.'

Jo snorted into her drink. Even Roger's mouth flirted with a smile.

'I said to Richard, "You don't have to pay me, but I've got to go home now."'

'You didn't even get paid?' Maddie rolled the gold foil into a ball.

'He gave me twenty quid. He was a decent bloke. Anyway! How are my eyebrows?' He thrust his face close to Jo's, then turned to Maddie. 'Final kick in the teeth, got back to the flat to discover I had a Denis Healey. Enormous great big long fucker. And it was…' he lowered his voice and exaggerated the lip pattern, 'silver.'

Roger was at the bar when a guy and girl came in wearing Santa hats.

'Got plans for later?' the guy asked Jo.

'Not sure.'

'All shots and bottles only a pound at the Garage tonight.

Interested?'

'Could be.'

'I'll fill you out some passes anyway.'

'There's three of us.'

'No problem.' The guy handed over the passes then he and the girl wove into the crowd.

Roger turned and shrugged. It was three deep at the bar and he wasn't having any luck getting served.

'It annoys me. How come you, me and Roger are struggling for work when there's so many duffers from our year in rep, or on TV?' Jo tried to balance the passes in a triangle. 'Lenny's got a film, for Christ's sake.'

'It's not like nobody warned us.'

'That's why I think we've got to do our own thing. I spoke to Roger about *The Tempest*. He's up for it, so I'm gonna contact the Tramway about that commission. It'd probably just be for a pilot production to begin with.'

'D'you need a hand with anything?'

'I dunno. I'd love to make it multimedia, find a filmmaker to work with…'

'When would it go on?'

'If we were lucky, I reckon about June or July next year, but it'd be great to start workshopping after Crimbo.'

'That'd be brilliant.' Did she dare let herself believe it would happen?

Roger looked over again, success. The barmaid pressed three glasses in turn up against the optic.

For a moment Jo's triangle of passes held in perfect balance, then they collapsed. 'What are you doing for Crimbo by the way?'

'Can't even bear to think about it.'

Jo rubbed her back. 'Fuck family. You should just do your own thing.'

'What are you doing?'

'Family.'

They laughed.

'But then I don't have a cunt like Rab in my clan.'

Maddie flicked the foil ball towards the ashtray. It bounced and skidded off the table. Folding her fingers into a temple, she rested her chin. The wax of the nightlight had turned completely liquid and the wick, unsupported, tilted until it was submerged.

Seven

Friday morning, Jo called round at 7:30, once again wearing the giant specs.

'Same problem?'

'No.' She pushed the frames up her nose. 'Eyes just feel like shit. Hoping to get more sleep in the car.'

Maddie led through to the kitchen, keeping her voice low. 'Quick coffee?'

Jo nodded. 'Feels like when we'd been out all night. Only a lot worse.'

'Maybe 'cos of the lack of vodka. We could do with a smoke.'

Jo produced her tin from the top of her rucksack. 'I probably won't bother, but feel free.'

Was it wise, when she was working later? There were hours of travel ahead, maybe it'd help her sleep. She took the small lump of hash from Jo's tin. It was squidgy – no need to heat, she could just roll a thin snake. 'What is it?'

'Black, I think. But pretty potent. Wren got it through his friend, Terry.' Jo filled the kettle then took a pint of milk from the fridge. 'Jeezo, since when did Callum start labelling all his stuff?'

'Shh.' Maddie pointed towards his room. 'Since he caught Mike helping himself to his Cornflakes.'

'Next he'll be marking the level.'

Smoke rose from the joint. Indigo.

Jo set the coffees down on the table. 'Too bad you didn't come to the Garage with us on Wednesday. The music was great. Roger was on top form.'

She wished she had. Mike woke her when he finally stumbled

in. They'd argued about money again.

She released her breath. 'Tastes almost perfumey.'

'Sod it. Let's have a toke.'

Some time later, she lifted her cup and was surprised to find only a mouthful of cold coffee in it. What had she been doing? Oh yes, wondering why, when she stared, the wall opposite turned from white to grey to ultraviolet. Up in the corner was a mesh of black lines – cracks in the plaster or a cobweb? Would be a fucking big spider.

Jo was standing by the window, peering down. She turned. 'Fuck, what time is it?'

'Christ knows. Where are we going again?'

Jo looked stricken, then her face crumpled. She sniggered. 'I don't fucking know.'

By the door, the rucksack Maddie had packed the night before. What was in it? 'Oh, man.' She started to snigger too.

On their way out, she considered saying goodbye to Mike. He'd only grunt, then turn away. Fuck it.

The streets were busy. People in long coats with briefcases and umbrellas hurried to offices. A queue of cars stretched back from the motorway traffic lights.

Jo adjusted the straps of her rucksack. 'Meet at the bloody bus station. Why couldn't Alison just have picked us up from yours?'

They parted as a big green street cleaner came towards them – a lawnmower for the city. A couple of newsagents were open, their windows neon displays of toy tigers, cheap lighters and plastic soldiers in clear souvenir tubes. Behind the gratings at Boots, a woman tore open a bag of change and tipped it into the till. Everyday – buying, selling, earning, spending.

Round the corner, Alison's car was in the lay-by.

'Shit.' Jo picked up her pace.

As they neared, the driver's door swung open and Alison stepped out. Her 80s-style bubble perm was scraped back into a banana clip. Seemingly her younger sister was an actor, but Alison didn't have the same opportunities growing up. She'd married at eighteen, had kids, and sold diet products for a while until, one Christmas at a work do, the entertainment was a murder mystery. A long-time lover of true crime books, she'd gone to bed reckoning she could do it better.

Jo swung her rucksack from her back. 'Sorry we're late. It's my fault, I couldn't find my keys.'

'Don't worry about it. The phone went just as I was leaving. That bloomin' Roger said his alarm didn't go off. He's probably going to be another ten, fifteen minutes.' She opened the boot.

Jo put her rucksack in. 'I'm just gonna nip over to the shop. Want anything?'

Alison shook her head. 'No thanks.'

As Maddie climbed in the back, Alison handed her some printed pages. 'Here's the plot and character notes. I'd have got them to you sooner, but it was a bit of a last-minute booking.'

She looked at the cast list. 'Who else is coming?'

'Imogen and Hugo. They're driving up from Perth. D'you know them at all?'

'Are they a couple?'

'They recently got engaged.'

'Really? If it's the same folk, they were the year below us at college.'

Jo returned with a breakfast of chocolate and crisps.

Maddie flicked through the pages. 'Who am I playing?'

'Audrey. The murderer.'

She turned to Jo. 'Apologies in advance.'

'Hey, don't worry about it,' Jo said. 'In the afterlife there's a bed, beer, TV…'

Alison spotted Roger first. He ran up, panting, his shirt half-hanging out his jeans. Alison wound down her window.

'I'm so sorry…'

Maddie caught a whiff of stale cigarettes and whisky.

As Alison put his holdall in the boot, he whispered, 'Not been to bed since I saw you on Wednesday. Ended up shagging *a woman*.' He grimaced.

'Any port in a storm, eh?' Jo said.

'How dare you. I must've been spiked!'

'Again?'

'Oh!' He held up a hand and turned to Maddie. 'Please let me sit in the back.'

Seemed he was in greater need.

Alison was edging from the lay-by when Roger gasped. She braked. 'What's wrong?'

'I've forgotten my shoes!'

'What d'you mean you've forgotten your shoes? What did you come here in?'

'My trainers.'

Alison twisted round.

'They'll do,' Jo said.

'No they won't. It's 1920s. I'm supposed to be the manager of the hotel.'

Gripping the steering wheel, Alison leant her head on her hands. 'For God's sake, Roger.' She indicated and pulled out. 'We'll just have to stop en route and buy you a pair.'

Maddie looked out the window and bit her lip. Would now be a bad time to mention she needed the loo?

Once on the motorway, the journey was fairly smooth. Directions were a little confusing after Inverness, but by late afternoon they were heading up a long winding driveway.

The hotel looked like a converted granite castle. Stone steps led to an arched entrance. The reception area was panelled with dark wood and strung with thick strands of red tinsel and gold baubles. Alison pinged a brass bell. Beside the curved desk, a tall Christmas tree twinkled. An open fire had burned low. Roger warmed the back of his legs. On each wall was a mounted stag's head. Grotesque, though when she looked again she realised one was made of papier-mâché and another carved from wood – were any of them real?

A lanky porter with streaked blonde hair took Alison's suitcase. They all squashed into a mirrored lift, then followed him along a dimly lit corridor where he opened rooms for Alison and Roger.

'And a twin room…?' He wielded a key. Striding ahead, letting them catch the heavy fire doors in his wake, he led the way up a narrow spiral staircase into a turret.

He unlocked a door. 'Need anything, dial zero.' His casualness had an air of disdain – inspired by their youth or the fact they weren't proper guests?

Their room was far from servants' quarters though.

Jo slipped off her rucksack and dived onto one of the beds. 'Bliss.'

On a mahogany desk was a tea-making kit, with a white teapot and a range of teas and coffees.

Maddie lifted a china plate. 'Homemade shortbread. A step or three up from the last hotel.'

Jo reached for the plate. 'Yeah, Alison said the do's for some big pharmaceutical company. Gawd knows what they'll make of us.'

A small diamond-shaped window looked out over lawns to the loch. On the far side was a forest of fir trees that stretched halfway up a snow-capped mountain, dusky purple in the fading light. It hadn't snowed in Glasgow since that night with Alex. They'd get most of their snow in February and March, though last year they'd had a white Christmas. It'd been bitter.

She touched her nose to the cold glass. 'I'd like to live in a little wooden hut halfway up that mountain.'

'Can't see Mike liking that.'

Mike? She flinched.

Jo licked the crumbs from her fingertips, then leant over,

pinched one of Maddie's pillows and positioned it behind her head. 'Hope you don't still snore.'

'I never snored!'

'The one who denied it always supplied it.'

'The one who smelt it dealt it. No, wait, that's farts isn't it?'

Jo pulled her clothes from her rucksack. Her tin clattered onto the carpet, landing on its lid. 'Definitely no farting. The last time I shared a room with Roger he hadn't eaten all day, then had an omelette for supper.'

'Too much information.'

Jo brandished a *TV Quick*. 'Wish we could just chill out in here watching films.'

'It's alright for you. You'll be dead by eight o'clock. I hadn't realised I'd basically have like the main part.'

'You'll be great.'

'I should look over the notes again.'

'You looked over them plenty in the car. Just relax and go with it.'

She righted Jo's tin with the toe of her shoe. Maybe a puff or two would help settle her. 'D'you think it'd be a bad idea to have a wee smoke?'

Jo looked at her watch. 'Maybe if it was a really weak one…'

They were halfway through smoking the joint when there was a knock at the door.

'Shit.' Jo stubbed it out in a saucer then called, 'Just a minute.'

Maddie wafted the bathroom door back and forth as Jo sprayed deodorant high into the air.

Jo opened the door. 'Hey, Imogen.'

'Oh my God, you guys are in the back of beyond up here. It's creepy.' She poked her head into the room. She had a china-doll face – creamy skin, rosebud mouth, bright blue eyes. 'Hi, Maddie.'

'Hi.'

'When did you guys get here?' Jo asked.

'We drove up early this afternoon.'

She looked quite ethereal standing there, half in shadow on the threshold. Any moment her lips might curl back exposing long, pointed incisors, dripping blood.

Pulling her mane of blonde hair over her shoulder, Imogen ran her fingers through it. 'Do either of you have your hair straighteners with you?'

Jo shook her head and turned to Maddie.

'No, sorry.' Like she even owned a pair.

'Bother. Fuzz alert!'

Jo leant against the doorframe. 'Do you know when we're meeting in Alison's room?'

'Oops, that's what I came here to tell you. Alison's got some stuff to sort out downstairs, so says can you come now?'

'No probs. Tell her we'll be there in five.'

'Will do.' Imogen drifted from view.

Jo closed the door. 'No, no, not now.'

Maddie stood, one hand on the wall. 'I need to get my brain together.'

In the bathroom she filled the basin and dunked her face, pulling up moments later, panicked for breath.

By the time they arrived at Alison's room, Imogen had donned a gold sequinned flapper dress. She twirled. 'Good enough to be Roger's wife?'

'Hmm,' Jo said, 'I hear the gent is not for turning.'

Roger, sitting on the edge of the bed wearing the disgusting patent leather lace-ups Alison had bought for him, glared.

Pacing up and down near the bathroom, still in his own clothes but wearing a deerstalker hat, Hugo raised a hand in greeting.

Maddie sat in a moleskin armchair in the corner.

Alison, now wearing a grey trouser suit with large shoulder pads, put some paperwork in a folder. 'Right, quick run through.'

Flopping on the bed beside Roger, Jo said, 'Did you say you had costumes for me and Maddie?'

Alison gestured to a suit bag hanging on the wardrobe door. 'Yes. Please tell me you've brought shoes and tights.'

Maddie nodded. The black Character shoes she'd bought for college would finally come in useful.

'Shoes, yes,' Jo said. 'But I don't remember you saying tights…?'

Alison tossed a bumper pack in Jo's direction. 'Anticipated.' She perched on the edge of the desk. 'So, everyone ready by seven. Then all but Hugo downstairs, welcoming guests, interacting. Jo and Maddie in the cocktail lounge serving snacks. At some point, about twenty minutes in, I'll give you the nod, Jo. Five minutes after that the gun will go off. Make sure you're in full view of everyone when you collapse. That's when you, Roger, need to take control and usher everyone out of the room.'

'Okay.' Roger caught Maddie's eye, crossed his legs, bounced his foot a couple of times and raised an eyebrow. She tried not to laugh, but burst with something that sounded like a cross between a cough and a sneeze.

Alison looked over. 'What's funny?'

'Nothing. Just a tickle in my nose.'

Imogen turned from the mirror. 'Hair up or down?' She showed both options.

'It'll have to be up,' Alison said. 'It's too long to be period.'

Hugo continued to pace, puffing on an unlit pipe. Maddie looked at Jo, but she'd sprawled on the bed behind Roger and was watching the mute TV.

Roger stood, shifted about in his shoes. 'Are you sure these are a size nine?'

'I'm positive, Roger.'

'They just seem a bit tight.'

Alison sighed. 'Oh, by the way, kids, I meant to say, I need to start doing things by the books. So, in regards to wages, can you invoice me and I'll send you out cheques? I can get them to you as soon as I receive your invoices.'

'No worries,' Imogen said through a bundle of hairpins held between her teeth.

Maddie slid her hands beneath her thighs. So much for buying Christmas presents.

Dashing over, Hugo switched off the TV. 'Ladies and Gentlemen.' He gestured to Roger, pipe in hand. 'Indeed you, sir, if you'll be much obliged. Will you do us the honour of revealing the total amount of time you have been manager of this 'ere establishment, otherwise known as "an hotel"?'

He'd always been a shite actor. Maddie glanced at Jo again, but she'd picked up the leather-bound Welcome to Castlebank Hotel, and was flicking through the poly-pocket pages.

Two hours later, Maddie and Jo headed down the spiral stairs in their maids' costumes.

In a mirror at the end of the corridor, Maddie checked her lace headpiece was secure. 'We don't look much like sisters do we?'

'Some sisters don't. Take mine – clearly the milkman's daughter.'

'Jo!'

'D'you ever wish you had siblings?'

'I wouldn't wish Rab on anyone else.'

'Imagine if your mum and Rab had had a child…'

'Are you trying to give me nightmares?'

A sweeping wooden staircase led down to the reception area. Five guests were standing by the Christmas tree, two men wearing tuxedos and three women in dresses like Imogen's.

'Alright, Audrey?' Jo asked.

She wiped her palms down the front of her pinny. 'Yep. Ready, Rita?'

'Nearly.' Jo leant against a garlanded bannister and hitched up her tights. 'Fucking value pack of twenty deniers.'

Charleston music came from the lounge. It sounded busy in there – chatter, laughter, glasses rattling on trays. An older man emerged from a passageway, his arm round a young woman's shoulders.

'Look at that,' Maddie hissed. 'Lecherous old git.'

He lifted the woman's chin and brushed something from her cheek.

Jo shrugged. 'Might be his daughter.'

Might it? The thought would never have occurred. What would it be like, to have someone to look out for you?

Alison appeared on the bottom step. 'For God's sake, you two, where have you been?'

'Sorry,' Jo said. 'We had some trouble with a zip.'

That was one of the things she loved about Jo – great improvisation skills, and always a hundred percent believable.

'Well, hurry up. Get yourselves in there. Mingle. Make sure everyone sees you before the gun goes off.'

The lounge looked like it'd once been a drawing room. The red walls were wainscoted, and hung with large gilt mirrors and oil paintings of rural scenes. Guests were seated on Chesterfield sofas and in wing chairs. In a far corner, Roger was flirting with a group of women beside an open fire. They let out a hoot of laughter. He pretended to be too hot and opened a window.

At the bar, Imogen was playing drunk, shouting for more sherry. She reached out and stroked the real barman's arm. He looked terrified. Catching sight of Jo, she turned and started criticising her shoddy work at lunchtime.

Roger appeared and took Imogen by the arm. 'Come along now, darling, wasn't one supposed to be having a little lie-down?'

Guests turned to watch as she struggled. He dragged her away, pinching Jo's bum as he passed. Jo giggled and fluttered her eyelashes.

The real barman slid a tray of canapés towards them.

'Well take it then, Audrey,' Jo said. 'I can't keep covering for you, lazybones.' She stalked off.

Maddie took the tray and edged into the room. Some guests ignored her. To others she was just a floating platter that they hawked over, wrinkled their noses at, or dismissed.

One balding red-faced man smirked. 'Ooh, maids. Are you available for room service?'

The men sitting with him laughed.

'Clive!' A woman swiped his arm.

Maddie curtseyed. 'I can only apologise for the service tonight, sir. My sister, Rita, has been totally unreliable again.'

'Hmm…' Clive fingered the top button of his waistcoat. 'A sister. Not twins by any chance? What's the likelihood of a bogof?'

Jo reappeared and sneezed into a hanky. That was Maddie's cue to make herself scarce. She handed over the tray and crossed the reception to the toilets. The stags looked on. As she passed a mirror framed with antlers, she too was momentarily crowned.

In the Ladies', a woman was kneeling on the chequered floor.

'Choker broke.' She held up a handful of beads.

Maddie retreated. 'Sorry I can't help. I'm needed in the kitchen.'

She dashed upstairs, along the corridor, up the spiral staircase to the safety of the turret room. Closing the door, she sighed and rolled her shoulders. Her shoe chinked against something beneath Jo's bed. The saucer holding the half-smoked joint. Just a puff might help give her a boost?

The diamond-shaped window was large enough for her to poke her head out. Downstairs, a bell rang and one of the real staff called the guests to gather before dinner. This was to ensure that no one was lingering when Hugo stole round to the open window to fire the gun. Sadly she was on the wrong side of the hotel to see Hugo.

Amber light bounced off wet gravel. Beyond, the loch was smooth, black as oil. A scattering of lights glimmered on the far shore. The bustle below seemed a strange tight capsule of light and noise held in the grip of a wide dark hush.

Bang! Even though she knew it was coming, it made her jump. Some kind of creature fled across the lawn. A bird flew from a tree. She blew the smoke high into the freezing night air. Was that a gibbous moon, gazing down so mournfully? The walls of the room pulsed. Why had she smoked the joint down to the roach?

Her shoes sunk into the spongy carpet as the spiral stairs led her down. Had there been so many steps before? Through a narrow door she found herself in a different passageway. She turned right. Right again. They'd be expecting her by now. Dead end. On a tartan wall hung a small silver stag's head. Beneath its chin, her face was stretched to a blur.

Which way now?

That depends a good deal on where you want to get to…

Noise hurtled down the corridors to her ears. Roger shouting, 'Dear God. Has someone telephoned the police?'

She tracked the low hubbub, the clink of glasses, and came out behind the sweeping staircase. Amongst the white lilies in the vase on the reception desk, tall red roses flexed their thorns like claws.

'Get yourself together.' She picked up a couple of empty champagne flutes from the mantelpiece.

The first thing that hit her was the heat. Everyone was gathered in the centre of the room.

'No,' Roger shouted. 'Keep her away.'

The crowd parted, showing Rita lying on the floor.

'Oh, what's she done now?' She stepped forward. 'Rita!'

Alison caught her eye. She mustn't take too long with this transition, the real manager was keen to get the guests seated for dinner.

'Rita…?' She saw blood. 'Oh my God, what's happened?'

Roger shook a tablecloth and laid it over Jo's body.

'What have you done?' She fell to her knees.

The stem of the flute in her right hand snapped. A shard pierced her index finger. Blood pooled. She wiped it down her pinny. Covering her face, she pretended to cry. Then a real wave of tears built in her chest, and burst out as a big bawling sob.

The room was silent. People liked real blood, real tears.

She crawled to Jo's body. 'Don't leave me…'

Roger tinged a glass. 'I'm terribly sorry, ladies and gentlemen. I can assure you the police have been called. I need to ask you to vacate the room.'

People murmured and started to drift away when Imogen's voice rang out. 'Wha's going on?' She staggered towards Roger. 'Your little ssslut. Drunk is she? Been at my sherry!'

Maddie was supposed to stay by Jo, weeping, till the guests had been cleared, but something kicked in her gut. She rose to her knees. 'How dare you. It's your husband that's the lech. Can't keep his big, greasy paws off the staff!'

Roger coughed. 'Mind your language, young lady. And have some respect.'

'Respect!' Imogen's face came close, her voice singsong. 'Little girls from the gutter don't know the meaning of the word.' A spot of spittle landed on Maddie's cheek.

Maddie shoved her away.

A gasp from the crowd.

Imogen snarled. 'That's it, you're sacked.'

Maddie launched herself. Imogen buckled beneath her weight. They fell to the ground, rolling over one another.

Maddie's cheek pressed against someone's gold slingback, they quickly stepped away. 'You're an ugly drunk.'

Some material ripped.

'You're a dirty little scrubber.'

She pinned Imogen to the floor. 'Take that back!' Saliva fizzed at her mouth as she swallowed the urge to call her Fuck-face. She tugged Imogen's hair. They'd had some stage fighting classes at college, she should really be using some of the techniques…

Hands grasped beneath her armpits. Roger lifted her off.

Imogen scrambled to her knees. Her hair, torn from its bun, fell over her face.

'For God's sake, someone restrain my wife!'

One of the real bar staff placed his hands gingerly on Imogen's shoulders.

'Okay, okay!' Alison called. 'That's everyone gone now.'

The empty room seemed unbearably bright.

Jo flipped back the tablecloth. 'Blimey, what happened there?'

'Ahhh!' Roger pretended to cower. 'The living dead!'

Imogen rubbed her elbow.

What *had* happened? A chill ran through her. 'Are you okay?'

'Meow.' Roger swiped the air. 'Ladies!'

Imogen didn't meet her eye. 'Think I'm still in one piece…'

Maddie crouched and pulled a hairpin from the carpet. Her skirt was torn. 'Oh no…' She looked up at Alison.

'Never mind. That was fantastic. Right, let's get Jo up the back stairs quickly, before anyone sees.'

Their dinner was brought to Alison's room. Imogen kept her distance, but Alison's continued praise seemed to help ease the atmosphere.

A call came from reception to let them know the guests were on their desserts. Roger checked the corridor was empty, then shepherded Jo to the turret. Alison changed into tweed jodhpurs and jacket for her role assisting Hugo.

Downstairs in the dining room, Hugo summed up what he, as detective, had discerned so far. Then he questioned Maddie's, Imogen's and Roger's characters. A few of the guests heckled, but Roger quickly won them over.

After a short break, Alison laid out some articles the officers had found in the victim's and suspects' rooms. A vial of poison; Rita's diary; letters; a samurai sword; a record of Roger's gambling debts. The guests were given the opportunity to question the suspects and examine the evidence.

At the end of the night, the troupe made their way to the turret room with a bottle of wine, courtesy of the hotel, to which Alison added two bottles of cava.

Jo had changed and was lounging on her bed. 'Hey, how'd it go?'

'Pretty good, I reckon.' Hugo flopped down in the armchair. Imogen settled herself on the floor, between his knees.

Maddie cleared the clothes from her bed, and Roger perched on the end of it, unlacing his shoes. 'Some of the guests were pretty stocious,' he said.

'Your innuendos kept them entertained though.' Imogen unpinned her hair.

Alison popped a bottle of cava. 'What was that old goat like who thought I was the culprit?'

'Totally blootered.' Hugo twirled his deerstalker on his index finger.

Jo looked at Maddie. 'So who's got wind it was you?'

'Not sure.'

Alison handed out glasses of pink fizz. 'So far, I think most of them think it was Roger.'

After a drink, Imogen and Hugo made their excuses to leave. Alison, who was exhibiting the effects of liberally topping up her own glass, taunted them.

Hugo ignored her. 'See you all at breakfast for the grand finale.'

Alison grumbled as she veered towards the bathroom.

'She's going to want to play Truth or Dare in a minute,' Roger whispered.

'Will she?' Maddie asked.

'Probably,' Jo said. 'This is a night out for her.'

Roger drained his glass. 'I'm sorry, but this is my third day without any sleep.'

The bathroom door swung open. Alison swayed slightly. 'So, come on. You guys are actors. Surely one of you must have some wacky backy?' She grabbed the cava and, despite Roger's protests, refilled his glass.

Maddie tucked her legs under her. 'I didn't know you smoked, Alison.'

'Well, years ago I had a puff or two at a party.'

Roger raised his eyebrows. 'How very Bill Clinton.'

She refilled her own glass. The last of the cava trickled from the bottle.

Jo produced her tin. 'I've got a little bit of something if you fancy?'

Maddie skinned up and passed the joint to Alison.

She broke into a coughing fit on her first inhalation, then held in the second till she looked fit to burst. Exhaling, she passed the joint to Jo. 'No, not doing anything for me. I think I must be immune.'

Five minutes later she'd monopolised the conversation, babbling on about how her husband had lost interest in sex. Then, mid-sentence, she came to a halt. Her face paled. She gripped the arms of the chair.

'You okay?' Jo asked.

'Something... from dinner... Feel slightly sick.'

'It's just a bit of a whitey,' Roger said. 'Relax. It'll pass.'

She looked frantically around. 'Need to lie down.'

Maddie shifted. 'Want the bed?'

'No. Need my room.'

Roger stood. 'I'll take you. It's past my bedtime anyway.' He helped her to her feet.

She clasped his arm. 'You'll make someone a very fine husband one day.'

'Huh. They'll have to revise the Matrimonial Causes Act first.' He waved goodbye to Maddie and Jo.

Alison pitched forward. 'Not too fast!'

'Okay. Step coming up…'

Jo shut the door behind them. 'That's sorted that problem.'

'D'you think she'll be okay?'

'Yeah, she'll sleep it off.'

Maddie changed into her pyjamas. They drank the wine and smoked another joint.

Jo slid her head onto the pillow. '*We are such stuff as dreams are made on; and our little life* rum-tum-te-tum-te-te…'

'*The Tempest*!'

She pulled the covers up round her neck. 'I've started to dream about it.' Her eyes closed.

When Maddie came back from the bathroom, Jo's jaw had slackened and her breath was slow and shallow.

Only a pinch of hash left in her tin, hardly worth saving. She rolled a single skinner.

The window was still ajar. The world had spun towards the moon and, reflected now on the loch, it cast a shimmering path. Far away a dog barked. Under this same moon… What was Keswick like? She'd never been to the Lake District. The night air was damp with frost. She closed the window.

As she folded back her covers there were footfalls on the stairs. Roger returning?

'I don't know what's wrong with her,' a man's voice said. 'All that anger.' He had an English accent.

She moved towards the door.

'They say she never grieved,' a woman said. 'I think that's where it comes from. A realisation that he's not coming back.'

'All a bit of a mystery.'

Mystery… Alex?

She eased open the door. The stairwell was empty. She ventured a few steps down. Halfway along the corridor leading to Alison's room, a white-haired man was tapping his fingertips on a door. His head hung low, chin to chest. 'Clarissa. Clarissa…'

Back in their room, something had changed. She shouldn't have left the door open. She forced herself to look under the beds, in the bathroom, behind the curtains, in the wardrobe. Nothing.

It was freezing, but no amount of fiddling with the valve coaxed the radiator back to life.

She climbed between the icy sheets. Eventually she turned off the bedside lamp. Wide-eyed, she lay awake for hours, her feet so cold they ached to the bone.

Eight

The next morning, when the reception phoned with a wake-up call, she felt as if she'd only just dipped down into sleep.

Jo murmured and rolled over. Okay for her, she got a lie-in, her breakfast brought to the room. She'd only have to appear downstairs to take a bow.

Feeling slightly revived after a shower, she made her way to Alison's room where Roger and Imogen were watching *Live & Kicking* on TV and Hugo was reading through some notes.

Alison had more make-up on than usual, a thick layer of blusher.

'How are you feeling this morning?' Maddie asked.

'Oh, fine. I think the fish was just a bit dodgy last night.'

Roger looked over. 'I hope it's not E. coli.'

Imogen slapped his knee. 'That's not funny. Fifteen-odd people have died from that outbreak so far.'

'Fifteen *old* people. Who knows if they were odd?'

'Roger!'

Downstairs, the dining room had been transformed into a breakfast room, gerberas instead of candles on each table. Several of the guests looked pale and puffy, hunched over their plates.

Maddie took a seat at the small round table that'd been reserved for them. A sheet of paper detailed a choice of cooked breakfasts. She felt queasy, maybe a coffee would do.

There was a strange atmosphere as Hugo started the session, like when she'd had that fling with the music student, raucous and fun in the pub, awkward as he pulled on his clothes the next morning. She was never sure whether to ask if she'd see him again.

One of the women tugged a heavy curtain to block the low winter sun that streaked across the white tablecloths.

Roger had slept well and livened things up. At the end, Alison read out the name of the woman who'd guessed correctly and she was presented with a bottle of sparkling wine.

After a bow, Maddie followed Roger into the reception area.

He migrated towards the open door. 'Fabulous day.'

Outside on the steps, he offered her a B&H, lit it for her, then blew two smoke rings. They elongated as they drifted towards the trees. 'Fresh air.'

The frosted gravel sparkled, and the leaves of the camellia shrub looked sugar-crusted. A thin layer of mist hung over the loch. Behind, the snow-capped mountain dazzled against a deep blue sky.

'So'—Roger nudged her—'what did you make of your first full murder mystery?'

'It was more intense than I thought it would be.'

'You really went for it. You should've seen the old guy sitting near you at the end. When you turned into psycho bitch from hell and grabbed the gun, he nearly sprayed a mouthful of tea across the table.'

'I quite liked having the gun.'

'Power lady.'

An image of pulling Imogen's hair sprang to mind. She cringed.

Some guests came out, carrying suitcases to their cars. The women hugged and the men shook hands. Boots and doors were slammed shut. Engines revved. Steam rose from exhaust pipes. The gravel crunched as a silver Jag reversed and swung a wide arc towards the drive. The passenger window slid down.

'Thanks for that,' a woman called, her eyes fixed on Roger.

'A pleasure.'

She twinkled her fingers as the car pulled off.

'Got yourself a fan.'

Alison appeared. 'Ten minutes to get changed, then hit the road?'

'Coolio.' Roger stubbed his cigarette out on a stone planter.

Alison squinted and blinked hard. 'Sure wish one of you was insured to drive my car.'

Sitting in the back, with the heating on full blast, Maddie drifted off. Coming to several times, head nodding, she caught snippets of conversation from the front, then she was running, running beneath trees strung with multi-coloured ribbons. The ribbons brushed her arms, gentle at first, then stroking like fingers, gripping, tangling her hair. She tripped and fell. A manhole at her feet was uncovered. Down she went, down, down, down. Echoing above she heard Rab say, 'Waste of time. It's all a bloody fad.' Her head bounced and she jerked awake. Pins and needles in her right foot. It took a moment to remember where she was.

Beside her, Jo slept, her cardigan folded into a makeshift pillow. She caught Alison's eye in the rear-view mirror.

'*Morning has broken… like the first morning!*' Her singing was slightly flat.

Maddie mustered a smile.

Rain was battering against the windscreen. The wipers squeaked back and forth, casting off waves.

'Where are we?'

'Coming into Glasgow.'

'Already?'

'Okay to drop you guys off at the station?'

'Sure.' She nudged Jo. 'Nearly there.'

Jo lifted her head, eyes still closed. Half her hair was bunched up.

'*Rivaling the glittering sunshine,*' Roger sang. '*With her glory of auburn hair!*'

Alison laughed.

'Piss off.' Jo pulled the cardigan over her head.

Having said goodbye to Alison, they sheltered for a moment in the entrance of the bus station.

Roger buttoned up his coat. 'What's everyone say to a drink?'

Jo nodded. 'A quick one wouldn't hurt.'

'Sounds good, but I think I'm gonna head.'

'Come on,' Roger said, 'a wee sly voddy?'

She knew one of them would stand her a drink, but it was mortifying always being skint. 'I need to get a few things in town.'

He shrugged. 'Suit yourself. I'm just gonna get some ciggies.'

Jo reached into her rucksack. 'Here. I won't say Merry Christmas, 'cos I know you hate it.' The silvery parcel was tied with purple ribbon.

'Oh no, I've not had a chance to get you anything.'

'I don't need anything.' She rubbed Maddie's arm. 'Just grin and bear it. It'll be over in a couple of days.'

Roger returned and they walked in the direction of the Atholl Arms, heads bowed, trying to keep the rain from their faces. Maddie stopped at the corner.

'What're you doing for Hogmanay?' Roger asked.

'No plans.'

'Give us a call when you've returned to civilisation.' Jo hugged her goodbye, a tight squeeze.

Roger kissed her on both cheeks. 'May something delightful fill your Christmas stockings.'

'Ho ho. And if the Christmas fairy visits, may he be well endowed… with gifts!'

'Oh'—he looked to Jo with mock disdain—'it's all so carnal with her.' As the traffic lights changed he spun and, with a flourish of his hand, called, 'Ta ra, angel.'

Along Sauchiehall Street she dodged the points of umbrellas. The last Saturday before Christmas, the place was mobbed. The rain was relentless, it'd soaked through her hood already. Stepping from the kerb, her trainer sank into murky water. A taxi sped round the corner, beeping its horn, soaking her from the knees down. She wanted to rage against the sky, like King Lear on the heath.

The flat was empty. No sign of Mike, no messages on the answering machine. In her room, a folded sheet of A4 lay on the floor. *Hey, Maddie, could really do with that £40 back before you go away for Xmas. Callum.* Bloody Alison, needing to do things 'officially'.

As she dumped down her rucksack, she saw two envelopes on the sofa. One was her dole cheque. The post office would be shut, she'd have to wait till Monday to cash it. She opened the second and a cheque drifted to the ground. Inside the envelope was a compliments slip. *With thanks again and best wishes, Margaret x*

Over summer, Roger had done some corporate video work. Strapped for funds, he cashed his cheque in a place off Argyle Street. All he needed was two forms of ID. They took a commission but he'd got his money right away. Rooting through the cupboard, she found her passport and a copy of the tenancy agreement and shoved them in her bag. If she went now, there might be time to get to the pawnshop. And she could give Callum whatever was left.

The Cheque Centre was easy to find. In the windows, posters advertised the services available alongside numbers and percentage signs. Inside looked like a building society – bright blue and yellow, sparse. She pushed open the glass and steel door and was blasted by an overhead heater. The place smelled of gloss paint and Shake 'N' Vac.

Behind a glass partition, two women were serving customers. Looking round at the darkening street, she willed them to hurry up. She was hot under her coat, but her face and hands were cold and damp, her throat raw from panting cold air.

She hoped the frizzy-haired woman would be free first, but the younger one, with dark hair pinned in a chignon, called her forward.

She slid the cheque beneath the partition.

The woman peered at it. 'What kind of cheque is it?'

'A work cheque.'

'Have you got a copy of your contract?'

'No.'

'What about a letter, or something with the company's address?'

She shook her head, reached for the chain of the stick-on counter pen and rolled it beneath her fingertips.

The woman pressed her lips together, pale coral lipstick. 'What forms of ID do you have?'

She pushed her passport and tenancy agreement under the partition.

'Just a minute.' The woman spun in her chair and walked to a filing cabinet where a bearded man was searching through one of the drawers. He looked at Maddie's documents, then glanced over. It'd been a mistake to rush down here, drenched and windswept.

The woman returned. 'We'll have to photocopy these, and I'll need to take your details for our records.'

The clock on the wall said quarter to four. She signed a declaration on the back of the cheque and fed it under the glass.

The woman opened a drawer by her side. 'Twenty, forty, sixty, seventy.' She dropped the notes into the metal box beneath the glass and drew back the lid so Maddie could access them.

Folding them quickly, she fumbled in her bag for her purse, then turned, almost colliding with an old man who was shuffling to take her place.

Round the corner, she hurried under the Hielanman's Umbrella, breathing shallowly to keep out the stench of chip fat and exhaust fumes. Outside one of the shop units was a basket of slippers with a sign sticking from it. *£1.99 a pair. Left feet only.* At the far end, a man was playing the saxophone to a backing track.

Rockin' Around the Christmas Tree…

The escalator to St Enoch's subway was packed with people, long rolls of wrapping paper poking from their shopping bags. She took the stairs. She didn't have coins for the ticket machine so had to wait in line at the kiosk.

The platform was crammed by the time the train arrived. People pushed ahead to get seats. She stood, squashed against a metal pole. The doors closed. With a screech, the train glided into the tunnel. On the seat across from her, a little boy in a parka jacket sat under the protective wing of his dad. He curled his ticket to make a miniature telescope. His dad reached into his coat pocket and gave him a Milky Way.

When he came to visit, before Rab appeared on the scene, her dad used to bring her Caramac bars as a treat. Beneath the paper sleeve, the bar was wrapped in gold foil. She always meant to eke it out, but invariably wolfed it down, like Charlie with that extra Wonka bar. Was that the one with the golden ticket? The train lurched to a halt and she was slammed against the pole. The ticket. She'd forgotten to bring the ticket. Chances are the lady with the bob would remember her, but without a ticket would she be able to locate the ring?

She fought her way out at St George's Cross and doubled back to the flat. Dark out now, rain catching in streaks beneath the streetlights. She ran till she got a stitch in her side.

Looking up at the flat windows, she could tell no one was home. She took the stairs two at a time. On the first floor landing, the light wasn't working. The one on the second floor flickered, creating a slow strobe effect.

Dropping her bag in the hall she went through to her room. The ticket was on a shelf in the wardrobe. A wave rushed through her. She put a hand on the wardrobe door and waited for the dizziness to pass. Had she eaten anything today? Time was short but she was bursting for the loo.

She was drying her hands on Callum's towel when she heard the front door shut.

'Mike?'

She looked in her room. No sign of anyone. Opening the front door she stepped into the stairwell. Someone was halfway down the stairs.

'Mike?'

The footsteps neared the bottom.

'Callum?'

The close door clicked shut.

Back in her room, she pulled up the window and leaned out. Some folk were getting into a taxi. A couple walked arm-in-arm, pressed together to fit beneath the arc of an umbrella. She pulled the window down and locked up.

Sandra was running a duster over the counter when she burst into the shop.

She flipped down her hood and swept her hair from her forehead. 'Hello.'

'Hi. I wondered who that was. I was just about to close up.'

Her heart beat fast. 'I've come to get my dad's ring back, if there's time?'

'No bother, I can do that for you.' She dropped the duster beside the till.

It was like the ones Maddie's mum used, fluffy orange cotton, edged with red blanket-stitching. She took the ticket from her bag and handed it over.

'Just a sec.' Sandra disappeared into the storeroom.

She placed her purse on the counter. Some thin blue tinsel had been sellotaped across the front of the glass. It hung in loops.

Sandra reappeared carrying a maroon box with a corresponding ticket held on top by an elastic band. She snapped off the band, opened the box and turned it to Maddie.

'Yes. That's it.' Relief flooded through her.

Sandra closed the box and lifted a calculator. 'Miserable day.' She punched in some numbers.

Somehow she'd forgotten she was soaked.

'Right, with interest, that's fifty-six pounds.'

'Okay.' She unzipped her purse. Inside was her old bankcard. Her fingers delved into the empty space.

Putting her purse back on the counter, she searched through her bag. She looked in her purse again, then checked her coat pockets, even though she knew the money wouldn't be there. 'I don't understand...' Undoing her coat, she patted the pockets of her jeans.

Hadn't she folded the notes and put them in her purse? On her way out of the Cheque Centre, she'd nearly bashed into an old man. Had she dropped the money? No, she couldn't have, she'd bought a ticket for the tube.

She unzipped the change section of her purse. Four pounds thirty-five. Someone must've gone into her bag, her purse, and taken the money. Someone on the tube.

She looked at Sandra. 'It's gone.'

Sandra placed her hand on top of the box.

Outside, the wind had picked up, hurling the rain sideways. She gasped down some air. Her eyes spilled over. Hardly anyone about to see, and, under the streetlights, her tears probably just looked like rain.

By the time she got home, she knew no one on the tube would've been able to take the money from her bag and buckle it back up. Which left one culprit.

She changed her clothes and carried the electric fire through to the kitchen, rehearsing how she might approach the subject. She felt sick, part nerves, possibly hunger. Fuck it, she'd have a slice of Callum's bread. The toaster had broken months ago, after Mike tried to fish a Pop-Tart out with a knife. She put the grill on. Channels of gas flared as they struggled to catch light.

In the back alley, something crashed. Too dark to see anything from the window. Probably just a cat amongst the bins. A burning smell… the toast, completely charred. She scraped it over the sink.

'Fucking, fucking thing.' She hurled it down.

Resting her head on the cold aluminium, she held her breath, swallowing the urge to cry.

She was sitting at the kitchen table staring at the wall when she heard a key in the lock.

'Hello?' It was Callum. He carried two Co-op bags through to the kitchen.

'Hi.'

'Stinking weather.' Water dripped from the bags onto the lino.

'Yep.'

He took two tins of beans from one of the bags and stacked them in his cupboard. 'Something burning?' He sniffed the air, then dropped three onions into a wooden bowl. He looked round. 'You okay?'

'Bit of a nightmare day.'

The onions bounced off one another as they settled.

'Want to talk about it?' He opened the fridge door and manoeuvred a bag of oven chips between the thick frozen sleeves of the icebox.

'I cashed a cheque but the money was stolen.'

He filled a saucepan with water and put it on to boil. 'No shit. How much?'

'Sixty-five quid.'

He whistled. 'Jeezo. Any idea where it was taken?'

'Here. Here in the flat.'

He turned. 'Eh?'

The electric fire was singeing a patch below her knee. She pushed it away with her foot. 'Where were you today, about half four?'

'At work. Why?'

'Someone came home. Just briefly. I was in the bathroom. I called down the stairs. Whoever it was didn't answer. When I went to take the money from my purse after, it'd gone.'

'Wait. Why did you ask me where *I* was?'

'You were annoyed, weren't you, that I hadn't given you your money back.'

'Well, yeah, but what's that got to do with anything?'

'I wondered if you might just have helped yourself.'

Behind him, steam rose from the pan. The water gurgled and clucked.

He stared. 'Have you gone mad? You seriously think I'd have gone into your purse? I mean, you're a total stoner these days. You probably just left the money somewhere.'

She couldn't believe it. 'Black-affronted' her mum would say.

'I tell you, Maddie, if there really was money, and it really was taken, from here, this afternoon, I know who I'd be pointing the finger at.'

The water began to bubble and spit. Drops hissed as they landed on the hob.

'You've always had it in for Mike, haven't you?'

'No. It's just I've seen what he is.'

'What's that?'

Callum sighed. 'A taker. He doesn't pay any rent, contribute to the bills…'

'You just can't bear to see us happy.'

'Happy? Don't make me laugh. I'm sick to death of hearing you scream at each other.'

'We don't…!'

'Reality check, Maddie.' He turned the gas down. 'Look, I've been meaning to say, a room's come up in my mate Gareth's flat. I'm gonna take it. I'll give a month's notice here.'

'No. You can't. Who's gonna take your room?'

He gave a wry laugh. 'That's hardly something for me to figure out.' He tore the top off a box of Cheesey Pasta. 'It used to be fun living here. But the last year or so's been a nightmare. The place has turned into a total dive.'

He was still wearing his coat. It was as if, after he'd had his tea, he was going to pack up and leave immediately. She might never see him again. She'd be left here on her own, in the dark. Her throat tightened. She couldn't let him see her cry.

'I still want my money back,' he called after her as she walked down the hall.

For a while she sat with her head on her knees. When she was all cried out, a desolate peace descended. She became as still as the chest of drawers, as the wardrobe. With any luck, she might just fade away.

Some dishes clanked in the kitchen and Callum's bedroom door shut. When the phone rang, he didn't answer it.

'Hi, Maddie, it's me, Mum. Just wanting to know what time you're thinking of getting here on Christmas Eve. Irene's coming over. Give me a call back when you get this, please.'

Irene? After all this time. Why now?

She lay on the sofa and closed her eyes.

The summer before that argument. The back door of Auntie Irene's cottage had been ajar. A long sash of sunshine draped the kitchen table. The air thick with the smell of large yellow roses, splayed in too short a vase, petals so open she could see their pale centres and seeded crowns.

'You've got your dad's eyes,' Auntie Irene said.

She gripped the yellow pencil and looked down at the picture she was drawing. Since Rab arrived, her dad wasn't talked about at home anymore. It felt a kind of sacrilege just to hear him mentioned. She chose a green pencil for the stems, waiting, but Auntie Irene didn't say anything else. Stupid picture. Stupid hopeful little girl.

One in the morning, Mike shuffled in. A surge of anger flooded back into her veins.

'Hey, babe.' The words slipped out the side of his mouth. 'The guys were all going up to Gnasher's, but I thought I'd come home early. See if you were back.'

'Got back this afternoon.' Her voice was flat and hard. 'Like I said I would.'

He leant against the chest of drawers, dug into his trouser pocket. 'Got you a present.'

Something small landed a couple of feet away. She reached for it. A lump of hash wrapped in cellophane. 'Where'd you get this?'

'Gnasher's flatmate.'

'On tick?'

He sighed. 'Thought you'd be pleased.' He grazed the doorframe as he headed for the loo.

Out on the street a group of guys sang, '*We wish you a Merry Christmas, we wish you a Merry Christmas…!*' Shouting was followed by the sound of breaking glass. She went to the window, but couldn't see anything.

'Want to skin up?' Mike took his jacket off and flung it on the bed.

'No.'

'What's wrong?'

They stood either side of a green pool cast by the lava lamp, which was working again. The red wax swelled to a peak, a blob separated from the mass and rose.

'I want it back.'

'What?'

'You know what.'

'You've lost me.'

'The sixty-five quid.'

'What sixty-five quid?'

She walked towards him. 'The fucking money that was in my purse this afternoon.'

'What money?'

'From my work cheque.'

'I don't know what you're talking about.'

'Admit it.'

'Admit what?'

'You know what. Admit it!' She pushed him. Her hands on his shoulders. Just lightly. He stumbled a couple of steps back.

'Hey! Turning into Rab now?'

The sound of the slap cut the air. He put his hand to his cheek. Their eyes locked for a second, then he grabbed his jacket. She stayed frozen as he walked out. Eyes wide. At her side, her right hand pulsed and started to sting. Snatched all the words from her throat.

Nine

The Christmas tree was standing in the same spot. Each year it looked a bit more bedraggled. Her mum had strung it with the old decorations. Baubles with chipped enamel, wiry tinsel, a string of fairy lights that was too short to reach the bottom tier of branches.

With the biscuit tin under her arm, her mum carried two cups of coffee through from the kitchen. 'I've only got you a couple of wee pressies.' She handed a cup to Maddie and set her own on the nest of tables. 'I thought money might be more useful.'

'I've only got you a wee something myself. I'll get you a proper present when I get paid.'

Her mum put her hand on the arm of Rab's chair and lowered herself into it.

'Knees bad?'

'Play up a bit in this weather.' Marshall rested his head on her lap, nostrils quivering. 'Sit down.' She yanked his collar. 'And stop scrounging.'

'What time did you say she's coming?'

Her mum glanced at the carriage clock. 'She said about four.'

'And why's she coming now?'

She lifted the lid off the tin. 'Biscuit?'

Maddie took a Rich Tea, snapped it and fed half to Marshall.

'For goodness' sake,' her mum said as he wolfed it down, slavering crumbs on Maddie's trousers. 'Messy beggar.' She took a packet of Superkings from her pocket. 'Oh, be a doll and get the ashtray, would you?'

On the dining table, the ashtray was brimming with cigarette butts and torn up scratch cards. She carried it through to the kitchen and emptied it in the bin. Her mum had started preparing vegetables for Christmas dinner. A pan of peeled potatoes sat on the hob.

'Mike going to his mum's?'

'Maybe.'

'Oh?'

The day after the fight, she'd gone over to Jo's. Jo was livid about the stolen money and insisted Maddie stay. 'You're not going back there till you promise to break up with him.' She'd kind of regretted saying anything.

'Here.' She sat the ashtray down.

Her mum offered her a cigarette and lit it. 'That's good about those bits of work. D'you think they might take you on full-time?'

'Perhaps.' She didn't have the energy to explain the random nature of the gigs. 'So did Irene just call then, out the blue?'

'She dropped me a card. Asked if I'd phone.'

'Rab doesn't mind her coming over?'

'Seemed no need to say. He's out with the boys from work. He'll not be back till late.'

She sipped her coffee. Sweet and soothing. 'Why has she got in touch now, after all these years?'

Her mum tapped the ash from the end of her cigarette and sighed. 'The highland dancer.'

'Really? Of what?'

'Cervix. Cervical.'

Irene arrived just after four, looking pretty much as Maddie remembered – the wide forehead, hazel eyes, deep laughter lines. She had a bit of a double chin. What had she been expecting, a stick woman? Her hair used to be straight and strawberry-blonde, now it was short, platinum with a wave in it. A wig?

'Jean...' Irene wrapped her arms around Maddie's mum. 'It's been too long. And look at this young lady.' She held Maddie by the shoulders. 'All grown up now.'

While Maddie put the kettle on, her mum and Auntie Irene made small talk, as if they'd just seen one another last week. Strange to think they were sisters – that they'd been children together, grown up under the same roof, shared a room for thirteen years. They didn't look overly alike. Same nose, maybe, and some similar gestures.

She carried the tea tray through.

'D'you remember when you were about five years old, you came on holiday with us to the Isle of Wight? You were quite a shy wee thing. To think you're an actress now!'

She had vague memories of travelling on a hovercraft, getting a giant stick of pink rock, having her photo taken beside a Womble. It'd been the first time she'd stayed in a caravan. One afternoon, noseying through her cousin Clare's things, she accidentally broke a strawberry ChapStick. 'No wonder your parents don't want you anymore!' That night she'd wet the bed.

Her mum nodded in her direction. 'You've had a couple of bits of work recently, haven't you.'

She sat on the sofa, next to Irene. 'Takes a while, after you graduate.'

'You're doing something you love, that's the main thing.'

She felt her mum bristle.

'How's your Clare?' her mum asked.

'Still working in the lawyers' office. She got married a couple of years ago to a nice young man from accounts. I brought these to show you…' Irene took a packet of photos from her bag and handed them to Maddie's mum.

'She takes after you.' Her mum passed them one at a time onto Maddie.

Clare was a willowy blonde in a giant puffball dress. 'She looks beautiful. Really happy.'

'She was a challenge, in her teens, but we get along fine now.'

'Teenagers, tell me about it!'

Anger flared in Maddie's chest. *Once* she'd told a lie, went to a party when she said she was going to a friend's, came home later than agreed, drunk. She ignored Rab when he shouted from the living room. He stormed into the hall, grabbed her shoulder, shoved her up against the bannisters. 'You're not too big to go over my fucking knee.' Her mum had stood behind him, silent.

Irene put her cup down and smiled. 'We were more than a handful ourselves, Jean, growing up.'

An hour later, Maddie offered to make more tea.

Irene looked at the pearly face of the gold watch, tight on her wrist. 'What time's *he* back?'

'Rab?' her mum asked. 'Not till late.'

Irene put her hands on her knees, spread her fingers, took a deep breath. 'You've been alright, have you, Jean?'

Looking down, her mum adjusted her cardie. 'Aye. Aye. Working away. You know how it is.'

'I hoped, all those years, I hoped I'd hear from you. A couple of times I saw you, in town.'

'Ach, bygones and all that.'

'At Mum's funeral, it felt ridiculous…'

Marshall, who'd been sleeping in front of the fire, sat up, ears raised. He sprang to his feet, barking.

Maddie's heart raced, she uncrossed her legs and put her feet flat on the floor.

Her mum stood and pulled back the edge of the curtain. 'It's alright. It's just next door. I thought it was too early…' Her voice tailed off. She turned, face pale. 'I s'pose I should be getting the supper on though. You'd be welcome to stay…?'

Irene reached for her lilac scarf. 'No, thank you for the offer. I need to get back. Donald will be home soon. And there's still a few things to wrap. Oh'—she indicated a bag at her feet—'Santa asked me to deliver these.'

'Irene, you shouldn't have. Just a wee minute, I've something for you too.' She made her way upstairs.

Leaning forward, Maddie gathered the cups.

Irene tied her scarf round her neck. 'I wasn't sure what you'd like, so I just got you a voucher.'

'You didn't need to get me anything.'

'Time goes so quick, Maddie. My mum, your gran, used to say that and I'd think, *Yeah yeah*... You don't understand when you're younger. It's as if the old folk have always been old. As if you'll always be young. And then...' She pulled her coat onto her lap. 'Clare and I didn't talk for a while when she left home. She was fiery, and I was stubborn I suppose. You can't get that time back, but you can make the most of what's left.'

'Yes.' She hesitated. No one had mentioned the cancer. Was it ruder to ask, or to ignore it?

Irene put a hand on her arm. 'I'm sorry I wasn't there for you, when you were growing up. If you ever need anything now... Even if you'd like to pop in, you'd be more than welcome any time.'

'Thank you.'

'My goodness, you're so like your father. Not just your eyes, your whole manner. You know, Maddie...'

Her mum appeared in the doorway, slightly breathless. 'Here we are. Just a wee something.'

Outside, the night air was heavy with moisture. Irene took her keys from her handbag. 'See the old boy's still challenging the National Grid.'

Through the fog, Mr Mackinnon's house blinked a blurry red and white.

'Santa's bloody grotto.' Her mum rubbed her hands together. 'Hope you have a good day tomorrow. Love to Donald. And Clare.'

Irene tucked the tail of her scarf inside her coat. 'You too. Merry Christmas, Jean.'

They hugged. Her mum's hands released, but Irene held her for a couple of seconds longer.

'Don't wait. Go in.' She unlocked the car door. 'It's too cold to be standing on the doorstep.'

After they'd watched Irene's car pull off, her mum shut the front door. In the living room, she plumped up the sofa cushions, then carried the cups through to the kitchen.

Maddie followed. 'I thought she looked pretty well, considering.'

Her mum switched on the radio. 'Now there's enough to be doing for tomorrow without pushing the boat out tonight, so we'll just have these…' She opened the fridge and pulled out two ready meals. Turning one on its side she muttered, 'For best results, microwave.'

When they'd finished eating, Maddie feigned a headache and went upstairs so she wouldn't have to see Rab. Not tonight, anyway. Her old bedroom had turned into a kind of junk room, but her mum had cleared an area round the bed. In a couple of boxes in the wardrobe, some of her old stuff: R.E.M. records, Morrissey, The Stone Roses; school jotters; some drawings from art classes, rolled up; a Holly Hobbie that her granny – her dad's mum – had given her; a few photos of Jay, her best friend from school – his hair spiked up like the singer from The Cure. Where was he now? Last time she got a letter from him he was working in a service station near St Andrews. She'd scratched a tiny proscenium theatre at the bottom of the wardrobe door. All the little ways she'd marked her territory. The gap behind the skirting where she used to post herself notes. She fished one out. Pink felt tip: *Come home*.

She lay down, the bed seemed tiny now she was used to a double. Her mum's jewellery box was just at the end of the landing. She could almost feel the space in the bottom drawer. Her dad's ring would be back in the pawnshop's storeroom, locked up, in the dark. Stupid to feel sorry for an inanimate object. She just needed to get it back before her mum noticed it gone.

From her rucksack, she pulled the present Jo had given her. The purple bow was iridescent, it shimmered green. Inside was a copy of *The Tempest*. A fancy hardback copy, with pictures and notes. A slip of paper fell onto her chest. *Fingers crossed for next year... xx.* Jo had drawn a sprig of holly in the top right corner.

Downstairs, Marshall started to bark. The front door opened.

'Shut up, for fuck's sake. Fucking idiot.' Rab.

Jumping up, she turned off the light.

When her eyes adjusted, the room was fuzzy orange, lit by the streetlight outside. With her curtain pulled back, it was just bright enough to read. She climbed under the covers, opened the book, and was swept into the midst of a storm, to a fantastical world of illusions, revenge, and reconciliations.

Ten

A week later, she was sitting in the back of Wren's car, squashed between Jo and Roger, travelling through to Edinburgh for Hogmanay.

Holding a half-empty bottle of Coke between her thighs, Jo attempted to pour vodka into it. 'Can you try and keep the car still?'

Wren glanced over his shoulder. 'Would kind of defeat the purpose of driving.'

She'd been staying at Jo's again since Christmas, unable to bear the thought of an empty flat, and not sure what she'd say to Mike if he were there. She spent most of the time staring at a book pulled off Jo's shelf, with The Cranberries practically on a loop.

'You're missing him,' Jo'd said. 'But there's nothing to miss.'

Beside Wren, his friend, Terry, was skinning up in the weak glow from the passenger light. 'Jesus, can we get some music on in here? It's like a fucking hearse.'

Wren pointed at the glove compartment. 'CDs in there.'

'So what's the plan?' Roger asked.

'Head along Princes Street,' Jo said, 'up the mound for the bells, see where the wind takes us after that.'

'A pal of mine's having a party in the New Town.' Terry sealed the joint and switched off the light. Smoke billowed from the front. 'Watch yourselves with this, kids'—his voice was reedy as he held in a lungful—'first-class Hawaiian Haze.'

Wren gave the joint a double take as Terry passed it to Jo. 'It's a fucking cone!' He wound his window down an inch and Maddie was blasted by freezing night air.

'So where's Mike tonight?' Roger asked.

'Don't know.'

Jo angled herself round. 'I didn't want to say on the phone, and besides, it's not my place to say really, but he stole from Maddie's purse.'

'No way.'

'*Yes* way!'

Somehow, in telling Jo the story, she'd managed to omit the part where she'd slapped Mike. He *had* stolen from her, she was sure of it, but it didn't excuse the slap.

'Woo hoo,' Terry hollered, 'I love this track.' The fast hi-hat of Leftfield's 'Black Flute'. Terry bumped the volume up and the seats vibrated.

Jo nudged her. 'Smoke?'

She took the joint and inhaled, making the cigar-sized tip glow orange, then handed it to Roger.

'Well, I'm sorry to hear that, sweet cheeks,' he said.

Jo leant forward. 'What did you call her?'

His words came out tangled, a stream of sibilant esses.

Jo whistled. 'What would Valerie Dawes make of that?'

'Valerie Dawes? She can smoke on my hot dog.'

'My hot daaawg,' Terry echoed.

Roger bobbed with silent laughter and a guffaw burst from Maddie.

'Enough!' Roger wiped his eyes.

'Hot daaawg,' Terry howled. '*Deputy* hot daaawg.'

The car leapt forward and her head hit the headrest.

'First-class stuff?' Wren asked. 'Well, let the ride commence.'

After driving around town for a bit, Wren finally found somewhere to park.

Lights were on in some of the smart Georgian townhouses, but blinds were down and curtains drawn. Globules of rain glistened on car roofs and bonnets. Ahead, Wren reached for Jo's hand.

Jo had been halfway through second year when she met Wren in Bar 91. He was a year above, at the art school. After a few dates, he suggested a trip to Arran. Spring came early and Jo said the two of them sunbathed on the deck of the ferry. Once there, they zipped their sleeping bags together and spent most of the weekend in the tent, emerging Sunday afternoon to climb Goat Fell. From the summit, they saw all the way to Ireland. 'My granda lives near Dundrum Bay,' Wren said. 'Give him a wave.' Staring at the viewpoint indicator, he asked what she thought about love at first sight. Even telling the story, Jo looked down, reining in a smile, making Maddie realise she'd never seen her blush before.

'You two lovebirds!'

Wren looked round. 'Alright, wee Madster?'

'Absolutely.'

Stretching out his arms, Terry wove ahead, turning back to look at her. '*I'm floating in the air…*'

'Walking.' Roger tutted. '*Walking.*'

Soon they were passing other groups and folk accumulated behind them, voices loud and shrill. She caught up with Roger and linked her arm through his. As they turned onto Princes Street, everything grew manic, close – people milling, running, wheeling about, shouting, squealing, laughing. Music made the air thick with pounding and everything smelling of fried onions and burnt sugar.

Terry clapped his hands. 'It's gonna be a helluva night.'

A feather boa brushed her face as five drag queens dashed past on six-inch lap-dancer heels.

Jo made them all huddle. 'We should have some kind of contingency plan, in case we get separated.' She looked round. 'Speaking of which…?'

'Over there.' Wren pointed in the direction of the Scott Monument, where Roger was chatting to a guy with spiky hair and a cropped fur jacket. He raised his hand, indicating he'd just be a minute.

'Someone you know?' Jo asked as he sauntered back.

He brandished a slip of paper. 'Not yet.'

'Okay, gang'—Jo hooked her thumb through a loop on Wren's jeans—'let's stick together.'

Roger was just in front and Maddie was reaching for his hand when a girl on stilts wearing a Pierrot costume stepped between them, hovering, shifting her weight from stilt to stilt. She held out a rose with a flourish.

'I haven't…'

'No charge.'

Were Pierrots supposed to talk? On her white face, below the waxy black teardrop, her red lips quivered into an odd smile. She extended her arm and Maddie took the rose.

'*Till a' the seas gang dry…*' With her smile widening, the Pierrot twirled and wove into the crowd.

A pink rose. A real one. It even had a scent.

'Hey, daydreamer.' Wren. He took her hand and led her up Princes Street to where Roger, Jo and Terry were waiting outside BHS.

'Phew.' Jo loosened the knot of her arms. 'Thought we'd lost you.'

Up towards the mound, with Roger's arm around her shoulder. 'We should put reins on you.'

'Same could be said.'

'Mmm, Tangerine-man.' He pulled the slip of paper from his pocket. 'He's got a pager. Maybe I should get a pager.'

'Didn't you get his name?'

'I was a bit distracted by his tight tangerine t-shirt.'

Terry indicated an open ziplock bag he was holding at waist height. 'Sherbet?'

'Rude to refuse.' Roger licked his finger and dipped it in

the white powder. She did the same, and brilliant tiny metallic tendrils crawled under her gums.

Her tongue numbed, fat and furry. 'What was that?'

Roger squeezed her. 'Better enjoy this anonymity.'

'Eh?'

'This time next year we might be superstars. Once we've done *The Tempest*, who knows where it'll lead.'

'We shouldn't get ahead of ourselves, though, should we. I mean, we don't even know if it'll get to go on yet.'

'We should totally get ahead of ourselves. How d'you know what to aim for if you don't dream?'

Her heart kicked and a thousand tiny bubbles fizzed to the surface of her face. She rubbed her jaw. 'Are you thirsty?'

'Parched. Got any chewing gum?'

She searched her pockets. The crowd pushed in. 'Nothing.'

He turned. 'What?' His expression had changed, his eyebrows furrowed.

'I've not got any gum,' she shouted, but something ahead distracted him. They came smack up against a wall of people. 'What's going on?'

He stretched his neck. 'Impossible to see.'

Someone kicked her heel.

'Sorry,' a woman said, jostling Maddie as she turned and shouted, 'quit pushing!'

Further ahead, someone cried, 'Move back, move the fuck back!'

She looked for the others but couldn't see them. People pressed in on all sides as the horde behind them swelled, driving forward, crushing her against a man's chest. His rough corduroy jacket stank of garlic.

'Jesus Christ.' He pushed out his elbows, pressing her head back. 'This is fucking ridiculous.'

'Ow.' She pulled her foot from beneath someone's shoe.

A ripple started to drag Roger away, she grabbed his shirt but it slipped from her grasp. 'Shit. Hold on, angel-eyes.'

'Stop fucking pushing, you fucking idiots,' yelled an Irish woman to her right, her red lipstick bleeding into fine downy lines around her mouth. She let out a war cry. Her breath, rising as a train of steam, smelled of aniseed.

A little boy, sitting on his dad's shoulders, burst into tears.

'I don't like this,' said a thin-faced woman squashed against her side. 'I don't like this at all.'

'Move back! Fucking move back!' So many voices, so many people. 'Folk are getting crushed up here!'

Someone blew a whistle, a piercing, incessant blast.

'We're trying,' a man bellowed, 'but the people behind can't hear us.'

The tide pushed back, but another surge drove forward. She tried to use her arms to protect her ribs, but they were mashed into her sides. Lifted from her feet, no longer in control of where she was going, she was swept away. People at concerts died like this, they tripped and were trampled by the crowd.

Everyone was shouting now, shrieking, the chorus of voices becoming a gale. Compressed, she was only able to take tiny sips of air. How much could a rib bend before it snapped? Above the bobbing heads, a phantom ship was tossed about on the waves. Miranda would implore Prospero to make it stop.

If by your art, my dearest father, you have
Put the wild waters in this roar, allay them.

She'd forgotten about the rose in her hand, now flattened against her chest. If only she could turn into a butterfly and flutter out of here... The water rose over her mouth and she struggled, fought, her ribs sinking in, a tight, sharp pain.

One last look up... Something prickled her nose. Small cool drops, soft flakes of snow, drifting out of the black sky...

She could breathe. The crush gave way. A calm came, an

easing. More space. The crowd relaxed. Her arms fell by her sides. People peeled off. Several turned to see if a disaster had been averted. The man took the little boy from his shoulders and cuddled him. The Irish woman doubled over, 'Jesus, Jesus, Jesus.' Two women hugged, one of them covered her eyes.

Folk walked back the way they'd come, a slow exodus, quiet, dishevelled. A snowflake landed on her eyelashes, refracting the streetlights into dark rainbows. She blinked, took a deep breath.

'Maddie!' Jo rushed over, Wren and Terry behind. 'Are you okay?'

'Yes. Are you?'

'Fuck. That was scary.'

'Thank God.' Roger emerged from up ahead and hugged her. 'After we were separated, I was nearly strangled by my own scarf!'

Jo rolled her eyes. 'You're so Isadora Duncan.'

'I don't know about you guys,' Terry said, 'but I could sure use a smoke and a serious drink.'

Getting to Terry's friend's flat involved a twenty-minute walk. A red glittery reindeer's head greeted them on the top floor.

'Cool.' Jo reached up and stroked its antlers, her fingertips coming away sparkly red.

Terry pushed the door open. Maddie wiped her feet on the mat and followed him in, stepping onto wooden floorboards that ran the length of a high-ceilinged white hall. The warm air smelled of dope.

From a doorway at the far end a dark-haired guy appeared. 'Hey, hey, Terence.'

'Yo, Duncan, my man.'

They clapped each other on the back.

Beside a tinsel-strung kentia palm, a tall girl with long blonde hair struck poses with a bowler hat. Her friends laughed and took photos.

'Good to see you,' Duncan said. 'Come on in.'

'For you.' Terry held out a carrier bag. 'Best we could get on the way over.'

'If we run out of booze, I'll eat Bunny's hat.' He nodded towards the tall girl, then extended his hand. 'Hi, I'm Duncan.'

'Sorry,' Terry said, turning. 'Jo, Wren, Roger, Maddie.'

'Throw your coats in there, then come through and get a drink.'

In the low-lit bedroom, a curved sail of gold silk rose from the head of a wrought iron bed, billowing slightly in the draft from the door.

'Look at these.' Jo stood before a mesh of fairy lights pinned on the wall in swirls. 'Must've taken some doing.'

'Duncan was sensible,' Terry said. 'Went into product design. Earns a proper salary.'

Taking off her coat and jumper, Maddie turned to Jo. 'Do I look okay?'

'Let's take your hair out of that scrunchie. In fact…' Jo opened her bag and pulled out her make-up case.

'Come on, guys,' Wren said, 'let's go and get a drink. Unless anyone else is lining up for hair and make-up?'

When Jo had finished applying her full range of pencils and powders she spun Maddie towards a mirror. 'Ta da!'

She lifted a hand to her cheek.

'Leave it.' Jo smacked her hand away. 'You look lovely.'

In the kitchen, folk were leaning on counters, chatting, smoking and drinking. What did you talk about at a party like this?

'Look at the choice.' Jo lifted a slender green bottle from the glass-topped table. 'Absinthe. Blimey.'

Duncan passed by. 'If you don't see anything you like there, ladies, there's a tonne of beer in the bath.'

'Thanks.' Jo lifted another bottle and turned to Maddie. 'Vodka-and-cranberry?'

'Perfect.'

The highball glass Jo handed her glowed invitingly. 'Right, let's go find the boys.'

Jo angled her shoulders to get through the crowded doorway and Maddie followed. The lounge had been cleared of furniture, apart from a set of decks in the bay window, where a guy with a ginger beard was sorting through some LPs.

They found the boys watching a game of table football in a small room just off the lounge. Bunny was playing some skinny guy.

'12-2,' Bunny shouted, spinning a celebratory circle and sliding the numbers along.

Maddie joined Roger in front of some CD racks. 'What have you ascertained so far, Miss Marple?'

'Difficult to say.' He glanced down. 'Wow, you look great done up like that.'

'Roger!' Terry called from an armchair behind the door, holding out another Camberwell carrot.

The football table rattled and Bunny shouted, 'Woo hoo, ya dancer!'

The joint went to Wren next, then to Maddie. Bunny leant in to say something, her hair tickling the back of Maddie's arm.

She turned to Roger. 'What did she say?'

'Okay,' Jo said, 'but bagsy defence.'

Someone tapped her shoulder. 'Hey, Miss Gluey-fingers.'

Had she really been hogging the joint? 'Sorry, Terry.'

'Hellooo?' Wren waved slow-mo in front of her face. 'What are you, chicken?'

'Right, that's it.' Roger cupped her elbow. 'Prepare to be decimated.'

Like a coconut. Flowers glowing beneath glass cobbles…

As soon as the ball was dropped, Roger started frantically turning the handles. 'Come on. Come on!'

Jo laughed. 'What are you doing? None of your players are anywhere near the ball.'

'Don't let her psyche you out, Maddie. Kick the fucker!'

Jo squealed. 'Stop it. I'm gonna wet myself.'

Maddie made her way to the door. 'Time out. Can't cope.'

The hall was packed with people. She needed some air.

Wren appeared at her side. 'Let's try the kitchen.'

It was crowded but they found a space by the sink. He pulled up a window and she leant out into the frosted night. The garden, still and shadowy. Snow hadn't settled.

'Drink?' Jo's voice.

Drawing herself back into the room, she took one of the glowing red glasses. 'Ta.'

Beside them, a girl wearing a blonde wig was chopping white powder with a bankcard on the back of a book. She swept the powder into three rows, sniffed up a line then proffered the note. 'Anyone?'

Jo shook her head.

'If you don't mind?' Wren asked.

'Go ahead,' the blonde girl said, nodding. She looked at Maddie. 'What about you, Rapunzel?'

She took the note from Wren and put it up her right nostril.

'Now close the other one over… and sniff.'

'Guys!' It was Roger. He beckoned maniacally. 'Come on. The bells. The bells!'

Linking her arm through Maddie's, the blonde girl said, 'Okay, Quasimodo, we cometh.'

The blonde girl pulled her into the midst of warm bodies, all facing the decks, chanting, 'Ten, nine, eight…' Beside her, a short-ass guy in a nylon top reeked gamey and acidic, taking her back to the school sports hall: Airtex tops, split crash mats, and the PE teacher tactfully trying to stress the importance of personal hygiene.

'Happy new year!' The blonde girl clutched her into the crook of her powdery neck.

An amplified voice. 'Okay, folks, let's get this party started.'

A guy with an elfish face bounced up, blew a stream of bubbles and demanded that they dance. How did you dance again?

'Maddie, this is *Simon*,' Roger overenunciated. What was the expression? *Say it, don't spray it...*

'Oh, *Tangerine-man*.' His low-cut v-necked t-shirt was tight, but the trousers... 'Wow, check out the goods,' she whispered in Roger's ear.

He gave her a stern look. 'Simon, my slightly wasted friend, Maddie.'

'I am not!'

'She's just split up with her boyfriend.'

His words hit sharp. 'Maybe, soon.'

Simon nodded. 'Having a bit of a blowout. You go, girlfriend, you don't need that motherfucker.'

Roger's eyes sprang bush-baby wide. She spluttered and Simon laughed too, holding out his bottle of Bacardi Breezer. The warm, melony liquid washed away the sour trickle that was sliding down the back of her throat.

Roger pulled the bottle off her mid-slug. 'Share!'

But Simon was lifting her other hand saying, 'Come on, princess, let's shake it out.'

As he spun her round, a space cleared. He drew her close, lifted her leg, placed it round his waist, then bent her backwards till her hair skimmed the floor. The inverted room made her feel as if they could be anywhere – London, Paris, Manhattan... Pulling her upright, he turned her towards Roger.

'*Dirty Dancing!*'

Roger cocked an eyebrow, but she was rising, unsteady on Simon's shoulders.

'Whoa.' Her hands formed a skullcap on his sticky tousled hair, then clamped round his thick neck as she tried to balance. His fine gold chain wrinkled beneath her fingers.

As Simon turned, she looked down on the bobbing stripes of scalp, where folk had parted their hair centrally, or to one side; and other ruffled heads with no parting; and Bunny up at the decks in her bowler hat, chatting to the beardy guy who was opening a window, letting in a rush of cold air.

'I'm a mirrorball!' Tinkerbells glimmered around the walls. She tilted back her head and watched the crystal drops of a chandelier dance and sway, lifting her hands to flutter her fingers amongst the stars, till she was tipped, the floor coming up to meet her as she fell like the tail of a comet, landing safely, cradled in Roger's arms. 'Woo hoo!'

Simon held something out towards her, hands cupped.

'Sniff,' Roger said.

She reached to take whatever Simon was holding but Roger brushed her arm away. 'Just sniff.'

A pungent gas – nail polish remover, bleach and oranges. As she looked between Simon and Roger, a buzz built in the soles of her feet, tingled from her knees to her hips, crackled in her gut, exploded in her chest, whizzed higher and higher till it blew the top of her head off and all of her, midnight and glitter, shot up like a broken fire hydrant, arching over the room, swooping out the window, soaring into the night sky to dance in the velvety blue-black with a star-limbed Orion.

Happy new year was chanted in for Cape Verde, then Rio de Janeiro. Roger and Tangerine-man were snogging. Where were Jo, Wren, Terry? She pushed through the throng, around the flat. The hall was heaving with folk, voices echoey, words slurred.

She locked the bathroom door and slid down it. The back of her eyeballs ached. In the bath, cans bobbed in an ocean of melting ice. If the ship had been sunk in the storm, Ferdinand – Miranda's future husband – must be wandering around here somewhere. *I would not wish any companion in the world but you...*

A large white-framed mirror hung above the square porcelain sink. She looked wild. Big hair, black eyes, smear of red lips. The mirror dissolved, leaving her face to face with a strange creature, standing upright on two legs.

She shivered, turned on the tap. Bang, bang, bang – in the mirror, the door shuddering.

'Hey, hurry up.' A girl's voice, muffled against wood. 'Some of us are bursting out here.'

'Happy new year, Santiago!' cried an amplified voice.

She dried her hands and slid back the lock. 'Sorry,' she said to the girl who was standing outside, shifting from foot to foot.

When the hall tilted, she used the wall to keep upright. The small window, a bit of air. She lifted herself onto the counter and folded her legs beneath her.

'I stayed in a bad relationship once,' Duncan said. 'Out of habit.' He took three cocktail glasses from a cupboard, rubbed a slice of lime around their rims and dipped them in sugar.

She touched her cheek. It was sticky. A scrunched-up tissue in her other hand. 'Have I been crying?'

Terry sealed a joint. 'Don't worry about it. Hogmanay. Emotional time.' He sparked up. 'Still, out with the old and in with the new.' He passed her the joint.

She took a toke. Stars danced around her head, a celestial daisy chain.

'I'll drink to that.' Duncan handed out the glasses, each dressed with a cherry and umbrella. 'Sláinte!'

They chinked.

She passed the joint to Duncan. 'Got anymore sherbet, Terry?'

'Sadly no. But I do have a wee something special put by. Another wee treat from the 'dam.' He took a small ziplock bag from his shirt pocket, opened it and shook out three white pills.

'What are they?'

He swigged his beer, then pretended to clear his throat. 'Shall I begin?'

'Please do.'

'Item number one, collection of the pound.'

'For what, dear Shylock?'

He undid the paisley-patterned bandana that was knotted round his neck. 'You know what for, you minx.'

Across from one another, like Miranda and Ferdinand playing chess. '*Sweet lord, you play me false!*'

He laughed and offered her his beer.

She took the bottle from him, sipped. Should she say she was seeing someone?

He lifted her chin. 'Your eyes are amazing. They're almost completely black.' He gestured to the wall behind. 'The fairy lights are reflected in them. Like stars.'

'All stars, and no moon?'

'Funny you should ask that. Yes, there is a moon. It's more than half, but not yet full.'

'If only there was a word for the moon in that phase.'

He pursed his lips and shook his head.

She tapped the bottle against his knee. 'What?'

Tying his bandana in a bow around her wrist, the look of mock disdain fell from his face. As he glanced up, a wave rose in her chest.

In the dance room they were chanting, 'Five, four, three, two…!'

He pushed back her hair and tilted towards her.

2
SPRING
1997

One

The bottom panels of the windows were painted yellow and orange and depicted scenes from nursery rhymes. She pulled one of them up – it rose just high enough for her to perch side saddle on the sill. The morning air was frosty, but smelled of spring. A robin hopped over the narrow back road that led to garages – nothing to hear but birdsong. She lit a single skinner and blew the smoke skywards.

The windows had been the first thing she'd noticed when she came to view the flat ten weeks ago, using the term 'flat' loosely – it was more of a bedsit really. Jo accompanied her, and pointed out the room probably *had* been the nursery, before the house was divided into flats.

Half nine, she should leave – it was walkable to Maryhill Community Centre, but she wasn't sure of the way. It wouldn't be good to be late, even if she *was* only meeting Jo and Roger. Her hand shook slightly as she lifted her coffee cup. Silly to be nervous. It was only a discussion day, workshops proper didn't start till Monday. She stubbed the joint out on the sandstone ledge.

Putting the play in her rucksack and pulling on her coat, she surveyed the room. Small, but far from dingy, especially since she'd put up some posters – the one of Miranda looking antique, rather than grubby, now it was in a frame. A programme from *Miss Julia* on the coffee table. Finally she'd got back to the theatre, seeing a couple of shows at the Citz. Why had it taken her so long to finish with Mike?

Two floors down to the entrance hall, where she checked the large mahogany chest for mail – nothing for her, then through the stained-glass door, down the steps, past the communal gardens with their budding rhododendron bushes, and out, out into the world, or at least Glasgow's west end.

After Hogmanay, she'd stayed with Jo for a few more days. Whether or not anything came from the night with Alex, she knew she had to deal with Mike, but when she rang the flat to speak to him, the phone kept going to the answering machine. She took a bus over there, found a letter from Callum on the kitchen table – horrible to push open his door and see his room laid bare.

In her own room, the duvet was bunched up. She sat on the edge of the bed. As daylight bled from the room and the temperature dropped, she listened to passing cars, the shudder of buses, and watched panels of artificial light slide across the darkening ceiling. When the phone rang, shrill, it took her a moment to identify the noise. The answering machine clicked in.

'Maddie, it's Jo, are you there?'

She went out in the hall and picked up. 'Hey.'

'Hi, we're in The Halt.'

'Mike's not here. I've been waiting for him.'

'I know. He's here.'

'What?'

'Here, in The Halt. With Gnasher and that crowd.'

She leant against the door of what had been Bea's room. Had the hall always been wonky, or had the building started to subside?

Jo continued, 'I know this is hard, but bite the bullet.'

Mike ignored her as she approached. She asked if they could talk and he said to go ahead. Gnasher and the other guys turned aside, but she could tell they were listening.

'I've been doing a lot of thinking.' She bent her knees slightly to try and stop her legs shaking. 'I think it'd be best if we called it a day.'

He laughed. 'Think I was gonna hang around and be a punching bag?'

Gnasher sniggered and handed Mike a rollie. Gulping down his pint, Mike turned his back on her.

The day after, she went back to the flat to get some things. A green streak down the wall where he'd hurled the lava lamp; the old TV face down on the carpet; drawers of her clothes tossed across the room. As she picked her way through the mess, broken glass crunched beneath her trainers.

Later, Roger called her at Jo's. 'I saw the wee shite,' he said. 'Got his keys off him for you.'

That night, Alex phoned from his folks' place near Keswick. The chat was brief, but he asked for her address and she gave him Jo's. Two days later, a large red envelope arrived full of silver stars. He'd written her a poem on the back of a postcard, and said he'd be in Glasgow for Burns night – did she fancy doing something? Over the next few days, in between viewing flats, she spent hours composing a reply.

Arriving now at the bottom of Dowanside Road, she passed an old man trimming a hedge with a pair of scissors, using a shoe for a level. She smiled, pleased with the quirky suburban-ness of her new home. Outside Greggs, she bought a *Big Issue*. Not that she had spare cash. There'd been a few murder mysteries at the start of the year, but she'd had to borrow the deposit and the first month's rent from Jo, Roger and her mum. Still, when her dole came in, it seemed only fair to share a little of it around.

She was first to arrive at the community centre. The janitor led through to the room Jo had booked and switched on the heaters. Jo's proposal had gone in to the Tramway, but it'd be a few weeks yet till they got a decision. The way Jo saw it, there was no harm in making a start, even just to workshop some ideas for themselves. High up, windows framed the springtime blue, and sunlight, coming in at an angle, highlighted floating fibres, making them miniature mobile studies of petrol on water.

'*Did you not see my lady…?*' Roger, leaning on the doorframe singing, a hand over his heart.

'Don't start.'

'But I heard the romance is galloping apace, *you fiery-footed steed!*'

'Likewise.'

'I may travel through to the east coast occasionally, but others of us have been south of the border – fraternising with the English!' He took a seat, unbuttoning his jacket. 'How long's it been now?'

'Two months tomorrow.'

'Hey.' Jo arrived, hauling a massive sack with bits of wood falling from it. 'Did you find the place okay?'

'Easy.' Roger rushed to catch some books that were slipping from under her arm. 'What the bejeezus have you got there?'

'Just some bits and pieces. We'll probably not use any of it till we start proper next week.'

They spent the morning talking through their first impressions of the play.

Maddie flicked through her copy of the text. 'Do you want us to start learning *all* the lines, or just the Prospero/Miranda scenes?'

'Don't learn any yet. What I really want to focus on first is developing the father/daughter relationship between the two of you.'

She curled the corner of a page – what would she have to draw on?

Roger glanced at her. 'You're not going to make us go round town in role or anything, are you?'

'No,' Jo said. 'We'll keep to the safety of the rehearsal room.'

'Good.' He sat back. 'I've never fancied myself as much of a Daniel Day-Lewis. I've always thought, *Method, sunshine? Try acting!*'

At lunchtime, she accompanied Roger to Safeways to buy sandwiches.

Linking his arm through hers, he said, 'I'll accept nothing but the full goss.'

'Where to start? His folks were nice. The cottage was pretty.'

'No, no, don't leap in there. Tell it from the beginning.'

Alex had been staying with her the week before, and, on the Thursday, they hitchhiked down to Keswick, where his mum picked them up. It was late, but she heated them up some lasagne before she went to bed. In the living room, Alex put a log on the fire and the flames roared blue and yellow.

After they'd eaten, they crept upstairs. His room was at the end of the landing, up an extra step. The walls were painted with trees.

She ran her hands over the layers of green, brown and yellow. 'Did you do this?'

'I was in my romantic phase.'

'And is that over now?'

He smiled, unbuttoning her cardigan.

The next morning, he negotiated the use of his mum's car. They drove into Keswick and parked, then took a bus half an hour out of town. Cutting up a lane beside a hotel, they joined a footpath that led over a bracken-covered hill.

She pointed. 'Is that the top?'

He laughed.

'What have I let myself in for?'

'Nothing to worry about.'

From the top of the hill, the path ran up to a sheer rock face.

'It's more of a staircase,' he said. 'When you get up close.'

Halfway up, they had to scramble. He showed her how to seek out good handholds.

'Where do we end up?'

'Back at the car.'

'Are you kidding me?'

From the top of what Alex announced was the first summit, the path undulated over several camel humps.

'Langside, Carl Side…' His finger traced a line up a steep pyramid. 'Skiddaw. The fourth highest mountain in England. High enough to be classed as a Munro.'

'I don't remember signing up for this.' Overhead a crow squawked, tipped and dived.

He kissed her palm. His nose, cold and damp. 'Slowly, slowly and all that.'

The scree crumbled beneath her feet, but only the top section was as vertical as it looked. And then, the view, layer upon layer, hills and mountains – green, brown, purple – set against a clear blue sky. Down, southwest, the tiny houses of Keswick were wrapped in a soft haze, and Derwentwater looked like a hole in the earth, mirror-lidded.

Standing behind her, he rested his chin on her shoulder. 'Wait till you see it in autumn.'

It was almost dark when they arrived back in town. The restaurant was fully booked, but in the office Alex's mum had laid a cloth across the desk and set it with candles. Alex chose a white wine and it came in a bucket with ice. Towards the end of the night, while he was in the bathroom, his dad came through from the kitchen and introduced himself. His hair, though greying, was still thick, and he had crinkles at the edge of his violet eyes, like a man who laughed a lot. He talked about the restaurant, asking what line of work Maddie was in. 'It's great having Alex helping out here,' he said, 'but secretly we're hoping he's going to return to art school in September and finish his degree.'

She'd replayed that line in her head a lot since. It'd mean he'd be back in Glasgow full-time.

Roger put a cheese sandwich in the basket she was carrying. 'It's so exciting. We might need to buy hats!'

She frowned but her smile was wide. 'Bit early days to be thinking about that.'

As they joined a queue he whispered in her ear, 'But you'd

have such cute babies together.'

'Roger! Behave.'

He nudged her. 'Look at your face – total beamer!'

Back in the rehearsal room, Jo had acquired some tables. 'I thought we could do some text analysis this afternoon,' she said. 'Stand us in good stead for getting up on our feet next week.'

They finished at 4pm and walked to the pillared entrance of the Botanic Gardens, where Roger said he was going for a bus.

'Wren and I are heading down Blackfriars later if you fancy?' Jo said.

'Cool. I'll see what Simon's in the mood for when he gets through from Edinburgh.'

Roger and Tangerine-man had been dating since Hogmanay, though Roger had asked Maddie to stop calling him that after Simon, distressed one night, confessed paranoia – he thought she'd been referring to his bottle tan.

'If not tonight, see you Monday.' Roger hugged them goodbye.

As Maddie and Jo walked on, Jo said, 'I like Simon enough, but I hope he's not a keeper. Is that awful of me?'

'He is a bit of a nippy sweetie.'

'For a guy who sells kitchens, he could sure out-drama-queen the lot of us.'

Maddie stopped outside the supermarket. 'I need to get some things.'

'Alex coming up tonight?'

'Yeah.'

'Last weekend sounded amazing.' She'd given Jo a fuller account on the phone. 'It's so cool, you guys. You know where we'll be if you fancy stepping out.' She turned in the direction of the tube.

'Hey, Jo…'

She spun.

'It's good to be in a rehearsal room again.'

Jo grinned. 'Feel free to jump in any time, I don't want to be dictatorial about things.'

She bought half a dozen beers and the ingredients to make enchiladas. Back at her bedsit, she put on her new LTJ Bukem CD, tidied round and opened the window to air the room. She rolled a joint and smoked half of it, drinking a beer and flicking through *The Tempest*. Jo had asked them to come up with three key images from the play to explore on Monday.

She was halfway through chopping an onion when the buzzer sounded.

'Shit.' Alex was earlier than anticipated. She rinsed her hands and wiped her eyes. No time for make-up.

As she hurried downstairs, the buzzer sounded again. A long tone, followed by several short jabs. Through the stained glass, only his outline was visible. She let loose her hair and swung open the door.

'Mike.'

He swayed slightly as his eyes slid to her face. 'So this is where you're holed up now.'

He was pissed. How had he found out where she lived?

Putting his hand on the doorframe he asked, 'So how's things?'

'Fine, ta. You?'

He shrugged and wiped his nose. 'Ob-La-Di, Ob-La-Da.'

She took the scrunchie from her wrist and tied back her hair. 'I'm actually just about to go out. I'm running a bit late.'

'Right. Yeah. I was just in the area. Thought I'd swing by and say hello. Reckoned it was time.' He shoved his hands in his jacket pockets. 'Anyway, if you're going out…' He half-turned. 'But could I just trouble you for a quick glass of water? I'm absolutely parched.'

As he followed her upstairs, she could hear his shoes scuff against the dusky pink carpet. 'Nice looking place.'

What was wrong with her, why hadn't she just told him to fuck off?

Standing in the centre of her room, he turned a full circle. She felt him take in the new TV, the CD player. She switched the music off.

He took off his jacket and slung it on the bed. 'See you've got it all kitted out.'

'I had to borrow a lot.' It wasn't a lie. She turned on the tap, let the water run cold, filled a glass. 'Here...'

'Thanks.' He collapsed on the sofa, setting the glass on the coffee table and picking up her copy of the play. '*The Tempest*?'

'Yeah. I'm doing some work with Jo and Roger.'

'Profit share?'

'Kind of. Probably.'

He sniffed, dropped the text back down and nodded towards her empty bottle. 'Beer.'

She bit her tongue to stop herself offering him one.

'Still smoking then?' Picking the half-smoked joint from the ashtray, he inspected it, then sparked up.

Had he looked this bad the last time she saw him? His hair was lank and there were dark circles beneath his eyes. His beard and moustache looked mangy. As he dragged on the joint, a smouldering lump of hash fell and melted a tiny crater in the carpet at his feet.

'Fuck, Maddie, what happened to me?' He stubbed out the roach then ran his fingers through his hair. 'I was the best fucking actor in that college. Now look. I owe money left, right and centre; I've not got ten pence to rub together; I'm homeless; I've not eaten in three days...'

She picked a hangnail at the edge of her thumb. It smarted. 'I can't... I haven't...'

'No, no, no'—he hugged one of the cushions to his chest— 'I'm not asking for money. I just need a place to crash, just for a couple of nights.' His eyes travelled over her double bed.

'Why don't you go to your mum's?'

'Ha! And have her do my head in?'

'What about Gnasher's then, or Ade's?'

'Too much temptation. I wanna go cold turkey, clean up my act.'

'I…'

'Look'—he put the cushion down and angled himself round—'we've been through a bad patch, but people work through worse. Tell me, I'm not the only one who feels we're still connected, am I?'

'Mike…'

'I'm sorry I messed up, Maddie, I really am. But I need you to believe me, I didn't take that money.'

She sighed, perching on the chest of drawers.

'I'm not condoning it, but I can see why you slapped me. I put you through the wringer, coming home late, drinking… But I can change, I'm ready to change.'

He stood, unsteady, knocking the corner of the coffee table as he edged towards her. Water spilled from the glass. 'How often does a love like ours come round? Once in a lifetime, if you're lucky?'

Crumbs in the corner of his moustache.

'No, Mike…'

'My mum said Raymond's waiting to hear from us about his wedding.'

'You haven't told him we split up?'

'What's the point? Come on, we've done our Oberon and Titania. I'm prepared to step down, offer the olive branch.'

The buzzer sounded. He spun round. 'Jesus! What was that?'

'Buzzer. Sorry. I said I was going out?'

'Can't you cancel?'

'No.'

'Okay, but I can stay, yeah? We can finish our conversation

when you get back?'

'I'm sorry.'

'Hey, I don't need straight back in the bed. I can do a night or two on the sofa.'

'Mike…'

He winced and rubbed his chest, leaning to one side. 'Maddie, I don't think I'm well.'

A knock at the door. She sidestepped Mike and opened it.

Alex stood there, face flushed, unicycle under one arm, a brilliant bright sunflower in his hand. 'Hey. A guy on his way out let me in.'

'Hi, good to see you.'

He leant forward to kiss her, but she stepped back, swinging the door wide. 'Alex, this is Mike. Mike was just leaving.'

'Oh, hello.' As Alex raised his hand in greeting, the head of the sunflower bobbed slightly on its stem.

Straightening, Mike looked between them. Did he take in the flower, the colour rising in her cheeks, the rucksack on Alex's back? He let out a short bitter laugh. 'I see.'

Walking to the bed, he picked up his jacket, then stared at her, eyes narrowing. 'You wasted no time, eh?' He laughed to himself, shaking his head. 'Well, congratulations'—he patted Alex's shoulder—'jump in while the bed's still warm.' Outside the door, he stopped and turned.

She glanced at Alex, then back to Mike. 'I'll see you out.'

He held up a hand. 'Don't bother.'

On his way down, he bashed against the bannister, his feet landing heavily on the stairs. From the floor below he looked up. 'Thanks.' He snorted. 'Thanks a lot.'

When he was out of sight, she closed the door and leant on it. 'Sorry about that.'

'So that was the notorious Mike.' Alex propped his unicycle up against the wardrobe and slid the rucksack from his back. 'He looks a state.'

'Yeah. He is. He wasn't always like that. At college...'

'Hey, come here.'

As he wrapped her in a hug, she breathed in the familiar smell of wood smoke and sandalwood.

She sighed. 'This wasn't how I envisaged the weekend starting.'

Pulling away slightly, he looked at her. 'Has he put you on a downer?'

'I just wanted things to be nice for you arriving.'

'I'm with you, how could things be nicer?' He held the sunflower beneath her chin. The tips of its petals tickled her neck. 'Look – you're practically *made* of butter.'

'It's beautiful.'

He popped it in the glass of water. 'Tell you what, I just got paid, why don't I take us out for something to eat?'

She glanced towards the kitchen. 'I was cooking.'

'Will it keep?'

'Yeah.'

When they stepped out, the slip of sky between the houses on the western horizon was lemon yellow, arching over their heads through cornflower blue to indigo. A scattering of stars had appeared.

He took hold of her hand. 'Have you noticed how the tips of the branches have turned scarlet, like blood's rushing into them? Soon they'll be bursting with leaves and blossom.'

A flutter in her stomach. She'd always thought she'd never get married, or have kids. But maybe, maybe...

Cottiers was busy with an after-work crowd, but they nabbed a table just inside the doors.

Alex handed her a menu. 'So what did Mike want?'

'To tap some funds, I think. Just chancing his arm.'

'Doesn't he have any family he can turn to?'

'He's worn his mum's patience more than a bit thin, and he's too proud to ask his brother.'

'Didn't look like someone suffering from a superfluence of pride.'

She looked at the menu. Why the strange desire to defend Mike? Slipping off her coat, she asked, 'What you gonna have?'

'The burger's kinda calling me.'

Beneath the raucous Friday night chatter 'Unfinished Sympathy' was playing. Alex went to the bar to place their order. Lighting a Silk Cut, she sat back, eyes tracing up the red stone walls, over the window ledges with their zigzag stripes to the arched windows. Hopefully that'd be it, Mike's one and only visit. She exhaled.

Alex returned with a vodka-and-cranberry and a pint of heavy. 'Cheers.' They clinked.

While they waited for the food to arrive, he told her stories about folk who'd come into the restaurant through the week, and she described the goings-on in the rehearsal room.

'Sounds like it's going to be an experience.' He set down his pint. 'On that note, how d'you fancy coming on an adventure with me?'

'Does it involve seven summits?'

'No, more genteel, more valley than heights.'

'Sounds promising.'

'Free next week?'

'Next weekend?'

'No, Wednesday-Thursday.'

'I'm working full-time over the next fortnight.' Hadn't she told him that?

'Here we go folks.' The barman set down some cutlery wrapped in paper napkins, followed by their plates and some sachets of sauce. 'Enjoy.'

Alex tore the corner off a ketchup sachet with his teeth. He gestured to the chips. 'Help yourself.'

'I'm good with this, ta.' She picked up a nacho. It remained attached to the rest by a lengthening string of cheese. 'So what's the adventure anyway?'

'Dartington.' His mouth was full of burger.

'Where's that?'

'Devon. Just outside Totnes.'

'What's happening down there?'

He chewed his mouthful and set the burger down. 'I wrote to the director of the arts college and he's invited me for a chat.'

A dollop of guacamole landed on the thigh of her jeans. She wiped it off with her napkin. 'What about?'

'You know how I'd been considering going back to art school?'

'Yeah...'

'I'm just not sure if Glasgow's the right place for me. It looks a lot more open-minded and interdisciplinary down there. I thought I should check it out.'

'Oh. Cool.' She lifted her drink.

'Shame you can't come. The countryside is s'posed to be really beautiful.'

A girl nudged her elbow and some of Maddie's drink spilled. The girl seemed oblivious. Maddie wiped her hand on her jeans. 'It's beautiful here. It's beautiful in Keswick.' Did her voice sound strained, defensive perhaps, or petulant?

Somehow, while eating and talking, Alex had managed to fold his napkin into a swan. He set it down between them. '*And I think to myself... what a beautiful world...*'

She could hear Roger correct him: 'Wonderful. *Wonderful!*' and felt an urge to run, but where to? She pushed the nachos to the side of her plate.

'So, fair lady, what's the plan for ce soir?'

'Are you tired?'

He licked his fingers. 'Nope.'

'Jo said she and Wren would be in Blackfriars, if you fancy?'

'Sounds good. And Hanna said a few of them are heading to the Subby later, if we want to make a night of it.'

They walked down Hyndland Street and along Dumbarton Road. By the time they reached Sauchiehall Street, the conversation had dried up. Ahead, a taxi driver beeped his horn as a white car pulled from a lay-by.

Leaning from his window, the driver shouted, 'Fucking arsehole!'

'Nice,' Alex said.

Through the massive windows of Mother India, diners were bathed in a soft glow, all laughing and chatting.

'We should go on a *proper* adventure together,' she said, though she'd no idea how she'd afford it. 'Maybe over the summer?'

He released her hand to button up his jacket. 'Remember I told you about that couple in Barcelona?'

'Yeah…'

'They've invited me back to work in their café. Maybe we could both go? It's an awesome city. I met some beautiful people there.'

She'd seen his photos. The tall, stunning Carmela, sitting on a low wall looking out to sea.

'Sure. That could be good.' Seeing as he hadn't taken hold of her hand again, she stuffed both of them in her pockets.

The other side of Charing Cross was busier. In a doorway, a girl in a skimpy dress was vomiting, her friend holding back her hair.

'What you staring at?' the friend shouted.

Maddie looked down.

As they walked on, Alex said, 'Welcome to Glasgow! I forgot about the carnage and the casualties. We should've got a tube.'

Beneath their feet were the glass cobbles with the backlit chrysanthemums. The lights had gone out behind a lot of them.

By the time they got to Blackfriars, she was bursting for the loo. Jo and Wren were sitting with a group of folk round a table up on the platform area. She recognised some of Wren's friends from art school, but couldn't remember their names.

'Hey, guys.' Jo hugged them. 'Wait till I see if I can find another couple of chairs.'

Maddie edged through the crowd gathered in front of the bar. Bolting the toilet door, she pulled down her jeans and sat heavily on the cold black seat. Sighing, she rested her forearms on her thighs and hung her head. The tiles on the floor were cracked and damp grime had built up in the grouting. On the wall, women had drawn love hearts, written daft limericks, and responded to each other's messages – they'd been raped, lost love, were still virgins, fancied their gay mates or their straight girlfriends, felt suicidal. A comment about John Major had been streaked through with something rusty-coloured.

A corner of white poked from her coat pocket – the swan Alex had made. She straightened it and sat it on the edge of the sink. Little swan… sailing away. When she turned on the tap, the water gushed so ferociously it splashed the front of her coat. The swan, sodden, wilted to one side. Stupid to feel sorry for a paper swan. She tucked it in the sanitary bin.

Back at the table, Alex was engrossed in a conversation with one of Wren's friends.

'Here, Maddie…' Wren held up a dark glass. 'Voddy-and-Coke?'

'Cheers.'

'Jo's just looking for another seat.'

A girl wearing a headscarf from which hung two long blonde plaits shifted along the bench. 'Squeeze in here,' she said. 'We're just talking about Glasgow losing the Mr Happy face.'

'I think it's a shame,' a guy said.

Another girl held the sides of her head. 'Are you mad? Copyright cost nearly thirty grand last year.'

The headscarf girl looked dreamily at the ceiling. 'I wonder if we can major in illustration…'

Folding a copy of *The Herald*, a guy who looked like Boy George said, 'The old Lord Provost's got a point though – does a wee round fatty really say healthy Glasgow?'

Everyone laughed, then broke off into satellite conversations, none of which she could hear.

At half eleven, folk gathered their coats to head to the art school.

'Come,' the girl with the plaits said. 'Word is Tricky's gonna turn up and play a set.'

She glanced at Alex, he was still busy chatting, drawing shapes in the air. 'I think we're meeting some folk down the Subby.'

Jo appeared at her side. 'Cool, we'll join you for a bit if we can get in before twelve.'

On the way to the club, Alex walked ahead with Wren.

Jo tucked her arm through Maddie's. 'Penny for them…'

'Mike came by.'

'No way! What did he have to say for himself?'

'He seemed under the impression we hadn't really split up, that we were more on some kind of break.'

'He's a fantasist.'

'Then Alex turned up. More than a bit awkward to say the least.'

Jo tugged her arm. 'Jesus, look at that…'

In the middle of the empty car park, a deserted shopping trolley.

'What?'

'A fox! There, behind the trolley.'

Sunk into its shoulders, the fox kept low as it padded across the open tarmac. It shot off in the direction of the river, leaving behind just an impression of round yellow eyes and a white-tipped tail.

Jo shook her head. 'Everything topsy-turvy.'

As they turned into Stockwell Place, Wren leapfrogged a bin.

'What's got into him?'

'Between you and me,' Jo said, 'he's been chatting with a friend about taking over some studios in King Street.'

'Wow. What would they do?'

'Renovate it, hire out some space, organise exhibitions. I think he really wants to stay here.'

The queue to get into the Subby stretched halfway to MacSorley's.

Wren turned and called, 'Just running up to the cashpoint.'

Dropping back, Alex asked, 'Would you guys mind holding a place while I nip up and see if there's any sign of Hanna?'

'Sure.'

Jo smiled. 'You guys look good together.'

'D'you think?'

Her smile became a frown. 'Did Mike intimidate you or anything?'

'No. It was all a bit mortifying, nothing more.'

'Don't let him get to you. He's history.'

The queue shuffled forward. 'It's not Mike bothering me, really. It's Alex. He's thinking of moving to Devon.'

'Is he?'

'He's got an interview at a college down there.'

'Is that why you're so dour?'

'I don't want him to go.'

'Hey, it's just an interview, right? Don't jump the gun. Worst-case scenario, you'll work something out. It's not Australia.'

'Hey, guys!' It was Wren. 'Hanna and Liam are nearly at the door. Alex said we should try swinging in up there.'

As they merged with Hanna and Liam's group, a girl shouted, 'Bunch of fucking chancers!' Luckily the bouncer let them through.

The door staff divided them by gender. A jowly woman with scraped back hair checked Jo's bag and Maddie's pockets, then waved them on.

As she walked down the dimly lit stairs, the bass thumped beneath her feet.

Alex was waiting at the bottom. 'Hey, I've paid you in.' He swung open the heavy black door, the music blasted, clear and loud, and they were sucked into a sweltering underground world of smoke and swirling lights.

'Wanna put your coat in?' he yelled.

'No, I'll just find a corner.'

'Cool. Vodka?'

'Whatever's on offer.'

He joined the crowd at the bar.

The first time they'd come here together, after the Burns supper, Liam gave them a pill each and they danced all night. Alex's eyes were massive pools, edged with a thin corona of blue. Flesh warm, damp, tactile, magnetic – his hands held hers, lifted them above her head, encased her hips, stroked her shoulders. They kissed, danced, ran hand-in-hand to the bar like kids to a fountain, and were unable to understand, when the lights came on and they were asked to move outside, where all the hours had gone.

Outside, snow lay on the ground, becoming banks of white as they walked west. They shared a pot of lemon and ginger tea in Café Insomnia. The smell spiked her nose as the steam rose from their cups in long spirals. Alex curled a lock of her hair round his fingers, leaning in, again and again, for a kiss.

In Kelvingrove Park, the bright white day was shocking, so early on a snowy Sunday they were the only ones there. Pulling a discarded piece of cardboard from a bin, they tobogganed down the hill, squealing, collapsing in a laughing heap at the bottom, near the frozen pond, where the snow angels they made were joined at the wing.

Back at hers, they sat with their knees up in a deep bubble bath. In the heat, his lips turned cerise. Wrapped in towels before the gas fire, he took a pen and drew a knot of roots and leaves on her wrist, then traced a stem up her arm, her neck, to plant a kiss on her cheek – a star of orange petals burst in her mind. He peeled the towel from her. The first time they'd made love. So slow, so gentle, she felt as if she might shatter with bliss.

'Making love!' Roger said, when she reported back to him and Jo.

'It was,' she said. 'What other word for it? It wasn't sex, it wasn't fucking – it was tender, considered, savouring.'

'Savoury! Like a pie?'

'Ignore him,' Jo said. 'He's just jealous.'

'Too right I am. Simon's desire for sexual gymnastics is exhausting me.'

Standing in the Subby now, she felt as if she were watching the crowds from behind glass. Alex came back from the bar with their drinks and, once everyone had gathered, they made their way along the edge of the dance floor to where Liam had spotted a vacant corner of sofa. He offered Alex and Maddie a pill, but Alex said he wanted to have a clear head for the following week. Probably wise. She declined too.

Liam seemed quite wasted, shouting in her ear about festivals. 'We wanna get a minibus this year. Get a whole posse down to Glastonbury. You in?'

She looked at Alex. He was absorbed in a conversation with Hanna. 'Yeah, maybe.'

In the centre of the dancing mass, Wren held Jo to his chest and they swayed like old-time lovers.

They all left the club before the end of the night. Jo and Wren headed south, and Maddie, Alex, Hanna and Liam walked west.

Alex put an arm round her shoulder. 'I was thinking of doing a bit of busking tomorrow. Would you mind?'

'No, I need to work on *The Tempest*,' she said, though she'd planned to do that on Sunday afternoon, after he'd gone.

Above, three seagulls cawed and screeched, swooping down

Hope Street, two of them in pursuit of one with something in its beak. Their underbellies were lit orange by the streetlights, and they looked massive, alien, here in the city.

After they crossed the M8, Hanna and Liam stopped to chat to another couple.

'Party on Rupert Street?' Hanna said, when Maddie and Alex caught up.

She turned to Alex. 'I'm a bit shattered, but you go if you want to.'

He shook his head. 'Nah, I'm about ready to hit the sack too.'

'Maddie and Alex up a tree,' Hanna sang, 'K-i-s-s-i-n-g!'

Back at her flat, she put her Portishead CD on. The crackle, and ponderous guitar, and scratching – like a distorted voice – filled the room with a blue pool burning red round the edges. She flicked on the kettle. In the bathroom, she reapplied concealer beneath her eyes, combed her fingers through her hair and ate a bit of toothpaste. Putting the tube back in her wash bag, the sight of her nail scissors reminded her of the old man she'd seen trimming a hedge that morning.

'Hey,' she said, pushing open the door to her room, 'funny thing...' But Alex was in bed, his trousers, waistcoat and shirt folded in a neat pile, his jaw slack and his breathing slow.

She switched off the big light and turned the music down. Sitting by the lamp, she skinned up and opened the magazine from last Sunday's paper. Difficult to think how she was going to pay the gas bill, reimburse Jo, Roger and her mum, clear her overdraft and student loans, retrieve her dad's ring. A job in a pub or a call centre would mean working all the hours and she'd still only earn about the same as housing benefit and the dole combined, and she wouldn't be available if any acting work came up.

Lighting the joint, she looked at Alex, the way he curled his hands beneath his cheek.

The very instant that I saw you did

My heart fly to your service, there resides
To make me slave to it

The wrong way round – they were Ferdinand's words to Miranda. A spongy numbness ran through her till she couldn't feel her breath. What did people breathe anyway? Invisible gases that you couldn't smell, feel. How could you trust, when you went to sleep at night, that air would always be there? She wanted to shake Alex – I can't breathe, I can't breathe!

When the wave subsided, she lay on the couch. Reaching across for his waistcoat she pulled it to her. It smelled of hay. Maybe if he went to Dartington they could still make things work. There were bound to be buses, they could hitchhike, he'd have holidays. Taking the sunflower from the glass, she counted its petals.

Two

After Alex left on Sunday, she hardly slept. Throughout the week in rehearsals she stifled her yawns as Jo tried numerous exercises to help encourage what she referred to as an *authentic* father/daughter relationship between Maddie and Roger. Wednesday evening, she skipped dinner, smoked a joint, stared at the answering machine. Would Alex be in Dartington now? She held the bandana he'd given her to her cheek. She couldn't smell him anymore.

On Thursday morning, Jo asked them to lie down and talked them through a visualisation. When they opened their eyes, they found she'd strewn wood and debris around the rehearsal room. As they started to build a shelter, Roger caught Maddie's eye and sniggered.

'Okay.' Jo drummed her pen against her notepad. 'Take a break.'

The next day she arrived with the proposal that Maddie and Roger spend a couple of nights on an island in Loch Lomond.

'I've done some camping in my time,' Roger said, 'but mostly down Club X. I like to think of myself as a little more debonair now.'

Jo rolled her eyes.

'Can we at least invite a few folk?' he asked, 'have a barbeque?'

'It's research, not a party!'

He glanced sideways at Maddie. 'I *knew* she was going to get methody on us.'

Jo sipped her coffee. 'Maybe you should've tried acting.'

At lunchtime, Maddie stayed in the rehearsal room and curled up on a pile of exercise mats. She was back in the derelict house, clinging onto the roof as rusted nails worked their way loose and slates tumbled into the dark eddies below.

After work, Roger suggested a drink, but she declined. Letting herself into her flat, she saw the answering machine flash a double beat. The first message was from her mum, the second, Alex.

'Hey Maddie, just calling from Dartington. My meeting went really well and the director's introduced me to some students, so I'm staying on for the weekend to see some kind of event thing they're doing. I'll try calling again later.'

Sitting on the edge of her bed, she replayed the message. Next door in Julie's room, music was thumping, but the volume was low enough to hear voices, excited voices that broke easily into laughter. Her room was so still. The only thing that had moved was the sunflower – its head dipped towards the table, some of its petals had dropped.

She loaded a joint and smoked it, but instead of becoming numb, her heart started to race. She touched things, solid things with her hands, and drank water, breathed in the cold evening air, let the heat from the fire scald her knees. Staring up at the cobalt sky, she finally understood. She was made from a bit of rubble, fallen from a star, and was lost.

Three days passed. Alex didn't call again till Tuesday night. On hearing his voice she lifted the receiver.

'Maddie? Hello…?'

Her breath bounced off the mouthpiece.

'Maddie?'

'Hi.'

'Hey, how are you?'

'Okay.'

He was back in Keswick, hyper and chatty. 'Dartington was amazing. You would've loved it. There was some kind of Easter festival on and a whole bunch of students had set up camp. There were mini plays, musical happenings, a girl in an ice-cream van writing on-the-spot poems... It had such a carnivalesque feel about it, really neat, and so interactive, you know, with the community. I thought, *They've totally got it right – this is what art should be, this is what it's all about.*'

Since when had he started using the word 'neat'?

'Sounds cool,' she said.

'So, you around this weekend?'

'Not sure.'

'I should be able to come up, if you like?'

She let his question hang.

'Shall I ring you tomorrow?'

'Yeah, okay.' But she knew she'd be away on the camping trip Jo had organised. 'I better get on just now.'

The kettle whistled in the background and she pictured his folks' kitchen, the stout blue and beige earthenware mugs.

After she hung up she paced the room, eyeing the items she wanted to hurl against the wall. A sharp grating sound and the mirror fell of its own accord. Such a fright, a volt behind her ears. Her eyes watered, then the sobs came. She wept till her lungs ached and her eyes were too puffy to cry anymore.

Putting the lamp on, she rolled a joint and smoked it. She'd been so scared, as a kid, of ghosts and poltergeists, of what she might see reflected in her bath water, up at the window when she drew close the curtains, in the mirror after midnight. She keeled over on the sofa, eyes sore, heart beating fast. Finally, when the sky began to lighten, she slept, a dark dreamless two hours before her alarm went off.

An hour later, she was walking down a narrow pier, the strap of her rucksack cutting across her palm. Her other arm swished against the blue padded buoyancy vest she was zipped into. Over barely rippling water, sky hung as a low grey haze.

At the far end of the pier, Roger was talking to an old man

whose fluffy white combover wafted in the breeze.

'You've used an outboard motor before?' he asked Roger.

'We went on a couple of trips when I was wee. I think it's fairly straightforward?'

The old man's bushy eyebrows twitched as he took his hand from his trouser pocket and pointed. 'You've got your pull-start system there. Use the lever for steering.'

Jo appeared at her side. 'Sure you've got everything?'

'Think so.' She dropped her rucksack. It landed with a clank at her feet.

'A note of the exercises I'd like you to do?'

'Check.'

'Extra layers?'

'Check.'

'Food?'

'Check.'

'And Roger's got the tent.'

'Yep.'

'You okay?'

'Just not been sleeping well lately.'

'All aboard,' the old man called.

Roger was in the boat and the old man, hunkered down, had the rope pulled tight so the prow nudged the edge of the pier.

'Hope it goes well.' Jo hugged her, but the bulky padded vest hindered her usual squeeze.

The boat rocked as she stepped down into it. She turned, resting her fingers on the damp, rotted planks. Jo handed her the bags.

'Just the two going?' the old man asked.

'Aye.' Roger pressed his lips into a flat line and gave Jo a mock scowl.

'Righto. You'll need to reverse out. Watch for the sailboats there. Nice and slow till you pass into the open.' As he threw the rope into the boat, a gust of wind lifted his hair so it stood up at

90°, an off-centre white Mohican.

She sat on the plank that served as a middle seat, clutching its edge. Behind her, Roger pulled the cord once, twice, and the motor kicked in. As they chugged away from the pier, Jo waved.

She lifted a hand, and Roger did his best impression of Rod Stewart's 'Sailing'.

He shifted the boat up a gear and they powered out into the wide stretch of the loch, tilting back and forth, casting small waves of spray up the side of the boat. 'Woo hoo!'

Hills and mountains rose up on either side, banked with forest, and all around spread a vista of islands, poking above the water-line like heads of broccoli. Wind-provoked tears streaked back from the corners of her eyes, wetting her hairline. She took a deep breath – sanded wood, flaked paint, moss, and a minerally smell of cold water.

Had she overreacted? Maybe she needed to focus back on herself. If she applied herself, she might make a brilliant Miranda, like Jo said. That agent might turn up and sign her to his books, she might get offered more work, maybe even a part in a low-budget film.

'See… fancy…?' Roger shouted, the wind snatching the words from his mouth.

She turned to him. 'See what?'

'…island you fancy?'

'Can we stop on any one?'

'Eh?'

She shouted, 'Are we allowed to camp wherever we like?'

'…spot… beach.'

'Okay!'

The wind was strong in the centre of the loch. It nipped her cheeks and stung the tips of her ears, making them ache deep down. Unclipping the top of her rucksack, she rooted around for the woolly hat Jo had lent her and pulled it on. It muffled the loud churning of the motor.

'How about that one?' She pointed to a small island that rose steeply in its centre.

'…house on it.'

Between the trees she could just make out what looked like the top of a granite castle.

He steered them left and shouted something that sounded like wallabies.

'There's hundreds of islands. How many are there?' She turned, but he was squinting into the distance, his curls flying back from his sharp-boned face.

Up ahead, a waterskier zigzagged behind a blue speedboat.

Her nose ran. She dabbed it with the end of her sleeve.

Slowing the boat, Roger brought them close to a long, thin island. 'This one's a possibility.'

The island had an appealing crescent-shaped bay. Just then, something white flashed through the trees. Two goats emerged.

'Hmm,' Roger said, 'best leave them to it.'

The next one had people camping on it already, but the one after that, he announced, was perfect. He steered them straight in the direction of the bay. 'Motor going off!'

They glided to shore, grinding to a halt with an alarming crunch. Roger leapt out and she followed. Grabbing the front of the boat, he lifted it and hauled it ashore.

'You're pretty good at this.'

'Don't expect such competency with the tent.'

They stood for a moment looking out over the water. Roger's breathing slowed, and little sounds surfaced from the silence. Lap of waves; rustling leaves; a distant caw of a bird in flight. If only there was a phone box, she could call Alex.

Roger lifted their bags from the boat and she unzipped her buoyancy vest. She was here to work, and it was stupid to panic. It wasn't as if Alex was going to disappear. They'd be back on the mainland on Friday. She'd call him straight away.

'So what's the order of the day?' she asked. 'Tent? Fire?'

'First things first.' Roger produced a bottle from his rucksack. 'Cava.'

She dug the cups from the bottom of her bag and Roger popped the cork.

He poured. 'Here's to a swift return to central heating.'

'I'll drink to that.'

As they sat side by side on the beach, the grey day darkened and the mainland became fuzzy. Roger talked about Simon, the way he threw tantrums if he didn't get his own way, often going AWOL, ignoring Roger's calls.

From a pocket on the side of her rucksack, she took out her tin and lit one of the single skinners. Alex might be calling her now. Her phone ringing and ringing…

Some time later she realised Roger had stopped talking. She gulped the last of the sour cava. The back of her throat felt raw, as if she might be getting a cold.

'I've brought us some tatties to bake,' Roger said. 'But they'll take a while, and they'll need a fire.'

She straightened her legs. Her trainers had got wet when she jumped out the boat and her feet were now frozen. 'It's baltic.'

'No wonder you're feeling the cold. You've no insulation. You've started to look like Skeletor's sister again.'

'Did Skeletor have a sister?'

'Who knows. Point being…' He staggered to his feet. 'We'd be wise to get a fire going before it gets too dark. Specially as muggins here forgot to bring a torch.'

She rolled on to all fours, feeling sparkly and lightheaded as she stood. 'That cava's gone straight to my head.'

'We need to gather some wood.' He pulled another bottle from his bag, peeled off the foil, untwisted the wire and lodged it in the sand at the water's edge. 'A wee incentive.'

Up from the bay, a bank led into a forest area. She turned back towards the beach, where Roger was clearing a space. She could imagine him raising his arms to command the elements, but it would be better if he were wearing a long robe and wielding a staff.

Difficult to see much amongst the grass, ferns and gnarled roots at her feet, but, as her eyes adjusted, she found a couple of branches and half a plank. It had been Caliban the slave's job to collect firewood, then Prospero set Ferdinand the task, pretending to punish him. Jo was still thinking about whether to engage more actors. Ariel the spirit and Caliban, she said, could just be aspects of Prospero's subconscious, or represented in sound, images, light.

Setting down her bounty, she put her hands on a tree trunk, ran them down the rough scales and furrows of its bark. Ariel had been trapped in a cloven pine when Miranda and Prospero arrived on the island, but what did that mean? Was he visible, or stuffed tight into the soft, moist wood in the centre of the trunk? She imagined detecting a nose, the ridges of eyebrows, lips so like Alex's she almost wanted to kiss them. Was that some kind of life force beneath the bark, or just the pulse in her own fingertips? Something splintered further off. Heart racing, she gathered up the branches and stumbled back to the bay.

'Alright, sweetpea?'

'I think there's something out there,' she whispered, 'in the trees.'

He'd dug a hole, filled it with twigs and leaves and built a teepee of sticks over the top. 'Probably just birds. Or rats.'

'Rats!'

He rolled a sheet of newspaper, lit it and pushed it into the centre of the teepee. 'Nothing to worry about.'

'How d'you know?' She set down the branches.

'I don't think anyone's been murdered on these islands since the days of Rob Roy.'

'You don't *think*!'

'Tell you what, if a big bad man comes, I'll protect you.'

'Not feeling any better.'

Some of the leaves curled at the edges as they singed and a few twigs glowed and crackled.

'Windshield. Windshield!' he cried.

Trying to feel which direction the wind was coming from, she knelt, opening her coat wide. A thin twist of smoke rose, followed by spitting and hissing as tiny yellow and orange flames licked up the sides of the sticks. 'How can you be sure we'll be okay?'

'I just am.' He stood. 'I think you're being a bit paranoid.'

You're a total stoner these days… She'd heard Callum was getting on well, been offered a full-time job at the Tron, started seeing one of the techies that worked there.

'You keep an eye on that,' Roger said. 'I'll make a start with the tent.'

A few feet away, he bent, picked up a stone and threw it to one side.

'It might not have been a man,' she said. 'It might have been an animal.'

'Luckily we no longer have bears and wolves and wild boar. If we get attacked in the night, it'll probably be by some rogue red-necked wallaby escaped from Inchconnachan.'

'I thought I heard you say something about wallabies.'

'Some Lady or other introduced them in the 1940s.'

'Are they dangerous?'

'Not unless you're a tree sapling.' He lifted the plank she'd found and levelled the sand with wide smearing movements. 'Firstly to prepare the ground.'

He pulled a large plastic sheet from one of the bags. 'The ground tarp.' He shook it, pulled at its corners till it lay flat then, unzipping a long, thin bag, announced, 'Next, the poles.'

He twirled a pole and presented it to her, bowing. 'Can you inspect that for me please, little lady, and tell the crowd if it seems to be a genuine pole – any wires attached, any trapdoors?'

He inverted the bag. 'Hmmm, should be two poles.' Setting the pole down, he pulled the tent from the largest bag, spread it out and checked its zips.

She looked into the darkness behind the trees, took another spliff from her tin and lit up.

'It's properly dark now, eh?' Roger said, coming over. 'The fire's going well.' He placed a couple of branches on it, then took two foil-wrapped lumps and tossed them into the flames. A flurry of orange sparks whirled into the night air.

She offered him the joint.

'Nah. I'm giving it a rest.'

'Why?'

'It was messing with my head.'

The joint glowed as orange as the fire as she inhaled. She held her breath for a moment then exhaled. 'I'd hate to see the mess my head would be in *without* it.'

'Hmm.' Roger walked back towards the tent and started feeding the pole through loops and fabric. 'There's definitely a pole missing. I could have a go at securing it somehow with the guy ropes, but it'd be more like a mosquito net than a tent. Especially with no flysheet.'

'No what?'

He dragged the tent towards a tree. 'Outer bit. Waterproof bit.'

Something glimmered at the corner of her vision, something fleeing through the dark, leaving a trail of red. 'Roger, *there is* something out there, I'm not kidding.'

Dropping the tent he walked back to her side. 'Where?'

'There.' She pointed. 'I saw it.'

'Saw what?' He ventured in the direction she was pointing.

'Something…'

'Hello!' he called. 'If you're out there, make yourself known please.'

'Shh, Roger. Don't.'

'See?' He turned to her. 'Nothing.'

Bang! White light flashed behind her eyes. 'Roger!' She scurried to hands and knees, cowering, tail between legs.

'Jesus!' he cried, then began to laugh.

'What what what…?'

Sprinting to the water's edge, he lifted the bottle of cava and sucked up the flowing bubbles. 'Popped itself!'

'I thought, I thought…'

'Hey hey, sweetpea, are you alright?'

Her eyes started to stream. 'No, not really.'

He put a hand on her shoulder, pulled her close. 'What's wrong?'

'I don't know.' His cold jacket smelled of aftershave, almost like Alex's. 'I just want to go home, Roger. Can we go home now?'

'Well, not right now, but in the morning.'

'I don't like it here. I want to get off this bloody island.'

'It's not so bad. Our tatties will be ready soon. There's a nice bit of heat coming off the fire now. Why don't you get in your sleeping bag if you're cold?'

'I don't care about the cold. It's not safe.'

'You know what the most dangerous thing here is? The water. In places, only five or six metres from the shore, it drops to a depth of eighty, ninety metres. The undertow can be so strong. Swimmers have just been swallowed up, even on fine summer days when the loch looks completely calm.'

'But we won't be swimming. We'll be in the boat.'

'I'm not taking any risks.'

'Fine, I'll go by myself then.' She pulled away from him, picked up her tin and stuffed it in her rucksack.

'You're not being serious?'

'Why not?'

'Don't be mad! You don't even know how to start the motor.'

Heaving the rucksack over one shoulder, she walked to the boat, legs shaking. 'I'll figure it out.'

Roger overtook her, stood between her and the boat. 'No way, Maddie.' He looked strange, his face half-lit, all copper and shadow.

'You can't stop me.'

'I can and I will.'

'What, you're going to physically restrain me?'

He rubbed his forehead. 'Just calm down. This conversation's gone crazy.'

'You're calling me crazy?'

'No, no, you're twisting things.'

'*I'm* twisting things! Who are you to cast judgement, to say what I can and can't do?'

'I'm not. The boat doesn't have a light. We've drunk a bottle of wine. You're stoned. End of.'

'I'll follow the lights on the shore.' She grabbed her padded vest and pulled it on.

'Everything else aside, you'd just take the boat and leave me here, on my own?'

'I've asked you to come with me.' Hands trembling, she struggled to engage the zip, turning towards the fire for more light.

'Maddie, why, why d'you have to go now?' His voice was soft.

Looking up, she saw he was holding out his arms. Her eyes filled with tears. 'Roger, I've done a terrible thing.'

'What, sweetpea?'

'I was horrible to Alex. I really need to speak to him.'

'What did you do?'

'I was distant when he came to visit. I was short on the phone. He'll be ringing me tonight, thinking I'm ignoring his call. He might just have enough, think it's all too much bother.'

'They're hardly the crimes of the century, babe. We'll leave first thing in the morning, you can explain to him then. I'm sure he'll understand.'

'It might be too late by morning.'

'You can't hold someone too tight, angel. Have you heard the expression, *If you love something, let it go free, if it comes back, it's yours*? I've seen Alex, he's smitten.'

She brushed away a tear.

He put an arm round her shoulder. 'Come back to the warm. Jo said she'd given you a flask? Let's have a cup of tea.'

Half an hour later, the feeling of desperation loosened its grip and she stopped shaking.

Roger used a branch to fish one of the foil parcels from the fire. The aluminium had turned amber and bronze. With his sleeves pulled over his hands, he unwrapped it. A mass of steam rose. One side of the potato looked raw, the other charred. He tested it with a plastic knife. 'Still hard in the middle.'

'I've got some crisps if you've got the munchies?'

'The munchies? I'm starving!'

She rubbed her face. 'Shit, Roger, I'm sorry.'

He wrapped the potato back up and returned it to the flames. 'Don't worry. These'll be ready soon.'

'No, not about the food.' She pressed between her eyebrows. 'It's like I can see what's gonna happen with Alex, but I can't stop it.'

'I don't think anything's inevitable. But if you fixate on your fears, you can make them come true.'

She nodded, but somewhere far off it felt as if the wheels were turning.

'Let me finish the tent. Have you got a note of the stuff Jo wanted us to do?'

She dug her notebook from her rucksack and leant towards the flames. Her body felt oddly divided – her face scorched, her back cold. 'Number one,' she read, 'imagine the waters in a roar, thunder, lightning, the two of you cast adrift on a raft, knowing you've been betrayed…'

'Cheery!' Roger said, dragging the tent.

'I wonder how much of it I'd remember.'

'They say the first three years of a child's life are the most important for emotional security.' Picking up a small rock, he staked a couple of pegs. The pole tilted. She sniggered.

He looked up. 'What?' Behind him, the vulnerable-looking structure collapsed. 'Oh no…'

'With that five-star accommodation you are spoiling us!'

He kicked at it, then started to laugh. 'No wonder I never made Chief Scout.'

'Though you clearly spent more than enough time on *Scouting for Boys*.'

'Slander,' he called. 'Slander!'

'Just leave it. We'll sort something out if we need to sleep.'

Clouds drifted in front of the moon, gauzy edges backlit, rainbow-fringed for a moment before their density swallowed the light.

Roger joined her in front of the fire. 'Do you remember much about your dad?'

'Not much.'

'Is that because you try not to think about him?'

'According to my aunt, I've got his eyes.'

'How old were you when he left?'

'About six. But for the last wee while he came and went. He wasn't there like full-time.'

'Where did he go?'

'I don't know.'

He was just like Prospero, in their first scene, asking Miranda what she remembered before they came to the island.

'Tis far off,
And rather like a dream than an assurance

That my remembrance warrants.

She wanted to smoke her last single skinner, but felt too self-conscious.

'My dad can be a cantankerous old git, but I wouldn't be without him. I think my mum feels the same.'

'Was he a good dad, when you were growing up?'

'He certainly did the basics. You know, made sure there was food on the table, a roof over our heads. We had the odd family day out, a couple of summer holidays in Largs. I remember I was mortified because Mum wanted me to wear my brother's cast-offs when I started at the secondary. He insisted I got a new uniform. I'll be eternally grateful to him for that.'

'D'you think they'd come and see the show?'

'Maybe. I'd wait till nearer the time before deciding whether to invite them.'

'In case it's shite?'

'In case it's too arty. D'you know what would've made my mum's year? If I'd have got that *Taggart*. I think it might've even secretly pleased the old man.'

'Why "secretly"?'

'He wasn't too chuffed when I swanned off to drama school. He'd gone out of his way to get me that job as a postie.'

'Is it the insecurity that bothers him?'

'Partly. His dad, my grandpa, was an actor and musician. So he knows what it can do to a family.'

He reached across, picked up one of the bigger branches and stoked the fire. Some of the sticks were glowing with cracked red centres. They shattered as he prodded them. The flames rose again from the pile and he balanced the branch on top.

'So you've never been tempted to go look for your dad?' he asked.

'Why would I? He clearly didn't care about me.'

'D'you think he never cared?'

'He used to come by sometimes to pick me up. He'd take me out swimming, down the river, heating up a couple of pork pies under the bonnet of his Cortina on the way. That'd be our picnic. Along with a jar of pickled onions.'

'Haute cuisine!'

'I loved it. I had a blue rubber ring with a pattern of white anchors. Sometimes he'd come in the water with me. Other times he'd lie on the bank while I paddled about.'

'See? You probably remember more than you think.'

What seest thou else

In the dark backward and abyss of time?

'I remember the last time. I went in the water without my rubber ring. I think I was only under a couple of seconds before he plucked me out. A woman who lived a few doors down from us arrived with her kids. She was a busybody. Made a big song and dance out of it. Told my mum, who went ape and said my dad was totally irresponsible, that she'd not let him take me out again. It's difficult to remember everything. It was me who found his wedding ring though, on the kitchen table. I think it was the next morning.'

'Was that the last time you saw him?'

'I think so.'

'Where is he now?'

She shrugged.

'If it were me I'd have to know. Maybe your mum or Rab scared him off.'

'D'you think if you really cared about someone, loved them, you wouldn't fight for them?'

'Maybe he thought he was doing the best thing.'

'I've had enough shit men in my life.'

'Not all men are shit.'

'Present company excepted. And Alex, of course.'

He shuffled over, put his arm around her.

176

She rested her head on his shoulder. 'You're the nearest thing to a dad I've ever had.'

'Hey!'

'You know what I mean.'

He gave her a squeeze, then wiped his cheek, rubbed his fingers together, looked up. 'Did you feel that?'

A speck landed on her nose. 'Rain.'

They put their hoods up. It came softly at first, then the heavens opened and a heavy shower fell, rattling pebbles, percussive, making the fire hiss. Roger ran to the tree, gathered up the ground tarp, sprinted back. He wrapped the tarp around them, over their heads. She peeked out. From across the loch there was a rumble of thunder as the next curtain of rain swept ashore.

'What are we supposed to do in a storm?'

'Erm…' Roger said, 'stay away from trees and out of the water?'

The sky cracked open with a double flash, lighting the loch and hills in negative.

'Jesus. I wouldn't last two minutes alone in the wild.'

Rain battered on the plastic above their heads.

'You don't have to,' Roger said. 'You've got me.'

When the storm finally receded to drizzle, Roger shifted over and lay on his side. His breath deepened and he inhaled half through his nose, a soft snore, occasionally puffing out through his mouth like a horse.

Dawn broke grey. She closed her eyes but saw an image of the loch bed, strewn with bodies, naked, swollen, glassy-eyed. Slipping from beneath the tarp, she walked to the woods. Large drops of rain dripped from the leaves. One splattered on her head, then slid an icy path down the side of her scalp, re-emerging at her temple like a cold bead of sweat.

Maybe it does matter, where you're from.

She turned. Had she heard it, or just thought it? No one to be seen.

'Who's there?' she whispered.

Nothing.

Something rustled high up and a bird rose from a tree.

Be not afeard, the isle is full of noises,

Caliban's words. Had Prospero always treated him abysmally, or only after he'd tried to rape Miranda? Trying to look calm, she strode back to the beach. She'd no idea what time it was, but it was certainly light enough to sail. Gently rocking Roger's arm to wake him, she remembered the feel of the slippery thin skin of her dad's eyelid as she prised it open early one Christmas morning.

Roger groaned. 'Bacon buttie please, no brown sauce on mine.'

Three

The following Thursday, sitting on a train on the way back from Aberdeen, she turned the pages of *The Tempest*. Her gaze slid from the text to the landscape passing outside – towns she'd never visited, buildings thinning on their outskirts as they gave way to fields then mountains. The blue sky was scattered with large white clouds and the sun, shining through the train window, felt summer-warm. She rested her head back and closed her eyes.

Roger had been a good sport about being woken so early. After they scooped some water from the boat, they headed back to the mainland. From a payphone in a hotel bar, she called Alex's folks' house, but the line rang out.

An hour later, she and Roger caught a bus back to Glasgow, then another to Roger's flat. Since second year, he'd lived in a small one-bedroom modern pad in the east end. They spent the day on the couch, under his duvet, watching *Reservoir Dogs* and *Withnail and I*. Then he made spaghetti hoops on toast for tea. That evening, she got hold of Alex and made her apology.

'Hey,' he said, 'no worries. I just thought you were caught up with work stuff.'

'Any news from Dartington?'

'Not yet.'

'Have you thought what you'll do, if you're offered a place?'

'I'd be sorely tempted.'

She twisted the coiled phone cord round her fingers. 'I'd totally understand if you wanted a fresh start.'

'It does seem pretty special down there, the whole ethos, not just the environment.'

She withdrew her fingers. The cord bounced. 'I mean, in regards to us.'

A slight pause. 'What?' he asked. 'Why?'

'Just might be the kind of thing you'd want to go into without any ties.'

In the living room, Roger rewound the videotape and played the first scene with Monty again. '*I happen to think the cauliflower more beautiful than the rose…*'

'I don't want to leave you,' Alex said.

She took a deep breath, feeling emboldened. 'Take some time, a week, two weeks, think about it.'

Later, when Roger had gone to bed and she lay on the couch in the dark, she wondered if she'd said the right thing.

The next day, the last day of workshops, Jo asked how they'd got on camping. Roger didn't mention the standoff. Instead he spun a story about the isolation. 'I could've been there for over a century and still not have managed to generate electricity,' he said. 'It's incredible, isn't it, how we benefit from generations of progress?'

Jo asked them to do an improvisation. Modern day, Roger, the single father who'd found drugs in a teenage Maddie's room. The initial conversation built to a row.

'You shouldn't have been going through my things!' she yelled.

'Well thank God I did! What were you thinking? This is serious stuff.'

'It's none of your business.'

'It certainly is my business. You're a minor. You're still under my care.'

'Like you care.' She sat down, swallowing back tears.

He knelt before her. 'Hey, hey… What do you mean? Of course I care.'

'You've hardly been here. After Mum left…' Her eyes spilled over.

'Ach, come here…' He cuddled her up, rocked her back and

forth. 'You're my best girl, my one and only. You know I've *had* to take on more work, right?'

She nodded.

'But you've got a point. My head's been…'

She pulled away, wiped her face with the flats of her hands. 'I'm sorry, Dad.'

When the improvisation came to an end, Jo clapped. 'Huh,' she said, 'take that, Mr Anti-Method. Something's definitely changed.'

They went for a drink in Curlers afterwards. Jo said Wren had recommended a filmmaker called Morven who might be interested in working with them.

'So I'd like us to start thinking about sections that could work well on film,' she said. 'For example, I'd love to recreate Prospero and Miranda arriving on the island, find a three-year-old Maddie for you to carry out the sea, Roger.'

'Hang on, hang on.' Roger tapped a beer mat against the edge of the table. 'Roughing it? Getting wet? These things aren't in my contract. Who's Equity Rep round here?'

Jo laughed. 'In your dreams.'

Back at Maddie's flat, the answering machine was flashing – one message. Praying it was from Alex, she pressed play.

'Hello, Maddie, it's Margaret here. I hope this finds you well. I'm calling to see if you're free to do a day's work in Aberdeen next Wednesday? You'd need to travel up on the Tuesday for the briefing session, and stay overnight on the Wednesday too. Give me a ring when you pick this up and I can tell you more about it.'

Over the weekend she forced herself to go out, to not sit by the phone. Saturday night she joined Jo and Roger for Theatre Babel's production of *A Doll's House*.

'Now Pete D'Souza would make a good Prospero…' Jo said afterwards. 'Bet you wouldn't catch him complaining about research.'

'Okay okay,' Roger said. 'Do with me as you will.'

When she left for Aberdeen on Tuesday, there was still no word from Alex.

The role-play followed a similar format to the one before, except this time the training was for mental health workers and she was playing a teenage girl with manic depression. The feedback session went on into the evening, followed by supper. After, in the double room she had to herself, with the crisp white sheets and power shower, she smoked half a joint and dialled Alex's number. *If they return to you, it was meant to be...* She'd put the phone down after the second ring.

The train drew to a halt. She opened her eyes. Dunblane. A woman got off, three folk got on. Next stop Stirling. On an impulse, she gathered up her stuff. She hadn't seen her mum since Christmas. Maybe Auntie Irene was right; she could make more of an effort.

Ten minutes later, the Wallace Monument slid into view. She used to go walking up there sometimes after school with her best friend, Jay. They'd take his dog up past the cliffs where women had been hurled off to see if they were witches. Jay knew all about the fault line, and the conglomerate rock that had once been the seabed.

'They've found whale's bones up here,' he said. 'Or the ancient equivalent of.'

Across the valley floor, the broad loop of the river Forth, they looked out at the power station, the castle, on up to Ben Lomond. One clear day, to the east, they saw a shimmer on the horizon – Edinburgh.

'Did you know Stirling's original name meant place of strife?' Jay asked.

She'd snorted. 'Fitting, that.'

Outside Stirling station, she turned towards the estate. It was colder out than it looked, especially now the sun was obscured by cloud. Would her mum be home? At the bridge she waited for a gap in traffic, wandering a little to the right, then headed along by the river, in the direction of Cambuskenneth.

How many years since she'd been here? Down by the picnic tables, she stopped to watch a small white feather twirling just above head height. Passing her hands above and beneath it, she detected no silken thread. How was it suspended? Alex never told her how he'd made the rose turn into a butterfly, perhaps he never would. Please, please, please let there be a message from him when she got back.

Along the riverbank, bright green grass was scattered with pink petals of cherry blossom. As she crossed the narrow footbridge, she hoped Auntie Irene had meant it, about popping in any time.

Three sharp raps, metal against metal, lucky horseshoe. The white cottage looked very still. No lights on, no sign of movement behind the net curtains. She was turning away when the wooden door eased ajar.

'Maddie?'

The door opened wider. Auntie Irene, in lilac velour jogging bottoms and matching zip-up top, looked thinner, drawn without her make-up on.

'Hi. Did I disturb you?'

'I was just having a wee nap.'

'Sorry. I'll leave you to it.'

'Not at all. All I seem to do these days is sleep. It's lovely to have a visitor. Come away in.'

The living room was as she remembered, low-ceilinged, a three-seater sofa facing the fire, an armchair to one side, photo frames along the mantelpiece with a cross-stitched *Home Sweet Home* hanging above.

'Make yourself comfy. I'll put the kettle on.'

The photos spanned a number of decades, but were all of Clare, from school to her wedding day.

'Up to see your mum?' Irene called from the kitchen.

'Not really. I was just on my way back to Glasgow from Aberdeen.'

'The Granite City? What were you doing up there?'

'A role-play job. Just a day's work.'

Irene carried through a tea tray. 'Must be a tough profession.' She set the tray down on the coffee table. 'Seen your mum lately?'

'Not since Christmas.'

Her pale eyebrows furrowed. 'Me neither. Ach well.' She sat in the armchair, shuffled to the edge of the cushion to pour the tea, then reached across to switch on the fire.

'Gas?' Maddie asked.

'Oh yes. We changed it years ago. Too much bother with logs and coal.'

Irene continued to bombard her with questions: where was she living these days; what were her friends like; did she have a boyfriend? She talked a little about Alex.

'How old are you now?' Irene asked.

'Twenty-two.'

'So young. And you know what they say, twenty is the new ten!' She laughed broadly at her own joke, then coughed and poured a second cup of tea. It had brewed to reddish brown. 'I mean, yes, some folk are married with children by your age, but really, what's the rush?'

Did her face darken as she said those words? Maddie wanted to ask about the cancer, but wasn't sure what to say. 'How are you yourself?' she asked.

'Ach, good days and bad. Donald's hoping to get a transfer at work. That'd mean he'd be home more. Fingers crossed for that.'

When had she last seen Uncle Donald? Her memory was of a quiet, bespectacled man in a leather-buttoned cardigan.

'I was trying to work out,' she said, 'when I was last here.'

'Oh…' Irene looked down, rubbed her hands together, then

glanced up at the corner shelves. She took down a silver photo frame, wiped the glass with the end of her sleeve and handed it across.

In the picture, two little girls sitting on a tartan rug having a tea party in the garden. Clare was pouring from a red plastic pot.

'I think that was round about the last time,' Irene said.

She peered at the other girl with the long dark plaits. 'I wouldn't have recognised myself.'

'Hmm.' Irene sat forward. 'I've something you might be interested in.' She stood, putting a hand on the doorframe as she left the room. Maddie heard her footsteps, slow up the stairs, the creak of the floorboards above.

Gas flames hissed up between the coals, creating a steady pattern of yellow and blue. Something wavered behind the net curtain, a shadow pacing up and down along the sill, the familiar coo of a woodpigeon. So quiet here in the countryside, like at Alex's.

'Wasn't where I thought it would be.' Irene reappeared, slightly breathless, a subtle rasping sound as she breathed in. She handed Maddie a white leather book. 'You have a look through that, I'll make us a fresh pot.' Placing the cups back on the tray she muttered, 'Bit stewed that last cup.'

'Can I give you a hand?'

'Oh no, the exercise does me good.'

Maddie opened the book. Inside clear plastic pages were a range of black-and-white photos. In one, a young woman was holding a baby that was wearing a white frilly bonnet and scowling. Maddie and her mum. She'd seen similar photos before. Two pages on, Polaroid pictures, a bunch of kids sitting on a car bonnet, a man standing in a paddling pool holding a little girl under one arm. The girl, wearing yellow towelling shorts, looked as if she was squealing with laughter.

'Look at you there,' Irene said, returning with the tea.

'Me?' She looked closer.

'Yes, you and your dad. You didn't recognise him?'

She looked at the man with the shoulder-length brown hair. Why hadn't it occurred to her that other people might have photos of him, memories of him?

His features were slightly blurred, but she could see there was a resemblance. 'Mum got rid of all the photos,' she said.

Irene sat on the sofa beside her and pulled the album half onto her own lap. 'Look at you laughing. You were such a cheeky wee monkey.' She flicked back to the start. 'There's your mum and dad when they started dating. That's him there on the moped.' She laughed. 'He got a fair amount of stick for that.'

Overleaf, she tapped a nail beneath a Polaroid picture. 'There's the three of you the day we went to Saltcoats.'

'How old was I there?'

'I'd say about three.'

Three-year-old Maddie was sitting on her dad's knee. They were both eating ice cream. Beside them, her mum was wearing a denim miniskirt and a sleeveless t-shirt. Enormous brown sunglasses covered half her face.

'Look at Jean's skirt!' Irene said. 'Our mum used to say a handkerchief would've covered more.' She sighed. 'Things were good then.'

Her heart beat fast. 'What went wrong?'

'Difficult to say exactly.' Irene sat back. 'They were both young when they met. Your mum fell pregnant pretty quick. There were rumours about another woman, who knows if they were true. Jean was fiery, that's for sure, had our mother's temper. Chris, your dad, moved back to his folks' place. Came and went from there. I thought they were going to figure things out, when your mum met Rab. Safe to say he wanted shot of your dad.'

Sitting forward, Irene poured two fresh cups of tea. Maddie looked at the photo.

'Here.' Irene handed her a cup, but, as she took it, the saucer slipped from her grasp. Tea splashed down her thighs, across the tabletop, the cup rolled and chinked against the fireplace.

'Oh my God!' She sprang to her feet.

'Quick, off with those jeans,' Irene said, rising and heading towards the kitchen.

Clumsy, clumsy and stupid. She picked up the cup, it was chipped and the handle had snapped off.

Irene reappeared with a bag of frozen peas. 'Come along, off with those trousers, let's minimise the scalding.'

She held the cup in both hands, it was warm, a dribble of tea seeped between her fingers. Her eyes brimmed. 'It's broken.'

'Hey…' Auntie Irene stroked her arm. 'It's just a cup. Besides, it's my fault for not handing it to you properly.'

It was after three when she left Irene's. Her jeans had been tumble-dried, but still felt damp down the thigh. Irene had given her some white tulips from the garden to take to her mum's. She was half-tempted to leave them somewhere and make a beeline for Glasgow.

As she entered the estate, some school kids overtook her. They hollered as they lobbed a textbook back and forth, its pages flapping like an injured bird. Running between them, a skinny boy with a crew cut tried to catch it. 'Give us it!' he shouted. She put her head down, crossed the road and walked faster.

The approach to her mum's front door was notable for the absence of barking. She knocked, waited, flipped up the letterbox – no sign of anyone. Rooting around in her bag, she found her keys and let herself in.

'Hello?' she called as she closed the door.

The only sound was the low hum of the boiler.

In the living room, Rab's slippers beneath the nest of tables. On top, a *Daily Record* lay folded beside a full ashtray. Shamed Tories and the war on sleaze... She set down her rucksack and the flowers, took the ashtray through to the kitchen and emptied it in the bin. The washing-up on the draining board was dry. She tried the back door. Locked.

'Mum?' She made her way upstairs.

From her bedroom window, she looked down onto the paved back yard. Marshall's rubber bone lay behind the rotary airer. Between the paving slabs, grass was pushing up – not soft green turf, that had been pressed beneath the concrete for too long, but tough yellow strands and spiky clusters of weeds.

In her mum's room, three carrier bags of clothes on the bed. Her mum always put her winter stuff away at the turn of the season. Kneeling, she lifted the edge of the duvet. The box was still there. She slid it out, lifted its lid. It was almost full now. On top were packets of photos. Christmas; her mum and Rab on holiday in Blackpool; someone's 50th; her graduation; Marshall: in the back yard, in the park, as a puppy.

Beneath the packets were albums. She opened one and flicked through it, trying to avoid looking at her gawky teenage self. The next album featured her mum and Rab's wedding – Maddie aged nine in a hideous peach nylon bridesmaid's dress. Rab often gave her a row for being a moping, miserable child, and she did look thoroughly depressed.

Finally, an album pre-Rab. As she recalled, mostly blank spaces, just a few pictures of her and her mum. Had it been her dad standing behind the camera taking those photos? In one of them, she and her mum wrapped in hats and scarves, her mum kneeling beside a snowman with Maddie on her lap. How old was she there, three, maybe four? She was grinning, but her mum was smiling weakly.

That was it. The box was empty. She ran her hand over the sheet of wrapping paper that lined the bottom of the box. Cartoon reindeers pulled Santa's sleigh across a dark blue sky. She felt a couple of bumps. Lifting the edge of the paper, she saw a corner of an envelope, then another. Six or seven envelopes in all. She picked one up. It was addressed to her mum. Opening it, she pulled out three sheets of pale pink Basildon Bond paper, torn from a pad, still bound together at the top. The handwriting, in blue ballpoint, sloped right. She skipped to the end:

With love, Dorrie xx

As she turned the pages, a musty smell rose, like potpourri that had lost its scent.

understand you need a fresh start

think he regrets many things

so sorry things have not worked out between you

There was reference to a Bert who spent most of his time upstairs practising the trumpet, or out shooting rabbits.

the thought of not seeing Maddie grow up makes me very sad. I know Bert feels the same, even though (like all men) he doesn't say much.

Some words were difficult to decipher.

If you change your mind, you'd be welcome over anytime.

It was from her dad's mum, her granny. Hadn't she and Grandpa had a narrow garden, with a rope swing hanging from an apple tree? Granny wore a floral apron, and let her spoon strawberry jam into pastry cases to make jam tarts. At the front of the house, in a dark living room, a budgie in a cage with a small round mirror, a bell, and a piece of cuttlefish. She'd once been allowed to inspect the cuttlefish. The edge of her nail sunk into it, it'd compressed like green blocks of oasis flower foam.

Out on the landing something thudded. She froze...

Silence.

She put the letter back in the envelope, opened another.

It was from Auntie Irene. She said she was writing because every time she phoned, Rab said Jean was out, and Irene didn't believe that was true.

I need you to know, Jean, I felt physically threatened by Rab that day, and that makes me concerned for you, and for Maddie. At least know I'm here if you need me. I can come and get you anytime. You'd be welcome to stay with us while you sorted things out.

Her hand shook as she angled the letter back into the envelope. She scanned the others. One more from Auntie Irene and two from Dorrie. Beneath those, two small white envelopes addressed in scrawly print. She opened one. A single page. At the bottom:

Please phone or write. Chris x

Her dad. At the top an address: 13 Silverbirch Drive, Lenzie.

Dear Jean,

Downstairs, a key turned in the lock, the door opened, slammed, a jacket brushed against the wall. Rab. Setting her dad's letters to one side, she put the rest in the box and smoothed the paper over them. Something clanked and rattled in the hall, then Rab moved through to the kitchen, ran the tap, filled the kettle, coughed a phlegmy smoker's cough. She placed the albums back in the box and gathered up the packets of photos. Some of the photos fell from their sleeves. No time to sort them. Rab started to climb the stairs. Shoving the lid on the box, she slid it beneath the bed, flipped down the duvet, then dashed along the landing to her own room.

Rab hauled himself up using the bannister.

'Hi,' she said, poking her head from her room, the letters held behind her back.

'Jesus!' He looked startled, then his features settled into their normal half-sneer. 'What are you doing here?'

'I was working in Aberdeen. Thought I'd stop by and say hello.'

'Where's your mother?'

'I don't know. I just swung by on the off chance.'

He reached the landing, breathing heavily through his bulbous nose. 'Work! You don't know the meaning of the word.'

He pulled the bathroom light cord. The fan began to whirr. 'What are you staring at?'

'Cup of tea?'

He grunted. 'But let it brew. None of your gnat's piss.'

'Okay,' she said, edging round the stair post.

She was about to step down when the letters were snatched from her hand. She spun.

'What's this?'

'None of your business.' She reached for them.

'Uh uh uh!' He lifted them higher.

'They're private.'

Stepping back, he looked between them. 'They're addressed to your mother.'

'I know. She gave them to me.'

Opening one of the envelopes, he pulled out a letter.

'No!'

His jaw tightened and the vein in his temple throbbed. 'Where'd you get these?'

'Mum gave them to me, years ago.'

'Bullshit.' Walking into the bathroom, he brushed against the side of the bath. The old towel that served as a bathmat slid to the floor. He flipped up the toilet seat. It clattered against the porcelain tank. Pulling out his Zippo, he flicked back the lid and struck the wheel. A steady flame jumped up, yellow, blue at its centre.

She stepped into the doorway. 'What are you doing?'

He held a corner of the letter over the flame. 'You're full of shit.'

'Don't…!' She wanted to grab his arm.

Beside her, the grimy light cord continued to swing and the plastic end ticked against the tiles. The edge of the letter browned then caught alight.

She took another step forward. 'They're not yours!'

Flames crept up the paper, gathering momentum. Rab's neck reddened. He dropped the letter into the toilet bowl and flushed.

Nothing she could do. She turned towards the stairs.

'Where d'you think you're going?'

She hesitated.

'Think you can fucking skulk off?'

What had she learned? Obey. Keep calm. Show no emotion. It didn't always work, but it was the best bet.

From the corner of her eye she saw him hold a flame beneath the second letter, then the envelopes. The stench of charred paper was overpowering, her eyes smarted with the smoke.

Rab flushed the toilet again, pocketed his Zippo and shoved a hand in her direction. 'Keys.'

'What?'

'This is my house. There's no reason why I should have to put up with you lurking about. Uninvited.'

'I wasn't…'

'Just give me your fucking keys!'

'They're in my bag.'

'Well go and fucking get them.'

She ran downstairs. In the living room, she shoved the tulips into the pouch of her rucksack and grabbed her coat.

'Don't make me come down there!'

She climbed the stairs. When she reached the landing, Rab walked towards her till she was cornered.

'Think I've not done enough for you and your mother?' He snatched the keys from her hand. 'That so-called fucking father of yours. Made your mother's life a misery. Made mine a fucking misery, having to take on a fucking halfwit like you. And what fucking thanks do I get for it?'

Fumes on his breath. Whisky.

'You gone deaf as well as dumb?'

'Sorry.'

'Tsss.' He looked as if he was about to spit. He pocketed the keys. 'Get out of my fucking sight.'

She didn't need to be asked twice. Running downstairs, she noticed Marshall's collar and lead hanging over the bottom post. Then she was out on the street, half-running, her breath fast and shallow, shuddery. Please God her mum wouldn't turn up now. The thought of her mum with her worried expression asking, Maddie, are you alright, love?

Don't cry, not now, not now... She swallowed hard and dug her thumbnail into the pad of her index finger. Someone shouted behind her, she dropped her head and started to jog. As she crossed the road, her foot landed awkwardly in the gutter, her ankle twisted, throwing her forward. She put her hand out. It slammed against the tarmac, her nose less than a centimetre from the road. Her ankle spasmed. Hauling herself back onto the kerb, she gripped her leg round the calf. A Jack Russell ran up, sniffed round her, hurried on.

Don't cry, don't cry, don't cry...

A few minutes later, the splitting pain became a swollen ache. Tentatively she flexed her foot. It was painful but didn't seem to be broken. She stood. Some of the tulips had fallen from her rucksack. She left them strewn across the pavement as she hobbled towards the train station, gradually putting more weight on her injured ankle. Rain started to fall as a fine mist.

At the station, she took a seat at the far end of the platform and pulled out *The Tempest* to hide behind, opening it at a random page.

All lost! To prayers, to prayers! All lost!

A shriek. She looked up. A girl ran down the platform chased by two neds. One grabbed the girl round the waist and the other lifted her legs. She was laughing, laughing and shrieking as they swung her, looking as if they were going to toss her onto the tracks. A shrill whistle made them glance round. A portly gent in a cap and navy blue uniform strode towards them, gesticulating wildly, his voice drowned by a two-tone blast of a horn as a freight train sped by. She was buffeted as it tore through the air. Beneath its roar was a steady thump of wheels, a high-pitched squeal. She half-closed her eyes, wishing she could close her ears.

When it'd passed, she saw a few folk had gathered on the opposite platform. If she ran and leapt, would she make it to the other side? She could see herself dangling mid-air, then falling onto the tracks. Another train would speed towards her, her laces would be caught in the metal clips that pinned the rails to the sleepers, she'd be struck, bashed with unimaginable force, turned, sliced, torso from legs. The blue-grey knuckles of her bones would be ground beneath the wheels. *Fee, Fi, Fo, Fum…*

A pigeon with a gnarled foot limped past, pecking at the spaces in the paving. How like a pigeon's foot her hand was, lying across the pages of the book. She lifted it. The heel was speckled with blood, studded with grit. It left a light rusted streak across the text, the shipwreck:

'Mercy on us!' – 'We split, we split!' – 'Farewell, my wife and children!' – 'Farewell, brother!' – 'We split! We split! We split!'

When the Glasgow train arrived it was packed with commuters. Halfway down a carriage, a man lifted his bag from a window seat so she could sit. She wiped a patch in the condensation, but the window was too dirty to see much.

At Croy she remembered a joke Mike had made about going out with a girl from there, named Helen.

'Helen of Croy.' She'd laughed.

'Yep. She had a face that'd lunched on a thousand chips.'

Leaning her head against the glass, she closed her eyes.

When the train next drew to a halt, she rubbed the window again. Lenzie. The word, painted black on white, looked different. It'd felt like some alternative world, some mythical place, where her dad lived. Not here, in this same geography, in this same time and space. Some folk alighted, men with long coats and briefcases, others with jackets and rucksacks. Could he be one of them? Could they have been on the same train, passed on the street before now, without knowing? The passengers exited towards the car park and the train pulled from the station, beating out a name: Silverbirch Drive, Silverbirch Drive.

She was cold and damp and her head was pounding by the time she got back to her flat. The answering machine was flashing. Four messages. She pressed play. The first three consisted of a slight pause, then whoever had called hung up. The fourth was from her mum. She sat on the edge of her bed and gripped her knees. What would Rab have said? How would she explain about the letters, about her dad's ring?

'I've tried calling you a couple of times.' Her mum sounded weary. 'I don't really want to leave this in a message, but we've got to go out now.'

Her ankle spasmed, a sharp, splintering pain.

'It's about Marshall. He's not been well. He had a funny turn last night. Rab took him to the vet's today. We had to let him go. Sorry to leave this in a message, love, but I thought I should let you know. Give me a call when you can, eh? I'll be about over the weekend.'

Not now, she couldn't deal with this now. The tape rewound. She pressed play again and listened to the brief spaces before whoever had called hung up. Was one of them Alex, or were they all her mum? She took off her coat and went to the bathroom. Julie must've just had a bath – the room was humid, the mirror steamed up, a crown of suds swirled on top of the plughole. She sat, the toilet seat damp beneath her thighs, put her head in her hands and breathed in lavender and eucalyptus.

She'd been about thirteen years old. Her mum and Rab were going out for the day. She was supposed to be going too but, at the last minute, she'd been made to stay at home and think about what she'd done. What had she done? Who knows. She was lying on her bed crying when Marshall snuffled at her door, pushing it open with his nose. She wasn't supposed to let him on her bed, but when he put his forefeet up she helped lift him – his back legs scrabbled, he was just a puppy. He sniffed her face, his big brown eyes looked as if he understood. Padding round and round he curled up, nose to tail, against her stomach. She stroked his velvety ears. His ribcage rose and fell. He was warm and smelled milky. Little Marshall, sweet soft puppy…

She pulled a length of toilet paper from the roll and pressed it against her eyes, crying silently, so Julie wouldn't hear.

When she was all cried out, she blew her nose and splashed her face. Her eyelids were puffy and sore, her right eye bloodshot. As she opened the door to her room there was a click followed by a whirr: the answering machine rewinding. She stood over it till it reset. Holding her breath, she pressed play.

'Hi, Maddie, it's me, Alex. Wondering where you are. Maybe you're away working somewhere. Anyway, just wondering if you got my note. I'm gonna have to leave here soon. I guess I'll try calling again when I get back to my folks'.'

What note? Putting the door on the snib, she ran downstairs. On the chest in the hall, a makeshift envelope with her name on it. She unfolded it.

Tuesday it said at the top. He'd been here two days.

Hi Maddie, rung a couple of times – no luck. I'll head over to Hanna's. Ring me when you get this? Hopefully catch you soon. Alex x

A kiss, but only one. Quite formal in tone. She ran upstairs and dialled Hanna's number. Please pick up…

After she'd pulled on her coat she tried the number again. She hung up after the seventh ring.

Outside, it was raining harder. By the time she got to Hanna's her coat, trainers and the bottom of her jeans were soaked.

Keith opened the door. 'Hey, wee Madster, come on in.'

Folk were sitting in the living room, shouting over a dark, edgy, industrial track layered with caws and hollers. The sub-bass beats made the floor vibrate. Liam was trying to play along to the fast breakbeats on the bongos.

He raised his hand. 'Hey, Mads.'

She waved back, scanning the room. No sign of Alex.

'Hey there, Maddie.' Hanna stood behind her, holding three mugs in each hand. She set them down on some upturned crates. 'Two more teas. Maddie?'

'I'll come through.'

In the kitchen, two guys were sitting at the table playing pick-up sticks. Three others were spectating. In an armchair in the corner, a girl wearing a red poncho chewed a pen and stared at a folded newspaper.

'Hey, that totally moved,' one of the guys said.

'Did it fuck!'

'It did and you know it. That yellow was shoogling all over the place.'

A guy wearing a hat like Jamiroquai's rubbed his eyes and sniggered. 'They're all fucking moving, man.'

She recognised his voice. The guy who'd danced with the dragon. Brendan.

Hanna filled the kettle. 'Tea, tea...'

'Is Alex about?' she asked.

Hanna glanced up, her eyes unfocussed. 'Alex? Oh! He's gone.'

'Shit. When?'

Pulling open the cutlery draw, Hanna peered into it. 'What am I looking for again?' She lowered her head onto the counter. 'Oh, those shrooms are shrinking my brain.'

Brendan curled his hands beneath his chin. *'I'm shrinking! I'm shrinking!'*

Melting! She could hear Roger correct him.

The girl in the red poncho looked up. 'He left about ten minutes ago. Said something about getting a bus.'

'Thanks.'

Iggy appeared in the doorway and opened his arms wide. 'It's my birthday!'

'Happy birthday,' she said.

Hanna sprang upright. 'We're having tea. I made a cake.' She looked about. 'Did I actually make a cake?'

'Yeah,' the poncho girl said. 'You put about an ounce of hash in it. It started to smoulder so I took it out the oven.'

Brendan banged his fist on the table. 'It's a tea party!'

'Hey,' one of the guys shouted. 'Watch the sticks, you big fucking numpty.'

Iggy pointed at Brendan. 'It's a mad fucking hatter's tea party.'

'I'm the mad fucking hatter, man!' Brendan threw his arms in the air. The sticks scattered, some rolling onto the floor.

'Brendan!'

'I've gotta go.' She edged towards the door.

'You can't go. It's my birthday.'

'I'll come back.'

'But wait… What's brown and sticky?'

A chorus came from the table. 'A stick!'

'Okay, okay… When is a stick not a stick?'

'Iggy, I'm in a rush.'

'What d'you call a boomerang that won't come back?'

'Iggy!'

'Fine. Fuck off then.' He stepped aside, then clutched her to him as she passed. 'I didn't mean it. I love you really!'

She ran down the stairs and out into the night. The roads were quieter. Black cabs with yellow lights on passed her. If only she had enough money to hail one. She jogged down Woodlands Road, her ankle twingeing with every step. Impatient at the traffic lights, she dodged between cars. One of the drivers sounded a long beep of his horn. She got a stitch in her side, but kept on running. As she passed Speakers' Corner she saw him on the other side of the road, rucksack on his back, unicycle under his arm.

'Alex. Alex!'

He turned, then waved his hand high. 'Hey!'

She waited for a gap in traffic then sprinted over.

'I've been calling you,' he said.

'I know. I've been away working.'

He tucked a strand of hair behind her ear. 'This rain…' He looked up, blinking.

'Monsoon season.'

'Currently running March to November, with a brief break for snow.' He adjusted the straps of his rucksack and put his unicycle under his other arm. 'I waited as long as I could. I've gotta get this bus. Walk with me?'

'Sure.' Why couldn't he stay? If she asked him, if she said please, if she told him about her day…

'Where were you working?' he asked.

'Aberdeen.'

'North of north. On *The Tempest*?'

'No. A role-play job.' Her throat was sore from breathing so fast and her mouth was dry. So much water outside. Raindrops smacked against the pavement, jumping a few inches back up. They passed Nico's, where they went that first night, before Christmas.

'I got a place,' he said. 'At Dartington.'

'Wow. Congratulations!'

He took a deep breath. 'I hoped we'd have more time together, to chat and stuff.' He glanced at her, half-smiled. 'But I guess you know what I'm gonna say.'

She held her breath.

'Shit, Maddie, you're so much wiser than me. I thought, *So what if I go down there, we could still go out, we could still date.* But I totally didn't think about it realistically, what it'd be like, trying to travel the length of the country to grab brief moments together, not fully committing to life where we were. We'd just end up limiting each other.'

Should she tell him her thoughts about moving, ask whether they could look for a flat somewhere in between?

He ran his hand through his hair. 'I've thought about it, what to do. Whether or not I should take up that place. I've gone on walks. I've sat on top of hills.'

He sighed. 'I've booked a ferry. Set sail tomorrow. I'm gonna hitch about for a bit, then head to Barcelona, work there for a few months. I thought, if I was totally away...'

He stopped and took her hands. 'You're the most amazing person.' His brow furrowed, he turned her injured hand. 'What happened?'

'Oh. Nothing. I fell.' Her voice wavered.

He traced a finger across her wrist, around the blood and grit. 'Looks sore.'

She swallowed hard but a large, hot tear spilled onto her cheek.

'Hey, are you okay?'

'My mum had to have the dog put down.'

'Shit. Shit, I'm sorry.'

She brushed away the tear. It must've been about here, where the Christmas tree was, where he spun her round, where feathers of snow had fallen.

'I'll write,' he said. 'I really hope, further down the line, we can be friends. But you're totally right, about where we're at in our lives just now. You're at the start of your career, and I'm going back to square one.'

Had she said that? Could she persuade him otherwise? Just for the summer, just for tonight even? She daren't speak.

He looked at his watch. 'I gotta run. I'm sorry. I'll call you tomorrow from my folks' place before I head off.' He hugged her, his sodden jacket against her cheek. The smell of wood smoke and something else... Pine needles. *Of all the trees most lovely...*

'Alex?'

He pulled away to look at her. 'Yeah?'

'Take good care.' She raised a hand and managed to turn before the tears started streaming.

'I'll call you!'

She walked west, cutting down back alleys so no one would see her. When she reached her flat, she couldn't bear to go in. Too many ghost-spaces – where he'd laid his head, where he'd folded his clothes, where he'd leant his unicycle. She made her way back to the city centre.

Why hadn't she run after him? If she'd said she was wrong, would he have changed his mind? Too late. He was speeding further into the night, every second widening the gap between them. Soon he'd be in the southern uplands, crossing the border, swallowed by miles and miles of land, amidst millions upon millions of people. She wanted to fall to her knees.

From Central Station, she walked to Roger's. Under the bridge, past the Tolbooth Steeple, a group of old men were standing in a circle, swigging from bottles of booze barely disguised in plastic bags.

Their conversation was all murmurs, then one of them shouted, 'Ya daft fucking cunt!'

She put her head down and crossed the road.

At Roger's, she pressed the buzzer. No reply. Up at his windows, the curtains were open, the living room dark.

From a phone box, she called Jo's. Her flatmate answered. 'I've no idea where she is. I've not seen her for weeks. Have you tried Wren's?'

She replaced the receiver and the top of her head flipped open, like when she'd sniffed those poppers at Hogmanay, but glittering stars didn't shoot out of her. Instead, a slow seepage of dank water, rotted leaves, sewage and silt. She pressed the cuts on her hand till the pain drew her back inside her skin.

By the Bridge of Sighs she climbed over railings and up the steep bank of the necropolis, bushes scratching at her coat. A path snaked up, flanked by solid shapes of gravestones, tall obelisks and pillars. Smooth tarmac became gravel, then larger stones that made her feet slip, a stabbing in her ankle. What did it matter, her pain?

Beside the floodlit statue of John Knox, she looked out across the dark city with its broken tendrils of light, south to the hills, down to the cathedral and the massive wall of the Royal Infirmary, hundreds of tiny rectangular windows, most lit.

A rustle behind. She turned. Nothing but statues and stone angels, then, 'Hey, sweetheart.' Two shapes weaving between the monuments. Two skinny neds wearing baseball caps.

'Fancy a chip?' She caught the sharp smell of brown sauce.

'Fancy a shag?' the other one asked.

She looked down, took small, quick steps, the grassy mound slippy with mud.

'Hey, we're talking to you,' the first one shouted.

Left, or better to head back the way she came?

'Silent type, eh? Prefer it when they make a bit of noise.'

She'd come up here with a group of folk one night after college, drunk. One of the techies said some of the burial vaults had collapsed and grass had grown over them. Please God she wouldn't fall into one now.

Behind, she heard the swish of denim. They were following her. 'Here, kitty kitty…'

She started to run, felt a hand on her shoulder, shrugged it off.

'Gonna be a wee fighter, eh?'

'Fuck off,' she whispered.

'What's that, ya wee hoor?'

She spun. 'I said fuck off!'

Was that her voice? It came from a full deep breath.

A man and woman appeared on the path.

'Everything alright?' the man asked. He was older than the neds, bigger.

'Ho, brother.' One of the neds held up his hands. 'Lady just can't take a fucking joke.'

'Best leave her alone then.'

The neds backed off, turned and walked away.

The one with the supper scrunched up the paper and threw it over his shoulder. 'Frigid fucking bitch, man.'

'You okay?' the woman asked.

'Yeah.' She tried to stop shaking. 'Thanks.'

Back down at street level, she headed to the bus station and sat on a bench. Passengers boarded the night bus, an empty coach pulled in, then everything was quiet until the clubs came out and a few folk careened across the forecourt to the taxi rank. The sky lightened.

'Hen.' A woman was at her side, holding out a plastic cup. 'Here you go.'

'Sorry?'

'Tea.'

'For me?'

'Aye.'

She took the cup. 'Why?'

The woman sat down, turning up the collar of her coat. 'Been watching you. Just finished my shift. Streets aren't easy for a young lass.'

The woman was older than Maddie first thought. She had short, dyed black hair. 'No, I...'

'Some folk would tell you to go home. Others of us know home ain't always kind.' She adjusted her large hoop earrings so they sat outside her collar. 'Case of the devil and the deep blue sea, eh?'

The tea was burning through the beige plastic.

'Best drink it while it's hot.'

She sipped, it was scalding.

'It's a rocky road, and a long one, but you *can* get yourself sorted. Eight years I was moving about, between hostels, on the street.' She took a packet of Regal Kingsize from her handbag. 'Take it you smoke?'

'Thanks.' Maddie took one.

'But I've not come over to chew your ear. I just wanted to give you this.' She handed over a piece of paper, torn from a diary. On it was written a name and an address.

'They're Christians, but they're good people really. You still look pretty smart, pretty sane. But take it from me, it'll eat you up. Eat you up and spit you out.' She patted Maddie's arm and pointed to the slip of paper. 'If you can take any shortcuts, do.' She stood. 'Wish I could do a Cher, me.'

Maddie looked up.

'Turn back time.' The woman smiled, gave a nod then walked away, tying her belt round her coat.

Heading west, Maddie passed people on their way to work. Nobody looked at her. Had she become one of the invisible ones, like the skeleton boy just ahead, sitting cross-legged on a grey blanket in a doorway? He only looked about fourteen. She had three pounds seventy in her purse. She put it in his cup along with the slip of paper the woman had given her.

Back at her flat, on the chest in the hall, an envelope addressed to her. Thick, quality paper. She waited till she was in her room to open it. The pawnshop. They'd have had her dad's ring for six months by the end of the month. Six months. She'd need to go down there, extend her loan. The answering machine was flashing. She pressed play.

'Hey Maddie, it's me, Jo. Hope things went well in Aberdeen. Just calling to say I've spoken to Morven and she's free to do some filming two weeks today. Give me a bell if it's a problem.'

She switched on the fire and huddled in front of it. Lucky to have a fire. Lucky to have shelter from the wind and rain; a lock on her door to keep out the nutters; hot water – she'd have a bath soon, soak her hand, wash out the grit. Lucky to have a bed to lie down on. A big empty bed, with two pillows. She folded her legs and wrapped her arms around them, rocking back and forth. Alex, Alex, Alex… She rested her head on her knees.

'My brave soldier, my brave wee soldier.'

Five years old, she'd fallen off her bike and grazed her knee. Her dad lifted her up, carried her indoors, sat her on the kitchen table, ran a basin of warm water and wiped the wound with a wet ball of cotton wool. Then he'd dabbed on some sticky pink Germolene.

She lifted her head. She'd forgotten about the photos Auntie Irene had given her. From her still damp rucksack she pulled out an envelope. Inside were three pictures, thankfully undamaged by the rain. The one of her dad on his moped; him standing in the paddling pool with her under his arm; the three of them in Saltcoats, eating ice cream. They'd faded over the years and, despite being kept in an album, were slightly dog-eared. Was there anything she could do to preserve them?

Four

Two weeks later, the morning of the filming trip to Ayr, she took Alex's bandana from beneath her pillow, folded it and put it in her bottom drawer. The buzzer sounded.

Outside, Wren's car was half pulled up on the kerb with Jo at the wheel.

Wearing shades and leaning on the stone pillar at the bottom of the steps, Roger was smoking. 'I hope you like roller coasters.' He nodded towards the car. 'The woman drives like a lunatic.'

'Hey!' Jo called out the open door. 'I'm just a bit rusty.'

Roger peered over his shades. 'Morning, angel-eyes.'

'Hey, handsome.'

She ducked to climb in the back. 'Hi, Wren.'

'Greetings.' Beside Wren, in the middle on the back seat, was a little girl with long dark hair. 'This is Cassie, my niece. Cassie, this is Maddie.'

'Hi, Cassie.'

Jo turned in her seat. 'Cassie, Maddie's going to be playing the older version of you.'

Cassie glanced up, her brown eyes fringed with long, dark lashes.

'She's four years old,' Jo said, 'but I think she's wee enough to pass for a three-year-old Miranda. She looks quite like you, don't you think?'

'She's prettier. I had a god-awful bowl cut at her age.'

Jo turned her attention back to Roger. 'Come on, Grandad. I want to get there before Morven does.' She caught Maddie's eye in the rear-view mirror. 'Someone had a rough night.'

'Oh?'

Pushing back the passenger seat, Roger climbed in. 'Least said the better.'

She gazed out the window. Goodbye, Glasgow, even if only for a day.

Alex had called the day after they'd said goodbye on Sauchiehall Street, but she let the answering machine take a message. He was at Dover, about to board the ferry. She lay in bed, smoked the last of her hash, drifted in and out of sleep, watched cycles of light build, stretch, then fade on the wood-chipped walls. Her mum, Jo and Roger left messages, but she couldn't summon the energy to speak to anyone; she even waited till the middle of the night to go downstairs and check for mail.

Five days later, a postcard from Alex. *Bières de la Meuse.* He was in Paris, had a hair-raising lift there, hoped she was well. She felt lightheaded reading his words. What had she eaten since he'd left?

The next day she was due to sign on. It took her hours to build up the courage to leave the flat. At the dole office she bumped into a guy who'd been a year above them at college, an older guy, a bit of a tough nut. He told her how one of the advisors tried to put him forward for a job as a kissogram. She laughed. After she'd signed on, she bought a loaf and a tin of soup, walked back to her flat. On the chest in the hall, her polling card – the election was only a couple of weeks away now. Upstairs, she returned some of the calls.

Roger came over that evening with magazines, wine and popcorn. 'His loss,' he kept saying. 'Just wait till we do our show. Handsome, eligible bachelors will be queuing round the block just for a glimpse of you.' She couldn't bear to think of ever being with anyone other than Alex. But the show, it was good to be reminded of the show.

Cassie wriggled.

'I spy with my little eye,' Wren said, 'something beginning

with…T.'

When the sea came into view, Jo whooped. The sky was clearer here, making the water a strip of sparkling blue.

Roger shook his head. 'It's going to be baltic.'

'But the weather's cheered up,' Jo said, lowering her sun visor.

'Oh how the Scottish April sun heats the Firth of Clyde.'

They passed the statue of Burns, then turned down a street of grand sandstone houses. Jo pulled up beside the pavilion. 'Clear run. We're a bit early.' She opened her door, stepped out and pulled her seat forward. Wren climbed out followed by Cassie, who ran straight to some cast iron gates and peered in at the miniature golf course.

Maddie hauled herself from the car. The sun was warm, promising a hot summer that'd never come. It'd be all floods by July.

Roger didn't move. Asleep? His head rolled to one side as a turquoise 2CV pulled up and shuddered to a halt.

Wren raised a hand. 'Here she is.'

A ruddy-cheeked woman with a head of golden spirals sprang from the car. 'Morning!' Her voice singsong.

She powered over, her patchwork coat billowing, grabbed Wren by the shoulders and kissed him on both cheeks.

He gestured. 'This is Maddie.'

'Enchanté.' Her eyes light blue, like a husky's. She crushed Maddie's hand as she shook it. 'You must be our lovely Miranda.'

The passenger door of Wren's car creaked open and Roger pitched out.

'Ah, the gent who's getting dunked.' Her laugh was like a bell flung to the wind.

Roger slipped off his shades and shook Morven's hand. 'I still can't remember having given my consent.'

'Hi,' Jo called, walking back with Cassie. 'Get here okay?'

'Fine. Could use a quick caffeine fix though before we get

started.'

They found a small Italian café on the esplanade.

As Wren pushed open the door a bell tinkled.

'First customers of the day. Welcome. Sit wherever you like.' A waitress gathered up six tall menus, her eyes on Cassie. 'Ciao, bella.' She looked between Jo and Maddie. 'Whose daughter?'

'My niece.' Wren slid into a window seat.

'Beautiful. Very like my Louisa when she was a bairn.'

After she'd brought their coffees, she returned with a lollipop for Cassie and two bendy straws for her lemonade.

'D'you want a croissant or something, Maddie?' Jo asked.

'No, ta.'

'What about some toast? Did you have any breakfast?'

'Yeah, I had some cereal,' she lied, taking a sugar lump from a small silver bowl and dropping it in her coffee.

As the others chatted, she twirled the sugar bowl and watched the café bend across its surface like in a hall of mirrors. The bright décor had a fairground feel to it, helped by the Dumbo kiddie ride chained to a railing outside.

When they'd finished their drinks, Jo asked the waitress if they could use the toilets to change in.

'No problem. Go ahead. Actors, yes? Making a *Braveheart* or something?' She laughed as she wiped down the counter.

Jo pulled some clothes from her rucksack. 'For you, Roger. And nightdresses for you, Maddie and Cassie. I reckoned since you were taken from your bed…'

Maddie frowned. 'But how would the dress have grown with me?'

Wren wiggled his fingers. 'Maaaagic.'

'For such a dreamer you're sometimes very literal.' Jo handed out the clothes. 'Put your jumpers and coats on over the top. Keep as warm as possible. Morven and I will go down to the beach and start setting up.'

Once they'd changed, Maddie, Roger, Cassie and Wren walked seawards, stepping over firm ripples of sand.

Cassie stopped by a pool of water and nudged a piece of bladderwrack with the toe of her shoe. 'Uncle Wren, what's this?'

'Ooh, I don't know.' He wandered over, bent down and tentatively picked it up. 'Could it be some kind of… sea monster?'

As he thrust it in Cassie's direction, she shrieked and ran away. Wren growled, following in a measured pursuit.

'At least you look nice in that dress,' Roger said. 'I feel like Robinson bloody Crusoe. I don't wish to over-compliment myself, but the trousers are rather tight in a certain area.' He kicked up a leg. 'Ouch! Mistake.'

'So, feeling the pinch?'

'Yes. And they're right up my ass.'

'No! I mean from last night.'

'Oh. You could say that.'

'Out with Simon?'

'Don't mention that name to me.' Reaching into the cuffs of his jacket, he pulled his jumper sleeves down over his hands.

'Really? Why?'

He puffed out some air. 'He wanted to bring a guy back with us from the club. I wasn't up for it. Maybe a few years ago, but not now. I want something more meaningful now, just two people. Is that too much to ask?'

'I don't think so.'

'Maybe because he's younger. I don't know. Anyway, he threw a bit of a hissy fit, said I was so bloody conventional I may as well be straight. I went to bed when we got in, but he stayed up and played Sheryl Crow at top volume, singing along and tanking the best part of a litre of vodka.'

'Nice.'

'Yes, charming. But the best bit was when I went through after my shower this morning. He'd disappeared, leaving the front door open and a pool of vomit on my rug.'

'Oh, man. Sometimes I think love has too high a price.'

'I don't believe that's love.' Roger tucked his arm through hers. 'I think we'll find better, you and me.'

Better than Alex?

My affections

Are then most humble. I have no ambition

To see a goodlier man.

Overhead seagulls darted over and around one another, squawking wildly.

'Gotta set some boundaries,' Roger said. 'Work out what's acceptable to us.'

Cassie squealed as Wren flung the seaweed away, caught her and swung her round.

'Cassie, Wren.' Jo beckoned as she strode towards them. 'Let's run through what we're doing.'

When they were all set, Maddie watched from a slight distance, guarding the jumpers, bags and coats. Roger huffed and puffed but eventually carried Cassie in up to waist height, dipping her gently so her hair got wet.

'Don't go too far,' she whispered. A mad desire to run, shout for them to stop.

Morven called 'action', and Roger walked out of the sea carrying a young Maddie, a three-year-old Miranda. His face looked tired, drawn. Was he acting, or just letting his true feelings show? Poor Dad. *Alack, what trouble was I then to you!*

A tingle, a half-memory – but when she reached for it, it vanished.

Morven moved the camera to a new position and Roger waded back into the water carrying Cassie.

After a few takes, a dripping Roger hurried over and gathered up his stuff.

'As cold as you thought?'

'Can't speak,' he said, teeth chattering. 'Must get dry.'

Wren carried Cassie over, wrapped in towels. 'Coming to get changed, Roger?'

'Too bloody right.'

She wandered over to Jo and Morven. The tide had gone out leaving a pattern of bare branches, a network of empty veins.

'Morven's spied a grassy bank a little further along the beach for your bit,' Jo said. 'Shall we check it out?'

'Sure. Want me to carry anything?'

'No need.' Morven slung a bag over her shoulder. 'It's just along here.'

'So what do you want me to do?' she asked Jo.

'Just look out to sea.'

'What should I be thinking about?'

'Maybe bits of things you can remember from before you came to the island.'

'But I don't remember much.'

'Well, make something up. We want pensive.'

Morven asked her to stand on a specific spot, then raised the tripod a little.

'That works,' she said. 'Can we shake her hair loose?'

Jo obliged.

'Better. Ready? And, action.'

What was the story Prospero told Miranda? Something about being driven from their kingdom at midnight, by a treacherous army.

Alack, for pity!
I not rememb'ring how I cried out then
Will cry it o'er again…

'Cut,' Morven said. 'I'd like to angle you a bit more.'

'This way?'

'Yep. Stop. Perfect. And if you can keep your head still for me.

The only movement I want is the shadow of thoughts playing across your face. But subtle. No stadium acting.'

'Okay.'

'Turning over. And, action.'

From her new perspective, she could see Roger, Wren and Cassie. Roger and Cassie had changed back into their own clothes. Wren was holding some kind of bundle in his hands – red and blue. He started to run, then launched it into the air. A kite. Roger let out the line and it rose into the sky, its tail snaking, fluttering. Cassie reached for the reel and Roger handed it to her, supervising as she got a feel for how the kite tugged. Then he stood back and he and Wren cheered. Would that be what it might look like, one day, if Roger had a family of his own?

'And, cut,' Morven said. 'Lovely. Except for the cheer in the background. But I'm guessing you're having music over the images?'

'Probably,' Jo said. 'Wren's working on something.'

After she changed, she walked back to the beach. Roger jogged up to meet her.

'How was that?' he asked.

'Easy life compared to you guys.'

'Yes. I hope I'll recover from my mild case of hypothermia. Anyway, me going on about Simon…how are you?'

'Ach. Still sore.'

He put an arm round her shoulder. 'I know it doesn't feel like it, but it'll get easier. I promise.'

Words from an agony aunt column, but she knew he meant well. 'Something I forgot to tell you. When I popped in to see my mum on the way back from Aberdeen, I found some letters, upstairs, from my dad.'

They veered towards where Jo was laying out a picnic.

'Blimey. What did they say?'

'I don't know. Rab came back and took them off me. But I

'memorised his address.'

'And?'

'Lenzie. But the letters were from years ago. I doubt he's still there.'

'Have you looked in the phone book?'

'No.'

'If you wanted someone to come with you…?'

'I couldn't just turn up!'

'Maybe a letter then. Might be good to write a letter even if you don't send it.'

They arrived at the tartan blanket Jo'd set with rolls, cartons of juice, packets of crisps.

'Lunch, you guys,' she called to the others. 'Here, Maddie, tuck in.'

After lunch they played frisbee, then, on the way back to the cars, stopped at the café for ice cream.

She was dithering over what to have when Cassie said, 'You get the same as me.'

Sitting outside on a wall, they looked out to sea. The sun was beginning to dip towards the horizon. For a moment they ate in silence, with just the sound of Cassie bouncing the rubber heels of her shoes off the wall.

'I forgot I've got my camera.' Jo fished it out her bag and stood in front of them. 'After three, say "cheese".'

Cassie budged up closer to Maddie.

The two of them, eating strawberry ice cream, with their pale faces and long dark hair. Maddie then, and Maddie now.

'Two, three…'

'Cheeeeese!'

On the way back to Glasgow, Cassie leant against Wren and they both fell asleep.

Jo dropped Maddie at her flat, getting out the car to give her a hug. 'We might go and see Tessa's play tomorrow, if you fancy?'

'Maybe.'

'You're coming to us for election night next Thursday though?'

'You bet.'

'Is there anything I can do…?' Her eyes were full of sympathy. Maddie broke the gaze, gathering up her stuff. 'I'll be fine.'

'I'll ring you tomorrow,' Jo said. 'Meantime, promise me you'll eat and sleep?'

'Will do.'

As the car drove off, Cassie waved from the rear window.

In the hall, copies of the phone book were stacked on the chest. She took one up to her room, made a coffee and rolled a single skinner before settling on the couch.

Strange to think of herself as a McGuire. She could remember learning to write it, Maddie McGuire, but it felt like a lifetime ago. She flicked through the thin, grey pages. MacDonald, Magee, McCormack… McGuire. C. He was still living at 13 Silverbirch Drive.

Taking her notebook from her rucksack, she turned past her *Tempest* notes to a fresh page. At the top of it she wrote *Dear Dad,*

The words looked odd. Rab had insisted she call him Dad, but the name never belonged to him. It felt strange, using it now, for a man she hadn't seen for sixteen years. She crossed it out.

Dear Chris,

That looked peculiar too. Formal and judgemental, like when her mum called her Madeline instead of Maddie. How else to start? Perhaps she could leave it, come back to it at the end.

Dear

I hope this finds you well. I imagine it must be weird hearing from me after all these years, and I'm sorry if this letter comes as a shock. Perhaps you're wishing I hadn't written, in which case

Bit convoluted. She hadn't even said who was writing. Perhaps she should put that at the top.

Sitting back, she smoked the joint. The sky was still light outside. Was there any possibility Alex would change his mind and rush back from France, saying he'd made a mistake? She wished she'd suggested doing more – galleries, plays, gigs. Maybe he'd got bored with pubs and clubs.

A bit of hash fell from the end of the joint and burnt a little hole at the bottom of the page. Would her dad want to hear from her? She lay on the sofa, her cheek on the notebook.

Dad. Dad, it's Maddie calling for you. Your daughter, Maddie. Remember me?

How could I ever forget? Oh, sweetheart, I've waited for this day, every day, for sixteen years…

There was a phone number in the book, but she'd never use it. It'd have to be a letter. She opened her notebook and looked at what she'd written. But now the light was fading, all the words seemed odd, seemed to be flying from their meaning, like a flock of starlings rising from a twilit field.

Five

The next morning, she left the flat early and walked into town. In WHSmith's she found an A–Z that covered Lenzie. Silverbirch Drive looked a short walk from the train station. She made a quick sketch in the back of her notebook.

By the time she arrived at Queen Street, it was starting to get busy with Saturday shoppers coming into Glasgow from the outlying towns. An Alloa train was due to leave Platform 1. She bought a return ticket.

Hardly any folk travelling on the line. She almost had a carriage to herself. Taking a seat by the window, she took her old Walkman from her bag and replaced the batteries. The mixtape was one Jo'd made for her. Putting her headphones on, she pressed play. A fast synth roll and a surge of bass, then Candi Staton's soulful voice: 'You Got the Love' – one of their favourite dance tracks when they used to go out every weekend.

The train pulled from the station, slow and steady through the dark tunnel, out into brilliant sunshine, picking up pace as it travelled between high-rise blocks, soon passing wide fields and scattered residential areas. The knobbled end of Dumgoyne came into view, leading to the smoother back of the Campsies. She rewound the tape and played the song again, letting her body sway with the finger clicks and disco beats, remembering Jo, bouncing on the balls of her feet, arms held high as if she'd just found Jesus.

She smiled. It was spring, a time of new beginnings, the upward curve of the cycle. Lambs in a bright green field. One took fright and gambolled back to its mother, ducking under her to feed, tail all a-quiver.

Far too hot now in the greenhouse of a carriage in her winter coat. She wiped her damp palms down the front of her jeans. The train announcer called Bishopbriggs, next stop Lenzie. She put the Walkman back in her bag.

Strange, alighting from the train, climbing the steps her dad might have climbed many times – unless he always took the car, which probably wasn't still the old Cortina.

She crossed the footbridge. Would her dad recognise her if she bumped into him? Probably not, after all these years. She tried to relax in her anonymity as she walked through the car park up towards a church, but clusters of daffodils proclaimed her arrival in bursts of vivid yellow.

According to her sketch, Silverbirch Drive was a cul-de-sac on the left. She was just going to walk to the end of it and back, catch a glimpse of number thirteen.

The houses in Silverbirch Drive were not as grand as Margaret's in Edinburgh, but they were attractive. Sandstone, semi-detached, front lawns bordered by hedges. A damn lot nicer than the grey pebbledashed affair where he'd left her and her mum. She took a deep breath. Auntie Irene said things had been complicated. She'd need to keep an open mind.

46, the brass number on the royal blue door on her right. Looking over, she saw she'd already passed number thirteen. Could it be the one with the white uPVC windows? She'd get a look on her way back. Ahead, a woman carried shopping bags in through an open front door and, further along, a man was waxing his old bottle-green Morris Minor. At the road's end, some kids were cycling round a hopscotch grid. She turned, praying no one would ask if she was lost.

Number thirteen *was* the one with the white windows. She slowed as she approached, knowing now why it was familiar. It was her granny and grandpa's house. Would they still be alive? Would the swing still be hanging from the tree in the garden?

There were no net curtains up, so she could see in. The dark living room looked bright now, with a large cream sofa, bookshelves, plants, pictures on the walls. The front door swung open. She opened her bag and pretended to be searching for something.

A woman came out, slim with blonde hair styled in a sleek bob, wearing casual weekend clothes. She opened the door of the Volvo in the drive and took something out. Maddie expected her to go back indoors, but instead she walked to a large blue BMW parked in the road, sat her handbag on its roof and took out a pair of sunglasses.

Then, as simple and natural as anything, Maddie's dad stepped from the house. His hair was silvery now and cut short. He wore jeans and a grey sweater. Pulling on a navy linen jacket, he pointed at the BMW and unlocked it remotely.

The strangest feeling swept through her, part recognition, part curiosity, part nerves, and something stronger running beneath it all…

The blonde woman climbed into the passenger seat. Who was she – a colleague, a friend, a girlfriend? Her dad reached to close the front door, but into the space framed by the curve of his arm stepped a young girl. She was tall, slim, maybe fourteen, fifteen, slightly Goth-looking with long brown hair tied in a high ponytail. Preoccupied with a magazine in her hand, she got in the back of the BMW.

Her dad locked up the house. As he opened the driver's door, he glanced in Maddie's direction. Doing up her bag, she walked on, head whirring. As she neared the road's end, the BMW overtook her, indicated and turned left. She caught a glimpse of him at the wheel before the car disappeared.

Hurrying to the train station, she scanned for a phone box. She wanted to call Roger. I've seen him, Roger – she was unsure whether to whisper or shout it. I've seen him!

Back at her flat, the words came more easily.

Dear Chris,

It's Maddie here. It's been a long time, and I hope you don't mind me making contact. It's hard to know where to start, but I'm an actress now – I studied for a degree at the RSAMD. I'm currently working on a production based on The Tempest (we're hoping it'll be on at the Tramway in June or July) and I'm playing Miranda, who was shipwrecked on an island with her dad for 12 years.

I guess some of the father/daughter stuff has got me thinking about things that have always been there, but perhaps have been easier to ignore. I have bits of memories of you living with us, and then coming over to take me on days out, and of Granny and Grandpa – more memories than I realised. And I've often wondered where you were and how you are. I suppose I thought – because you left and didn't keep in touch – that you didn't care about me. But I realise, now I'm older, that things aren't always that simple.

I know you might have another family now, of course, and that this may come as an intrusion. But I wanted you to know, if you wanted to make contact again (even just to go for a coffee), that I'd like to see you. I've put my address and phone number at the top (I rent a little flat in Glasgow's west end now).

Hope to hear from you soon.

With best wishes,

Maddie

She read over what she'd written, double-checked her contact details, crossed out *'like' to see you,* and wrote *'love'*, then changed it back again. Wondered whether to say *love from* rather than *best wishes* at the end, her pen hovering over her name – should she sign off with a kiss?

She put the kettle on and stared out the window. The horizon was a yellow streak against peach haze. A buzz in the air, the smell of summer coming – warm tarmac and cut grass. Jo had left a message saying she and Wren were meeting Roger for a bite to eat before Tessa's play – did she fancy joining them? She'd have a cup of coffee, write her letter out in neat, then call back.

It was eleven o'clock by the time she finished. Even though there wasn't a postal collection from the nearest post box on Sundays, she wanted to get the letter off before she changed her mind. Pulling on her coat, she jogged out into the night. The sky was black, studded with stars. Halfway round the crescent, a window was pulled up. The room was full of people. Music, chatter and laughter spilled out. Could the gaping hole she carried around most of the time just be loneliness? Something rustled in the bushes. She ran to the end of the street. At the post box, she made sure the letter was thoroughly sealed and pressed the stamp down again. The envelope slipped from her hand.

Six

Thursday evening, she followed the line of red balloons down Jo's hall. The sun had dropped but the clouds, still aglow, flooded the kitchen pink and amber.

A lot of the folk standing about were friends of Wren's, but, by the alcove, Roger was talking to Tessa and a few others from college.

'Hey, Maddie.' Jo opened the fridge door. 'What would you like to drink?'

She held up a carrier bag. 'I've got some beers with me.'

Roger made his way over. 'How's my angel?'

'Good!'

'Any word?'

'Not yet. Early days. How are you?'

'Okay. Sad. Relieved. Finishing with him was definitely the right thing to do.'

The buzzer sounded and Jo called, 'Roger, could you get that?'

She set the bag of beers on the table and a girl with red dreads introduced herself, offering her a bottle opener. She said she'd been at art school with Wren and was now doing an MFA.

Maddie flipped the cap off a beer. 'I'm always meaning to go to more exhibitions. Sometimes I feel like there's several layers to the city, you know? And I've just been living on one of them.'

High tings rang above the conversations. Folk turned towards where Jo was standing on a chair. 'Ladies and gents. If you'd like to make your way through to the living room, the last election of the century is about to commence!'

In the large, rectangular lounge, furniture had been pushed

to the walls and the TV positioned between the windows. Jo turned the volume up. Dramatic, marching music accompanied swooping shots of cliffs and fields. The cameras pulled out to show the images were on a screen in a studio. A multi-screen montage: Paddy Ashdown; Tony Blair; John Major; a ballot box; Big Ben; Number 10 – followed by an '*e*' for election '97.

'Check out the big *e*,' Terry said. 'Anyone for a big *e*?'

Folk shushed him.

Wren clapped his hands and rubbed them together. 'Here we go, folks.'

David Dimbleby made an introduction then passed to Jeremy Paxman.

Maddie pulled at the neck of her jumper. 'Anyone else hot?'

Wren put an arm round her shoulder and whispered, 'I feel sick.'

For a while, folk were silent. She could feel someone's breath on the back of her neck, the pressure of the group behind as they swallowed, sniffed, pawed the ground like a herd of cattle held in a pen.

Referencing the exit poll, Dimbleby said, 'Tony Blair is to be prime minister and a landslide is likely.'

Folk cheered.

'Remember '92 though, guys,' Wren said. 'Counting chickens and all that.'

Some people by the door started to whisper and drifted back to the kitchen.

Tessa came over. 'Maddie, long time no see.'

They hugged. Tessa's blonde curls, crispy with hairspray, smelled of sugared almonds.

'I hear your play went well at the Tron.'

'Sold out.'

'Sorry I didn't get to see it.'

'Looks like it's gonna transfer to the Festival, so you'll get a chance to catch it there.'

For some reason, Jo had always got on well with Tessa. She seemed so confident, talking now about an audition she'd had at the Arches. Everything just seemed to gift itself to her. How nice to grow up in a big house with a brother and sisters, a mummy and daddy, dogs, cats, rabbits, a pony. Did she have a pony?

'Maddie'— Jo tapped her arm—'Sally Magnusson's in Stirling.'

'Who?'

'BBC reporter.'

Maddie turned to the screen. 'Lucky her.'

'Who's for another beer?' Terry called.

She looked over. 'I'll come through.'

In the kitchen, Wren was fiddling with the aerial of Jo's old portable telly. 'We should sign the contract next week,' he said to a couple of guys sitting on the two-seater sofa in the alcove.

'What's that?' she asked.

'Talking about that bid a couple of us put in to take over the King Street studios.'

One of the guys offered her a joint.

'Ta.' It was skinny. She perched on the arm of the sofa and inhaled. Mostly skunk, pungent, tarry buds.

Wren pulled up a chair. 'So Jo and I have been talking about getting a place together.'

'Like buying somewhere?'

'Maybe just renting to begin with.'

'In Glasgow?' She passed him the joint. She'd only had a couple of tokes, but somehow there was only an inch or so of it left.

Wren pointed to the screen. 'First results. City of Sunderland.'

Folk quietened, then erupted into cheers when the declaration was read out. Eighteen years of Conservative rule. She'd been a kid when they came to power. Her dad still living at home with them in Stirling. What had he made of her letter?

Jo hurried through. 'Good start.' She slid a pizza into the oven, then turned the volume up on the telly. 'Hamilton South results, guys. First in Scotland.'

When George Robertson was announced as having a majority of over fifteen thousand, Wren jumped to his feet. 'Still'—he turned, wagging a finger—'remember '87, remember '92.'

Another joint came round, then Terry appeared at her side. 'Beer?' He held out a bottle.

'Don't be giving her too much booze,' Jo said. 'She needs to eat. Here.' She nudged Maddie's arm with a plate of garlic bread.

It looked so greasy. 'Just need to nip to the loo.'

Leaning against the door, she waited for her heart to stop thumping. The long, narrow bathroom was like a shrine to the sea. Even the shower curtain featured a starfish design. She could just curl up, in the bath, pull the curtain round and sleep, safe, for the night, or the week. She imagined waking, hearing her dad in the kitchen, him and Jo laughing and sharing stories.

She'd go through and he'd smile. 'I've come to take you home, love.'

Down at the big blue BMW, she'd climb into the front seat.

'I wasn't sure how you'd like your room, so I've done the best I could.' He put on some classical music. 'There's so much to talk about, but we've got our whole lives. The important thing now is for you to rest. You've got a play to do.'

His face so familiar, though he'd aged.

At number thirteen, he carried her bags upstairs.

'I know it's a bit childish, but it's been there a long time.' He nodded to the nameplate on her door, with its watering can filled with flowers.

'It's perfect,' she said as he pushed the door open. And it *was* perfect. A massive sleigh bed with a big soft duvet; a glass of snowdrops on the bedside cabinet; a dressing table with mirror and stool, and some kind of black case leaning against it.

'Oh'—he'd noticed her gaze— 'I always thought you'd like to

take up the violin. Never too late, of course, if you'd like lessons?'

Swathes of cream gauze at the side of a tall sash window, where she'd be able to look down onto the garden she'd played in as a kid.

As she turned to him, he wrapped her in a big bear hug and kissed the top of her head. 'Welcome home, love.'

'Thanks, Dad.'

Thudding behind her, the door vibrating against her back. 'Maddie?' It was Roger. She blinked. The bathroom seemed so bright.

'Yeah?' Her throat was raw.

'Just checking. I'll be in Jo's room when you come out.'

Roger had gathered some pillows behind him and was stretched out on Jo's bed, flicking through a book. He looked up. 'Hey, sweetpea. So... exciting times?'

She sat beside him. 'Maybe.'

'Oh my God, Maddie, to think you might have a half-sister!'

'I know, but I was thinking, it could have been anyone really – a friend's daughter, a neighbour's daughter...'

'But you saw your dad. Aren't you excited?'

'Yes...' She twirled a tassel of Jo's cotton bedspread. 'What if he doesn't want to know me?'

He sat up, took hold of her plait and waggled it like he was ringing a bell. 'Got to think positive. Who knows what'll happen. Worst-case scenario, you'll always have me.'

She laughed, her eyes spilling over. 'Shit, sorry.' She brushed the tears away. 'I'm feeling happy. I'm feeling hopeful, Roger, I really am.'

'Me too. It's time something good came your way.'

A cheer went up in the living room and kitchen. Roger stood, an ear inclined towards the door. 'Blimey, Michael Forsyth's lost Stirling.' He held his arms out. 'Big changes afoot, Ms Maddie, for the country, for you...'

'And you?'

He lay along the bottom of the bed, propped up on one elbow. 'I got a phone call this afternoon from my agent. I've got an audition next week for a commercial – I could be the new face of Bell's Scotch.'

'Hey, that'd be brilliant!'

'Fingers crossed. It would be a good few bucks.'

A massive cheer.

The door swung open. 'Hey guys.' Jo beckoned. 'Edinburgh Pentlands – Lynda Margaret Clark's won on a ten percent swing. There's no Tory seats left in Scotland!'

'Woo hoo!' Roger punched the air.

'Jo,' Wren shouted from the hall. 'Portillo, Enfield Southgate!' She rushed out.

More people had arrived and the living room was packed.

In a gap between people's necks, Maddie caught a glimpse of Michael Portillo. A few folk booed but Wren called for quiet. The mayor announced nineteen thousand one hundred and thirty-seven votes for Portillo. Folk in front of her shifted and she saw a young dark-haired man onscreen look away, down to his right.

'Stephen Twigg of the Labour party… twenty thousand…'

A roar went up, folk in the room joining the folk on TV, cheers from a flat above, whoops from across the street. Jo flung her arms around her, then Wren was there, his arms around both of them. Roger's face appeared as he called, 'Group hug, group hug!'

'Shh,' someone said, turning the volume up.

Stephen Twigg had finished speaking and Portillo was now at the mic. 'But I would like to do whatever I can from the wings…'

Folk jeered.

'See? *All the world's a stage,*' Tessa said.

Jo nodded. '*And the men and women on it merely players.*'

'*They have their exits and their entrances…*' Roger did his best Simon Callow. '*And one man in his time plays many parts.*'

Terry shook his head. 'Bloody actors.'

Dimbleby announced Labour had the overall majority it needed and Piccadilly Circus lit up with news of the Labour victory.

Jo distributed some party poppers and the air filled with red and white streamers. Wren started singing 'Auld Lang Syne' and a chain of arms dominoed around the living room and out into the hall as folk joined in, bouncing, charging towards one another at the chorus.

Squashed between two big guys, Maddie's fingers were crushed, her wrists twisted. A strand of her hair caught round one of their cardigan buttons and, when the singing stopped, her head was attached to the guy's chest. She had to yell to stop him walking off and tearing her hair out.

After four, people started to leave. In the kitchen, a friend of Wren's was holding court, talking about how he didn't really trust Tony Blair.

Wren leant back in his chair, his feet up on the table. 'It's got to be an improvement on that old grey muppet though.'

'And think what it'll mean for Scotland.' Jo opened a bottle of Baileys and sniffed it.

'Now John Smith,' Terry said. 'He was a leader.'

Outside, a loud bang. Crackling white sparks drifted over the rooftops. Jo lifted the window and Maddie pressed beside her, leaning out. A small group standing in the communal garden. They whooped and Jo cheered. One of them lit the fuse of another firework. It fizzed, then a rocket soared into the night sky and burst into a glittering gold umbrella.

Just after five, Blair arrived at the Royal Festival Hall.

Roger rubbed his face. 'Happy days, but I think I need my bed.'

Everyone looked to be sagging. 'I'll get a taxi with you,' Maddie said, though personally she'd got a second wind.

Outside, the dawn was an intense blue and birds sang loudly in the trees. Roger climbed in the back of the cab and she followed.

'Where to?' the driver asked.

Roger gave his address, then turned to her. 'The sofa's all yours if you want to crash? I can assure you the rug has been laundered.'

'It's okay, ta. I quite fancy the walk back to mine.'

The streets were almost deserted and Glasgow, with its mishmash of architecture, looked noble and inviting.

The taxi pulled up, they climbed out and hugged goodbye.

'Speak over the weekend?' Roger asked.

'Yeah. Sweet dreams.'

Halfway home, she regretted her decision to walk. Her legs were stiff and heavy, her eyes ached. The alley of flowers in Kelvingrove Park became a treadmill. She arrived back at her flat, tired and thirsty, collapsed on the bed and pulled the duvet over her.

When she woke, she was unsure for a moment where she was. She drank a coffee, then ran a bath and lay in the warm water, cocooned in pink and orange as sunlight illuminated the blood in her eyelids. Friday. How would she spend the day? She dried, wrapped her hair in the towel, and dressed. As she was leaving the bathroom she heard her phone ring.

Rushing to it, she picked up. 'Hello?'

The silence was live, then a woman said, 'Hello, could I speak to Maddie, please?'

She made her voice sound bright. 'Speaking.'

'Hi, Maddie.' The woman spoke slowly. 'It's Chris's wife here, Carolyn.'

Chris's wife…?

'I'm calling because I got your letter.'

Her dad's wife? He *had* remarried then. To the blonde woman she saw?

The woman continued, 'I've been deliberating for a few days about what to do. I thought I should give you a call.'

Had she intercepted the letter? Why are you calling, she wanted to ask, but the question seemed too direct, too rude.

'Are you still there…?'

'Yes.'

'Maddie, I rang your family home in Stirling just over three years ago and spoke to your stepfather – is it Rab?'

She flinched at Rab being given the name. 'Yes.'

'Did Rab tell you I'd called?'

'No.'

It sounded as if the woman was changing hands. A tapping sound, like a nail against plastic, a rustle as she pushed the receiver to her other ear.

'Does your mum or Rab know you were writing to your dad?'

'No.' Why did she keep mentioning Rab?

'I think you need to tell them that you wrote, and that I called.'

'Why? What's it got to do with them?' The words came out unfiltered. She wished she hadn't sounded so petulant.

'Well, they're your guardians.'

'I'm twenty-two.'

'Yes, yes I realise that. I'm just thinking now that they might have had their reasons…'

'Reasons for what?' Enough of the riddles. 'Has Chris seen my letter?'

'No, no he hasn't.'

'It was addressed to him.'

'Yes, I know that.'

'Why hasn't he seen it?'

The woman sighed. 'This is all a bit of a muddle. I'm sorry, Maddie, perhaps I should have phoned Rab first. I didn't really think this through properly.'

'No! No, you shouldn't. Rab as good as kicked me out. I haven't even spoken to my mum in weeks.' Her voice trembled.

'Oh.'

Something wavered at the window. A bird on the ledge. 'Should

I not have written?'

'It's not as simple as that.'

'I don't understand...'

'I'm sorry, Maddie. This shouldn't be coming from me.' The woman took a deep breath. 'There's no easy way to say this. I'm afraid Chris died, three years ago.'

'Sorry, what?'

'I'm afraid he died. He's been dead for three years.'

She sank onto the edge of the bed. 'Oh.' A silly little noise to make, as if they'd just gone over a bump in the road.

'I phoned your house after it happened and spoke to Rab. I thought you had a right to know.'

The towel turban on her head began to slip backwards, tugging at the roots of her hair. She loosened it and it landed with a damp thud on the bed. Her hair fell in tangles around her shoulders. 'How...?'

'He was working in the Outer Hebrides. It was January 1994. There were terrible storms. His car was swept into the sea. It was... shocking. A terrible tragedy. Right out of the blue.'

'Nobody said. Nobody told me.' Her eyes started to stream, then she remembered the man she'd seen coming out of number thirteen. How could she ask about him without letting on she'd been spying?

'I'm so sorry no one spoke to you about this, Maddie. That it's had to come from me. Have you got anyone with you just now?'

A fresh wave of tears. 'No.'

'Have you got someone you can call?'

'Yes.' Where had her voice gone? It was barely a whisper.

'Is there anything I can do? Anything you want to know?'

Her mind, blank. 'No, thank you.'

'Will you call someone now?'

The bird on the ledge chirruped. 'Yes. Yes, I better go.'

'I'm so sorry. I'll post your letter back to you.'

'No. Thank you. Just bin it.'

After the woman hung up, she listened to the silence. It buzzed. 'Hello?' she whispered.

Nothing. She placed the receiver back in the cradle.

Running her finger along the sill, she created a path through grains of grit. The house was made of large sandstone bricks. Would it return one day to its original state? *I'll huff and I'll puff...* The room darkened as clouds slid across the sun, the walls lengthened and the cornicing melted, reset.

She snatched up the phone and dialled Roger's number.

'I'm sorry I can't come to the phone. Please leave a message after the tone.'

'Roger, it's me, Maddie. If you're there, can you pick up?'

Please, please, please... He was probably still sleeping. She put the phone down. What to do, what to do... She tried to stand but her legs were jelly. She dropped to the floor.

Up at the window, the bird had gone. She hadn't really studied the painted panels before. Humpty Dumpty and Little Bo Peep. Humpty was still whole, sitting on a wall, an egg in a buttoned-up jacket, large shoes at the end of his skinny legs.

Little Bo Peep was standing in a meadow, by a pond. She held her crook in one hand, the other cupped round her mouth as she hollered.

January 1994. She'd been at college, halfway through second year.

A loud ringing made her jump. She waited till she heard Roger's voice before she picked up.

'Maddie?'

'Hi.'

'Hi, babe. Are you okay?'

'No.' She gasped. 'Roger, he's dead. My dad's dead.'

'What?'

'A woman called. His wife. She said he's been dead three years.'

'Oh no. No no no…'

She blotted her nose with the end of her sleeve. 'But I don't understand. I saw him.'

'Oh, sweetheart. It must've been someone else you saw.'

'Like who?'

'I don't know. The woman's brother. A friend?'

'You don't think she's made it up because she wants me to stay away?'

'No.' He sounded firm. 'No, angel, I don't think people make up stuff like that. Look, I'll pull on some clothes and come over.'

'I think I need to get out of here. Can I come to you?'

'Of course you can. Shall I phone you a cab?'

'I'm gonna walk for a bit. I need some air. I can't breathe.'

'Have you got money for a cab?'

'Yes. I'll walk for a bit then flag one on the street.'

'When will I see you? Are you coming now?'

'Yes. I'll be an hour at the most.'

'Okay, babe.'

'I've just got to put my coat on, my shoes on. Is that right? What else do I need to do? My hair's still wet…'

'Babe, I think I should come to you.'

'No. I can't stay here. I can't wait.'

She pulled on her socks, her left trainer. She really needed a smoke, but her tin was empty. She wandered round the room. What was she looking for? Her hairbrush. It was on the floor by the broken mirror. She raked it through the damp knots.

Ae fond kiss, and then we sever…

What a thing to remember now, her dad singing that to her.

Ae fareweel, alas, for ever

Holding her, dancing in circles.

Deep in heart-wrung tears I'll pledge thee…

Dropping her back at her mum's.

Warring sighs and groans I'll wage thee.

Driving off in his Cortina, beeping his horn, waving.

'Hold on, hold on,' she whispered to her reflection. 'Even just till we get to Roger's.' She grabbed her coat and stepped out onto the landing, staring for a moment at her sock. Idiot, she'd need her other shoe.

Outside, the wind had got up. It blew her wet hair across her face, chilling her scalp. She tucked strands behind her ears, stuffing the bulk of it down into the collar of her coat.

Papers outside the newsagent's showed Tony Blair, grinning, waving.

Things Can Only Get Better…

But it wasn't her dad she'd found, just some random stranger. How could she have got it so wrong?

January 1994. How long after he'd died had Carolyn phoned Rab? Had Rab told her mum? She eyed a phone box. Perhaps she should call now.

How dare you! she'd yell, once more that little girl shouting, Look what you've done! This time she'd shove him, push him hard so he'd tumble down the stairs, crack his head off the stair post, snap his neck.

An old woman walking a schnauzer looked up at her.

What! she wanted to shout. What are you looking at? Instead, she folded her arms and walked faster. Wait till her mum found out. Maybe that'd finally make her leave Rab. But should she speak to Auntie Irene first? Clearly Auntie Irene didn't know.

The lights were changing at the crossroads. She sprinted across and strode up University Avenue. The storms of 1994. Where in the Outer Hebrides had her dad been, and what was he doing there? Where had his car been swept into the sea? Who raised the alarm? How long did it take them to find his body? Was he buried or cremated? Why hadn't she thought to ask Carolyn anything?

A smoke, she needed a smoke. A ciggie would have to do.

Up at the counter in Raju's, a guy wearing a purple beanie was talking to the shopkeeper.

'They'd been drinking tea all that time,' he said, 'wondering why it tasted weird. None of them knew the old biddy had been heating up her hotdogs in the kettle.'

The shopkeeper laughed.

'Can you imagine, her fucking hotdogs, man?'

His voice was familiar. He turned. Brendan.

'Hey,' he said. 'I know you, don't I? What's your name again?'

'Maddie.'

'Go ahead'—he gestured to the counter—'I'll wait on you.'

She bought ten Silk Cut, pulling her hair from the collar of her coat.

'So what's the news?' he asked as they left the shop.

She chewed the corner of her lip. 'Bad news. Just found out my dad's dead.'

He sucked in some air, sharp, as if he'd touched something hot. 'No way, man. Heavy scene.' He patted his jacket pocket. 'Wanna head up the hill there, smoke a pipe?'

'I'd kill for a smoke, to be honest.'

From the top of the hill, she looked out over the spires of the uni and the turrets of the art gallery as Brendan told stories about what he'd got up to last night, some club he ended up in, then a party in a block of flats somewhere.

'I scarpered when a fight broke out between the guy who'd invited us and his neighbour. The neighbour pulled a knife, for fuck's sake. Besides, it was all too heavy for me. Smack and all sorts. Dirty drugs. I'm not into downers. I mean, hallucinogens, yeah bring it on, man. But just leaking your life away? Life's short enough as it fucking is.' He touched her arm. 'Sorry.'

He passed her the pipe. The bowl of it, shaped like an upturned bluebell, was a cool weight in the palm of her hand. He lit it for her and she breathed in a smoke that was floral, like incense. The world flew into focus and her heart stopped, then thumped a double beat, and she melted, exhaling, feeling as if she could keep on breathing all of her soul or spirit or being out of the dry, tired shell of her body, fly out to join her dad somewhere, two swirling wisps soaring over fields and mountains and seas.

A nudge. Who was this man by her side, with the tufts of hair on his chin? He looked faun-like. Probably hiding goat horns under that hat. His neck stretched into the swirling blue, mouth moving but no sound coming from it. The big green carousel picked up speed and she gripped the sharp grass. The faun held out a hand, a large scooping starfish that reached down into the water's depth and pulled her up by the elbow. She broke the surface, gasping, tall on spindly stilt-like legs.

By the fountain, a pixie balanced on a rope.

'Dad dead,' the faun said to two gnomes who were squatting like frogs.

A long-bearded wizard nodded to a silent song as he pulled a needle and thread, stitching feathers onto a strip of beige cloth.

She picked up a feather. 'A bird came. I think it had a message.'

The wizard's eyes were pale. 'There are messages everywhere. You just have to know where to look.'

A roar. A long jet of orange shot from the faun's mouth. Was it time to dance with the dragon? Beat, beat, a heartbeat under the earth. The gnomes had bowls between their knees and were striking them with the heels of their hands, with the flats of their fingers – what were they called again, those bowls?

The wizard was speaking, but what was he saying? One of the gnomes came close, holding out a bowl. A drum, that's what it was called. He tapped, waited, tapped with his speckled hands with their hard yellow calluses. Then he lifted her hands, placed them on the skin of the drum and tapped again. Was it some kind of code? She copied, like Simon Says, like Follow the Leader.

Don't worry, the code said, there's new things to learn. The rhythm flows through all, it never ends.

The other gnome and the faun twirled fire sticks. A damp tin in her hand. Beer.

'Where'd this come from?'

Maybe it was magic beer. She laughed.

The pixie sprang down. 'What's the craic?'

She looked round.

'What's funny?' he asked.

What *was* funny? What was she doing here, with these guys? Dirt under her fingernails.

'What time is it?' She tried to stand. Her legs were numb. 'What day is it?'

The faun appeared. 'Here…'

Two black stars in the shell of his hand. Stars where there should have been pearls.

'They might help you find some answers.'

She picked one up. Tiny between forefinger and thumb. He put the other on the tip of his tongue, took a swig of her beer.

'I wanted to dance with the dragon too.'

He nodded. 'Dance, fly, dive, ask, seek.'

She swallowed the star. A squirrel ran up, sat on its hind legs, bounded away. She scrambled to her feet and followed.

At the water's edge, she crawled through the long grass, listening to the wizard.

'You think the river makes a noise, but there's strata, at least six layers – trickling, bubbling, gurgling, rushing. When you listen deeper, you realise it's a language, a language beyond thought.'

Small rocks were set in a circle. How had she not noticed them before? Each was like a mountain in miniature, nooks and crevices, shades of brown, grey and green. On one, a ladybird with two spots struggled over mosses that were expanding into deep sponges. She fell down with the ladybird into the jungle of them, down into their laced labyrinths of trees and vines.

Ladybird, ladybird, fly away home,

Your house is on fire,
Your children shall burn!

A low tone behind. She turned. The world exploded, massive in scale, the wizard at its centre, all ages rising, morphing in his face, newborn to death mask.

'I'm going to draw you a portal.' His voice echoed from the sky. He was Merlin. He was Gandalf. Then she knew who he was – he was Prospero, the first one.

'Beyond you will find the answers you seek.'

He traced a line, leaving a neon green oblong in the air.

'Step through.' He gestured with a wide arc. 'Ask your questions.'

She stepped. The world faded to black and white, then flooded blue. The rocks were no longer solid, they were shifting, rising into shapes of people, then reforming into tigers, dogs and swine. They were the ancient ones, the guides. They were everywhere. And all this time she'd felt so alone.

Bowing her head, she listened to muttered conversations about day and night, light and dark, good and evil. The base of the rocks flowed into the grass, into the earth, up into the trees – electric ligaments linking every living thing. She stared and the world vibrated, separated into particles like a pointillist painting. Everything bleeding into everything else. But there was something bigger too. A central core of truth. If she could stand completely still, she might be allowed to draw near it.

When the voice came, it was like a rustle of leaves.

'After the storm, the shipwreck, Prospero scatters the courtiers around the island.' The earth creaked. 'Alonso thinks his son has drowned. What does he learn?'

She blinked and the world flashed orange. 'He learned remorse.'

The wind whistled. 'And you?'

She'd pretended she didn't care, she'd left it too late. Was there a way to undo things, if you learned your lesson, if you realised your mistake? In the play, Prospero returned Ferdinand to his father Alonso. He hadn't really drowned after all.

A sweet smell filled her nose. Honeysuckle. Hovering above the rocks, a woman wearing a bright coral sari, black hair hanging in long plaits. Juno – Queen of the Gods? She held out a hand. 'You're asking the right questions.'

Against a sapphire sky, silhouettes danced around a fire. She ran, flung her arms to the air. She'd dance it out – the shock, the sorrow, her remorse. The dragon was coming, but first the faun trotted over.

You'll feel the heat of his breath on your belly right enough, but you ain't gonna come to no harm.

A tree trunk hollowed to hold them as words tumbled from his mouth, and she talked too, talked and talked though her head couldn't hold a thread of sense and her clay tongue dried and cracked like a riverbed in drought.

'You're on your way,' the faun said. 'You're nearly there. Keep searching.'

One of the gnomes turned, the sockets of his eyes pulsed with maggots. She didn't have long on this side of the door, she needed to find her dad and pull him back through. Light already in the sky.

'Thank you.' She jogged towards the gate, then started to run, picking up speed, her feet swift over grass, along pavements, across roads, almost fast and light enough to fly. Which way? She tracked gutters and drains, channels of underground streams, listening for water in pipes.

Up, up and up the buildings soared. Stone faces gazed down at her, and, on street level, flesh faces stared. How much variation in a face – they had the same components, but there were no two identical in all the billions and billions. It was as if an axe had been taken to the face of God, and it had splintered, spawning endless variations. All the noses seemed to be growing towards her, like Pinocchio's. She looked down. Crouched down.

Someone bumped into her, a man in a suit, his face bubbling rage. 'What are you doing!'

What was she doing? Joining splats of chewing gum with straws and sticks to make constellations. They were spelling something. But he was right, time was passing and she was falling from it. All the buildings would still stand, but a whole generation of people would crumble to dust. It would be too late. She ran.

One street led to another led to another. Where was she? Blocks of red sandstone flats, a pub at the corner, two little girls drawing on a pavement.

She hunkered down. 'We've got to find our dad.'

The girls looked up, yellow and lilac chalk in their hands.

'Quick.' She took hold of their small, soft hands. They stood.

'Dad,' she shouted. Letting go of their hands, she ran to a door and knocked on it. 'Dad!'

The girls stood on a wall, their faces pressed between black railings.

'Don't worry,' she said. 'I'll find him. Here, take these.' From her pockets she pulled fistfuls of stones and glass, petals and feathers. The girls cupped their hands to catch them. 'These will keep us connected.'

Running from house to house, she banged on the doors. 'Dad!'

The windows of the pub were boarded up. She tugged at the door handles, battered on the boards. Perhaps she wasn't yelling loud enough. 'Dad!'

Round the corner, in front of a row of shops, a man was propped against a green metal litterbin, begging. She crouched down. Might he be hiding? All she saw in the man's face was distorted pain.

'Spare change, miss?'

How stupid, she'd been thinking only about what she could gain, rather than what she could give. 'Here.' She handed him her purse.

On a patch of worn grass at the road's end, she knelt and dug up stones, refilling her pockets with bottle caps, sweet wrappers and cigarette butts. In a bus shelter, she spread out everything she'd gathered and tried to explain to a white-haired woman what she'd learned, but the woman clutched her bag to her chest, turned and hurried away.

A narrow bridge took her to St Enoch's Centre and up to Central Station. The streets were filling with people now, too many people rushing by, a river in flood, full of conflicting currents. She closed her eyes.

How the shock of cold had struck her chest, risen over her head, filled her mouth with river. She'd gulped, a big painful gulp, a bubble of air forced down by water. Struggling, she broke the surface, choking and spluttering, sore at the back of her nose, eyes stinging, streaming as the river sped her towards the weir. She kicked her legs, but from the freezing depths a hand reached up and wrapped its watery grasp around her ankle. It tightened its grip as it dragged her down, then spun her round. She was bursting, her chest crushed, her head about to explode. But which way was the surface? Which way was up?

Full fathom five thy father lies,
Of his bones are coral made;

Her eyes sprang open. Noise burst into her ears. Cars and buses, the shudder of engines, horns blasting, voices: *Evening Times*! See you tomorrow! *Big Issue*! The train arriving at platform four... But beneath it all, a noise like static. The churning of the weir.

Now she knew. Her dad had saved her from the river that day. But she hadn't been there to save him. She needed to go back to the river, to take her remorse to the moment of drowning. That's where she'd find him, find him and pull him back through the door, to the world of the living.

Above the cacophony, a creature wailed. A boy in full highland dress, playing the bagpipes. Behind him rose long-feathered electric-blue wings. Ariel.

That's my noble master.

What shall I do? Say what: what shall I do?

She'd forgotten, Roger – her Prospero – he'd have something for her on this journey. Turning in the direction of Argyle Street, she ran.

By the time she reached the close door of Roger's flat, her lungs were sore. Old, cracked leather bellows. Which was Roger's bell? She pressed them all.

'Hello?'

She said her name and someone buzzed her in.

As she climbed the close stairs, something thundered above. They met on the first floor landing.

Roger's face blanched white. 'Oh my God, Maddie, where have you been?'

She started to tell him about the park.

'Come in, come in.' He led her upstairs. 'Look at your hair, it's all matted. You're covered in mud.'

He wanted her to sit down.

'What can I get you, something to drink, something to eat? I'll need to phone Jo. Oh my God, I've been worried sick. I've been calling you. I went to your flat. Jo's been calling everyone.'

Time was short, but she sat, hoping to placate him.

'Oh honey, what happened to you?'

She told him about the first Prospero and the portal, what she'd seen, the opportunity she'd been given.

'Sweetheart, you're not making any sense. You've had a terrible shock. You'll be in shock. Have you been drinking, have you been smoking something?'

What did it matter? Why was he asking such trivial questions? Didn't he realise what this meant? She'd seen things. She'd discovered a way.

'I don't know what you're talking about, honey.'

She pulled her collection from her pockets and laid out pebbles and lollipop sticks, explaining about all the layers of reality, about how she only had a short time on this side of the door.

'Look at your lips, they're all split. Aren't they sore? Try and rest your eyes for a moment, babe. I'm just gonna put the kettle on.'

Cutlery rattled as he pulled open a drawer, a cup clinked against a saucer. Water ran from a tap. 'Go to the window,' it said.

There was a wasteland opposite, vans parked either side of a skip. A white pigeon landed on the sill and paced up and down. As it took flight, the beat of its wings called for gifts. Of course – they were the city's messengers, they needed things to take to the ill, the homeless, the heartbroken. On Roger's shelves, a brass Buddha, a crystal vase, three nightlights. A paisley-patterned scarf hung over the back of a bentwood chair.

She gathered the gifts, opened the window and lined them up on the ledge. Take joy, take beauty, take healing…

She gestured from her heart, to the gifts, to the birds in flight.

'Maddie? Maddie, what are you doing?' Roger was standing in the doorway, a plate in one hand, a cup and saucer in the other. His brow puckered.

She tried to reassure him.

Setting the cup and plate on the coffee table, he walked to the window.

'Dear God.' He reached out and picked up the vase and the Buddha.

She tried to explain.

'Sweetheart, these could fall and seriously hurt someone.'

Why wasn't he listening?

'Okay, honey, okay. I'll leave the scarf out there, okay?'

He led her back to the sofa. 'Try and drink something. Look, there's a nice teacake there too.'

Didn't he understand? She didn't need food. She didn't need

drink. His eyes darkened as if the fear in them was stretching its roots all the way back to his brain. A cold shiver ran under her skin.

'Why don't you lie down for a bit? You can use my bed. I'll make you a hot water bottle. You might feel better after a wee sleep?'

Ah, now she knew what he was doing! She giggled. Why hadn't she realised he was just playing his part? She put a finger to her lips and whispered that she understood.

'Honey, I've no idea what you're talking about.'

this swift business

I must uneasy make lest too light winning

Make the prize light.

She joined her hands together in prayer and bowed her thanks.

In the bathroom, she was unable to pee. Maybe there were no bodily functions this side of the portal. She flushed anyway. In the mirror, everyone she knew rose in turn to the surface of her face. Her mum, Jo, Auntie Irene, Roger. She put her fingers on the glass and looked deeper. Rab. He opened his mouth, his broad smile growing. His jaws full of sharp, pointed teeth. Was he the crocodile, the ticking clock, true death itself? She looked down and, with shaking hands, turned on the tap.

The water gurgled at the plughole. 'Time's short,' it said.

As she opened the bathroom door, she heard Roger's voice in the hall.

'Doesn't seem well at all. Shocked, tired. Looks like death.'

Yes, but she'd be the phoenix rising from the flames. She'd come back from the other side, bringing her dad with her.

'She's in the bathroom. Yeah, I'm pretty worried, she's not making much sense. I don't know. It's like she's off her head on something. Oh, all sorts of nonsense. Riddles. Something about finding her dad in a river. I know. Would you? That'd be great. Cool, see you soon.'

The shiver ran down her arms as water knocked in the pipes.

'You've got to go now,' it said.

Back on the sofa, she closed her eyes but opened her ears, listening to Roger carry the plate and cup back through to the kitchen, listening to him creep to the bathroom.

Seven steps to the front door. Down the stairs and out into the roar of the street. Turning in the direction of the city centre, she ran towards the river. All rivers connected, all rivers to the sea.

Passing pubs, shops, past the courts. The massive arch at Glasgow Green warned of the portal, of the shortage of time. She wanted to leap from the middle of the bridge, to be cloaked in sequins, like a mermaid, on her way down. But there wasn't time. She sprinted across the paved area, vaulted the railings, ran down the bank and dived in.

A smack of cold. Her ears plugged, her nose filled with river. Bursting for air already. Nothing to see, it was all grey-brown. Something tugged her elbow and she knew not to struggle, she must go with it. A dark wisp darted away. Her dad. She followed him down, hauling herself lower with wide sweeping arms, kicking her legs. A rush of icy water pulled her and all light vanished. In the thick black, she heard children's voices, chattering, giggling.

A beat pounded the inside of her ears.

Her eyes opened to spinning blue.

She coughed, spluttered, heaved a breath, turned on her side, retching. The roots of the grass were yellow and between the blades the grainy earth was dry and cracked. An earthworm lay motionless, swollen purple at one end, grey and papery at the other. Someone was pulling her shoulder.

'Maddie… Maddie?'

She looked round. 'Dad?'

A man was kneeling beside her, dripping, shaking. He had red curls, faint stubble. He rubbed her back. 'No, honey. It's me, Roger.'

'Did I get him?'

'Don't talk. Just breathe.'

She tried to sit. 'Where is he?'

'No, Maddie. No. You can't find him, love. You can't. He's gone.'

She shrugged off his hand. 'You're lying.' She scrambled to her knees.

He clasped her arm. 'Stop.'

'Let me go. It'll be too late.' She pulled and twisted. She'd have to show him, prove how much she was prepared to fight. She shoved his arm, ducked under it, found her feet and began to run. But something seized her, she tripped, the grass flew up to meet her, her face slammed onto the earth. Her hand crept to her cheek. Thick, warm, red trickled between her fingers.

'Shit, Maddie. Shit.' He took off his shirt and pressed it to her eyebrow.

'I have to. I have to.'

'No, Maddie. It doesn't work like that. I'm not gonna let you.' His voice trembled as water filled the bottom of his eyelids then spilled over, chasing streaks down his face.

'Hey…' A girl with red hair, voice soft, eyes big.

'Thought we'd lost her, Jo.'

'I saw you running.'

Then another voice bounced from somewhere. 'You don't have to die for me, Maddie.'

Her dad? Maybe it was okay. Maybe she'd found him after all. She let go.

'You alright?' A woman knelt before her. Fluorescent yellow stinging her eyes.

Tugging at her coat.

Hand inside her t-shirt, burning cold circle against her chest.

'When can I see my dad?'

Jo's hand on her shoulder. 'Shh, Maddie.'

Voices all around: 'What happened?' 'When?' 'Does she have any health problems?' 'Has she taken any drugs or alcohol?'

Her wrist pinched. Thick black band inflating, squeezing her arm. Something in her ear – that worm? She shook her head.

'Keep still for me.' Hands clamped her head and turned it. Blinding light in one eye, then the other. Blurred shapes floating.

Her coat pulled off. Rough hands rubbing her head, back, arms.

Lifting...

'Roger?'

'It's okay, babe.' A hand held hers. 'I'm here. I'm here.'

3
SUMMER
1997

One

All so white here, but soon there'd be preparations for the reunion on Saturday – streamers, banners, balloons. She drew a boat, ripped the page from the notebook and tore it up. On a fresh page she drew a galleon, then began to shade it in. In the outhouses, they were making her a dress, sewing on sequins and pearls.

'Speed bonnie boat like a bird on the wing
Onward the sailors cry
Carry the man that's born to be king…'

The woman with the stern face, who'd raked a brush through her hair, tearing at the tangles, strode down the room, her rubber-soled shoes sucking at the grey lino.

'Quiet now, Maddie. Others are trying to sleep.'

Two beds down, the girl with the long blonde hair was caught in a ritual of muttering and shaking, rubbing her hands together like Lady Macbeth.

Out, damned spot!

Maddie's soft striped cardigan, blue and white, like the rubber ring she used to have, could serve as a float, as a holdfast. She wrapped it round the girl's shoulders.

In the bathroom, she stood at a large, square, white sink and undressed before the frosted window where branches brushed the glass with their rain-wet leaves. Roger had brought her strawberries. She washed them under cold running water till her fingertips stung. No mirror here. She pulled on a pair of cotton pyjamas. Back at her bed, she tugged the stiff white sheet out from under the corners of the mattress so her legs wouldn't feel so bound.

She hadn't wanted to stay here. She fought, but strong arms restrained her. Trying another tack, she lay still.

'Good girl,' they said. 'That's better.'

They drew her curtain round, and she waited till all was quiet, till the lights dimmed, then she sprang from the bed and climbed up to the window. With a scrape and a clang, the metal rings flew back on the pole as her curtain was swept aside.

'Thought that might happen,' the stern woman said.

They pulled her down, put her back in the bed, watched to make sure she swallowed her pills.

She didn't want to stay, but she understood she needed to rest. The reunion was on Saturday. She'd need all her energy. Her dad would be getting ready now, now he'd seen how much she cared. At last, at last.

Nobody died in the storm – not a single courtier or member of the ship's crew. Not Alonso, not Ferdinand. Nobody died.

Though the seas threaten, they are merciful;

Two beds down, the girl with the long blonde hair, wrapped in blue and white, curled up, a soft curve of sea and surf, whimpering.

Oh! She could give him back his ring.

Jo stood in the doorway, a carrier bag in one hand.

She beckoned her over. 'Jo, Jo! Quick!' She told her about her dad's ring, drawing a diagram in her notebook. 'Here's the door, the bed, the windows, the chest of drawers.'

She marked an X on the chest of drawers. 'The ticket's in there. In the top drawer, in an envelope.'

She started to draw Great Western Road, to show Jo where the pawnshop was. 'D'you think they'll still have it? D'you think they've sold it? Please God they haven't sold it.' How much time had passed? How long had she been here?

'Hey, hey, relax. Breathe.' Jo sat on the edge of the bed and stroked her hair. 'How are you feeling, how have you been?'

What did it matter how she was? There was no time to talk. 'Please, Jo, go now. Run. You must get it.'

Jo squeezed her hand. 'Okay, honey. Okay.'

Sitting with three others around a table, all wearing their pyjamas, playing Ludo. An old man had a tartan blanket over his knees. The dice rattled in the black plastic cup before it rolled out across the board.

Shake and roll, shake and roll.

She took the cup from the old man. If she got a six, her dad would be nearly here.

'A six!'

She threw the dice again. 'A six!'

And again. 'Another six!'

A woman, like the stern woman but kinder, thinner, placed a hand on her shoulder. 'Move your piece along now, Maddie, and give the dice to Diane.'

'But it's a six.'

'No, it's a three. Look. Come on, let everyone have a go.'

'But he's nearly here. Will everything be ready?'

'Just hand the dice on.'

A wave of fatigue washed over her. It was impossible to keep her eyes open. The back of her shoulders ached.

'Come on, Maddie, wake up. It's not bedtime yet.'

One evening, after dinner, her mum walked through the doors and sat in the chair by the bed.

'She's looking a bit better,' her mum said to the stern woman.

'Aye, that cut's healing up nicely. And she's got a bit of colour back in her cheeks.'

Maddie glanced between them. 'Better than when?'

The stern woman lowered her clipboard. 'Your folks came to

see you the day after you were admitted. Don't you remember?'

'My dad? He's been already?'

Her mum smoothed the crumpled sheet. Maybe she wasn't supposed to tell everyone.

When the stern woman had gone, she swung her legs out the side of the bed. 'So you've seen him?'

Her mum picked a bit of skin at the edge of her thumb. 'Don't be getting yourself in a tiz again, love.'

She tucked her hands beneath her thighs. 'Have we to keep it a secret?'

Her mum took a large bottle of Lucozade from a plastic bag and placed it on the bedside table next to the pink carnations. 'I better go. The traffic was bad on the motorway, and Rab's had a long day.'

'Rab?'

'He's waiting outside in the car.' She stood. 'I'll come again soon.'

'Yes, to the reunion on Saturday.'

She was grey around the eyes.

'It's going to be alright, Mum. Aren't you happy? What are you going to wear?'

'Soon.' She kissed the top of Maddie's head and hurried away.

The girl with the long blonde hair sat on the end of Maddie's bed, still wearing the cardigan. How long had she been wearing it now?

'You can wear that on Saturday, if you like.'

The girl blushed, pinker than the carnations, and smiled a little. She pulled her knees up, wrapped her arms around them, rocked back and forth and smiled wide.

'Come on, Ruth.' It was the thin woman. 'Back to your own bed, please.'

Ruth's face darkened. She stood up and shuffled off.

Jo came again, with Roger.

She sat up. 'Have you got it?'

'Yes, I've got it. Here.'

Jo handed her the maroon box. She opened it. There it was, her dad's ring, a circle of gold, with its scratches, its tiny dent. She tried it on. It was too big on all her fingers, even her thumb. Would it still fit him?

She looked from Roger to Jo. 'You're both coming, aren't you?'

Roger sat on the bed and swept back her hair. 'To what, sweetheart?'

'To the reunion.'

'Honey, there is no reunion. You're here to get better.'

She wrapped her fist round the ring and clenched until it cut her palm.

'But my dad's coming?'

'No, babe. No.'

A wave built in her chest. 'Why would you say that?' Drops and speckles on the sheet.

'It's okay.' Jo held her.

'What should I have said?' Roger asked.

Jo rocked her gently. 'I don't know.'

The sticky sound of the stern woman's shoes. 'Leave her now,' she said. 'Come back another time. Maybe tomorrow.'

When everyone had gone, she turned to the wall, her hands clasped around her dad's gold ring, holding it tight to her chest.

A thin strip of blue and white edged into view. Ruth sat in the chair, placed a hand on her leg, started to hum a lullaby.

Two

When she moved to the modern place, a woman sat on a chair at the end of her bed, knitting. She followed Maddie everywhere, even keeping the toilet door wedged open with her foot. But, day by day, she was allowed to do more by herself. Jo and Roger, appalled at the canteen food, brought her supermarket dinners, and now she was even allowed to use the microwave.

One afternoon, the suited man called her in for another interview and told her she was there voluntarily.

'Great,' she said, standing up, already imagining packing her bag.

He interlaced his fingers and leant on the desk. 'If you try to leave though, we'll have to section you.'

She sat down. 'Then I'm not free to go.'

'Yes, you are,' he said. 'You're here voluntarily.'

He made her head hurt, but he was friendly, not like the stern woman at the last place.

'You're a bright girl, Maddie, but you need to stay away from psychoactive drugs.' He looked over the rim of his glasses. 'That means, *all* drugs.'

'Yes. I understand that now.'

It was best to agree, to behave, to be polite.

When he'd first interviewed her, he asked her to tell him what'd happened. She didn't mention she was waiting for her dad. She'd made too much fuss about him in the last place. He was probably waiting now till she got out, when there'd be less eyes watching. She needed to get out.

In the evenings, she sat in a room with a telly in the corner. The space looked like a common room, filled with chairs, all facing the TV. Nearly all the chairs had people sitting on them. The air was thick with smoke. She sat with two older women, Sue and Dawn. Sue was tall and skinny with a hard, leathery face. Dawn was short and chubby. She was like Sue's sidekick, there to supply fags and make Sue laugh.

They'd first joined Maddie one dinnertime, asking a lot of questions.

'You remind me of my sister,' Sue said. 'Sadly no longer with us.'

'That's how Sue's in here,' Dawn said.

'It's one of the reasons.' Sue pushed a plate of mashed stuff away from her. 'It all started when I finally got my own place. It was good to be away from The Bastard, but I was lonely. My dog got run over, then my sister died. I thought, I'll just have a couple of wee drinks to cheer myself up. But it doesn't work that way, does it?'

Maddie's throat was raw from smoking so much, but she went with them for a cigarette. They'd kind of been a trio after that.

One time in the lounge, Dawn asked, 'Did you hear Yvonne last night?'

'No,' Sue said. 'I think they've changed my meds. I've been sleeping the sleep of the dead.'

'She was running up and down the corridor shouting, "Let me out!" Going crazy. She got as far as the gate before they caught her. They dragged her back and took her shoes off her. That's how she's been going round in her socks. She says to me, "Can I try your shoes on, Dawn?" I says to her, "Keep away! I've only got the one pair, and they won't suit you."'

Sue snorted, then coughed.

'I told her, "You could always go in your slippers." But she hasn't got any slippers. Next week, when we start this pottery shite, I'm gonna make her a pair of clay clogs. But then they'd hear her going, wouldn't they? Rat-a-tat-tat down the corridor.'

Maddie wanted to go, she was desperate to go, but she had to bide her time.

Another night, the three of them smoked in silence. Ribbons of blue-grey twirled up, blending with the low-hanging fug. *Coronation Street* was on the telly.

'I miss my kids,' Sue said.

Maddie dropped her shoulders, relieved someone was going to talk.

'I spoke to my mother and I says, "Don't tell me the whole report, just tell me the bottom line." And she says, "Access has been cancelled." No, hang on. She said, "Access has been *suspended*." That's not so bad then, eh?'

'Not so bad,' Dawn said.

One day, after lunch, she fell asleep at the dining table. A woman with a basketball woke her, and a few of them were marched across to a hall that she didn't even know existed. They were told to stand in a circle. A man with thinning grey hair lay down. Someone made him stand back up.

The basketball woman described a game they were going to play. It was like a drama warm-up game. They had to say someone's name, then throw them the ball. Maddie didn't know anyone's name.

'Let's go round,' the woman said, 'and tell everyone our names.'

Some folk said their names, others didn't. Maddie couldn't hear some of the names, and couldn't remember any of them. The woman gave an Indian guy the ball. He threw it. It bounced in the middle of the circle.

The woman picked it up and handed it to the man with thinning hair.

'Senga,' he said, dropping the ball and lying down again.

Everyone looked round.

'Billy, there is no Senga,' the woman said, standing him back up.

No one could remember any names, and no one had the strength to throw the ball. The man with the thin hair lay back down.

Was it a test? If you remembered the names, would they let you out?

A few days later, the suited man called her in for another interview. Dr Patterson, his name was. A psychiatrist.

'When can I go?' she asked.

'You can go anytime.'

'Yes, but when can I *really* go?'

He shuffled some papers and asked how she was feeling.

She tried not to panic. 'Will it be days, months, years?'

'It's important to rest,' he said. 'To let things run their course.'

Would she be here forever? She gripped her knees but didn't say anything in case it made him extend her time.

That afternoon, she was sitting at a table modelling a mermaid out of Plasticine when her mum arrived. A nurse pulled up a chair for her mum to sit on.

She asked how Maddie was, and she answered politely, returning the question.

'We got a new puppy,' her mum said.

'That's nice.' She looked out the window. Pansies and primroses in the flowerbeds, but the sky was grey, it didn't look like summer at all.

When the nurse was out of earshot, she turned to her mum. 'I think I saw him, Mum. Last night. Out there, waiting behind that tree.'

Looking down, her mum rubbed the knuckles of one hand against the palm of the other.

'Mum?'

She sighed. 'Perhaps we should have told you. But you had

exams or something coming up. And I thought, what's the point of going to the funeral of someone you hardly even knew? I thought it'd just unsettle you, for nothing.'

Shh, shh, quiet… If she kept believing, anything could happen. She rolled a thin snake of yellow for the mermaid's hair. Stupid-looking mermaid, nothing about it was right. She squashed it into a ball, all the colours ugly against each other.

'I didn't think it would be like this in here,' Sue said that evening. 'Have you seen some of them? Drugged up to the eyeballs. Mary hasn't moved for days, she just lies there, like a zombie. She got up at five o'clock last night, had a ciggie by the window, then went back to bed. They just leave you to it. What good's that? Before I came in, I thought there would be nurses and doctors that'd come and talk to you. How's anyone supposed to get better? Seemingly, during the week, there's activities to do – cake baking and the like. I've never seen anything.' She snorted, then coughed. 'Papier-mâché! What the fuck use would that be anyway?'

The next day, after the trolley came round, she hardly had enough energy to sit up. They said she was there to get better, but was she really there to die? A woman arrived with a tape recorder and asked them all to lie down on their beds. Smooth waves of sound rippled over her body.

'Feel the light travel up from your feet,' the woman said. 'Up your legs, through your pelvis, into your stomach, growing brighter in your chest. Breathe deeply, letting all your tension go.'

Were they preparing her for death?

She teetered on the brink, then tumbled. As she fell into the heavy black, a hand held hers. She was side by side with someone. Sinking, but peaceful, not alone there in the dark.

Another day, just before teatime, Jo came to visit. She smelled of cold air and cut grass.

'Roger sends his love,' she said. 'He got that advert. They're filming in the Cairngorms.'

'Cool. That's great. And have you had any news from the Tramway yet?'

'Yes, we got the go-ahead.'

'No way! Amazing. What are the dates?'

'They're not set in stone. I've got to go in for a meeting next week.'

'I'll say to Dr Patterson, I'll tell him I've got to go now because of the play. Will you say to him too? Maybe you could write me a letter?'

'Don't worry about that now. Just concentrate on getting better.'

'But the play…?'

Jo wandered to the table and picked up the Plasticine ball. 'Making something?'

She took it from Jo and tossed it in the bin. 'I just want to get back to normal.'

'I know. But don't put too much pressure on yourself. You've been through a lot.'

Pulling the ring box from her pocket, she said, 'I owe you for this.'

'We can sort it out later.' Jo sat on the edge of the bed.

Maddie sat beside her, took out the ring, placed it on her knee. 'Do you think he's out there, Jo?'

'What d'you mean?'

'My dad. D'you think he's waiting for me to get out?'

Jo sighed a long, slow breath. 'No. I think he's gone.'

'Gone where?'

'I think he died, three years ago, like the woman said.'

'And nothing I did helped?'

'Things don't work that way, honey. You got a bit muddled.'

'How do we know he really died in the first place?'

'I spoke to your mum. One time Roger and I were leaving, we met her in the car park.'

'She might have got it wrong. That woman might have lied.'

'There was an obituary. A funeral.'

She traced round the ring. 'So I'll never see him. Never ever ever?' She looked up.

Jo pushed her fingers into the corners of her eyes. 'I'm so sorry, Maddie.'

She nodded and placed the ring back in the box.

Two days later, her mum returned.

'I brought you some magazines.' She held out a bag, then set it on the bedside cabinet.

'I'm tired.' Maddie lay on the bed, facing away.

'That's okay.' A rustle of plastic, then pages being turned. 'I'll just sit here and read for a bit.'

Her eyelids quivered, it was hard to keep them shut. She listened to her mum sniff then clear her throat. Her cheeks burned as the words kicked in her brain: You knew, you knew, you knew.

Waking at 4:38 am, with everyone else still asleep, she walked to the TV room. A girl was sitting in there, drawing. She was wearing navy pyjamas with stars on them, her auburn hair loose around her shoulders.

'Hi.' Maddie sat down.

The girl looked up.

'Can't sleep either?'

'I hardly ever sleep.'

'That must be awful.'

The girl shrugged.

'My name's Maddie.'

'Hi, I'm Sylvie.'

'What are you drawing?'

'There's a nest out there in the bushes.' Sylvie pointed towards the window.

'Can I see?'

Sylvie handed over her pad. Sketches of trees, and studies of birds and leaves. 'Are they blackbirds?'

'I think so.'

She turned back a page. 'Hey, these are really good.'

Sylvie half-smiled. 'Thanks. It's for my art project.'

'Are you at college?'

'No, it's my last year at school.' Taking the pad back, Sylvie folded her legs under her.

A strange sense of déjà-vu, the joint interview sessions, only this time Maddie wasn't the child. She got up and walked to the window. Colour had yet to come into the garden, it was all awash with pre-dawn blue.

She was turning to head back to the ward when Sylvie asked, 'How long have you been here?'

'I'm not sure, to be honest. Maybe a few weeks. What about you?'

'Three days, so far, this time. Why are you here?'

She leant against the wall and ran her hands along the radiator. It was cold. 'My dad died three years ago.' As she put her weight onto the heels of her hands, the sharp metal ridge cut into them. 'Nobody told me.'

'My mum's dead. But I was only like two years old when she died.'

Maddie sat back down. 'Too young to remember her?'

Sylvie laid her pencil on her pad and rolled it back and forth. She talked about her mum, her step-mum, her dad, her younger sister. She asked about Maddie's family, about where she grew up. The conversation turned to music, books, TV. Maddie did some impressions from *The Fast Show* and Sylvie laughed. She had a beautiful smile, but it would've seemed odd to say.

The morning fog cleared and the rising sun filled the room with strong yellow light.

Maddie shielded her eyes with a hand. 'So you've been here before?'

Taking a bobble from her wrist, Sylvie tied back her hair. 'I don't know what's wrong with me. I just feel horrible most of the time.' She pulled up a sleeve and showed her scratches and scabs and scars.

Maddie wanted to hug her. 'You know, you'll feel differently one day. You'll finish school and leave home. You'll make the life you want.'

How could she make the words sound more sincere? She thought of her flat, about the Tramway, the play, what might happen if the show went well, and felt the tiniest, tiniest spark.

'I can't imagine ever feeling differently.'

'You will.'

Someone passed the room then doubled back. One of the nurses. 'Time to get dressed, girls, and go to breakfast.'

Maddie stretched her arms high into the air. Warmth in the sun.

'Thank you,' Sylvie said.

'Thank you, it was nice to chat.'

'No,' Sylvie said. 'Thank you for giving me time.'

In the small square-tiled shower room, she found a scrap of paper on the floor. A bit of someone's shopping list. Eggs, milk, butter. It wasn't giving her a message, or directives, or hiding any kind of code. It was just a list, fallen, maybe, from someone's pocket. She placed it on the orange plastic chair, undressed and turned on the shower. When the water had heated, she stepped under and let the warm spray run down her face, her arms, her legs, over her feet and away. Washing it all away.

Three

The following Friday, she hugged goodbye to Sue and Dawn, did up her coat and lifted two carrier bags of belongings from the end of what had been her bed. As she walked down the corridor, she looked for Sylvie. She hadn't seen her again since that encounter in the TV lounge.

Dr Patterson had recommended Maddie stay with a relative for a week or two before going back to her flat. 'Give you some time to adjust,' he said. 'And the company would do you good.'

Jo and Wren came to pick her up.

'Take good care now,' a nurse said as she neared the front doors. 'Let's not be seeing you again.'

Once outside, she rushed to Wren's car, anticipating a firm hand on her shoulder. The world seemed shockingly large.

Glancing back as they pulled from the drive, she asked, 'How long was I in there?'

'Just over two weeks,' Jo said.

It felt much longer.

Jo turned in her seat. 'You okay?'

'Yeah. How did you get on at your meeting?'

'What meeting?'

'At the Tramway?'

'Oh, don't worry about that. We'll talk about it later.'

The first three nights she stayed at Jo's, but Jo's flatmate was around and it was tiring trying to remember what a normal conversation was like. All she wanted to do was sleep.

Monday, Jo and Wren drove her back to her flat. She opened

the door and saw the room she'd fled from. Her duvet bunched up with her bath towel half-hanging from the bed; the phone at an odd angle on the floor; her hairbrush on the sofa; the clothes she'd worn to Jo's election night party in a heap by the chest of drawers. The air was stale and smelled of damp cardboard.

Jo opened the windows. For a moment, she wanted to flee again. But where would she go? She set the carrier bags down at the end of her bed, picked up the towel and folded it.

'Shall we stay for a coffee?' Jo asked.

'I'm not sure if I've got any.'

'Can we do a shop for you then? What d'you need?'

'Nothing. I can't think. I'm okay to go out if I need anything.'

Wren put his hand on her shoulder. 'Wee Mads. You know to phone any time?'

'Yeah. Sorry. I just feel shattered.'

'Okay.' Jo hooked her thumbs in the loops of her jeans. 'I'll call you later.'

They headed for the door.

'Jo?'

She turned.

'What about the play?'

'Oh, you rest up. We'll find some time to talk about it in the week.'

After they'd gone, she drew the curtains, stripped to her t-shirt and pants and crawled into bed.

When she woke it was cold and dark. She switched on a lamp, slowly recognising her flat, closed the windows, pulled on some pyjama bottoms and turned on the fire. Upending the bags, she inspected the strange mix of stuff she'd brought back from the hospital. A packet of Plasticine; some clothes Jo had brought her; a notepad filled with scribbles; a fluffy pencil case that looked like something a child would own; the ring box.

If she were Prospero, she'd be able to conjure something with these items.

Graves at my command

Have waked their sleepers, oped, and let 'em forth

Walking to the kitchen for a glass of water, something pierced the ball of her foot. A splinter of mirror was lodged in her skin. As she pulled it out, blood stained a line under her fingernail. Something crashed in the kitchen. She dived to her bed, pulling the duvet over her mouth. She hadn't meant it, about calling on the dead.

When her heart slowed, she crept to the kitchen. A mug had fallen from the draining board and was lying in three pieces.

At 11am she woke with a start, drenched in sweat. The sun was beating at the curtains and she'd forgotten to turn off the fire.

Several days passed in a haze. Jo and Roger called in, but she didn't have the energy to chat for long. As she saw them out, she noticed a letter on the chest addressed to her.

Dear Maddie,

I got a call from your mum and we met for lunch. I'm so sorry to hear you've been through such a terrible ordeal, and can only hope you're starting to feel a wee bit better. I was shocked to hear about your dad, and am truly sorry. I had no idea, and can't believe Rab and Jean had thought it best to keep the news from you. But then, in truth, us mums often get things wrong, even when we really believe what we're doing is for the best.

Auntie Irene wrote about her course of radiotherapy, and that she was feeling a bit brighter, fingers crossed, so was thinking of coming through to Glasgow soon to look for some summer outfits.

Let me know if you're free and would like to meet up. It'd be really lovely to see you.

Her mum had called and left messages a couple of times now. She really ought to let her know things were okay.

By the weekend, the ulcers in her mouth had gone and the glue fell away from the cut on her eyebrow, the scar hardly visible. She took some clothes to the launderette. It was the first Saturday in June, the leaves on the trees were at full stretch and there was sweetness in the air. Sap, nectar, cut grass.

Back at her flat, she bathed and put on a clean dress.

Her mum answered on the second ring. 'Hello?'

'Hi, Mum, it's me.'

'Oh, Maddie, I've been worried. Are you okay?'

'Yes. I've been sleeping a lot, but I'm starting to feel a bit better.'

'That's good, hen.' A rustle. Her mum lowered her voice. 'I was wondering if I could come through and visit you? Maybe just for an hour or two? I could get the train.'

Since when had she started using trains? She picked up the photo of her mum, dad, and self as a kid. 'Okay. I could come and meet you at Queen Street.'

'Or I could get a taxi to your flat, it'd be nice to see your wee place.'

She propped the photo back up. 'No. I'll meet you. How about sometime midweek?'

'Wednesday would be good for me, if that'd work for you?'

'Aye. Let me know what time you'll be arriving. Just leave it in a message if I'm not here.'

That evening, she was halfway through cooking chilli when there was a knock at the door. Wiping her hands on a tea towel, she padded to the CD player and turned the volume down.

'Maddie?' A man's voice.

'Hello?'

'It's me.'

She opened the door an inch. 'Mike?'

'Hey. I heard you'd been to hell and back.'

She opened the door wider. He'd had his hair cut and was clean-shaven. The blue shirt he was wearing still had a grid of creases across it from the packet.

'Come in.'

'How are you doing?' he asked, walking to the windows.

'Okay. Getting there.'

'I'm sorry to hear about your dad.' He picked up one of the photos. 'Is this him?'

'Yeah.'

'You look similar.'

'Same eyes.'

'General face shape.' He put the photo down, turned and perched on the chest of drawers.

'You look different.'

He laughed. 'Yeah, been through my own baptism of fire. Moved back in with my mum. Been drug-free for a couple of months.'

'Huh.' She sat on the arm of the sofa.

'Anyway, I was wondering if you'd like to come out for a drink?'

On one of their first dates, they went to Whistler's Mother. It felt quite exotic, venturing away from the college pub to the West End. He'd made her laugh all night, doing impersonations of the college tutors.

'I *say* come for a drink,' he added, 'but it'll be a softie for me. I'm not really drinking anymore either.'

'Really? Cool.'

He crossed his legs. He was wearing new shoes, a trendy pair of trainers. 'Well, maybe that's a bit of an exaggeration. A man's gotta have some vices!'

She laughed, folded the tea towel and laid it across her knee. 'To be honest, I'm still pretty wrung out. I seem to be able to stay upright for about an hour at a time.'

He looked at the bed, then pushed himself to standing. 'No worries. Perhaps when you're back fighting fit.'

As she walked towards the door, she wondered whether to ask him to stay for dinner. The company would be nice. They could sit on the sofa with the summer night air drifting in through the windows and watch some nonsense on TV.

He zipped up his jacket. 'Heard that wee punk you were seeing was a bit of a shit. Couldn't deal with the grief after your dad died, so did a disappearing act.'

'No.' She swung open the door. 'That's not what happened.'

Downstairs in the hall, he opened his arms for a hug.

She held him lightly, patting him on the back. 'Take care.'

As he stepped out, his half-smile was tinged with something.

Remorse, a voice said in her head. She tried to ignore it.

At the end of the street, he waved and she raised her hand. She exhaled as she closed the front door, but a heavy weight settled in her gut as she made her way back upstairs to her room, alone.

Four

Wednesday morning, she took a tube into town, staring into the dark, catching glimpses of cables bolted to curved walls. It was difficult to imagine how the underground system had been built, burrowed out beneath the city. All those layers of earth. She pressed her damp palms against the prickly brown and orange seat. If she couldn't hold it together, maybe Jo would find someone to replace her in the show. After all, she was still avoiding the subject.

The train ground to a halt. A man glanced up from his paper and caught her eye. The lights went off, then double-flashed back on. Four weeks ago she would have read a message into that. She bit the end of her tongue. Saliva seeped into her mouth.

Mortifying, remembering running wild through the town, babbling to strangers, what she'd put Roger through. The thought of Jo and Roger seeing her in hospital, prattling on and on. If she could get some work, even in a bar, she could at least pay them back for her dad's ring. She squeezed her jacket pocket, the ring box was still there. The train rumbled on.

Alighting at Buchanan Street, she took the escalator up. Wasn't it ridiculous to feel nervous about meeting your own mother?

Her mum was one of the last to step from the train. She looked so small, glancing about anxiously. Her face relaxed a bit when she saw Maddie, she gave a little wave, then slipped her handbag up her forearm so she was free to give her a hug.

'Hello, love.'

'Hi, Mum. You smell nice.'

'I treated myself to one of those wee imitation perfumes. I could get you one if you like? I know someone who's got a birthday coming up.'

'That's okay, I don't really wear perfume.'

'Maybe we'll see something for you today then, if you've got time for a wee look round the shops?'

'Maybe.'

She took Maddie's arm as they walked along Sauchiehall Street, chattering about the new puppy, work, the changes in Glasgow city centre since she'd last been.

Dino's was busy, but there were free tables through the back in the small square space. The red and green neon light bouncing off the mirror-clad walls was dazzling.

A waitress appeared. 'Hello, ladies. Do you know what you want, or would you like to see the menu?'

Glancing at Maddie, her mum said, 'The menu, please.'

The waitress handed them one each. 'I'll be back in a minute to take your order.'

'What'll you have?' her mum asked, putting on her pearly reading glasses that made her look like Deirdre in *Coronation Street*.

'A coffee. But I'll get it.'

'No, it's my treat. No arguments. Have something to eat as well.'

'I don't want anything to eat, ta.'

'At least have a doughnut, make me feel less of a greedy guts.'

After the waitress had taken their order, her mum took off her glasses. 'So how are you feeling?'

'Okay. Better. Still a bit bushed.'

'Staying away from the drugs though?'

'I took a couple of paracetamol last night for a headache.' She was being obtuse, she knew what her mum meant.

'No, love. I mean the party drugs.'

Party drugs! She swallowed the urge to laugh. 'Aye. Though I'm not sure how much they were to blame, really.'

Frowning, her mum said, 'But that's what the doctor told us – acute drug-induced psychosis.'

'So the circumstances had nothing to do with it?'

Her mum looked down. 'I don't think... not to that degree...'

'Let's not talk about it.'

The waitress returned with their coffees and two chocolate iced doughnuts.

Tearing open a sachet of sugar, her mum emptied it into her cup, then poured in milk to the brim. 'I should've said not too strong.'

Maddie pulled the ring box from her pocket. 'I've something I need to give you.' She set it on the table between them. 'I took it. I didn't really mean to. I'm sorry.'

Her mum reached for the box. It creaked as she opened it. Sighing, she closed it and pushed it back towards her. 'You keep it.' She leant forward and sipped her coffee till the level was low enough for her to lift the cup. 'We really thought we were doing what was best, love.'

'You, maybe. But Rab?'

Opening her bag, her mum took out twenty Superkings, offered her one and lit it for her.

'When your dad left, I mean, when it was finally over, I was terrified. What I earned cleaning was barely enough to cover the weekly shop, never mind rent, never mind bills. I thought we were going to be out on the street. Then Rab...'

'Why didn't you go to Irene? Or Gran?'

'They might've been able to help out for a week or two, but what after that?'

'We could've moved in with Gran.'

'Ha! I'd like to have seen the old goat's response to that idea. She was put out enough one time we stayed for just a night.' She sliced her doughnut in two and picked at a bit of chocolate icing. 'What can I say, love? Rab seemed like a good option. I thought we were lucky. Yes, he's got a temper, but… I said to your dad, "She's still your daughter, you're free to come and visit, to take her out."'

'And I wonder what Rab said.' She curled the edge of a paper napkin. 'About two months ago, on my way back from a role-play job in Aberdeen, I stopped in to see you. No one was home. I found some letters. I was looking in the photo box, under your bed.'

'I know. Rab told me.'

She looked up.

'When Jo phoned to say you'd gone into hospital, that you'd had a phone call from Carolyn about your dad, I was confused. He told me then. He didn't know where you'd got the letters from, but he knew I'd kept them. He was pretty angry.'

'*He* was angry?'

'I know, love, I know. But you've got to see things from his point of view.'

'Which is?'

'He took us on. He's worked hard all his life to provide for us, often taking on extra shifts. He thought we were flouting his good will. You know how touchy he is about that kind of stuff after what happened with his first wife.'

The one that got away. Though she might have gone further than his younger brother's. She tapped her ash into the cut glass ashtray. 'He took my keys off me.'

'Did he?' Her mum rubbed between her eyebrows. 'I don't want to make excuses… I know he'd had a bad day. He'd just come back from the vet's.'

Excuses, excuses. She sipped her coffee. Across from them, a little girl squealed as her mum tickled her. The waitress carried an ice cream sundae to their table.

'Look at that!' the man sitting opposite the little girl said. 'Who's a lucky girl?'

Her mum stirred her coffee. 'Not gonna take your jacket off, love?'

'No. I'm feeling the cold.'

Pulling the ashtray towards her, her mum stubbed out her cigarette. 'What can I do, to make things better?'

She shrugged. On the red-and-white chequered tablecloth, a raised circle where somebody must've placed their cup to the side of their saucer, searing the plastic. She ran her finger round it.

Her mum took an envelope from her bag and slid it across the table.

'What's that?'

'For you.'

'But what is it?'

'Open it.'

She stubbed her cigarette out and picked up the envelope. Inside was a small wad of twenty-pound notes. 'What's this?'

'One of the days I came to the hospital I met Jo. We got talking about what she was up to, work and that. I know you said you needed to get photographs done.'

'I'll get them done when I can afford to get them done. I don't need something else hanging over me.'

Her mum reached across and put her hand on Maddie's. Her palm was warm, slightly waxy. 'Please, love. I know what the acting means to you. Make a go of it. Get those photos done. Send them off. Do everything you can. If it doesn't work out, hey ho, have a look round for something else. But give this a real go first. Do it for me.'

'With Rab's money?'

'No. This is mine. I put a bit by. An emergency fund.'

'Then keep it for an emergency.'

Her mum laughed. 'This is an emerge and see.'

The envelope lay next to the ring box, nudging Maddie's plate. They finished their coffees. She ate half her doughnut, then went to the Ladies'. Returning to the table, she saw the envelope had gone.

'Take the ring,' her mum said. 'Please. I've got nothing else of his to give you.'

'Are you sure?'

'Yes. I am.'

She put the box in her jacket pocket. So many questions she wanted to ask, she didn't know where to start. Would her mum even have any answers?

Outside, it was drizzling. Taking an umbrella from her bag, her mum said, 'Fancy a wee look round the shops?'

'I'm a bit shattered to tell the truth.' It wasn't a lie. Halfway through coffee her eyelids had started to droop.

'Walk me to the station then.'

At the station, her mum hugged her goodbye. 'Maybe we could do this again sometime?'

'Maybe.'

Clasping Maddie's hand, she said, 'Go easy, eh love? Keep in touch.' Then she hurried down the platform, not looking back.

As she zipped up her jacket, something crinkled in her pocket. The envelope of money. Her mum was boarding the train. Should she run after her? Perhaps she'd been too harsh. Maybe it was like Auntie Irene said, her mum had done her best. The guard blew his whistle and the train pulled away.

Unable to face the panic of the tube, she walked back to her flat.

Halfway down Woodlands Road, she heard her name being called.

Hanna arrived by her side, slightly out of breath. 'Hey, Maddie. Long time no see.'

Chatting away, she asked what Maddie had been up to. Maybe word of her exploits hadn't reached that quarter yet.

'I hope you've not been staying away because of what happened with Alex?'

'No, I've just been busy.'

'What are you doing now? Wanna come up for dinner?'

The kitchen would be full of folk, laughing, shouting over each other, drinking beer, smoking. What she'd give for a smoke. 'I can't just now,' she said. 'I've got some friends coming over.'

'Just a quick coffee then?'

It'd be bad form to pop in and smoke other folks' hash without buying any. She was pretty skint, but she did have the envelope in her pocket. Was it true what Dr Patterson said? *Were* all drugs psychoactive? Her flat would be silent and empty, there were no friends coming over. But the play... She needed to be well, to give herself the best chance.

'I'm running a bit late as it is,' she said. 'Otherwise I'd have loved to.'

Hanna put a hand on her arm. 'Another time, then. Don't be a stranger.'

She walked on. Had Hanna said don't be a stranger, or don't be strange?

As she climbed the stairs to her room, she heard her phone ring and the answering machine kick in. She ran the remainder of the flight and unlocked her door.

'Hi, Maddie, it's Jo. Just wondering...'

She lifted the receiver. 'Hi.'

'Hey there, how's you?'

'Good. Been out to meet my mum. Just got back.'

'How'd it go?'

'So-so.'

'I was wondering if you fancied a visitor?'

'Definitely.'

'About seven?'

She started getting ready at six. Washed and blow-dried her hair and put some lipstick on. Did that make her seem saner?

The buzzer made her jump. Putting her door on the snib, she ran downstairs.

Jo was on the doorstep, wearing shades. 'Why does Glasgow wait till after five to get sunny in the summer?'

She shrugged. 'Something to do with being built in a valley?'

'It's still warm. Fancy going for a pint down The Wickets?'

On the way down Clarence Lane, Jo talked about flats. 'There's one just off Belmont Street we really liked. We've left a message with the landlady. Hopefully she's not already given it to someone else.'

'When would you move in?'

'Next month, if we could.'

They arrived at the hotel and walked through to the bar. Jo slipped off her shades. 'What'll you have?'

'Just a cranberry juice, ta.'

'Vodka cranberry?'

'Minus the vodka.'

'Okay, cool. Fancy seeing if there's room outside?'

There was a free table in the corner of the tiered courtyard. She sat, listening to the hubbub of conversation. A wild rose poked its head over her shoulder. Beside it, a tall leafy plant with yellow flowers near its tip. One of the flowers began to unfurl. When would the world stop seeming so trippy?

Jo climbed the steps carrying their drinks. 'Cheers.' She handed the highball glass to Maddie and clinked her beer bottle against it. 'How've you been doing anyway?'

Maddie talked about her mum, about resisting the temptation to go up to Liam and Hanna's.

'I've cut right down on dope myself,' Jo said. 'Amazing difference in my energy levels.'

A couple edged past them.

The guy stopped in front of the yellow flower. 'Check this out.'

'Oh yeah,' the girl said. 'Evening primrose. They open after dusk.'

Jo swigged her beer. 'Don't think I've ever seen a flower open before.'

As Maddie glanced over, it jolted to full bloom.

Jo leant on the table. 'So I've been wanting to chat with you about *The Tempest*.'

Maddie swirled the ice in her drink with the blue and white straw, then took a sip.

'We've got some dates. Rehearsals start a week on Monday, but I'm wondering how you're feeling about it. I've identified someone who could step in for you.'

'Have you changed your mind about wanting me to do it?'

'No. No, it's not that. It's more that you've had a lot to deal with lately. Understatement. It's still early days for you.'

She rubbed her hands over the rough wood of the bench. 'Does Roger not want me to do it?'

'We both just want what's best for you. We've only got a week to put the piece together. It's only gonna be about forty, fifty minutes long, a taster, but you know what it's like, the entertainment business, paradoxically one of the most stressful professions going.'

'I've been looking forward to it.' She'd practically been living for it.

'I know. But it's not even just a question of learn your lines and avoid the furniture. There's still some devising to do. I'm envisaging something quite unconventional, more like physical theatre with bits of *The Tempest* woven through it.'

'Sounds cool.'

'Yes. But it'll demand more of the performers. Then there's all the stress of production week, opening night, being in front of an audience. And some of the subject matter...'

Was she trying to talk her out of it? Taking ten Silk Cut from her bag, she offered one to Jo.

'Ta.'

She lit it for her, then lit her own and exhaled. 'I met this girl in the hospital... The long and short of it is, I don't want to escape anymore. I want to be right here, creating good work, being involved in good projects, making a difference. I want to do this.'

The moon appeared above the treetops, a slender sickle, pearly, with a single star to one side.

Jo stubbed her cigarette out and took a sip of beer. 'I'd want to see if the other girl would consider understudying.'

'Yes.'

'And I'd want you to tell me if you got cold feet, or the minute you felt uneasy about anything.'

'Yes.'

'Okay then.'

'Okay?'

'Yes.'

'It's a yes?'

Jo laughed. 'Yes!'

She sprang from the bench. 'Oh my God, Jo, you won't regret this, I promise. I'm gonna work so hard...' She grabbed Jo round the neck, swallowing back tears.

Jo stood. 'I know you will.'

They hugged. Gathering back Maddie's hair, Jo pulled away and looked her in the eye. 'Well, Ms Maddie, let's make this something damn bloody good.'

Five

Arriving early at the Tramway on Monday morning, the first day of rehearsal, she saw Roger weaving through the white pillars at the back of the building, smoking.

'Hey.' She ran towards him.

'Angel-eyes.' He swung her round, then put her down and patted her sides. 'Pleased to report you're feeling a bit more substantial.'

'Talk about a backhanded compliment, Oscar bloomin' Wilde.'

'It's a good thing. You're still a bloody stick after all.'

All morning she'd been plagued by voices in her head, asking whether she was up to the job. But on the journey to work, she'd put her headphones on and listened to the single she'd bought last week in Fopp – The Verve's 'Bittersweet Symphony', its opening orchestral chords melancholic, but the melody, as it faded in on strings, hopeful. A sudden rush had tingled down her arms.

Roger dropped the end of his cigarette and gestured towards the door. 'Shall we?'

They signed in and one of the jannies showed them through to Tramway 4 – a long black studio space with a concrete floor. They sat in the front row of the seating bank.

Roger slipped off his jacket. 'Oh my God, we're on in here next week.'

'Shh.' She slapped his knee. 'One day at a time. How did you get on finishing up filming?'

'Good. Wait till you see me, striding through the heather in my kilt. Then I was back in Gandolfi, down to earth with a bump.'

'If they're ever looking for new staff, will you let me know?'

'You searching for a job?'

'After this I thought I would. Reckon it might do me good. And I'd like to start paying my way in the world, pay you and Jo back.'

'No rush for that, sweetpea.'

Jo and Wren arrived with a stocky guy in black jeans and t-shirt.

'Hi,' Jo said. 'Maddie, Roger, this is Ben. He's one of the resident technicians here. He's been assigned to our production. Ben, the actors.'

They shook hands, then Ben opened the doors at the back of the space. Light flooded in and a cool breeze circled the room. A girl in a flowery knee-length dress peered round the door.

'Suzanne,' Jo called. 'Come on in. Folks, this is Suzanne, she's here on placement. She's going to be assisting me, and she'll be ready to jump in if either of you'—Jo glanced between Maddie and Roger—'come down with smallpox.'

Suzanne laughed, winding the cord of her headphones round her Walkman.

Morven squeezed through the downstage door with several bags, and Jo called the meeting to begin. As Ben talked through some housekeeping issues, Morven assembled a model of the set. She placed a wooden shell-like structure in the box that represented the theatre, and hung layers of cloth behind it that looked like maps. Then she positioned some tiny suitcases and books, and propped two stick people up amongst them.

'Hi,' Maddie whispered to Suzanne. 'Have you come far?'

'No. My flat's literally ten minutes' walk from here.'

Roger leaned over. 'Have you worked on something like this before?'

'I've just finished my second year at the RSAMD. I've been involved in a couple of devised pieces this year.'

Morven talked through the set and costume designs, then Jo took a folder from her bag and handed out some stapled pages.

'This is what I've got so far in terms of a script. It's bits of *The*

Tempest mixed with a range of Scottish poems. I've written some text to tie it together, focussing mostly on exile and return and colonial stuff.'

Maddie flicked through the pages. 'You've been busy.'

'I drew a lot from our development time. So, a read-through this morning, see what we think, then up on our feet this afternoon?'

At the end of the day, Jo dashed off to a meeting.

'Anyone for a drink?' Wren asked.

Roger nodded. 'I'll come for one.'

She packed her bag. 'I'd love to, but I want to make a start on these lines.' She was tired, and felt as if she had a headache coming on.

As they walked through the building, Wren dropped back beside her. 'Did Jo say, we got that flat on Belmont Crescent?'

'No. Nice one!'

'Yeah, we're pretty excited. Moving's gonna have to wait till the show's over, but we pick up the keys this weekend. If I can get some basics across, the last night party'll be at ours.'

'Cool.'

All that hash and speed and coke and who knows what else... She shivered. Then again, Jo's election night party wasn't too drug heavy. Surely it wouldn't be *that* hard to pass a joint on?

She smiled. 'It's such an exciting new stage for you guys.'

They stepped out into the dusty car park, blinking in the light.

'See you tomorrow, sweetpea.' Roger kissed her on both cheeks.

Back at her flat, her answering machine was flashing. Two messages. She pressed play.

'Maddie, it's Mum. Just to say I hope your first day went well. Irene phoned, she was delighted with your card. She said she'd love to see your show, and she could drive us through, if it was okay with you. Let me know when you get a chance, but no rush.

I know you're busy.'

She pressed save.

'Hi, Maddie, it's Margaret here. I got a lovely invite from Jo to your pilot production at the Tramway next week. I hope it's going well. I'm phoning to see if you're booked for the Festival? If not, I'd love to snap you up for the last two weeks of August. I won't prattle on just now. Give me a ring back when you can.'

Pulling up a window, she leant out and took a deep breath of summer evening air. Two weeks' work. That'd surely be enough to pay back Jo and Roger. She'd have a bite to eat then return Margaret's call. She filled a pan with water and put it on to boil, then lay on the sofa with her script, hugging it to her chest.

Six

Through the course of the week, the piece came together. Wren played sections of music as they rehearsed, coming in each day with new tracks. Jo was always there early, pacing the room, looking as if she was figuring something out.

Wednesday, planks of wood and scaffolding appeared at the back of the space. Thursday, Ben rigged some lights. Thursday afternoon they had a costume fitting.

They did a rough stagger through on Friday morning. Jo sat at the back of the auditorium with Morven. Maddie tried not to let their low-level chatter put her off.

After lunch, some of the backcloths were hung. Ben tilted the projector.

'There's still a bit of spill,' Morven said.

Maddie's face flashed up, looking out to sea.

Roger gasped. 'Wow, that looks fab.'

At six o'clock, Jo asked them to pull their chairs into a circle. 'I'm so impressed with what everyone's done this week,' she said.

Roger shunted his chair forward. 'See on Monday...?'

Jo raised her hand. 'There's probably a lot of questions, and I do want to answer them, but we need to clear out of here just now, and I've got a production meeting. Tomorrow, we can't use the theatre 'cos folk are building the shell, but Wren and I are getting the keys to our new pad first thing, so Maddie, Roger, Suzanne, can we meet there at ten? There's sod all there, but the living room's large enough to walk the piece through. I've got a few notes to give you from today, and we can do a couple of line runs and talk about next week.'

'That'd be fab.' Maddie looked at Roger and he nodded his agreement.

'Are there any actor questions that can't wait till tomorrow?'

Roger shook his head.

'Okay, thank you very much.'

Morven started to clap and everyone joined in. Roger whooped.

After dinner, knowing Rab would be in the pub having a Friday night drink, she gave her mum a call. She recounted some of Roger's antics that she knew would make her laugh.

'Did you get my message, about me and Irene coming through to see it?'

'Yeah. We get two comps each and I can put mine aside for you. What night would you like to come?'

'Irene can make Wednesday or Saturday. Which would be best?'

'Wednesday's opening night, so why don't you come Saturday, once it's had a chance to find its feet?'

'A Saturday night out. That'll be the first in a long time.'

'What'll you tell Rab?'

'I'm going to tell him that I'm off to the theatre with my sister, to see my daughter in a play.'

Untangling her fingers from the spirals of the phone cord, she smiled. She couldn't believe, when she put the phone down, they'd been chatting for almost an hour.

The next morning, she walked to Jo and Wren's new flat. It took her less than twenty minutes. Number eleven was halfway round the crescent, looking out over a communal garden. Jo buzzed her in. The flat was on the first floor.

She walked from room to room. 'There's so much light.'

Jo pushed open a door next to the lounge. 'A wee guest room. We could get you a nameplate.'

'But you're a westender now, I won't be needing to stay.'

Jo shrugged. 'Could be a home from home.'

Roger and Suzanne arrived, Suzanne holding a pregnant belly – a watermelon, green and lime tiger-striped.

As they stood in the kitchen chatting about the week ahead, Suzanne hacked at the watermelon with Roger's penknife. Jo frowned as juice dripped off the worktop. She caught Maddie's eye as she looked back up and they shared a smile. It felt years since they'd been daft young carefree students. Though Maddie had never really felt carefree.

The following week, Monday and Tuesday flashed by. Tuesday night, she lay awake for hours, thinking about the following day, anxious she'd wake up and her lines would be gone.

When she finally fell asleep, she dreamt she was running through the corridors of the Tramway. At the back of the building, she flung open the stage door, but what had been the car park was now ocean. She clung to the doorframe as a gale tore through the theatre, ripping away the roof, punching away the walls, making the building a bare timber frame that tipped and swayed...

Had I been any god of power, I would
Have sunk the sea within the earth or ere
It should the good ship so have swallowed, and
The fraughting souls within her.

She woke. Her dad had died saving her. No. Stupid thought, still tangled with sleep. It was a different time, a different place, years later. And not for thinking about today.

She washed, dressed and gathered up her stuff. On the chest in the hall was a postcard. A Barcelona postmark.

Buena suerte, senorita. A xx

Alex. Two kisses. She turned it over. The Gaudi tower on the front looked like a mermaid's palace. Shh, now. She put it in her rucksack and walked down to the tube.

At Bridge Street station, she was first off. The long opening chord of 'Hyperballad' playing in her ear – lights glimmering round the edges and bass notes that made her feel slightly sick, little electronic birds and a sudden burst of drum-and-bass beats, skittering, fast waves over pebbles crashing again and again against rocks. She ran up the stairs, buffeted by the wind from the tunnel, and stepped out into the sunshine as Björk's voice rose, fragile but strong. Looking up into the deep dome of blue, she strode out.

Signing in, she had a quick chat with the janny. The backstage area and dressing rooms were empty. Tramway 4 was in blackout, but she heard Jo say, 'Let's see it now…'

A blue light faded up, creating a pool centre stage. The transformation was nearly complete, the space even smelled different. Still, hard to believe there'd be an audience tonight.

Rona, one of the technicians, was up on the cherry picker. 'I could nudge the top shutter down a bit more, if you like?'

Maddie hurried round the side of the seating bank to where Roger was sitting.

'Hey, honey,' he whispered. 'Tonight's the night.'

'Going off cans for a minute,' Jo said. The seating bank rattled as she clomped down the steps. 'Hi guys, how's it going?'

'All good,' Roger said.

Maddie nodded. 'Ready for action.'

'We're just sorting a few things from yesterday's run. Why don't you get yourselves a coffee? In costume and back here ready for a dress at eleven-thirty?'

A woman from the box office came in and stood behind Jo, clearly wanting a word.

'Great.' Roger gathered his bags.

In the green room, Maddie flicked on the kettle. Even the cleanest-looking mugs were stained. She took them through to the kitchenette and gave them a scrub. On the way back, she stopped at her dressing room and ran her hands down her costume. The dropped-waist tartan dress was a bit scratchy, but it looked like a designer number, something Tilda Swinton would wear.

At eleven-thirty they made their way back to the theatre. Roger stood centre stage, humming and rolling his shoulders. She wove around the shell. It was bigger than she thought it'd be. Slightly disorientating when she was up there, in the dark, with no focal point.

Rona cleared away bits of gel. 'Look at you two enjoying the lights. A right pair of moths.'

Wren's score was more like a soundscape than music. He'd recorded them speaking bits of text and layered it. Every now and then a blast played through the speakers. The screen came alive for a moment. Roger carrying Cassie. Bits of text rose through the image.

Jo appeared onstage and Maddie and Roger drew close.

'We're about ready to go. You've still got the run this afternoon, so don't knock yourselves out on this one. My attention's going to be more on tech things, so use this time to play. Start getting a sense of ownership.'

They walked to opposite sides of the stage, where they'd be waiting as the audience came in. A pre-set of lights illuminated the shell, house lights on the seating bank. The soundscape was playing. Waves, the odd tinkle, low-level synths. Someone whispered at the back of the theatre and the volume inched up. Across the stage, in the wings, Roger was just a shape. It was impossible to make out any of his features, but she knew he'd be focussing, getting in character, becoming Prospero, her father.

'Everyone ready?' Rona called.

'Ready,' she and Roger called back.

'Okay. I'll open the house, the audience will come in. Stand-by LX one point two, sound two…'

The lights faded to black. Rona must've gone on cans.

The first hint of blue shone in the floorlamps and another track faded in, with whispered lines. She listened for a specific line: *Have you a mind to sink?* Then she'd walk on, open a few books. Film footage would play behind her, projected waves catching her legs, arms and face. What were her opening lines again? Her palms were damp and she wanted to run, but she heard her cue and walked out. The lights were hot, and the gulf of the auditorium met her with anticipation and energy. How much more alive it would be tonight. Then she vanished. Words came, but from Miranda's mouth.

A little later, she surfaced as Roger fluffed one of his speeches, wondering, fruitlessly, if she could help. Again, near the end, she crept back, asking where she was, what she was doing? But she was pulled under once more.

Blackout. Two or three people gave a quick round of applause. The lights lifted for a curtain call, dimmed, then came full circle to the pre-set state.

'Thanks, guys,' Jo called.

They walked back on stage.

'Well done,' Jo said. 'I'm just going to give some tech notes now. D'you fancy changing out of costume and I'll meet you in the green room in fifteen?'

'I totally ballsed up that bit in the middle,' Roger said. 'Sorry.'

'Don't worry about it. If you're going to make mistakes, now's the time.'

After Jo had given them their notes, they wandered over to Somerfield's to buy sandwiches. They ate their lunch then did a speed line run in Roger's dressing room.

The run in the afternoon felt clunky.

'Don't fret,' Jo said afterwards. 'I know it's ready, and when the adrenaline kicks in tonight... Better to have the last dress under par. Means you've got something to reach for. Technically it's all running smoothly. So take a few hours' rest. Get focussed. Do a thorough warm-up. Then let's kick some ass.'

She was flicking through a copy of the *Evening Times* when the woman from the box office came through.

'Maddie?'

'Yes?'

'There's a girl in the foyer asking to see you.'

'Oh. Thanks.'

Roger was stretched out on the sofa with a scarf over his eyes. He lifted a corner and peeked out. She shrugged, then followed the woman down the corridor into the foyer. The woman pointed to a girl with dark hair who was looking at a wall of flyers advertising the show.

'Hello?'

The girl turned. She looked like a sixth-former. 'Maddie?'

'Yes.'

Her eyes were wide. 'I'm Beth.'

She couldn't place her.

'Your half-sister.'

Her breath froze as she took in the lacy black dress, stripy black and purple tights and black Doc Martens. Beth was slightly taller, but they were of a similar build and colouring, and her eyes...

Maddie blinked fast. 'Oh. Gosh. Well, hi.' She laughed, short and high-pitched. 'Sorry.'

'Oh, no, I'm sorry... maybe I shouldn't have just turned up, without letting you know...' She was shifting from foot to foot, rubbing the material of her dress between forefinger and thumb.

'Not at all. Really, it's fine. Shall we see if we can get a coffee? Have you got time for a coffee?'

The café wasn't due to open till an hour before the show, but the guy who was setting up offered to make Maddie a cappuccino. Beth asked for a Coke. They sat on a corner seat by the window.

'I tried writing a letter,' Beth said. 'But everything I wrote just sounded stupid. I didn't know what to say.'

'How did you know where to find me?'

'I saw your show advertised in *The List*.'

'But how did you know I was doing a show?'

'Your letter.' There was a flyer on the table. Beth curled a corner of it. 'I hope you don't mind that I read it. Mum had it on her dresser. I snooped. I heard, when she rang you. She doesn't know.'

The barman brought over their drinks.

'There you are, ladies.' He set them down. 'You an actress too?' he asked Beth.

'No.'

'The sensible one.' He flipped a tea towel over his shoulder. 'I'll be in the kitchen. Shout if you need me.'

Sisters then, clear for all to see. Though Beth's chin was more pointed, and her lips slightly more defined in their cupid's bow.

'So your mum doesn't know you're here?'

'No. I was coming to meet some friends in town today.' She looked Maddie in the eye. 'You didn't know Dad had died?'

'No.' Maddie scraped some of the chocolate-sprinkled froth from the top of her cappuccino and licked it off the spoon. 'My mum remarried. Between them they thought it best not to tell me.'

'Jeez…' Beth sipped her Coke, fished out the slice of orange and put it in the ashtray.

'I don't like fruit in Coke either.'

Beth half-smiled then glanced away. 'Dad had said that your mum met someone else. He also said he hadn't been a good dad, back then. He was young, wasn't he, when they met?'

'They both were. Younger than I am now.'

'He always hoped you'd come and find him, when you were older.'

A pain, sharp, between her ribs. She put the spoon back on the saucer. 'But he didn't keep in touch.'

'I think he thought that might be easier for you, a new start…'

How well that'd worked out! She spread her fingers on the table. It wasn't Beth's fault. It can't have been easy coming here; she was braver than Maddie had been at her age. 'Are you still at school?'

'I've just finished,' Beth said. 'I'm hoping to go to Glasgow uni in September.'

'That'd be cool. What would you study?'

'English and History.'

A group of folk passed the café, looking as if they were being given a tour.

'I feel bad, just turning up…' Beth said.

'Please don't.'

'But you must be busy.'

'I'll probably have to get back soon.'

She looked down at the table and Maddie followed her gaze. The segment of orange was crusted with ash. Had she sounded nonchalant? She hadn't meant to.

'I've a couple of things I wanted to give you.' Lifting her bag onto the table, Beth took out a photo album, an envelope and a small bundle of tissue paper. 'These are the photos he kept of you.' She pushed the album towards her.

Maddie flicked through it. Mostly copies of photos she'd seen before. 'Are Granny and Grandpa…?'

'Oh, they died, like years ago.'

Closing the album, she slid it back towards Beth.

'No, the album's for you. But I wondered if I could keep this one?' She took a photo from the envelope. Maddie in Primary 1, her hair in pigtails with red bows at the ends. 'I used to keep this by my bed when I was wee, and wonder what my big sister was like.'

Sunlight flooded through the window and bounced off a framed poster on the wall. It threw panels of blue and green across the table, casting Beth's face in turquoise. She looked like a mermaid, but then she was the daughter of a drowned man. In the shimmer of the empty café, it was easy to feel as if this were a dream, that she was imagining this girl, making her up.

Her hands tingled, she rubbed them together. 'I'm sorry. It's all quite a lot to take in.'

'Sorry.' Beth put the photo down on the envelope, then glanced up. The corner of her mouth twitched. 'You didn't know about me?'

She shook her head.

'You were never a secret in our house. But as I got older I stopped asking questions. I could see it upset Dad. And it made my mum uncomfortable.'

'What was he…?' It seemed an unfair question to ask.

'…like? If you want, I'd be happy to tell you about him.'

She hesitated. There'd only ever be versions of him now. A group of three people arrived, looking as if they might be audience members. 'I better get back.'

Beth's hand drifted to the photo.

'Oh, sure. Yes, keep it.'

Beth slid it back in the envelope, back in her bag, just leaving the tissue paper bundle between them. Her hand hovered over it. 'I made this for you. A few years ago. I kept it, in case we ever met.'

Maddie opened it. Inside was a friendship bracelet, pink, red and black threads deftly woven together.

'It's beautiful.' She tried to fasten it round her wrist by slipping the loop over the glinting glass bead, but her hand was trembling.

'Oh, you don't have to wear it. You don't even have to keep it, if you don't want.' Beth looked down, still cast in blue, but maybe blushing slightly.

'But it's lovely. You've made such a great job of it. Will you do it up for me?'

'Okay.' She had slim, nimble fingers. Her short nails painted purple. Her shiny hair smelled of peaches.

'Thank you.'

She gave a shy smile, reminding Maddie of Sylvie.

They walked back to the foyer.

'Well...' Beth angled her body towards the door. Had things not gone as she'd hoped?

'Would you like a quick tour round?'

Light jumped into her eyes. 'If you're sure you've got time?'

She showed her through to the dressing rooms, then opened the door to the theatre. The working lights were up and Rona was sweeping the stage.

'Reckon we can have a quick look.'

Beth followed her in, put her hand on the shell, turned a full circle. 'This is so cool.'

'Would you like to come and see it?'

'That'd be amazing! How long's it on for?'

'Tonight, tomorrow, Friday and Saturday. It's just a pilot production at the minute.'

'I think I could come on Friday, I'd need to check...'

'Sure, we'll ask at the box office on the way out, make sure there's tickets.'

In the green room, Roger was still stretched out on the sofa.

'Hey, Roger. This is Beth.'

He whipped the scarf away.

'My... sister.'

Beth grinned. 'Hi.'

'Well, hello.' He stood and shook Beth's hand.

Jo popped her head round and did less well at disguising her shock. She peered between them. 'You do look really similar,' she said, then got a grip of herself and asked, 'are you coming to see the show?'

Back in the foyer, the woman at the box office said there were still tickets available, though it was nearly sold out on Saturday.

Maddie wrote her phone number down for Beth. 'If I'm not in when you call, just leave a message letting me know if Friday suits, or if another night's better. I can put a ticket under your name.'

'That'd be brilliant.' Beth stared at the slip of paper, folding it carefully and putting it in her bag. 'Hopefully, come September, I'll be in student digs. Then I'll have a phone number too.'

'Cool.'

'Thanks for…' She gestured a half-circle.

Should she give her a hug? Too late. Beth headed for the door, then turned and waved.

Could she have been more welcoming? Should she have thanked her for coming?

Backstage, Roger and Jo were waiting in the corridor.

'Bloody hell, sweet cheeks,' Roger said. 'Are you okay?'

'Yes. Yes, I think I'm fine.'

'Fuck,' Jo said. 'You've always been Maddie. Just Maddie. On your own.'

'I know!' She rubbed her cheeks. 'But early days. And hey, we've got a show to do tonight.'

'You're right.' Jo tucked her notebook under her arm. 'I better get in there and make sure everything's okay.'

In her dressing room, she sat in front of the mirror with the bulbs round it.

Hi, a voice said.

Who was that speaking?

So she found you.

'Shh,' she said to the voice. 'Shh, now.'

She dotted some foundation on her nose, forehead and chin and blended it in, a smile spreading across her face.

Once she'd got into costume, she did a salute to the sun, hummed a few scales and spoke a couple of tongue twisters. 'Lemon liniment; round the rugged rock; a big blue bucket of blue blueberries…'

A knock at the door. Jo was standing outside with Morven and Roger.

'Just wanted to say break a leg,' Morven said. 'I think it's looking the bizz.' She held up two bottles of cava. 'Something to celebrate with after. I'll put them in the fridge.'

'Cheers, Morven,' Roger said. 'I love what you've done with the footage.'

'And set and costumes,' Maddie added.

'A pleasure!' She waved a bottle over her shoulder as she walked off.

Jo looked between them, then took a deep breath. 'Time's come, kids.'

Her eyes welled up. She looked at Roger, he looked weepy too. They held hands, the three of them.

'I'm so proud of you,' Jo said.

Roger nodded. 'I'm proud of me too.'

They laughed and she quickly wiped away a tear.

'Go for it,' Jo said. She gave Roger a hug, then hugged Maddie.

'Hey, luvvies,' Rona said, 'that's your fifteen-minute call.'

'I'll be rooting for you,' Jo said. 'You'll be fab.'

She gave a thumbs-up. 'We'll do our best.'

Jo smiled and headed in the direction of front of house. 'Oh, Wren says, "Knock their socks off!"'

Roger sighed, turned to her and raised his eyebrows. 'Five minutes, then head through?'

'Sure thing.'

Back in her dressing room, she checked her hair was pinned securely. Could she wear Beth's bracelet onstage? Probably best take it off.

Next door, Roger hummed, opening out to a 'ma, may, me, may, ma, maw, moo, maw, ma'.

One final check in the mirror.

I think you're going to be okay, the voice said. Eat. Sleep. Exercise. Be patient.

She took a deep, full breath, then blew it all out, all the stale air, right to the bottom of her lungs.

She was about to knock on Roger's door when she heard him say, '*Be cheerful, sir.*' Was he speaking to himself, psyching himself up? He continued:

'*Our revels now are ended. These our actors,*
As I foretold you, were all spirits, and
Are melted into air, into thin air.'

As he found his pace, his voice built, started to swoop, glide, broaden:

'*And, like the baseless fabric of this vision,*
The cloud-capped towers, the gorgeous palaces,
The solemn temples, the great globe itself,
Yea, all which it inherit, shall dissolve,
And, like this insubstantial pageant faded,
Leave not a rack behind.'

He held the moment, then came back soft, intimate:

'*We are such stuff*
As dreams are made on, and our little life
Is rounded with a sleep.'

It was from her favourite Prospero speech. It hadn't found a place in the show. She was standing, half-mesmerised, when he belted out, '*There's No Business Like Show Business…!*'

She tapped on the door. 'Roger Stevens to the stage, please. Roger Stevens to the stage.'

When they were ready in the wings, Rona checked all was well.

'Break a leg, fair Madeline,' called the shadowy figure across the way.

'And you, Mr Stevens.'

The lights were pre-set. The soundscape was playing. Rona gave clearance to open the house. Her heart thumped. There were just a few voices to begin with, low-level conversation, murmurs, the rattle of the seating bank.

From front of house came the echo of the tannoy. 'The show

will commence in two minutes…'

A stampede. The chatter was loud. Someone shrieked with laughter. Margaret would be out there, Alison, Jo's agent, directors, press, funders. Her mum would be there on Saturday night with Auntie Irene, Terry, Tessa and a bunch of folk from college. Would Beth come on Friday, or at some point? On each night, the rowdy bunch would become their confederates. She envisaged the soles of her feet growing roots into the floor, breathed deeply, became grounded. It seemed to take ages for the auditorium to fill. Then the house lights dimmed. The babble died down and anticipation gathered in the dark.

Blackout.

The second track came in, with its whispered lines. She waited for her cue. The blues faded up. It was coming. The wide centre spot, into which she'd walk, slowly lifted. It was nearly here. She took another deep breath. It was here. Her cue. *Have you a mind to sink?* She couldn't hold it, couldn't hold back time. She had to step out, step out now. So she did. She stepped out.

With thanks to:

Adrian, Laura, Robbie and all at Freight Books; Rodge Glass;
staff and fellow former students from the University of
Glasgow, particularly Elizabeth Reeder, Michael Schmidt and
Colette Paul; and fellow writers, including Em Strang, Defne,
Becks, Dorothy and Lady Jess. With love and appreciation for
Heather Andrews; David Trotter; Kate Dickie; and friends near
and far.